PROTECT

BOOK ONE OF THE UNWELCOME TRILOGY

R.D. BRADY

SCOTTISH SEOUL PUBLISHING, LLC

BOOKS BY R.D. BRADY

The Belial Series (in order)

The Belial Stone

The Belial Library

The Belial Ring

Recruit: A Belial Series Novella

The Belial Children

The Belial Origins

The Belial Search

The Belial Guard

The Belial Warrior

The Belial Plan

The Belial Witches

The Belial War

The Belial Fall

The Belial Sacrifice

Stand-Alone Books

Runs Deep

Hominid

The A.L.I.V.E. Series

B.E.G.I.N.

A.L.I.V.E.

<u>D.E.A.D.</u>

The Unwelcome Trilogy

Protect

Seek

Proxy

Be sure to <u>sign up</u> for R.D.'s mailing list to be the first to hear when she has a new release and receive a free short story!

"The strength of a family, like the strength of an army, is in its loyalty to each other."

- Mario Puzo

"God, give me strength each day to fight for my family."

- Nehemiah 4:14

1

Thirty-Five Years After the Incident

Lyla Richards crouched down, her head tilted to the side as she strained to listen. Her dark brown ponytail swung over her shoulder with the movement. She narrowed her blue eyes. The forest around her had gone silent. But she had heard something this way.

"What is it? What do you hear?" whispered Jamal Nguyen, one of her closest friends and fellow Phoenix as he crouched next to her. At twenty-four, Jamal was one year older than Lyla, but he deferred to her.

Since joining the Phoenixes at age seventeen, Lyla had quickly established herself as a top-rate fighter, hunter, and tracker with almost supernatural skills. She gave him a disgruntled look. "A very loud man talking to me and drowning out any other noise."

Jamal cringed and shrugged. *Sorry*, he mouthed.

She shook her head. She and Jamal had been on guard duty at the northern end of the camp for hours. This part of the camp opened out into dense woods. There was thick underbrush and the trees had grown closer together, making it difficult to see anything creeping up on you until it was too late, which was why you needed to listen as well as watch.

It had been quiet. But she'd heard a shuffling noise, which she'd been trying to pinpoint just now. It wasn't an animal. It was larger, although she supposed it could be a bear. She gestured for Jamal to stay where he was as she crept around the trees to her right, staying low to the ground, using the trees and brush for cover. Her olive-green cloak blended in with the lush woods around her.

She passed through the trees and then paused. There. She turned to her left, crouching low behind a dwarf Alberta spruce.

A huff sounded from ten feet to her left and she recognized the sound—human. She pulled out her staff and moved forward silently, her senses on high alert. She thought there was only one in the immediate vicinity, but that didn't mean he didn't have a friend or two nearby.

Seconds later, a man stumbled into view only ten feet away. His sweat-stained clothes were shredded and he wore only one shoe. Dirt marked his face, and hair sprung from his head like it was trying to escape. He mumbled to himself as he walked. "Monsters. They're coming. They'll get me." He let out a cry and sank to his knees, tears rolling down his cheeks. "They got Shelly. I'm sorry, Shelly. I'm sorry!" he wailed.

A branch snapped and the man whirled around, nearly losing his balance as he lurched to his feet.

She watched him from her hiding spot, trying to determine the best approach. Was he deranged or sick? Either way, they couldn't risk bringing him into the camp. *I'll send Jamal for—*

"You okay there?" Jamal asked as he stepped into view.

Damn it, Jamal.

The man's eyes grew big and he let out a shriek as he flew at Jamal. "You have to run. They'll get you, too. Their ships— the skies are theirs. They'll kill us all." The man grabbed

Jamal's shirt with both hands. "You have to go. They're coming!"

Jamal stumbled back, but the man held on. Lyla burst from her spot. "Let him go."

But the man didn't seem to hear her. He pulled a knife from under his shirt. "They came from the sky. They're monsters. They'll kill you. You should die before they can."

"No!" Lyla slammed her staff into the man's arm and he screamed and dropped the knife. She swung the staff up and snapped it into the back of the man's head. Jamal caught him as he dropped, lowering him to the ground.

"What the hell was he talking about?" Jamal asked.

Lyla didn't look at Jamal. She scanned the area around them for anyone who might be with the man. "I don't know."

"Should we bring him back to camp?"

Lyla shook her head. "No. Get Simon and Frank. He's not going anywhere until Simon looks him over."

Simon Tolliver took off his glasses and wiped them on his shirt. "It's rabies. Advanced. He doesn't have much longer."

Lyla's stomach clenched at the pronouncement. Even if he had been in the beginning stages of the infection, rabies was a death sentence. Maybe in the Before they could have done something, but now, now there was no hope.

"Did he say anything else?" Frank Raffe, the head of the camp, stood with his arms crossed over his muscular chest. His deep, commanding voice was that of a man responsible for the lives of nearly two hundred people. White hair and lines in his face were testaments to the seriousness with which he'd taken the job for the last three decades.

"He mumbled something about ships and monsters. I couldn't really make it out," Simon said.

"Anything that can be done for him?" Frank asked.

"No. I could give him some meds to make his last few hours comfortable, but we are running low as is."

"Understood." Frank looked over at Jamal, who stood guard over the man. They had carried the man into a cave that was a few hundred yards from camp. Now they all stood at the entrance of the cave, the man on a stretcher farther in, a blanket covering him. "Jamal, escort Simon back to the camp to grab some meds. We'll give him a little, but it might be more humane to just put him out of his misery."

Jamal nodded to the man. "What about him?"

Frank's voice rang with authority. "He's *not* coming into the camp. We don't need people worrying about what's out here. There's enough tension because of the move. We'll keep him here until it's over."

Lyla stayed quiet during the exchange and said nothing as Jamal and Simon headed back to camp.

Frank glanced her way. "You're awfully quiet. Does that mean you agree?"

Lyla looked up at Frank. He'd been their camp leader for years, but she'd known him her whole life. He'd been her father's best friend. And when her father passed, he'd unofficially stepped into that role. "I don't disagree with any of it. But I hate that these are the choices we have before us."

"This world is not an easy one."

The man tossed and turned. Sweat rolled down his face as he mumbled. "They're coming. Run, Shelly. Don't let them get you."

"What do you think he means?" Lyla asked. "He said there were ships in the air. People from the sky."

"He's hallucinating. You know that technology no longer exists."

True. At one point, planes, cars, and computers were so much a part of everyday life that people didn't even think of how remarkable they were. But ever since the asteroid, the world had

changed. It was nothing like the Before. There were no governments. People banded together, creating camps, trying to eke out
a living and defend against other camps. And Mother Nature.

Lyla wasn't sure who was the bigger threat. They'd had to
fight more than one group trying to steal their resources. But
Mother Nature—there was nothing they could do to stop her.
Swarms of tornados and waves of earthquakes decimated areas.
Torrential rains could appear from a blue sky and wipe out a
valley without notice. The asteroid had killed most of the world's
population and now the aftereffects seemed to be trying to finish
the job.

"The ships are coming! Run!" the man yelled, struggling to sit
up, but the yell proved too exhausting. Tears rolled down his
cheeks again. "Shelly."

The man's pain was difficult to watch, and Lyla couldn't help
but wonder who Shelly was. Was she a figment of his imagination, too?

"Your shift's up. Why don't you—"

"No," Lyla said quickly. "I'll stay."

Frank narrowed his eyes, searching her face. "You took a
double shift already."

"Yes. But we both know that this needs to be kept quiet. No
more people should be let into the loop than need to be. Just do
me a favor and stop by and let Muriel and Riley know, okay?"

Lyla knew Frank wanted to argue with her. But he also knew
she was right. Finally, he nodded. "Very well. I'll send Jamal back
with some food, all right?"

Lyla was not looking forward to the night ahead, but she
nodded. "Great."

Frank headed back to camp and Lyla settled down by the
front of the cave, her back against the wall.

"They're coming. You need to run." The man's voice was soft,
but the words were desperate and sent a chill up Lyla's spine. *It's
just his imagination,* she reminded herself again and again as he

rambled through the long night. Finally, as dawn broke, the man went silent and he found peace.

And Lyla wondered why his hallucinations had taken the shape they had. *Why ships? Why monsters?* She looked at the man one last time as she pulled the sheet over him, preparing him for burial.

What did you see out there that made you hallucinate something so impossible?

Two Days Later

T welve-year-old Riley Quinn hurried down the path of tents
 toward the one he shared with his mom and his aunt Lyla.
He ducked through two tents side by side. "Come on, Dave," he
called, looking over his shoulder at his friend, who followed him.

Dave grimaced, his limp a little more pronounced than when
they'd started out. "I'm coming."

Riley slowed. *Shoot.* He always forgot about Dave's leg.
Normally the limp was barely noticeable. It was only when he
ran that it became truly obvious. Dave had broken his leg when
he was around five, and it hadn't set correctly. Back then, the
camp hadn't had a doctor and no one even realized it was broken.
They thought he'd just banged it up good. By the time they realized what had happened, the damage was done.

Riley glanced past the last row of tents toward the barn.
The camp was spread out over an acre on the edge of a long
lake. The tents were at the western part with the crops to the
east, nearer to the lake. It was a freshwater lake, meaning it
worked for watering. A fifteen-foot wooden fence surrounded

the crops, with only one entrance. The barn was north of the tents. But that wasn't their destination. They were heading past it to the training yards to watch the Phoenixes, the camp's security force.

David hurried to stand next to Riley. "Why did Mr. Tolliver have to keep us so long today?"

Riley shrugged. "You know Mr. Tolliver. He gets into certain subjects." Mr. Tolliver, the camp doctor, was also their schoolteacher. And he did have a habit of going off a planned subject if he got distracted by something else. Riley wondered if he'd ever pick up on the fact that kids sometimes introduced those subjects just to get him focused on something else.

Today, it had been ancient Egypt. And Riley had to admit, he loved when Mr. Tolliver took them with him into the ancient past, back before the asteroid, when the world had created incredible things. Ancient Egypt held a special interest for Riley. Pharaohs, the pyramids, the Great Sphinx—he couldn't get enough of it.

He dreamed of one day going to see it all with his own eyes. But he knew that was just a dream. No one crossed the ocean anymore. Besides, who knew if Egypt even still existed? The Great Pyramid was right next to the Nile River. It was probably underwater. So much land was now underwater that Mr. Tolliver couldn't even show them an official map of the world. He'd crossed out a lot of places he knew were underwater from reports before all the electricity and worldwide communications systems went out.

"Did you hear what Mr. Tolliver said about electronic libraries? A machine with thousands of books in it, but it could fit in your hand. Can you imagine?"

Riley shook his head. "No, I can't." And he really couldn't. Whenever anyone talked of the Before, it all seemed so incredible. Cars that could transport people miles in minutes, planes that flew through the air, even machines that made food.

"Man, I would give anything to see that." David grinned at

him and then his eyes lit up. He nodded down the road. "They're coming."

Riley looked to where David motioned and saw them—the Phoenixes. Mr. Tolliver explained that the Phoenixes had been named so because they stepped out of the ashes of the destruction to help people survive.

He and David ran to the edge of the path and stopped as the group of warriors marched past. They were in charge of protecting the camp's residents—everything from humans to animals. Each had a brown or green cloak that helped them blend into the trees. Each had a sword strapped to their side, and each carried a tall staff. They trained every day without fail, and there were always a handful patrolling the perimeter of the camp.

Each soldier was tough as nails and ferocious in a fight. Jamal and Addie Hudson, Lyla's closest friends, went by, giving both boys a grin.

Riley stood on his toes, trying to see through the group. He grinned when he caught sight of his aunt and nudged David. "There she is." Lyla stood in the middle, dwarfed by the Phoenixes around her.

At twenty-three, she was one of the youngest and looked it. She was the smallest warrior by far. But Riley had seen her take down everybody she'd ever gone against. She was fearless and respected by every single Phoenix. Even the older Phoenixes asked her for help. And Riley knew one day she'd be in charge of all of them.

Lyla caught sight of Riley and gave him a smile.

He waved. "Have you started your training yet?" he yelled. "Can we watch?"

A few of the warriors grinned at his yell.

She said something to the man next to her before jogging over to Riley. She reached out and ruffled his hair. "We haven't started yet. Weren't you supposed to go help your mom get ready for the move?"

Riley groaned. "We have two whole days."

"Two days is not a lot of time to get things done. We're even cutting our training time down so we can get the camp ready. It's going to take *all* of us"—she looked at each of them—"to make this move happen."

"Sorry, Lyla," David murmured.

Lyla looked over her shoulder at the Phoenixes as they disappeared behind the barn, then turned back to the boys. "Tell you what, if you guys get done what you need to get done, you can come watch."

Riley grinned, opening his mouth to thank her.

Lyla put up a hand. "But then you will help us get the camp ready."

Riley and David were already nodding before Lyla finished speaking.

She smiled. "All right. Go. I'll see you in a little bit."

3

Lyla caught up with the Phoenixes as they entered the training area. The 'training area' was really just an open piece of ground between the barn and some of the wooden cabins. Otto Swingler glanced back at her and then waited until she caught up, falling in step with her. He leaned down, way down, and whispered, "Can we meet up tomorrow morning?"

"Yeah. By the old oak."

He nodded.

"See you then." Otto hurried toward the rest of the group.

Addie caught the exchange with a raised eyebrow. She grinned, the sunlight shining off her dark skin. Lyla knew Addie thought something was going on between her and Otto, but Lyla was pretty sure his tastes did not run in her direction. No, Lyla was helping Otto with his fighting skills. He was easily a foot taller than any member of the camp and built of solid muscle, which made him a target whenever they got into skirmishes with other groups. Most people figured they should take out the big guy first.

With Otto, that was relatively easy to do. He had no feel for fighting. He needed to know exactly what he should do in each

situation to respond. He couldn't make it up on the spot. But the
bigger problem was that his heart wasn't in it. Otto's size was
impressive, but he was a gentle giant. Lyla could only get him to
fight by reminding him he was protecting other people. It was
why it was so difficult to train him—he never went full out or
even close to full out during training. He was too worried about
hurting someone.

Lyla had spoken with Frank about it. But Frank knew that just
the sight of Otto could be a deterrent, so he asked Lyla to work on
getting his fighting skills up. Lyla had been working with him, but
she hadn't really seen any improvement.

She caught the gaze of the head of the Phoenixes, who stood
in the middle of the training yard, his legs braced. Allan Carter
looked at her and then looked away. Allan was another big guy,
but he liked to fight, maybe a little too much, in Lyla's opinion.
Allan had made it clear that he viewed being in charge of security
as a stepping stone to camp leader. And the fact that Frank had
made clear his preference for Lyla taking over one day had not
helped improve Allan's opinion of her. It also didn't help that his
ego always seemed to need feeding.

But as much as he would like her out of his way, Lyla wasn't
really worried about Allan. After all, she knew she was good, and
so did everybody else, including Allan. So while Allan may
dislike her, when push came to shove, she was the first one he
called up when he needed someone at his back.

Allan waved everyone toward the stable and Lyla frowned as
they all headed that way. Addie and Jamal bookended Lyla as
they headed in.

"What's this all about?" Lyla asked.

"It's probably about the ship from yesterday," Addie
whispered.

Lyla stopped still, meeting Jamal's gaze, the words from a
dead man ringing through her head. "What?"

"Oh, right, you two were out on patrol," Addie said. "Saul was out gathering herbs for the kitchen when he claimed some sort of ship flew overhead. It was probably a big bird. Saul's not exactly comfortable in the woods."

"I'm sure that's it," Jamal said quickly, flicking his eyes to Lyla and away again. Lyla could hear the nervousness in his voice.

A second person claiming to see a ship? What was going on?

Addie scoffed, oblivious to the tension in both Lyla and Jamal. "Please, there have been no ships in the air since the asteroid. I think Saul was drinking."

"He doesn't drink," Lyla said.

"Well, then it was a big bird. I mean, what else could it be?" Addie asked.

The eighteen Phoenixes were spread out across the space, leaning against walls, sitting on bales of hay, all facing Allan, who stood in the hay between the stalls. Lyla, Addie, and Jamal quickly sat on some bales near Otto. There were thirty-six Phoenixes in total, but the rest were on guard duty. Frank had doubled the guard. Lyla thought it was in response to the rabies scare, but now she wondered if there was an additional worry occupying Frank's thoughts.

Allan gestured for quiet, and all the murmurs stopped. "We've had reports that the Tanners lost most of their crops to an earthquake swarm."

"Oh no," Addie murmured next to her. Lyla felt the same despair at the thought.

Allan put up a hand for quiet. "We will aid them if we can, but we will also need to make sure our own food stores are protected."

Allan wasn't talking about protecting them from the swarms. They all knew that was impossible. When Mother Nature struck, all you could do was sit back and wait until she was done. No, Allan meant we might need to protect our food from the Tanners. We traded with them and occasionally shared news. But when hunger hit a camp, there was no telling what people would do.

They'd had other camps attack them in the past after a crop devastation. It was the reason the crops had a fifteen-foot wall surrounding them.

"What about refugees?" called out Montell, a tall African-American Phoenix a few years older than Lyla.

"If they make it down to the new camp, we'll take in anyone willing to work, the same as always." Allan looked around, making eye contact with most of the Phoenixes. "We'll need extra guards on the food supplies as we head south. I expect you'll all volunteer?"

Everyone nodded back at him. Food was life. It was that simple. But this year it would be even more important. An advance group had gone down ahead to begin setting up the camp, but it was new land. There were no guarantees the crops would take right away. They might need to make this year's yield stretch.

Allan paused. "Now, there is another issue which you no doubt have heard about. Saul claims to have seen a ship in the sky. Frank sent out some runners yesterday in that direction. They reported no further sightings. However, we are going to keep extra guards on duty for a while as a precaution. In addition, the silence rule applies. No one in the camp is to know about the sighting. Right now, it looks like Saul was mistaken, and there's no point having everyone jumping at shadows for no good reason."

"Are we going to send anyone toward the coast? Saul said the ship was heading in that direction," Shane Summers called out.

"Frank and I have discussed it. And we will be looking for volunteers. Until then, we need to discuss the new guard schedule. I'm afraid you guys aren't going to like it too much."

Lyla tuned him out, turning her head toward the front gate with a frown. What was that? There was a strange noise under the normal sounds of the camp.

"I'm sorry, Lyla, are we boring you?" Allan asked.

Addie nudged her shoulder.

Lyla stood, the hair on the back of her neck rising. "Something's wrong."

Allan might not like Lyla, but he trusted her instincts and was immediately on alert. "Where?"

"Front gate."

He pointed to a group of Phoenixes to his right. "You six, front gate. The rest of you span out."

Lyla moved at a jog along with the rest of the Phoenixes, trying to figure out what exactly was on her radar. But she couldn't pin it down. She just knew something was wrong.

A whistling sound came from overhead as a ball of light skimmed through the sky.

Lyla whirled around. "No!"

The ball of light slammed into the stable. Lyla was flung into the air before being slammed onto her back as shards of wood pierced the air.

Her head ringing, Lyla rolled to her feet, pulling her staff from behind her back. Lyla stumbled forward to where Allan lay. "Allan, are you—" He stared straight ahead, a gaping wound in his neck and chest, his right arm gone.

Lyla looked across Allan's body and saw more Phoenixes down, at least five by her count. Screams sounded behind her, followed by that strange noise, but this time it was louder and closer.

Then the first one stepped into view. Lyla blinked, thinking she'd hit her head too hard in the fall. The creature was at least eight feet tall in a dark suit, a helmet covering its face.

It leveled a weapon at Lyla. Without hesitation, she rolled, and a ray of light burst from the staff. It engulfed Allan in blue light for only a second before reducing his body to ash.

4

Riley and David were headed away from the stables with the intent of going straight home. But then they'd started messing around with one of the moves Lyla had shown them to disarm someone. As Riley landed in the dust at David's feet, he grinned up at him. "That was awesome."

David stepped back with a grin. "Yeah." He glanced back toward the stables. "We better go check with our moms or we'll never get to see the training."

Riley rolled to his feet, wiping his dusty hands on his pants. "Hey, maybe they'll let us practice with them."

David's eyes lit up. "Yeah. I'll go get my sword." David's sword was really just a stick. Each of the kids had one. They trained three times a week with them.

"Five minutes," Riley called over his shoulder as he took off on a run to get his own and beg his mom to let him watch the training.

Riley ran down the path, dodging other people who were carting vegetables and lugging bags. He swerved around a group who was setting up the tables for dinner. Most gave him a smile as he passed. He turned down the row of tents that bordered the back of the camp. Stopping at the fourth to the last one, he peeked in, hoping his mom was out.

His mother raised an eyebrow at him. "Yes?"

His mom looked just like Lyla, with the same blue eyes and the same pale skin, though she usually wore her dark brown hair down.

Shoot. "Um, can I go watch the Phoenixes train?"

She smiled but shook her head. "You know we need to pack up. There's a lot to do."

Riley kicked at the ground, but he'd known she was going to say that. The camp had gotten too big to survive another cold winter. Riley still remembered how hungry he'd been most of the last one. And he didn't like to think of the people who hadn't made it. Now that all the crops were in, they were to begin their migration south.

His mother sat on her cot and waved him over. He dragged his feet on his way to her. Once in reach, she pulled him down next to her, wrapping her arms around him. He leaned into her. He was probably getting too old for her to do that, at least in public. But in private, he was okay with it.

She placed a kiss on his forehead and squeezed him tight. "Tell you what. You get all of your clothes and books in your pack and then you can go play with David for a little while."

He grinned up at her. "Thanks, Mom."

She ruffled his hair as she let him go. Then she stood up, looking around, her hands on her hips. "Okay. Let's see. I need—"

A loud noise rang out and the ground trembled. A gale force wind slammed into the tent as his mom threw herself over him. "Riley!"

5

S hock robbed Lyla of movement for a moment, but as soon as two more beings appeared behind the one who had annihilated Allan, she was all action. She swung up to her feet and dodged to her right as the being aimed at her.

And the whole time, she assessed. *Strong, tall. Need to get him off balance.* She slipped in at it from the side, slamming her staff into the side of its knee. It wobbled. Sliding her knife from its sheath, she plunged it toward its ribs.

And it broke. *Oh my God.*

The being grabbed her by the throat and lifted her up. She kicked up, catching it in the groin. It loosened its grip slightly. She kicked off its chest with both feet and threw herself backward, landing on her back. Rolling to her side, she kicked at the side of one of its knees and then the other. A shadow passed over her and her head jerked up as another took aim.

Without thought, she rolled between the creature's legs, keeping it between her and the other one. She stomped on the back of its knees and it crashed to the ground. Then she slammed her foot into the back of its head. It pitched forward. The second one, unable to get a shot, raced toward her.

Lyla tensed, ready to face it, when a blur of motion sped in from the left and Otto tackled the being to the ground. Lyla rushed forward as the being caught Otto in the chin with its staff. For a moment, the thing raised its chin, revealing its neck. Lyla slammed her staff into the opening and the thing convulsed. Otto rolled off of it.

In the distance, she could hear that horrible blasting noise repeating over and over. And she knew with each sound that someone was reduced to ash.

"Otto, go. Evacuate the camp. Now!"

Otto stumbled to his feet, looking dazed. She pushed him away from the creature as it started to get to its feet. She wasted no time. Her staff crashed into one side of its head, twirling back to hit the other. She brought the end of the staff toward its neck, but it dropped its chin and the staff slammed into the helmet instead, jarring her painfully.

I can't hit them. I can't hurt them.

She swept the staff toward its knees, but it met her with its own staff. *Don't let it get a shot.* She attacked and it blocked every move. Now it was on the attack, pushing her back. She defended, knowing she needed to get control of this fight or she was done for.

She backpedaled and then feinted to the right before shifting left and catching it in the knee. She slipped behind it, slamming her staff into the back of its legs, causing it to stumble forward. But it whipped around. She dove to the ground to avoid the staff swinging at her head. She slammed her heel into its right knee and then into the front of its left. Wrapping her left foot around its ankle, anchoring it in place, she kicked at its knee with her right.

Windmilling its arms, it toppled to its side. She lunged forward, her staff raised, but a blast sent her stumbling back. Her head whipped to the side and another creature, this one even larger, approached, its staff sending out bursts.

Lyla sprinted toward the trees, shifting direction to avoid getting hit, but some blasts came way too close. She didn't slow down as she hit the trees and circled to the left. They weren't defending the camp anymore. The camp was done. They needed to get out. And she needed to find Muriel and Riley. But guilt, strong and deep, accompanied her.

We should have listened. We should have warned everybody.

Riley lay still as the ground tremors stopped. The back half of the tent had collapsed around them.

His mom groaned, pushing the tarp away from them. "Riley? You okay?"

Riley blinked hard, his head ringing. He spit dirt out of his mouth and pushed his hands against the ground, still on his knees. "What was that?"

His mother wrapped her hand around his arm and pulled him up without a word. Fear flashed across her face and a trickle of blood dribbled down from a cut on her forehead.

"You're hurt."

His mom swiped at the blood and then kicked back the tarp. She pulled him toward the tent's entrance. Outside, people screamed and some sprinted past the tent toward the camp center. In the sky, a cloud of smoke drifted upward from the north side of camp.

Riley's heart began to pound. "Mom?"

"You stay right by my side, okay?" she ordered, a tremor in her voice. She grabbed her scabbard from her cot, looping it over her shoulder. Riley stared at her. She rarely ever carried her sword.

"Mom?" he asked again, fear spreading through him.

She grabbed his hand and gave it a squeeze. Her bright eyes stared into his. "It will be okay. Just stay with me. You do not leave my side, do you understand?"

He nodded before his head jerked toward the center of camp. Louder screams echoed from the camp along with a blasting noise. "What's that noise?"

She shook her head. "I don't know, honey."

He peeked around her. More blasts sounded from the center of town now. People ran past their tent. He saw Thad Williams run by, his arm bloodied. And he could see more people running in the distance.

He pictured the people in the middle of the camp. That's where the school was. He'd run past over two dozen people on his way home. Had they escaped? And then his stomach clenched.

The Phoenixes had been there, too. He grabbed his mom's arm. "Mom. Lyla. She was there. She was training."

His mom patted his hand, but he could see the tremble in it. "Don't worry about your aunt. She'll be fine, and she'll come find us. We need to run now, okay?"

She didn't give him a chance to argue. She just grabbed his hand and pulled him away from the center of camp, toward the trees. Riley sprinted next to her, but his mind kept going back to the picture of his aunt with the rest of the Phoenixes. What was happening? Were they all right?

That strange noise sounded behind him again. What *was* that?

A man jostled into him in his haste. Riley nearly went down, but his mom kept him upright.

They were almost at the end of the row of tents when his mom yanked him to a stop, pulling him behind her.

"Mom, what are you—" The words died in Riley's throat as he looked beyond her.

Ahead of them stood a man. No, that wasn't right. The thing was over eight feet tall, wearing a skintight suit of dark blue fabric, a matching helmet covering its face. In its hands it held a long brown staff with a white bulge at the end.

A man next to them ran to the right, trying to get around the thing. The being turned and a bolt of energy escaped its staff. The man exploded, disappearing in a blink of blue light. All that remained was a pile of ash.

Riley could feel his mom shaking. She reached back and touched his arm. "I love you, Riley."

The being raised its staff and pointed it at them.

R iley felt the breath leave his lungs as the being leveled its weapon on them. Then a dark figure darted from the forest behind it. Riley's heart clenched. *Lyla.*

Lyla swung her staff at the side of the being's legs. It stumbled back, trying to regain its balance. She hit it under the chin with her staff. It flew off its feet, landing with a thud that made the ground shake.

Another swing and her staff landed on the being's throat. Lyla kept all her attention on the creature at the end of her staff. "Run, Muriel, run!"

His mom grabbed Riley's arm and yanked him into the trees. A blast hit a tree next to him, leaving a scorch mark on the base.

Riley glanced behind him. Another being was sprinting toward them. It fired at Lyla, but she twirled out of the way.

Two more Phoenixes appeared between the tents. One had the beings' weapon. It fired. The being didn't turn to ash, but it did stop, clutching its side.

"Look out, Riley!" his mom yelled as they went over a rise and down a steep hill.

Riley's hands flew in front of him. He slid down a few feet, trying to keep his balance. But he was moving too fast. He tripped over a rock jutting out from the ground and landed hard on his side. His momentum kept him moving forward. He rolled, bouncing down the hill. Each time he hit the ground he let out a grunt. And it seemed like every time he touched the ground, he managed to slam into a rock or branch hidden in the leaves.

At the bottom, he rolled to a stop, his back resting against a tree, his body feeling like one giant bruise. His breathing came out in ragged pants and he couldn't seem to stop shaking. That thing had tried to kill them. And Lyla was still back at camp with God knew how many of them.

And for the first time, he feared that Lyla was going up against an opponent she couldn't beat. And if she couldn't beat them, then who could?

His mom skidded to a halt next to him, branches and leaves stuck to her hair and clothes. Scratches and smudges of dirt ran along her cheeks, but she seemed oblivious to her own cuts, too focused on him. She ran her hands over him, checking for any injuries.

"Are you okay?" she asked, even as she pulled him to his feet. She shot a glance back up the hill where the blasting noises continued to ring out. "We have to keep going. Can you?"

He barely had a chance to nod before she grabbed his hand and pulled him away. Riley ran with his hand in his mom's, and with each tree he passed he expected one of those things to step out. His breathing turned choppy, and it was only fear that kept his legs churning.

When the trees grew too dense for them to run side by side, his mom took the lead. She never hesitated, she just kept moving. He followed her as they moved over downed trees, pushed through brush, dashed through creeks and streams. Even as her breathing became labored, she didn't stop. She silently pushed him on, urging him to keep moving every time he thought about stopping. But it wasn't just his mom's determination that made his feet move. It was the memory of that being etched into his brain. If it caught them, they were dead. So every time Riley wanted to quit, he made himself run faster.

Finally, after what seemed like hours, his mom pulled him to a stop at the edge of a stream. Riley bent at the waist, trying to catch his breath.

She stood panting beside him, taking in huge lungfuls of air as she scanned the forest behind them and looked up and down the stream, holding on to the trunk of a maple tree for support. She turned to look at him, her cheeks red but the rest of her face abnormally pale. "We're going to get some water, but we need to be quick. Okay?"

He nodded, his heart still racing, and suddenly he became aware of how dry his mouth was. His mom pulled her sword and scanned the riverbank again before nodding. Riley walked next to her, scanning as well.

They reached the water's edge. She continued her vigilance, her gaze continually surveying the area around them. "Go ahead. Get some water."

He dropped to his knees, plunging his hands into the icy water, and pulling cupped handfuls to his mouth as fast as he could manage.

She put a hand on his shoulder. "Not so fast. But hurry, we can't stop for long. We need to keep moving."

He slowed his drinking, knowing she was right and that drinking too quickly would only give him a stitch.

Riley stood up and she leaned down to drink. A shadow moved by a tree. Riley's heart rate doubled. He stumbled back. "Mom!"

In one graceful move, she pulled Riley behind her, the sword extended in front of her.

"Just me," Lyla said, stepping from the trees.

His mother let out a cry and ran the short distance to his aunt. She pulled Lyla into a hug. Riley wanted to do the same, but he held himself back. But he did let himself smile. Lyla was okay. She'd found them. It would be all right now.

His mother pulled back, studying Lyla's face. "Are you all right?"

Riley could see the cuts along his aunt's face and palms, the bruise on her cheek. There were holes in her cloak and it was singed around the edges. He swallowed. She had just missed being hit by those things.

But Lyla nodded, giving them both a small smile. "I'm okay."

"The camp?" his mother asked.

Lyla shook her head. "Scattered. And those that didn't scatter ..." Her words died away.

There was a catch in his mother's voice. "How many?"

Lyla's gaze shifted away. "Hard to say. But we lost a lot. Any survivors are grouping at the Old Mill tomorrow morning, then heading south."

"What were those things?" his mom asked.

Lyla's eyes were troubled. "I don't know. But they're hard to take down—really hard."

The enormity of what had just happened hit him. They had been attacked. The camp was gone. Riley felt light-headed, and he swayed a little bit, his throat feeling tight. "David," he said. "What happened to David?"

Lyla darted a glance at his mother before walking over to Riley. Putting her hands on his shoulders, she looked into his eyes. "I'm sorry, Riley. He's gone."

Riley stared at her, not really comprehending her words. His vision became fuzzy at the edges. He backed away from her. Why would she say that? David couldn't be gone. It wasn't possible. "But ... he can't be. He's my best friend. He's not gone."

Lyla took his arms again, not letting him retreat any further. She kept her gaze steady as it met his. "I'm sorry, honey. I saw him. He's gone."

He shoved at his aunt. "But why? Why would they kill him?

He never hurt anybody. He never—" His words choked off, the tears in his throat making it impossible to talk. "You're wrong. He's not dead."

Lyla didn't move with his shove. She looked into his eyes again. "Riley, he is. And if you want to be mad at someone, be mad at those things. They're the ones that did this to him, to our home."

Riley's knees went weak at her words. David was dead. It wasn't fair. He was small for his age, and he never hurt anybody. His chest heaved. He stared at his aunt, feeling the tears roll down his cheeks. "Why David?" He threw his arms around her neck and sobbed. "Why? Why him?"

Lyla wrapped her arms around him and rocked him. "I don't know, but I *will* find out."

8

L yla sat on a rock just inside the cave, her eyes peeled to the forest for any sound, any movement, even as she fought off her exhaustion. She had led Riley and Muriel through the forest, keeping a grueling pace for hours. She needed to get them far enough away from the camp that they wouldn't be followed but also get them close enough to Old Mill that they would be able to meet up with everybody.

And with every step she took, she thought of the people they had lost. She pictured Allan, his eyes staring out at nothing. She heard the screams again and again and felt powerless again and again.

Addie and Jamal had been heading in the direction of the front gate just before the attack. They'd headed straight for them. *Damn it.* She closed her eyes, trying to get control of her emotions. She'd managed to avoid thinking about them all day. But now with the world quiet, there was nothing to distract her from her fears.

You don't know that they were killed. They could have survived. They have to have survived. She raised her head, staring into the star-filled sky, taking a deep breath. She willed back the tears that wanted to fall. There was no time for grief right now. Grief was a luxury of the safe. And they were not safe. Not yet.

Lyla glanced back into the cave. Muriel sat up against the back wall. Riley was curled into her side. Lyla had called a halt about an hour ago. She had wanted to keep going, but neither Muriel nor Riley were ready for this kind of hike. They needed to stop.

Lyla had found the cave. It was the best they could do for cover. It was more of an outcropping than a full cave, but it would at least keep them covered for the night.

Lyla had covered the opening with tall branches. Now it would be almost impossible to find the entrance unless you already knew it was there.

Her gaze roamed over Riley and Muriel, feeling that protectiveness for them that she had felt for as long as she could remember. She had been terrified today when those things attacked. Not just because of how hard it was to take them down, but because when that explosion went off, she hadn't known where Riley and Muriel were. She'd been terrified that Riley had doubled back to watch them train. When Riley was born, Lyla had been amazed at how such a tiny little boy could make her smile with one little look. And that joy at his presence in her life had only grown over the years.

There were only eleven years between them, and he'd become, in her mind, a little brother. Which meant it was her job to protect him. Ever since she was little, she'd felt a driving need to protect, even with Muriel, who was the older sister by six years. But for as long as both of them could remember, Lyla was the one to step in front of Muriel, keeping the danger from reaching her —because the idea of someone hurting her family was too unbearable for Lyla to face.

The world they lived in was hard. Strangers could bring death by weapons or disease. A simple cut left untreated could become infected and quickly be beyond the scope of their limited medical skills. Storms cropped up out of nowhere, sometimes bringing swarms of tornados or earthquakes, sometimes both. Three years ago, a tornado swarm destroyed the crops just before harvest.

That had been a cold, hard winter. They made it through because they had each other. She knew that. Lyla spent that winter hunting for every small piece of game she could find and bringing it back to feed the camp. She still remembered how cold she'd felt, her toes and fingers going numb. But she'd pushed on, knowing lives depended on her, knowing the two lives of her little family depended on her.

Lyla looked back at her sister, who ran a hand through Riley's hair. Muriel was the softness in this cold world. If Lyla was the fist, then Muriel was the heart. And the fist wasn't much use if the heart stopped beating.

Lyla pulled her gaze away, not liking where her thoughts were heading. *They're alive. Focus on that.* But the fear wouldn't leave her.

She had been a warrior for the group for seven years, fully initiated when she was eighteen. But so far that had meant fighting off humans and animals. In all of those fights—and there had been many—she had never been as terrified as she was today. She couldn't kill those things. All she'd been able to do was throw them off balance, allowing people a chance to escape.

Lyla studied the forest floor below. It was quiet, but not too quiet. Every once in while an animal would dart out. But their occasional appearance did nothing to distract her mind. Ever since those things attacked the camp, one single question flashed continually through her mind: *What are they?*

The shortest one she saw had been at least seven feet tall. The tallest was close to ten. And they were incredibly strong. *And we cannot get through their suits.*

There had been no warning of their approach, despite the guards that always surrounded the camp. No warning except the ravings of a man on the edge of death. And Saul, who said he'd seen a ship flying overhead the day before. They must have been doing reconnaissance on the camp.

Lyla closed her eyes. She had no doubt those perimeter guards had been the first to die today. And despite all their training, it had been done silently and efficiently. *Might as well have had no guard for all the good it did.* One minute everything was normal and the next, all hell had broken loose. The first blast had taken out five Phoenixes and the ones left were barely able to defend themselves, never mind the camp.

All their precautions to keep the camp safe had proven worthless. The fighting skills that worked against humans and animals had failed spectacularly today. But how did you prepare to fight an enemy you never knew existed?

At the snap of a branch, she whipped her head to the right as a small deer wandered out. It found of patch of grass it liked and contented itself with eating. Lyla relaxed, knowing the deer wouldn't be standing there so calmly if those things were nearby.

Above her, a full moon shone down. It was a beautiful sight, all bright and luminescent in the dark cloudless sky. Beautiful as it was, she wished it wasn't quite so bright. While it made it easier for her to see, it also made it easier for her to be seen.

She squinted and could just make out the face in the moon. Long ago, her father had told her that the man in the moon was real and that he watched over them. When she was a kid, whenever she was scared, she would look up at the Moon and remember her father's words.

Nothing can happen to you when the man in the moon is watching.

She smiled, but then the smile faded when she remembered finding his body four years ago. He had gone out hunting with Chris, Muriel's husband. It should have been fine. Spring was in full effect. But a snowstorm had sprung up out of nowhere. They had never returned.

When the snow stopped and they still hadn't returned, Lyla

had gone looking and she'd found them both. She closed her eyes against the pain the memory still elicited.

She glanced back at the Moon, the memory of her father's words about the man in the moon no longer provided her comfort. She let out a sigh, pulling her legs up and wrapping her cloak tighter around her. How she wished she could believe her father's words now.

But now I think it may be the man in the moon we need to worry about.

Muriel joined her at the entrance of the cave, peering out into the dark night. "Anything?"

"All quiet." Lyla tilted her head toward the back of the cave. "How's he doing?"

Muriel sat next to her with a sigh. "He's asleep. The one good thing about all that running is that it tired him out. But today was rough."

Lyla nodded, not turning. "For all of us."

Silence descended as they both stared out. Lyla watched the deer. It finished its meal and wandered back into the trees.

"Lyla, what were those things today?"

Lyla glanced over at Muriel, whose eyes were full of fear. Lyla tried to keep that fear out of her own eyes. It had always been that way. Lyla was the one who swallowed down her fear and kept a brave face, even when she was terrified. Her strength allowed Muriel to feel her fear and pass through it.

Today she pulled on all those old habits and shoved her fear away. But she couldn't help remembering plunging her knife into the being's chest. It would have been a killing blow if it had landed. Instead of a dead opponent, she'd been left with a shattered knife. Lyla liked to think that she could handle anything, face anything. But at that moment, she had been powerless. All her training, all her hard work, and she couldn't kill the thing.

Lyla strove to keep all emotion out of her voice and just report on what she knew, which wasn't much. "I don't know what they were. All I know is our swords can't cut through whatever armor they were wearing. The best we can do is knock them off balance."

"They can't be human, can they?"

Lyla paused before speaking. "I don't see how. I mean, occasionally you might see a tall human. But a group of them that are eight feet tall or taller?" Lyla shook her head. "No. They can't be human."

"So what does that mean? Robots? Aliens?"

Lyla thought of the things she had taken down. They had been warm, and although strong, they were soft, like skin. "I don't think they're robots. As for aliens ..." She shrugged. "I just don't know."

Muriel went silent. Lyla pictured the fight back at the camp. They hadn't been able to fight the beings—not in any real sense. She'd seen seven of her Phoenixes get evaporated and countless others. She closed her eyes. *How are we going to defeat these things?*

The ash itself brought back horrible memories. It reminded her of the five years when ash had covered everything. Her father said a volcano must have erupted. Even when the ash stopped falling it took two more years for it to disappear entirely. It was in the water, the food, everywhere. Muriel, who'd been pregnant at the time, had been terrified that it would affect the baby. When Riley was born happy and healthy, they had all breathed a huge sigh of relief.

"Did you know anything about them?" Muriel asked.

Lyla looked up, guilt eating at her. She sighed. "Two nights ago Jamal and I found a guy just outside the camp. He was sick, delirious. Simon thinks it was rabies."

Muriel gasped, her hand flying to her mouth.

And it was just that type of reaction that had led Frank to decide to not inform the rest of the camp about the man. Nothing terrified a group more than a disease with no cure. "He was ranting. We thought it was just the fever talking. He said they came in

ships. He said they would kill us all. We thought he was hallucinating. And then yesterday Saul said he'd seen an airship. But it
all just seemed impossible. That type of technology doesn't exist
on this planet anymore." Lyla paused. "But it might exist on
another one."

"Is that what you think they are?"

"Crazy as it may sound, it's also the most logical explanation."
She sighed. "Damn it, we should have warned people. We should
have—"

Muriel put her arm around Lyla's shoulders and squeezed.
"You can't blame yourself. I mean, there have been days when
getting a fire lit has proven almost impossible. So how could you
believe a sick man ranting about flying ships? I mean, look at how
we live. Some days it feels like we are one step removed from
Neanderthals or cave dwellers." Muriel looked around, her voice
dry. "Says the woman hiding with her family in a cave."

A small smile crossed Lyla's lips.

Muriel shook her head. "I'd settle for some electricity or an
indoor toilet. But spaceships? They shouldn't exist here. Not
unless someone brought them from somewhere off this planet.
You couldn't have known."

"But someone had to have known about them. Maybe other
groups saw them first. We can't be the first ones they attacked."

"You still couldn't have known. We don't have communication
with any other groups, at least not regularly."

"But that's the problem," Lyla burst out. "If something
happens, we don't learn about it until it's too late. We need to be
working together with other groups, not isolated from them."

"But with the distance, it's too difficult to maintain that
communication. I mean, if we had radios or computers like
before the asteroid, it would be easy. That's assuming we could
find people we could trust."

Lyla closed her eyes, picturing the last group of people they'd
had trouble with. The men had barely been human. They'd had

trophies of their kills around their necks. And they had decided their camp was their next target. It had been a bloody fight, but eventually Lyla and her people succeeded. But it reinforced why they needed to stay isolated.

Lyla sighed. "But we need to do better than this. We're barely surviving. It's not enough."

"Maybe we should join up with another group. Safety in numbers."

Lyla shook her head. "Not now, not with those things out there. That just means they'll find us sooner. Smaller is probably safer."

"But that will make basic survival that much more difficult."

Lyla nodded, feeling even more exhausted all of a sudden. She rested her head on her knees. "I know, I know. Damned if we do, damned if we don't."

Muriel pulled her into her shoulder.

Lyla sighed, letting herself lean on Muriel, both physically and otherwise, for just a little bit. "There has to be a better way to survive than this, though. And we have to figure it out. We're all living from day to day. I *have* to believe there's a better way."

"Even with the aliens?"

"Well, maybe not *with* them," Lyla said. "But maybe some group figured out a weakness. That would be something we all need to know. Right now, one group could figure it out, and we'd never know."

"Do you think they have a weakness?"

This time Lyla's voice was confident. This answer she was sure of. "*Everything* has a weakness."

Muriel took Lyla's hand and squeezed it.

Lyla looked up into her sister's eyes.

"I need you to promise me something," Muriel said.

Lyla didn't like the tone of her voice. "Okay."

"Whatever happens, you take care of Riley."

"Of course I'll take care of him."

"No." Muriel's eyes were intense. "You're a better fighter than me. If things go bad, you get Riley and run. You don't think about me."

Lyla yanked her hand away, shaking her head. "No. I'm not leaving you behind. We'll all get out."

"Lyla, you know as well as I do that if these things keep coming, you have a better chance of surviving than I do. Which means if Riley is with you, *he* has a better chance of surviving. You have to promise to take care of him. You can protect him better than I can."

Lyla wanted to argue with her. She wanted to tell her that it would be fine. That they *would* all get out of this. But that wasn't true. The strongest would survive. And she was stronger than Muriel. She gripped Muriel's hand. "If it comes to that, I'll protect him with my life. But it won't come to that."

Muriel studied Lyla's eyes for a moment before she reached up, pushed a stray hair off Lyla's forehead, and placed a kiss there. Then she leaned her head into Lyla's, just like she'd done since they were kids. "I love you, Lyla."

"I love you, too." Lyla let herself close her eyes for just a moment and enjoy the feel of her sister with her. Because she had a feeling—and she knew Muriel did, too—that this moment of comfort would be their last for a while.

9

The dream faded as Riley blinked his eyes open. He reared back at first, seeing a figure leaning over him in the dark. His mom's voice cut through the fear. "Riley."

He closed his eyes. Mom was here. It was all right.

But his mom just shook him again. "Riley, it's time to get up."

He groaned, his whole body feeling heavy.

"Riley, we need to go now."

Riley opened his eyes, the dim light in the cave enough to confuse him. *Where—* He stared at the rock ceiling and then his mom before the memories from yesterday rushed back to him all at once. He sat straight up, his pulse racing.

His mom put her arm around him. "Shh, honey, it's okay. You're safe. I'm here. Lyla's here."

Riley looked to where his aunt stood at the entrance of the cave, her staff in her arms, her sword strapped to her side, her cloak covering her. He felt better at the sight of her. She looked like she always did—strong, confident.

He remembered her taking down that thing from yesterday. She'd defeated it. His pulse calmed a little. As long as Lyla was around, they were safe. He pushed off the ground, his legs already tired. But he knew his mom was just as sore. He didn't ask about breakfast because he knew there would be none today. "I'm ready. Where are we going?"

"To meet everyone else," Lyla said.

But Riley heard the words that hadn't been said. *To meet everyone who is left.*

Lyla looked at him. "You ready?"

He nodded. "Let's go."

Lyla led the way. The Moon gave them enough light to see by, especially once his eyes got accustomed to it. Lyla moved like she had night vision. She never stumbled, never got caught on a bush. She moved soundlessly through the trees.

They walked in silence in the dark for an hour before dawn broke. The sky shifted from black to blue with angry slashes of pink. But they didn't stop as the sun rose higher in the sky. It felt like they'd been walking for hours before Lyla put up a hand for them to stop. They had not seen a soul, which wasn't unusual. But Riley had hoped they'd come across some people from camp. They'd just come over a rise, and Riley knew the Old Mill was just over the next one.

Instead of heading there, Lyla gestured toward a tall series of bushes. She slipped behind one and was completely hidden. Riley and his mom followed suit.

Lyla glanced over at them. "The mill is just ahead. I'm going to make sure everything is all right. You two stay here, out of sight. If you hear anything you don't like, you two get out of here and I will find you."

His mom pursed her lips together at Lyla's order but eventually nodded. Lyla squeezed his mom's arm and ruffled Riley's hair before she slipped away.

He watched the spot where his aunt disappeared. In his mind, he pictured her being ambushed by those things. He started to tremble and couldn't make himself stop.

His mother wrapped her arm around him, rubbing his arms. "She'll be fine. It'll be okay."

Riley hated when adults said things like that. They were empty words. There was nothing fine about any of this. Things were *not* going to be okay. But for now he let himself be lied to. And he let a small part of himself believe his mother was right.

Riley lay down, staring up at the sky as time dragged on. He wanted to sleep, but he was too scared to even think about closing his eyes. He started counting, his fear for his aunt making it hard to stay silent. When he passed five thousand, he began to shake. "Something's wrong. We need to go find her."

His mom shook her head. "No. We stay here."

"But—"

Without warning, his aunt reappeared, and Riley felt relief flood him.

She smiled. "Everything looks okay. Let's go."

"How many people are there?" his mom asked.

"About twenty," Lyla replied.

"Only twenty?" His mom's eyes grew large, her face paling.

Lyla squeezed her arm. "Yeah. But that doesn't mean it's everybody. People were scattered. They could be being cautious. They know where we're heading. They could meet us down there."

She nodded, blowing out a little breath, a small tremor running through her.

"Now let's go. They're getting ready to move in a few minutes." Lyla started to jog. Riley stayed behind her with his mom, not liking how worried she looked. Ahead, he saw the Old Mill.

It had once been a lumber mill. The old saws inside were rusted over. Most had crashed to the ground. One wall had collapsed and the other three leaned precariously into one another. Trees had begun to reclaim the space, an oak growing in the middle of the building, its top branches reaching just below the ceiling.

Riley scanned the area but didn't see anyone. Where were they? His heart clenched. Had something happened?

His aunt turned to the left just before they reached the clearing around the building. Riley heard a dull murmur and his heart raced. People. There were people ahead.

Riley smiled just before a scream split the air.

10

L yla clamped onto Riley's arm as soon as the scream sounded
and dragged him into the trees. Muriel was right behind them.
And then Lyla heard the blasting noise.

"Move," Lyla whispered furiously as soon as they were hidden
by the trees. She grabbed Riley's hand and sprinted forward.
Muriel stayed glued to their heels.

A scream sounded in front of them followed by the blasting
noise. Lyla yanked Riley to a stop and paused, trying to listen over
the sound of her pounding heart.

She could hear someone coming behind them. And they were
not coming quietly. And she knew there was also someone ahead
of them. *Right or left?*

Riley stared up at her with big eyes, his breath coming out in
pants. Muriel stood waiting, trusting her. Lyla tugged him to the
left. "Come on."

They took off again, dodging through the trees. But Lyla could
hear someone still giving chase—someone big. "You two keep
running. I'll be right back, okay?"

Riley stumbled, shaking his head, his eyes huge. But Muriel

took him by the arm, pulling him forward. "She'll be right back." She gave Lyla a nod.

Lyla turned and climbed the maple near her, scampering up like she'd done a thousand times in training. She crouched low on a branch fifteen feet up and scanned behind her. There was a cliff face ten feet to her right. She couldn't tell how high it was, but she could see the flow of water beyond it, letting her know it would be high enough for her needs.

Crashing sounded through the brush. She tensed, taking a few deep breaths to center herself. *Whatever is going to happen is going to happen. Don't anticipate. Just react.*

One of the beings sped into view. The thing was big—close to nine feet tall. And it was broad—almost four feet wide at the chest.

Lyla swallowed as it raced toward her—raced in the direction that Muriel and Riley had disappeared. Fear swelled up in her chest. She shoved it down. She would let herself be scared later. Right now, she had to protect them. That came before everything else.

She tensed, waiting for the being to approach, not sure what she would do if it looked up and saw her. But it didn't look up, too focused on the path ahead.

As soon as it was under her hiding spot, she swung from the branch, slamming her feet into its back. It was like hitting a tree. It stumbled forward but didn't fall.

Lyla hit the ground but quickly rolled to her feet, pulling her staff into her arms.

The being turned, but Lyla was already moving. She sent her staff up between its legs. The being paused, and then its legs buckled. Lyla slammed the staff into the back of its legs, its ribs, the back of its neck. The being jostled with each hit. It raised its weapon and Lyla brought her own staff across its hand with all her might. Using her staff, she twisted its hand, and then with a quick snap of her staff, disarmed it. Its weapon went flying into a bush.

The being paused as if in disbelief. Lyla aimed another shot at its groin, but the being sidestepped and reached out, one hand wrapping around Lyla's neck. Her staff slipped from her hand. Her feet lifted off the ground, kicking and not finding purchase. Fear poured through her as her mind scrambled for something, anything, to do against its strength.

It's stronger. You're faster and lighter. Use it. The voice barking in her head sounded exactly like her father.

She kicked out, hitting it in the groin again, then grabbed it by the back of the head with one hand and punched it in the throat with the other. She ran her feet up the being's chest, slamming the heel of her boot into its chin and using the momentum to flip herself over and out of its grasp.

She rolled as she hit the ground and grabbed her staff in one fluid motion. She moved forward, never stopping her strikes—knee, groin, ribs, neck, side, groin, stomach, neck. Over and over again, she struck, not giving herself a chance to pause, not giving it a chance to do anything but back away.

Lyla adjusted her grip and slammed the end of her staff into the middle of its neck. It grabbed at its neck as it stumbled back and tipped over the cliff's edge.

Lyla didn't wait to see if it survived. She took off after Muriel and Riley. But part of her couldn't help but cheer.

She sprinted through the trees, her eyes peeled for any sign of Muriel and Riley's passage. A broken branch here and a footprint there pointed the way. She picked up speed as she rounded an oak and saw them up ahead.

Muriel whirled around as Lyla approached, her face determined despite her fear. But her face melted at the sight of Lyla. Lyla didn't pause as she caught up with them. "Keep going."

But she did take the time to run her hand over Riley's hair.

Together they ran, no one speaking. Then Riley tripped, tumbling to the ground.

Lyla was at his side in an instant. "Are you okay?"

He nodded. The blasting sound came from ahead.

Lyla went still. Another blasting sound came from their left, maybe a hundred yards.

Lyla directed them to the right, her eyes scanning for any threat. They ran in silence, but Lyla still couldn't hear anything over the sound of blood pounding in her ears. Even as she ran, she tried to calm her breathing, forcing herself to breathe in cadence with her steps. *Focus, breathe, listen.*

And too close, she heard the sound of someone running toward them.

Ahead, the ground rose sharply. A wall of rocks. It was a thirty-foot-high retaining wall left over from the Before. The rocks jutted out, making it easy to climb, but the moss covering it would make it slick.

"This way. Quickly," Lyla said. She headed to a small alcove, hidden next to the wall, pulling Riley and Muriel in with her.

Muriel looked out. "Shouldn't we—"

"Shh." Lyla nodded outside. Muriel's eyes grew wide. One of the beings stepped into the clearing. Lyla slowly eased Riley back toward her and slipped her hand over his mouth. His breaths were coming out in loud pants. He turned to her. She gave him a small smile with a nod.

It'll be okay, she tried to tell him with her eyes, but inside she was shaking. She couldn't think of a way to get them out of here. And if those beings looked too closely, they'd see their hiding spot for sure.

A second being stepped into the clearing. The two seemed to confer before one started heading to the right. The other took up position thirty feet away from them. The path leading back to the Old Mill was open, but there was no way they could make it without that thing seeing them.

Maybe I could outrun them. I could head to the mill, lead it away, and then somehow get back to Muriel and Riley. Even as she thought it she knew it was a suicide mission. And then it hit her. *We're not going to make it.*

Muriel shifted so that she was closest to the exit. She turned to Riley, running a hand over his face.

And Lyla's heart broke. Muriel knew this was the end, too. They wouldn't be able to escape this time. Lyla's heart tripped as she looked into Muriel's face, the face that looked so much like hers.

Muriel gave Lyla the smile that reminded Lyla so much of their mother as she leaned over Riley's head to kiss her cheek. A tear slipped down Lyla's cheek, but she nodded at her sister and took a breath. They would face this together, just like always.

Muriel's eyes were bright with tears. "Remember your promise."

Lyla's stomach dropped and the world seemed to stop. She reached for Muriel's arm. "No, Muriel."

But her hand touched only air as Muriel sprinted from their hiding spot and out into the clearing.

11

"No!" Riley yelled, lunging for his mom. Lyla clamped a hand over his mouth and yanked him away from the alcove opening.

Riley struggled against his aunt's grasp, but she held on, not giving him an inch. His whole body shook with fear and horror as he watched his mom race away from them.

No, Mom. No!

He struggled against his aunt, but she held him so tightly. He was shaking so hard he could barely stand. All Riley could do was watch as his mom disappeared down the path, one of the things charging toward her as it caught sight of her. A second being appeared and took off after her as well, and Riley felt his knees give out. But Lyla held him tight, not letting him fall.

Riley felt the tears rise in his throat. *Mom, come back,* he begged silently. *Mom.*

Lyla lowered her head, her voice fierce in his ear, but even then he could hear the tears she held back. "Do *not* throw away her sacrifice. You run, God damn it."

She grabbed his hand and pulled him into the clearing, and they headed in the opposite direction his mother had disappeared. Behind them, he heard the blasts from the things' spears. His heart seemed to stop. But his aunt just tugged him harder, pulling him farther away.

Riley got his feet under him and started to run, a picture of his mom frozen in his mind. His aunt set a grueling pace, never letting go of Riley's hand.

At one point, Riley stumbled, going down hard on one knee. Lyla was in front of him immediately, kneeling down. "Get up, Riley. Get up."

Grief and fear rose in him, tears rolled down his cheeks. "It hurts."

Lyla's face held not an ounce of compassion in it. "Yes, but it doesn't matter. Not right now. Later, you can let yourself feel the pain, the hurt. Right now, you survive. So get. Up."

Riley looked at his aunt, who always had a smile for him, a laugh. But she wasn't laughing now. Her face was set like stone.

"We need to go back. Mom needs us—"

"She's gone, Riley."

"You don't know that."

"Yes, I do, and so do you. And we need to move. You want to be a Phoenix? Show me you have what it takes. Get. Up."

With a shuddering breath, Riley got to his feet. His knee buckled, but he waved his aunt off when she reached out a hand. "I got it," he spit out.

"Good. Let's go."

She took off again, and Riley was right behind her. He didn't utter a single word of protest as they cut over hills and slogged through streams. She led them on, never stumbling, never questioning where she was going. Riley followed behind her, a sense of unreality falling over him. He kept replaying his mom running out into the clearing over and over again, trying to find a way that his memory was faulty, something to assure him that she hadn't done that. Tears streamed down his cheeks, but he left them unchecked as they trekked on.

Mom, come back.

They ran until the sun sank below the horizon and the sky had turned pink. He leaned against a tree, exhaustion falling over him like a blanket. He couldn't remember ever being so tired in his whole life. He just wanted to close his eyes and see his mom when he woke up. His aunt disappeared from view for a moment. He knew he should probably be sacred, but he was too tired, too numb to feel anything, even fear.

Lyla reappeared seconds later. "I don't think anyone's following us. We should be good. We'll sleep here tonight." Lyla pointed to a tree with low branches that would act as cover.

Riley only nodded, too tired to do anything else.

Lyla looked at him and her expression softened. "Come on."

He blinked hard, forcing his eyes back open. He'd nearly fallen asleep while standing. "I thought we were staying here."

"We are, but there's something we have to do first."

Lyla led him around a small rocky hill. She climbed up about six feet, waving him up behind her. There was a large flat rock at the top. She pulled him up and then took a seat, her feet dangling over the edge. She patted the rock next to her. "Take a seat," she said softly.

He looked up at her. This Lyla was the aunt he knew, not the warrior. This was the one who always had time for a hug or a laugh. Tears laced her eyes and Riley felt the grief take him over. When she was the warrior pushing him, it was easier to shove his own feelings away, to not give in to them. But now? Now she was Lyla and he felt his eyes burn with tears.

Even so, he hesitated, fear of what could be lurking holding him back. If Lyla thought it was safe, though, it must be. And while part of him worried about being out in the open, another larger part of him couldn't work up the energy to care even if there was one of those things in the trees.

On automatic pilot, he climbed and sat next to her, feeling the warmth of her arm through his shirt. Neither of them spoke.

They simply sat and watched the sunset. It was a beautiful one. The sky was a blaze of color, pale blue to orange, pink, red, and finally black, dotted with stars.

Riley watched it all, almost numb. *She can't be gone. She can't be.* He repeated the same phrases over and over in his mind, each time picturing a different ending. He grabbed his mother to keep her from leaving. He ran after her. He yelled and distracted those things making them follow him instead of her. On and on his mind teased him with all the possibilities. But they didn't matter. He'd done none of that. And his mother was gone.

Riley looked over at his aunt, surprised to see tears streaming down her cheeks. She looked down at him, wrapping an arm around his shoulder. "Your mom gave us that sunset and every one we see from this day forward. It's our job not to waste them."

Riley watched the night sky through his own haze of tears. Memories of his mom, her hugs, her laugh, what seemed like every moment with her went through his mind in an unstopping reel. And the dam he had built up over his emotions during their escape burst wide open.

"I don't want her to be dead," he sobbed.

Lyla wrapped both her arms around him. Her tears dripped onto his neck, her voice thick. "Me, either, Riley. Me, either."

12

Five Years Later

Seventeen-year-old Miles Jones walked down the row of shelters in the Attlewood camp, books cradled in the nook of his right arm. His left arm, which stopped just below the elbow, was pressed on top of the stack to keep them from falling.

Two of the Phoenixes, Rory and Angel had returned from a scavenge and had managed to find some medical texts. Miles knew one of them was useless—all about laparoscopic surgery. He was lucky if he had a sharp knife, never mind anything more advanced. But the other one on infectious diseases might end up being useful. And who knew? Maybe someday the laparoscopic one would be as well. There were some places that managed to get electricity up and running, at least sporadically.

The shouts of a group of boys drifted down toward him. Four teens walked down the dirt path, jostling and pushing each other. In front, Adros Ryder, a muscular boy with unkempt blond hair and the ringleader, spied Miles.

Miles groaned, picking up his pace. He didn't need this today. He ducked his head, attempting to skirt past the group.

Adros stepped in front of him. "Hey, Gimpy, reading more books?"

"Leave me alone, Adros." Miles tried to walk around him.

Adros put out an arm, blocking his way. His friends lined up next to him, also blocking Miles's path.

Adros snorted, glancing at Miles's pile of books. "*Laparoscopic Surgery, Infectious Diseases,* and *The Gods of Ancient Egypt.* Think you're so smart, don't you?"

"He is smart. And we're lucky he is." Riley Quinn stepped out from between the cabins next to them. With dark brown hair lightened by the sun and bright blue eyes, Riley was in appearance the polar opposite of Miles with his dark skin, hair, and eyes. Yet there were no two closer. They were brothers in every way except biology.

Riley stepped onto the path, his arms crossed over his chest. The action pushed out his biceps, making them look even larger. Miles knew it wasn't an accident. With Adros, it was always important to remind him when a fight would be evenly matched.

And Riley was the only one who was a match for Adros physically. But Adros had never been able to take Riley down in any training exercises. Because unlike Adros, Riley used more than just muscle when he fought. He actually used his brain. Which probably made it unfair for Adros, because Miles was pretty sure he didn't have one.

"There a problem here, Adros?" Riley asked, coming to halt next to Miles.

Adros's friends took a step back as if to signify they had no allegiances to him.

Adros put up both his hands with a smirk. "No problem, just talking." He whacked Miles's right arm, sending the books flying. "See you later, buddy." With a laugh, Adros walked away, his minions following behind him.

Miles squatted down to get his books. "Asshole."

Riley crouched down next to him, reaching for a book. "Yeah."

"I got it." Miles's voice was rough. He felt his face burn.

Riley ignored him, picking up the books. "Hey, he's a jerk. Don't let him get to you." Riley stood, reaching down his hand.

Miles clasped it, letting Riley pull him up. "Thanks."

Riley handed him the books. "You're worth ten Adroses."

Miles smiled. "Only ten?"

Riley shrugged. "I could be talked into twenty."

Miles laughed, feeling some of the tension leave his chest.

"Why don't we go down to the training yard? You're getting pretty good with that sword and shield."

A few months ago, Riley had surprised Miles with an attachment for his half arm that Hilda, the metal smith, had created. It was a metal sleeve with a sword at the end. At first, Miles had balked at using it, but Riley had needled him until he agreed. And Miles had to admit, he liked having the use of two arms in a fight instead of one. It had been awkward to use in the beginning, but now it was a like another appendage. And it made him feel powerful. Not an emotion he was used to.

Miles wanted to go with Riley, but duty came first. He shook his head. "No. Maybe tomorrow. I need to go through these. One of the Carolina kids is sick. I'm trying to figure out why."

"Fine. But I'm going to hold you to it."

"Ah, gentlemen. Just the men I was hoping to run into." Simon Tolliver, the camp teacher, walked down the path, his legs moving fast. Simon was a few inches shorter than Miles's six feet, with a very thin frame. Miles figured it was probably nervous energy or brain energy that kept him from gaining weight. The man was always moving, always thinking.

"Hi, Simon," Riley said.

Miles nodded his greeting. "What's going on?"

Simon came to a stop next to them, his cape swirling around him. "It seems some of my students are under the impression that

Phoenixes do not need to know anything from books. I thought you two could come and disavow them of that notion."

Miles shook his head. "I'm afraid I can't. I need to go see Dixie."

Simon's smile dimmed. "I heard she was sick. Any ideas what it is?"

Simon had been the camp doctor for years, more out of default than anything else. But when Miles had shown an affinity for the work, he'd happily handed over the reins, even though Miles was only seventeen.

Miles had a few ideas about Dixie's illness, although as he hefted the textbook, he knew he needed to check a few more things before he was sure. "I'm close. Hopefully I'll know by the end of the day."

Simon nodded before turning to Riley, his expression bright again. "I guess that just leaves the two of us, Mr. Quinn."

Miles could tell Riley was scrambling to come up with a way out of the request. It's not that Riley wasn't smart; he just hated being the center of attention. But at the same time, having Riley support Simon would go a long way in demonstrating how important education was to the kids.

"Don't forget you promised to help me with Dixie in a little bit." Miles turned to Simon. "I need some help moving her and her cot."

"Oh, no problem. I'll have him back to you in plenty of time." Simon looked at Riley expectantly. Miles shrugged at Riley behind Simon's back. *Best I could do, buddy.*

Riley sighed. "Okay, Simon. Let's go."

Simon nodded. "Wonderful, wonderful." He latched on to Riley's arm before he could escape.

Riley looked back at Miles, and Miles struggled not to laugh. Riley, undeniably the toughest of the young Phoenixes, looked miserable. Facing a legion of aliens was not a problem. Standing in front of a classroom full of kids—terrifying.

13

Riley let Simon lead him toward the school tent, his hand still on Riley's arm. Riley would have shaken off anyone else who tried to pull him this way, but he couldn't with Simon. The man meant no offense, and Riley had known him since he was a kid. He was family.

Up ahead, the school tent had its flaps open. The sounds of children wafted out toward them. Riley remembered sitting next to David and then Miles, spending his days learning what he thought were useless facts when all he wanted to do was learn how to fight. Funny, though, the more he'd learned to fight, the more important what he learned in school had become.

Simon patted Riley's arm before they walked in. "I just need you to look serious. I won't draw too much attention to you."

Riley should have known Simon wouldn't make him uncomfortable. "Whatever you need."

Simon walked into the tent first, and Riley followed, although he had to duck under the fabric. As soon as he stepped in, all talking ceased. Riley's eyes roamed over the group. There were fourteen kids. No wait, thirteen. Dixie wasn't here. Riley knew all of the kids—all were younger than fourteen. They were the Jingle kids.

He winked at his sister, Maisy, who sat in the front row. They thought she was eight but couldn't be sure. They'd found her floating down a river five years ago right after the Unwelcome attack that had killed Riley's mom. For three years, she didn't say a word. But she was a pretty happy kid, at least during the day. At night, though, she'd find her voice and her fears. Thankfully, the nightmares had lessened over the years, especially since Lyla had started her defense training.

Most of the kids were too young to fight, but his aunt insisted all kids have some initial training at evasion. Two days a week, they met in the forest to learn how to move through the trees soundlessly. As they got older, bells were attached to their shoes and belt. They had to move without making a sound. Maisy had proven to be particularly adept at slipping through the forest without even a soft jingle of a bell.

Simon gestured to the back of the tent. Riley headed to an empty seat back there. An old chalkboard had been propped up in the front. A quick glance at it told Riley the topic: The Incident.

Riley sighed. He knew the kids had to learn it, but it seemed so unfair that they had to learn about such a horrific topic at such an early age. But as his aunt often reminded him, this generation of children knew of the harshness of the world since birth.

"Class, I've invited Riley to see how well you are learning your lessons. He has often told me how important it is for a soldier to think well."

As he took his seat, Riley arranged his face into a serious expression, although all the big eyes staring back at him made that difficult. "It's true. We need solders who can read situations, understand complexities."

Simon smiled, nodding. "Now, class, can someone tell me what was the initial event that resulted in our planet's instability?"

A dozen hands shot up in the air. Simon chose a small girl in the front with long, curly, dirty-blonde hair. Alyssa Ryder, six years old and Adros's sister. Alyssa clutched her doll to her chest. "The asteroid."

Simon beamed. "Very good, Alyssa."

Although correct, it was a highly simplified answer. The real answer was greed. Back in 2026, NASA had pulled an asteroid into the Moon's orbit and mined it. They found a treasure trove of new elements and minerals.

It didn't take long for the private sector to recognize the financial gain of asteroid mining. But unlike NASA, ByerTech didn't want the expense of wrangling an asteroid into the Moon's orbit. They decided it would be cheaper to pull one into the Earth's orbit.

NASA hadn't done that because they judged it to be too dangerous. One miscalculation, and the asteroid could crash into the Earth, setting off a worldwide catastrophe. Governments across the globe had argued against the actions. But no one controlled space. And legally, there was no way for any of them to stop ByerTech. By the time the countries managed to draft laws to block them, ByerTech had moved all the technology they would need into orbit.

Ignoring the worldwide condemnation of their actions and with potential profits clouding their view, they decided to go ahead with the cheaper operation, arrogance abundant in their ability to control every variable. That arrogance had resulted in the deaths of billions within a few weeks and millions more over the next few decades as the repercussions kept spiraling out.

Simon nodded, his thick gray hair unmoving, but his glasses slid down to the end of his nose. He pushed them back up, directing his attention to the rest of the class. "Correct. The asteroid hit in Europe in 2026, destroying most of the world's population. What exactly were the physical effects?"

A flurry of answers rang out. "Giant tsunamis."

"Volcanoes erupting."

"Earthquakes."

"Erratic weather patterns."

"Countries sank."

Simon gestured for quiet. "Very good. What country do we currently live in? Mr. Raffe?"

"The United States," Dart Raffe replied.

"And what has changed about the US? Ms. Chambers?"

"We no longer have a federal government, our elevation has increased due to crustal displacement, we have less land mass, and we no longer have machines."

Simon beamed. "And why don't we have machines?"

"The poles switched."

"Yes. The electromagnetic field shifted, making all electronics null and void, for the most part."

A horn blasted from somewhere outside the tent, followed by two others in quick succession. Everyone froze. Emergency signal.

Heart racing, Riley leaped to his feet. "Everyone stay here until you get your assignment." He rushed out of the tent, knowing Simon would keep the kids together.

He sprinted for the warning post. Six Phoenixes stood gathered there. Each wore a green or brown cloak, carried a long wooden staff usually slung over their back, and had a sword strapped to their waist. Lyla, the leader of the Phoenixes and the camp, stood in the middle of them. Her blue eyes met his with a nod. She had been in charge of the camp for the last three years. And although he now towered over her, he never questioned her authority, and neither did anyone else, at least not for long.

"What is it?" Montell asked.

Lyla's voice didn't waver as she met each person's gaze. "We have intel that the Unwelcome are planning an inspection. Riley, you and your unit get the Jingle kids to the cave. Go."

Riley nodded stepping away with his group who had fallen in line silently behind him as Lyla issued instructions to the others.

His mind organizing what needed to be done, he scanned his group, There were five of them. Himself, Petra, Shane, Miles, and Adros. "The kids are at the school. Adros and Shane you get them. Petra, we'll grab the supplies and meet at the cave. Miles head there now and make sure the entry is clear."

Everyone dispersed quickly without a word, even Adros. In moments like this, there were no disagreements, no questions. Everyone did what needed to be done. Because when the Unwelcome showed up, they weren't looking to take the camp's resources or even to take people with them.

No, when the Unwelcome showed up, they had only one thing on their agenda.

To kill the Cursed.

14

Lyla's skin tingled and her blood thrummed through her veins as she made her way toward the main gate. But she focused on keeping her expression calm, knowing she would help either stir up panic in the camp or calm it down. Lyla made eye contact with all who looked her way giving them a nod of assurance. Inside, she prayed that the visit went well. Their camp, named Attlewood, for a rusted sign unearthed near one of the camp's wells, was finally doing well. When they'd first started the camp, they'd had little more than a hundred people, one house standing, and lots of determination to make the place work.

Now they had ballooned to over two hundred people, had about two dozen freestanding wood cabins, a community kitchen, a stable, training area, and acres of crops. Everything was encircled by a strong fifteen-foot-high wooden fence. And every time the Unwelcome arrived, all that hard work was put in jeopardy. But like everything else, they'd prepared for these moments. Now all that preparation would either pay off or sign their death warrants.

Campers crowded the sides of the path, emotions ranging from fear to hate, usually both. Lyla was no different. She hated this, hated them. Five years ago, when she'd learned of the Unwelcome, she had been terrified. All they seemed to want to do was kill.

At that time, the Unwelcome had seemed to kill indiscriminately. And then she'd learned that they'd created a city along the coast. There'd even been rumors they'd done the same in other areas of the country, where cities had not been too badly destroyed. They'd fixed them up, returning power to them and allowing humans to live in them as well. Of course, there had been a price for that kindness—each human had to bring a child with them and hand them over to the Unwelcome.

Which was when the Unwelcome's killing pattern changed. No longer was everyone a target. Now it was clear they had one primary target: children between the ages of eight and thirteen. Those children were killed immediately, vaporized to ash. Younger children were taken into the city and adopted by people trying to wash the stain of their actions away.

Now, five years later, they were interested in those between the ages of thirteen and eighteen, the children known as the Cursed. Lyla's chest felt tight at the thought—Riley and Miles were in that age range.

And although Maisy was seven years old, Lyla wasn't taking any chances with her or any of the other kids. Some kids looked older than they were, some younger. She didn't think the Unwelcome would take a human's word as to the age of the kids, so anyone school age was hidden away when the Unwelcome arrived.

Lyla took a breath, her anger mounting as she thought of her three children—Riley, Miles, and Maisy. It had only been a few years ago that a few members of their camp had tried to take them along with another dozen kids to trade in. Lyla and the Phoenixes had stopped them, but Lyla had vowed never to allow the camp to be that vulnerable again. She'd initiated the Jingle Program, and they'd moved even farther inland. Simon had even figured out a method to create water from the movement of air that allowed them to stay away from all water sources.

All new members were carefully vetted and watched for months to make sure they weren't an Unwelcome spy. It wasn't a perfect system, but it had kept them safe all these years. But eventually the Unwelcome had found them. And they dropped in every three to four months, sometimes even at night. The image of the Unwelcome striding through the camp in the dark of night was the stuff of nightmares. The smallest one she had seen was over seven feet tall. And they were always covered from head to toe in a skintight navy-blue uniform with a dark helmet covering every inch of their faces.

After all this time, no one knew what the Unwelcome looked like under their uniforms. They were a complete unknown. And the terror she'd experienced the first time she'd seen one was still with her. But now that feeling of terror was surpassed by another feeling—hate.

Lyla didn't know how many had been killed when the Unwelcome first arrived, but the numbers had been huge. Her sister, Muriel had been one of the casualties, as had Miles's mother and sister. And she believed Maisy's family had been killed by them as well.

At the first sign of the Unwelcome, the Jingle kids and the Cursed disappeared into hiding at a spot they had searched long and hard for. It was far enough away that the Unwelcome would not stumble over it, and hidden enough that from the air that it would be unnoticeable. But Lyla didn't have time to make sure they reached it safely. She had to trust Riley and the other young Phoenixes to do their jobs, because right now, she had another job.

She was the welcome committee.

15

"Okay, you guys are doing great," Riley said quietly, glancing back at the kids that filed silently behind them. He and Petra had grabbed some bags of food and skins of water, then they'd hustled out of the camp. They'd caught up with Shane, who had a group of six kids. Adros had already gone ahead with another group of older kids and some supplies. Miles would be helping getting them all settled.

Ahead, he saw the entrance to the cave. It was wedged between two tall trees and a large boulder. It was actually a cavern under the ground. The trees were full of branches, which should give them cover from the air. He glanced back at Petra. She nodded at him to show she had all her kids.

Riley let out a breath. Good. He ushered all the kids into the large cave entrance, the air immediately cooling. There was a long tunnel that sloped downward almost imperceptibly. It was wide and deep, so all the kids could fit, with room to spare.

Riley stopped next to Adros, who stood at the entrance, ushering the other kids inside, taking a head count as they passed him. When the last one filed in, he looked over at Adros with a nod. "Six."

Adros's mouth dropped open. "I only have seven. That's thirteen. We're missing someone."

"Count again," Riley ordered, but Petra was already running down the tunnel to do just that. Riley scanned the trees surrounding them. How had they missed someone? Had someone fallen behind? They had done this drill thousands of times.

Petra ran up to him. "We're missing one Jingle kid. And Miles isn't here, either."

Riley stared at her, shock rooting him in a place for a moment before his mind shifted into gear. Miles was supposed to be the first one here. If there was a kid missing though, Miles must have gone after the other child. But who ...

Then it hit him. "Dixie Carolina—she's sick. She's in the med cabin."

16

Miles struggled to get Dixie up into his arms from the cot. She didn't weigh much, but it still wasn't easy with only half an arm. He'd been halfway to the cave when he remembered she was here.

"Miles?" Dixie asked, her blue eyes peering out from a face that was still flush with fever. Her blonde curls hung limp next to her face. She'd been in the med cabin for five days. Although only eleven, she was tall for her age, making her appear older— old enough to be mistaken for a Cursed.

"It's okay." Miles forced a smile onto his face. "I'm just taking you for a little fresh air."

Dixie nodded her head, her eyes closing again.

Miles got Dixie into his arms and hoisted her over his shoulder. *Thank God she's light*, he thought as he looked out of the tent. The coast was clear. Everyone was lined up near the entrance, although he knew the Unwelcome were most likely patrolling the forest as well.

Taking a breath, he darted out of the tent and headed for a loose board in the fence. He pulled the board back, turning sideways to slip the shoulder with Dixie over it through first. He yanked his foot back as he released the board, just barely missing pinning it there. He didn't even look around. He was out in the open here. He sprinted for the tree line. He stepped beyond one of the giant oaks and leaned against the tree to adjust Dixie. Now yells called out and better yet, no blasters, so he let himself a moment to feel some relief. *So far so good.* But his pulse still raced and sweat rolled down his back.

Pushing himself from the tree, he adjusted Dixie as she started to slip, and she let out a little groan. He winced. "Sorry, sorry. Shh, it's okay."

Miles looked around and realized he was off course. He needed to head more north if he was going to get to the cave. He changed direction and stepped on a branch. The crack sounded like a thunderclap. He went still. *Please let no one have heard that.*

He waited, but everything remained quiet. Too quiet. The hairs on the back of his neck rose. No birds, no chatter of small forest animals. Everything had gone silent.

Miles's heart began to pound. It sounded so loud in the still forest. He moved carefully, racking his brain to think of someplace he could hide Dixie, knowing that the cave had been a ridiculous idea. He'd never get them there without being seen.

Down by the water, there were some downed trees. He could probably put her in one of those and then cover her. She'd fit. *She* was small enough. He wouldn't, but he'd worry about that after he had Dixie hidden.

He felt a little better with a plan, but not by much. *Focus on what you can do. Worry about everything else later*, he warned himself.

He stayed off the path, knowing if the Unwelcome were nearby they would follow it. And besides, staying off the path made it easier to hide his footprints in the forest floor.

His shoulder began to ache, but he didn't dare move Dixie to the other one. He wouldn't be able to prop her up with his half arm. He shoved away the resentment that always surfaced whenever his arm kept him from doing things. He didn't have time for self-pity now.

He reached the edge of the tree line and paused, leaning against a tree to give his shoulder a little break and to give him a chance to scan the area. Trees lined the river on both sides, which was twenty feet wide where he was. The other bank was higher and covered with large rocks. This side, there were very few rocks making it a great spot for swimming in the warmer weather. Right now, the water meandered by slowly with no urgency. With the sun shining down, it looked incredibly peaceful.

No one seemed to be around, but the hair along his neck and arms refused to settle. He glanced around again. To get to the downed trees he'd have to travel open space. But there was no other option. He took a breath. It was now or never. He stepped from behind the tree just as an Unwelcome stepped from behind its own tree across the river.

17

L yla walked to the entrance of the camp, Frank Raffe at her side. Frank had been close friends with Lyla's father and was like a second father to her. He'd also run the camp until three years ago. He'd moved into the second's position, saying it was as close to retiring as he was ever going to get. But Lyla knew he needed the break. His leg hadn't healed properly from a gunshot wound he'd received protecting the camp, and he now had a permanent limp. He was still as strong as an ox, but these days he was an ox who needed to sit down a little more often.

Lyla glanced at her Phoenixes, who stood at varying points throughout the camp's population that had lined up for inspection. But her gaze searched for two in particular—a young muscular African-American woman and the lighter-skinned man next to her with almond-shaped eyes. Her best friends, Addie Hudson and Jamal Nguyen, gave her a nod as she headed for the front gate.

"Okay, Annie," said Lyla. "Open it up."

Annie, who stood by the lever, pulled it down, and the gate began to rise, revealing their guests.

Two Unwelcome stood flanking a smaller man—a human.

The human was wearing a deep purple velvet robe. Rings on his hands glistened in the sunlight. And his round stomach spoke to his lack of fear for going hungry. He looked like a medieval lord, which was no doubt how he viewed himself.

And the rest of us are his serfs.

Lyla gritted her teeth. She could almost understand the Unwelcome. They didn't owe her species anything. They weren't human. They probably didn't even have emotions. Humans like him, though, they disgusted her. They traded the lives of their own species for material gain.

"Vulture," Frank muttered, his eyes full of hate as he looked at the man.

Lyla didn't have time to respond but just gave him a curt nod to let him know she'd heard him and agreed.

Both of the Unwelcome towered above the man. One stood close to nine feet tall. The 'short' one probably measured out at eight feet. Both wore the tight navy-blue suits they always wore and helmets with the flat glass that acted as a mirror that completely covered their faces, their anonymity making them even more terrifying.

Lyla found herself wondering yet again what they looked like underneath their coverings. If they had eight eyes or two. Hell, they could have six tiny heads under that thing. Lyla studied the shorter Unwelcome's helmet, but it was just as opaque. Not a sliver of what was underneath could be seen.

Lyla and Frank stopped when they were five feet away.

The man in the robe nodded at Frank. "You are the leader?"

Frank shook his head, tilting it toward Lyla. "She is."

"Ah, my mistake. Apologies." Insincerity dripped off the man's words. "And what a lovely leader you are." The man's gaze raked Lyla from head to toe. She had to practically bite her tongue to keep from telling him what she thought of him. The happy image of yanking each of his eyeballs out kept her in her place.

Done with his inspection, the man gave a small bow. "I am Chad Keyes, liaison with the Naku."

Lyla crossed her arms, saying nothing, but she did wonder. Two years ago, they had learned the aliens were called the Naku, but by then the name the Unwelcome had fit too well for people to change it. But the fact that they had a name, that they had communicated that name somehow, that was intriguing. Did that mean they could speak? Because in all her time and all the stories she'd heard, she had never heard of one speaking.

Chad stared at her, and Lyla realized he was waiting for her to introduce herself. Lyla just stared back at the men. *It's going to be a long wait, buddy.*

Chad's cheeks turned red. "Yes, well, we are here to inspect the camp and make sure there are no undesirables being hidden."

"You mean *children*?" Lyla asked.

Chad narrowed his eyes. "As you know, we have bartered a truce with the Naku. In exchange for removing any undesirables, we are allowed to live our lives in peace."

Frank snorted next to her.

Chad raised his voice so it carried to the members of the camp who were watching. "Anyone who trades in an undesirable will be given lodging, food, and a job in New City. The offer holds regardless of the biological affiliation with the undesirable."

Lyla translated his little political speech in her mind. *Feel free to trade in any child you come across to live a little more comfortably.*

Chad waited a few moments, but no one said anything. "Very well." He waved the two Unwelcome forward. Each peeled off, walking along the crowd. Lyla held her breath as the nine-foot Unwelcome approached Susie Jenkins and her newborn. But the Unwelcome kept going, uninterested.

Only children between the ages of thirteen and eighteen. Lyla looked at Susie's little girl. Big brown eyes stared out of a heart-shaped face.

Why? What is so different about those kids? Her heart lurched as she pictured Riley and Miles. *What's so different about mine?*

18

M iles darted back behind the tree, his heart pounding.
Oh my God. Oh my God. There was no way that thing didn't see him. He was right there. Miles hugged Dixie to his chest, his mind scrambling desperately for a way to keep her safe.

Don't look. Don't look. He knew if the thing hadn't seen him, the safest option was to just wait and hope it went away. Looking would only raise the chance of it finding them.

A branch snapped to his right. Miles head whipped to the side before he dropped to the ground, crouching low over Dixie. A dense yew bush hid them from view as yet another Unwelcome stepped out.

No, no, no, no.

There was no chance they'd be able to get out now. He looked down at Dixie, but her eyes were closed, her breathing deep. Carefully, he laid her on the ground and gently pushed her under the bush. Silently, he grabbed some branches and leaves, placing them over her. It was not a great hiding spot but it was better than nothing. Maybe he could lead them away. Maybe the one across from him didn't realize he'd been holding someone. It was a slim hope. But it was all he had.

He placed a hand on Dixie's arm and gave it a little squeeze. *Stay quiet, Dixie, please.* Then he crouched, ready to run, when he heard a thump from the other side of the bank. He pictured the Unwelcome leaping across the river. He could run straight, but if they came around the oak, there was a good chance they'd see Dixie. *Damn it.*

He could hear the Unwelcome walking through the leaves. His heart continued to pound. Through the bush, he could just make out the Unwelcome from across the river joining the other one. They stood near each other, and Miles had the impression they were communicating, although he didn't hear anything. Then the two started to walk back toward the camp.

Miles's mouth dropped open. What the hell? Had the Unwelcome actually not seen him? The first Unwelcome disappeared into the trees. The second stepped for the tree line and then turned, looking directly at Miles's hiding spot.

Miles froze in fear. Sweat rolled down his back. His heart pounded so loud he was surprised it didn't wake Dixie. He tensed, ready to fight even as he knew it was a fight he couldn't win. But then the Unwelcome simply followed the other one, disappearing from view down the path.

Miles's stayed crouched, waiting for them to reappear, but neither did. He strained to hear anything, but it was silent, and eventually the normal sounds of the forest returned. Miles sank onto his butt, his back against the tree. He couldn't seem to stop shaking.

It saw us. It knew we were here. He shook his head. *No. It left. It couldn't have seen us.*

But how was that possible? He and Dixie had been in the thing's direct line of sight. For another twenty minutes, Miles sat with Dixie, too afraid to move, waiting for that thing to come back.

Then a blast of the all clear rang out from the camp center.

Miles looked around, stunned. It had to have somehow not seen him. That was the only thing that made sense.

I guess it doesn't matter, he thought as he pushed the debris off Dixie and pulled her from under the bush and into his lap. With effort, he got her into his arms and stood.

Don't look a gift horse in the mouth, Miles. Just say thank you.

19

As soon as the all-clear horn rang out, Riley and Petra sprinted back to the camp, leaving Shane and Adros to escort the kids. Riley had been crawling the walls of the cave waiting for Miles to show up or the all clear to blow. He was so scared he was shaking. Miles and Dixie had never shown up at the cave. Riley had tried to go look for them, but an Unwelcome ship flew overhead just as he was about to leave the cave. He couldn't risk all the kids in the cave, even to find Miles.

Now he and Petra sprinted through the woods, not saying a word, but he knew they were thinking the same thing: *Please let them be all right.*

Riley knew the chances of that were very slim. Miles was a good fighter, even with half an arm. And he was smart. Honestly, he had so many facts stored in his brain it was amazing. But he was not good at stealth. It was like he had cement blocks attached to his feet. And if he had to sneak past the Unwelcome ...

Riley shook off the thought and picked up his pace. He and Petra didn't slow as they sprinted through the western gate. He skidded to a stop in front of Edna and Emma, the first members of the camp they saw; they were headed back to the kitchen.

Edna, big boned with strawberry-blonde hair, looked between the two of them. "Hey, you two, where's the fire?"

"Did they find anybody?" Riley asked, his tone breathless.

"What? No," said Emma. "All you kids—" Her eyes grew large. "Who's missing?"

"Miles and Dixie. They never showed up," Petra said.

Emma and Edna turned around. "We'll head to the med cabin," Edna said. "You check with Lyla."

Riley was already running. Petra was right beside him. *Damn it, Miles, where are you?*

Petra grabbed his arm, yanking him to a stop and nearly pulling his arm out of its socket at the same time.

"What the hell?" he yelled, glaring down at her.

"Look." She nodded to the entrance as Miles came in with Dixie in his arms.

Relief flooded Riley so quickly that his knees shook. He ran a hand over his face and took a deep breath, trying to calm his breathing. Petra jogged over to them. Riley reached them as Petra was taking Dixie from Miles.

Miles looked up and must have read the worry on Riley's face. "We couldn't make it to the cave. I was halfway there when I remembered Dixie was at the med cabin."

"I'm going to take her back." Petra looked at Miles. "You did good."

Miles ducked his head. "Thanks."

"Yeah," Riley said, his voice a little ragged. He cleared his throat. "You did."

Miles shrugged. "It wasn't anything."

Riley punched him lightly in the shoulder. "Yeah it was. Now come on, let's go see what the Unwelcome took."

Miles frowned, looking back at the entrance.

Riley paused. "Everything okay?"

"Yeah, good. It's just—" Miles shook his head. "It's nothing. Let's go see what the damage is."

For a moment Riley considered pushing Miles to see what he had been going to say, but Miles was already moving away. It was probably nothing. Besides, he was still pretty shaky, and he couldn't really think clearly. He blew out a breath. Miles was safe. Dixie was safe. That was all that mattered.

20

Two days after the Unwelcomes' visit, Lyla rolled her shoulders as she approached her house. She had the only large house in the camp. It was a two-story colonial left over from the Before. She liked to imagine the house in its heyday, with flower boxes at the windows and newly painted siding and shutters. These days, there were only remnants of that past with its faded paint and one shutter left standing on a window at the side of the house.

But still, it was a real house. It was also Command Central. Meetings were held in the old dining room, and the parlor was now the camp office. And she had an open-door policy. Today was one of the few days she wished she didn't. One of the Phoenixes, Shayna, had gotten sick last night, so Lyla had taken her shift. And if today was like every other day, she knew sleep was far in her future.

The whole camp had been unsettled by the Unwelcomes' visit. The kids were safe, but the Unwelcome had taken half of their food provisions from the kitchen. Luckily, last year, after the Unwelcome had first started visiting, they'd taken to hiding their food stores, so it wasn't as bad as it could have been. The taking of the provisions bothered Lyla, but what really got to her was that she was pretty sure they didn't need them. The 'tax' as they called it was a punishment for not providing any kids. In other camps, when kids had been found, nothing had been taken.

We can make up the food loss. We can't make up the kids.

Lyla hadn't even made it to her front door before she saw the first headache awaiting her. Frank stood unsmiling, one foot on the bottom step of the porch as he spoke with a man. He was slim and muscular, but not Phoenix muscular, and from the hat he had crumpled in his hand at his side, she knew he worked the fields. As Lyla drew closer she realized it was Sheldon.

She paused mid-step, tempted to run and hide. She wasn't scared of Sheldon, but all the man seemed to be able to do was complain. He'd joined the camp two years ago along with his brother, and both of them seemed to get great joy in expressing how unfair everything was. But they were good workers, and the complaints never went beyond that, so they stayed. But Lyla really wasn't in the mood to deal with him right now. Last time he'd complained that Edna was intentionally giving him rolls smaller than anyone else. It didn't help that when she'd mentioned it to Edna, she said she actually did do it once because he'd criticized her beef stew.

Lyla slowed her steps, but Frank raised an eyebrow at her, and Lyla knew he knew what she was thinking, so she straightened her shoulders and continued forward.

"-apparently not all of us have to." Sheldon turned so abruptly Lyla had to step to the side or get run over. Crushing hit hat back on his head, Sheldon gave her a hard look as he passed.

Lyla watched Sheldon storm off , before turning back to Frank. "I'm probably going to regret this, but what was that all about?"

Frank sighed. "There's been some grumbling about the Phoenixes not pulling their fair share."

Lyla gritted her teeth. Cal had started all of that ridiculousness five years ago in an attempt to take over the camp. He hadn't succeeded, and Lyla later killed him after he'd kidnapped a large group of children, but the rumors were never completely squashed.

"How can anyone say that? The Phoenixes spend every day training and on guard on top of regular daily chores. They do more than their share."

"Well, some folks are taking issue with guard duty. According to them, standing around looking for non-existent threats is not taxing work."

Lyla opened her mouth to defend her Phoenixes and then shut it, trying to see the issue from the complainers' perspective. It was true. They hadn't had any threats to fight off in a long time. But that was in large part due to the reputation the Phoenixes had earned in defending the camp. Their past bloodshed had bought them peace—with the humans, at least.

Lyla sighed. "I can see that. We've been playing defense so long we haven't realized the landscape has changed."

Frank's eyebrows rose. "You don't think we should reduce the number of guards, do you?"

"No, of course not. But maybe we could open some of the positions up to more people, maybe start with a guard tower or two. Put people in place who are good with a bow and arrow as well as responsible."

"It's a good idea. How do you want to start?"

"Let's draw up a list of people who might be able to do the job. Then we'll have to figure out some sort of training. People always think they'll keep their heads in an emergency, but until that's tested, we can't be sure. We can't put someone up there who's going to freak out at their first sighting of an Unwelcome ship or an unfamiliar face."

"So how exactly do we train for that?"

She grinned. "I have no idea. Let's just start with the list and we'll think on the process for a little bit."

"Sounds good to me."

They headed inside. She opened the door and pulled her scabbard over her head, laying it against the door.

"By the way, you look like hell," Frank said.

A laugh broke from Lyla's lips as she headed into the dining room. "Please don't sugarcoat it."

"You work too hard. Someone else could have taken the shift."

"Everyone had already been on double shifts."

"Yeah, but they are off in between shifts. You take a shift and then take care of the camp all day." Frank nodded at the table. "Brought you breakfast."

Lyla looked at the long, scarred wooden table that had a tray on one end loaded with one of Edna's signature breakfasts. She looked back at Frank, who had perched his glasses at the end of his nose as he took a seat and began reading over the schedule for the day at the other end of the table.

Lyla walked over and kissed him on the cheek. "I don't care what anyone says. You are a sweet old man."

Frank glared at her over his glasses. "You tell anyone that and we're done."

She squeezed his arm. "Wouldn't dream of it."

Lyla walked over to the table and sank gratefully into the world's ugliest chair, which was also her most prized possession.

Miles, Petra, and Riley had given it to her one Christmas about three years ago. They'd found it in an abandoned house and lugged it back to camp. Then they'd dug up some extra foam for the seat and back and done a makeshift reupholstering job with a staple gun they had found God knew where with scraps of material. Corduroy, leather, faded cotton fabric with large blue, yellow, and orange birds adorned it, which made it slightly hard on the eyes. But it was awfully comfortable.

Lyla pulled the napkin off the tray and nearly groaned with joy. Eggs, bacon, even an apple. *Man, am I hungry.*

She picked up her fork and took a bite of the eggs. Heaven,

even if they were a little cold. There was a small knock at the
door. Lyla closed her eyes with a groan. *Oh, please go away.* She
looked over at Frank. "Guess we should see who that is."

Frank headed toward the window that overlooked the porch,
glancing out. "Whoever it is can damn well—" He cut off in mid-
sentence and hurried to the door.

Concerned, Lyla stood up, crossing the room. Frank opened
the door. Two girls, ages nine and six, stood framed in the doorway.
The sun shone behind them, showing their skinny frames through
their calf-length cotton dresses. They had matching dirty-blonde
hair that cascaded down past their shoulders in a tangled mess.

Lyla pasted a smile over her concern. "Rachel, Alyssa. What a
nice surprise. Come in, come in."

Alyssa clung to her sister Rachel's hand, her eyes as big as
saucers. Frank ushered them in, his tone unusually gentle. "Hi,
girls. Is everything all right?"

Alyssa moved behind her big sister, only her little face
peeking out. Rachel took a small step forward, her little shadow
moving with her.

Lyla smiled encouragingly as she gestured to the bench along
the side of the table. "It's okay. Come on over here."

Rachel took another three steps in, staying just out of Lyla's
reach. *Or just out of striking distance,* Lyla thought.

Lyla took care to keep her movements and voice non-threat-
ening. She gently placed her hands on the table, in plain sight.
"You two are out early. Does your dad know you're here?"

Alyssa ducked her head back again.

Rachel shook her head. "He's asleep."

"Okay. Well, have you two had breakfast? I was just about to
eat mine. But I'm not very hungry. Would you guys mind
helping me?"

The two girls slid closer to the table, their eyes on the tray.
Lyla's heart dropped. They looked so hungry.

Lyla darted a glanced at Frank. His face was mutinous, but she knew he wasn't angry at the girls. Oh no, his anger was directed at the girls' father.

The two girls climbed onto the bench next to Lyla, their eyes occasionally straying to Frank, who had shifted his gaze to his papers again, although Lyla could still feel his anger. She hoped he'd keep a lid on it while the girls were here.

Lyla pushed her plate toward them. "Like I said, I'm really not hungry this morning. You guys would be doing me a favor if you helped me eat this. I don't want Emma and Edna to think I don't like their food."

Alyssa looked at Rachel, who nodded. Timidly, they each reached out a hand and pulled off a piece of bacon. The girls' eyes widened as they swallowed and soon their hands were moving incredibly fast, trying to get all the food in. Lyla wouldn't have been surprised if they licked the plate clean when they were done.

Lyla grabbed the mug of coffee, taking a sip. She struggled to keep her features composed but inside she was seething. *God damn you, Brendan.* She pictured their father, with his gut hanging over his pants while his girls starved. People had come to her with suspicions that he was taking their food rations, but there had never been any proof. And he never let the girls out of his sight.

Across from her, the girls finished. A blush bloomed across Rachel's cheeks. "I'm sorry. We ate it all."

"You were supposed to," Lyla said before standing and grabbing a box from the windowsill. "In fact, there's something else here you two could help me with. Edna made these for me, but like I said, I'm not really hungry and I don't want to hurt her feelings. Do you think you guys have room for a few cookies?"

The girls' eyes lit up and Lyla cursed Brendan again. Cookies should bring happiness, but not this level of happiness. Retaking her seat, she opened the box and the unmistakable aroma of sugar cookies wafted out.

The girls' stared at the box. Lyla smiled, handing each of them one.

Rachel put hers in her pocket.

Lyla looked at her, eyebrows raised. Rachel read the question in her eyes. "I'm going to save it for later. If that's okay."

"I think that's a great idea. A little treat for when you're hungry again." Lyla closed the lid on the box. "Now, I'm glad you guys came to visit me. But I think maybe you might have something to talk to me about. Is that right?"

Rachel nodded, her gaze glued to the tabletop.

Lyla reached out a hand but then pulled it back without touching the girl. She had a feeling a touch might not be what the moment called for. Instead, she just waited.

Two minutes passed before Rachel said anything. And when she did, Lyla had to lean forward to hear her.

"My dad. He hits us." Rachel darted a glance at Lyla before looking down again. Her whole body was shaking.

"When did this happen?" Lyla asked, keeping her voice calm, unthreatening, even as her anger began to build.

"Last night," Rachel whispered. "But ... it's happened before."

It was a struggle for Lyla to keep her voice even. She took a breath. "I see. Are you two all right?"

Rachel nodded, darting a glance at Alyssa. Her words came out in stutters. "It wasn't me this time. This time, he went after Alyssa. He kicked her in her belly."

Discipline kept Lyla from gasping. But behind her she heard Frank's sharp intake of breath.

Lyla moved slowly, walking around the table, kneeling down in front of Alyssa. "Alyssa, could you show me where he hurt you?"

Alyssa looked at Rachel, who nodded. Alyssa climbed down

off the bench and slowly lifted her dress. A mass of purple colored her abdomen.

Lyla tightened her mouth, letting out a small breath. She reached out and carefully lowered the girl's dress. She looked at Rachel, who now had tears running down her face.

"He's done this before?" Lyla asked.

Rachel nodded, wiping at her tears.

Lyla reached out and squeezed Rachel's arm. "It's okay. Everything's going to be all right. Is there a reason you didn't you tell me sooner?"

Rachel looked at Alyssa, who buried her head into Rachel's side. "Dad said you wouldn't believe us. And if you did, you'd get rid of all of us. Not just him."

Lyla reached out, pushing the hair out of Rachel's eyes. "No, sweetheart. The rule is no violence. And those who are responsible for the violence must be punished. But they're the only one."

The violence rule was one of the first rules they'd created when they'd established their camp. There was too much violence in this world, and people needed to have a place where they felt safe, especially the children.

Lyla glanced away as images of Brendan hurting his daughters flashed through her mind. *Damn it. I should have known. I should have done something sooner.* She didn't like Brendan. The man was obnoxious, lazy, and cruel. But she'd had no proof, only suspicions.

Until now. She swallowed down her anger, because right now, making sure the girls were safe was the priority over anything else.

Pasting a smile on her face, she turned to the girls. "How would you two feel about living here with me and my gang? I have an extra room upstairs we could turn into a bedroom. Would that be okay?"

Rachel looked at her, hope blooming across face. "You mean it?"

Lyla nodded.

Rachel looked down at Alyssa and squeezed her hand. "Yes."

"Then it's settled. We'll move you in here. We'll just grab your stuff—"

Alyssa and Rachel took a step back, fear flashing across their faces. "We don't want to go back there. He'll be angry."

Lyla knelt down in front of them, reaching her hands out for them. "Shh, shh. It's all right. I'll have your stuff brought here. You don't have to go back. You don't have to see him again."

"You promise?" Rachel asked.

"Look at me. Both of you." Lyla waited until Alyssa raised her eyes to meet her gaze. It broke her heart to see the tears trickling down her cheeks. "I will never let him hurt you again. I promise."

The girls stared at her for a moment before they became a flurry of motion.

Before she could brace herself, Rachel and Alyssa threw themselves at her. Lyla stumbled back, nearly falling, but she wrapped her arms around them, feeling the tremor run through their small, thin bodies. She rubbed each of their backs, murmuring to them. "You're safe now. I won't ever let him hurt you."

They stayed together for a few moments before Rachel pushed back, her expression becoming dark. "But what about my dad? He's going to be angry."

This time Lyla couldn't keep the anger from her voice. "You leave him to me."

21

Riley grabbed the pole, the two buckets balanced precariously on the ropes at each end. He had to walk carefully, so as to not spill every time he took a step. The well was a good four hundred yards from the kitchens. The more he spilled, the longer he'd spend walking back forth with the day's supply. He reached the kitchen tent and unloaded his buckets in one of the giant tubs.

Edna looked up from where she was peeling potatoes with a smile. "Thanks, Riley."

"No problem. And only five more trips to go." He stepped out of the tent and rolled his shoulders. That had been his sixth trip and already his shoulders were sore. His aunt was right. He was slacking in his training. He put the pole back on his shoulders and started heading back to the well.

"Riley!"

He turned around to see Frank hurrying toward him, practically leaping with the use of his crutch. A sweat had broken out on his brow with the effort.

Riley lowered the buckets. "What's happened?"

"Your aunt. She's gone to confront Brendan. He's been hitting his girls."

Fear clenched in his gut. It wasn't that he didn't think his aunt would win if it came down to a fight, it was just he didn't trust Brendan Ryder to fight fairly. "Where?"

Frank pointed. "She was heading to their tent."

"Where are Jamal and Addie?"

"They're on a scouting mission. They should be back any minute. I'm going to find some other Phoenixes, but—"

"I'll go now." Riley took off at a run. He sprinted past a startled group of children and rounded the corner, almost running into his aunt coming from the other direction.

She stepped out of his way as he stumbled to a stop and raised an eyebrow. "Frank?"

He nodded.

"With me, then. Keep an eye on Adros. Don't interfere, but don't let him interfere, either."

He fell into step with her, wishing he had stopped to grab his sword. He felt at his waist. His dagger was still there. Small, but it would do in a pinch.

Some of the camp had noticed their passage. A few had even started to follow them. No threat, just curious.

Up ahead, the Ryders' tent came into view. To get a cabin, you had to help build it. Brendan had never bothered. The tent was set back from the rest of the camp. No one wanted Brendan as a neighbor. The man himself was just stepping out. He let out a big yawn, raising an arm to scratch the underside. His shirt was stained and there were rips at the armpits. His hair lay plastered against his head.

"Brendan Ryder," Lyla said. The camp behind him seemed to go silent with her words, as if everyone had been waiting for this moment. And she supposed they all had. Brendan had three children—Rachel, Alyssa, and Adros. Because of them, they'd let Brendan use excuses for why he couldn't contribute as much as the other members of the camp. The girls, at least, were sweet and always trying to help. But whenever someone mentioned to Brendan about not pulling his share, he suggested he and his kids should go. All of them knew the girls would not survive for long with Brendan, so they let it go.

But this, hitting the girls, that couldn't be allowed. Lyla stepped forward. "You have been charged with striking a child. You are banished from the camp."

Brendan sneered. "Banished? You mean you're going to send me and my kids out to fend for ourselves?"

"No. Your girls have asked to stay, and if Adros wishes to, he may as well. But you will be leaving."

"And who's got the stones to make me go? You?" His eyes shifted to Riley. "That little prick behind you?"

"The job is mine. And you will go." She pulled out her staff. "Either voluntarily or involuntarily."

Riley searched the crowd that encircled Lyla and Brendan. Adros wasn't among them. Where was he?

Brendan dropped his cup. "You know what? I've been looking forward to this. You walk around here like you're some big shit. You're nothing. Everyone bows and scrapes at your feet. Well, not me, and that's why you're trying to make me go."

"No, you are going because you struck Rachel and Alyssa."

He sneered. "They'll never survive without me. Who'd want them? Worthless little wretches."

"*I* want them. They're under my protection now."

Brendan narrowed his eyes. Riley scanned the crowd. Where the hell was Adros? Movement to his right drew his attention. Adros was emerging from between two cabins at a run, his friends at his side. Riley made his way over, blocking his way.

Adros glared at him. "Out of my way."

Riley held his ground. "Don't interfere, Adros."

Adros reached out a hand to shove Riley out of the way. Riley grabbed Adros's wrist and twisted it, stepping to the side. Pushing on Adros's elbow, he forced him to bend at the waist.

"Let go!" Adros yelled.

Riley leaned down until his lips were almost touching Adros's ear. He pictured Rachel and Alyssa and felt anger flow through him. He spoke through clenched teeth. "Your dad has been hitting your sisters. If Lyla finds out you knew, you'll be punished as well. So think very carefully about your next move." He released Adros and stepped back.

Adros whirled around, his hands up. Riley stared him down, not moving an inch.

"You don't know—"

Riley said nothing, but his hands itched to hit Adros. There was no way he couldn't have known. He let his sisters get hurt. In his mind, he was no better than his father. When he spoke, his voice was whisper soft. "Try me."

Adros stared at him before his gaze flicked back to his father. He gave an abrupt nod, not meeting Riley's eyes.

Riley studied him for a moment, trying to judge if he could trust Adros to hold himself back. His eyes met Shane's gaze behind Adros's back. Shane gave him the smallest of nods, agreeing he'd keep Adros in check.

Riley stepped out of the way, letting Adros continue to his tent.

He fell in step behind him. Adros came to a halt at the edge of the group who'd gathered around Lyla and Brendan. Riley noticed with some relief that Frank was now here, along with two Phoenixes, Montell and Otto.

Brendan hadn't moved much from his spot. Montell stepped forward. "Lyla? Do you want us to remove him?"

Lyla waved him back but didn't take her gaze from Brendan. "No. Brendan's going to leave on his own."

Brendan grunted, turning away and then sprinting back to Lyla and diving for her legs.

Lyla stepped aside, slamming her staff onto his back, twirling it so it caught him under his chin and slammed him onto his back. She stood with the staff resting on his throat. "You will leave. You have ten minutes to gather whatever you need and go."

Brendan looked up at her with hate in his eyes, then he nodded.

Lyla stepped back, letting him get to his feet. She gestured to Montell and Otto, who stepped forward and escorted Brendan back to his tent, standing guard as he collected his things.

Lyla caught Riley's gaze for a second before her gaze shifted to Adros, who stood stiffly next to him. She walked up to him. "Adros, your father has been banished because he has been abusing your sisters. Your sisters will be staying with me for the time being. You know we do not tolerate violence of any kind here. You are welcome to stay as long as you follow our rules and not the example of your father."

Adros wouldn't meet her gaze but gave her a nod.

"Speak with Frank and he'll let you know where you can bunk." She paused. "You are your own man, Adros. No one judges you for what your father has done."

He met her eyes, and Riley could have sworn relief flashed through them before he covered it. Lyla turned to Riley. "Walk with me."

Riley fell in step with her. He glanced back and saw Adros staring at his father, who was placing his belongings into a sack. He turned back to Lyla, keeping his voice low. "You know Adros knew about the abuse."

Lyla nodded. "Most likely."

"Well, I don't understand. How can he escape unpunished?"

Lyla didn't stop walking, and Riley had to hurry to catch up with her. Lyla looked at him from the corner of her eyes. "Do you really think the girls were the only ones he abused?"

Riley stopped short, his mouth hanging open. He hurried to catch up with Lyla. "But Adros is bigger than Brendan."

"But he wasn't always." Lyla sighed. "Adros has had it rough. But he's a good kid at heart, and one day, he'll be a good man. We can help with that or we can guarantee he becomes just like his father. Which would you rather do?"

Riley hated when she did this. He wanted to be mad at Adros for picking on Miles and being a bully. But he couldn't ignore the thought of Adros cowering from his father. He sighed. "Help, of course."

Lyla linked arms with him. "Good, because now he's your special project."

"What?!"

"Train him, give him responsibility. See how he does."

"Why don't you just ask me to teach the sheep to dance?" he muttered. "It'd be easier."

Lyla laughed. "Well, Sisyphus, I have faith in you."

"I think Sisyphus may have had it easier, too," Riley mumbled.

22

Montell and Otto escorted Brendan to the front gate. Riley had climbed one of the watch towers to watch him go. Brendan shook off Otto's hand at the gate and then spit at Montel's feet. Montell reached for his staff, but Otto held him back. Brendan gave them a smirk, but as he turned the smirk dropped, and Riley was pretty sure it was fear he saw on the man's face.

For a moment Riley felt pity for him. But then he pictured Brendan's daughters and the pity hardened, although it didn't completely disappear. Brendan had brought this on himself.

Riley watched until Brendan was out of view. Then he slowly climbed down. He still couldn't believe his aunt wanted him to work with Adros. At the same, he still couldn't keep the picture of Adros getting hit by Brendan out of his mind, and things started coming back to him. When Adros had first joined the camp, he always had bruises under his shirt. Riley saw them when they went swimming, although Adros almost always left his shirt on. Now Riley was afraid he knew why.

"Crap," he said as he kicked at the ground.

"Hey," Miles called out. "What did the ground ever do to you?"

Riley grinned. "It fails to cushion me softly every time I fall."

"Maybe you should stop falling."

"A little hard to do when people are swinging staffs at your head."

"Always with the excuses." Miles looked around and then lowered his voice. "I heard about Brendan. I'm worried."

"It's okay. He already left."

Miles shook his head. "That's not what I'm worried about,"

Riley sighed. "Yeah. Come on. I need to talk and I don't want to talk here."

With a nod, Miles fell in step with Riley. They gave Angela, the Phoenix at the gate, a wave as they headed out. Within the last year, Lyla had allowed them to leave the camp unsupervised during daylight hours.

The two of them slipped into the forest, neither one speaking. They walked for thirty minutes before they came across the old highway. In its day, it had had four lanes, but Mother Nature had done a number on it. A deep trench had swallowed the far lane, probably from an earthquake. The rest of the road was uneven, with larges rips in the cracked asphalt. Trees had sprouted through some of them. Even in its sad state, it was both Miles and Riley's favorite place to walk. They liked to imagine the lives of the people who'd once used the road. Riley liked to think that maybe one day it could be their life too.

As soon as they stepped onto the asphalt, Miles demanded a full accounting of the showdown with Brendan. When Riley finished, Miles shook his head. "I don't get why Brendan joined our camp. Why didn't he take the kids to New City? He seems like the type."

"New City is good, but they expect people to work. Brendan got to skate by in our camp by using the girls as his excuse. That wouldn't have worked there."

"True. So what do you think's going to happen now?"

Riley shook his head, but worry dogged his steps. His aunt had done the right thing. He didn't doubt that. But he knew there would be repercussions. "I don't know. But I don't see Brendan walking away quietly. It's not really his style."

"What about Adros? Do you really think he can be a good Phoenix?"

Riley sighed. "I don't know. But Lyla thinks he will be one day."

Miles shook his head. "I don't like it."

Riley looked over in surprise. "You think Lyla's wrong about Adros?"

"No, I think she's probably right. But she has an awful lot of faith in human nature. I'm not sure it's always warranted."

"You worried about her?"

"Yes. No." Miles sighed. "Trust me, I know how capable she is. It's just that Brendan is sneaky. Lyla isn't. She's about as straightforward as they come. If Brendan is setting something up, I don't know if she'll see the trap."

Riley nodded. He'd been thinking the same thing. He knew Brendan was going to strike back. It wasn't if, it was *when*. And just like Miles, he worried his aunt wouldn't see it coming. Because Miles was right, if there was one thing Brendan was, it was sneaky.

Riley looked at the asphalt, letting his mind drift to when cars had driven over these roads. What had that been like? To cover miles in minutes rather than hours? To not have to worry as much about the weather? To be able to put lights on at night? To be safe?

Miles grabbed his arm. "Riley."

Riley's head jolted up, his arm reaching for his sword, reacting to the alarm in Miles's voice.

Two Unwelcome emerged from the woods in front of them, only ten feet away.

23

The trees seemed to be pressing in on Brendan. He jumped at the snap of a branch and then again when a squirrel darted across the path behind him. Brendan wiped his forehead with a shaky hand. He did not like to be out here. He'd never really learned how to survive outside the walls of a camp. Truth was, he'd been protected from the outside world most of his life. He'd been ten when the world was destroyed. His dad had taken him, his mother, and his sister to their home in the hills, far away from civilization. They'd stayed bunkered down there for years, along with the house's staff.

The staff had taken care of them. But then sickness had come when he was a teenager and took most of the adults. After that, it had only been him and Sheila, the maid's daughter, who'd survived. Sheila took care of him after that.

A flood had finally taken the house, and they'd gone to their first camp with their kids. Sheila got to work, but she hadn't done enough and they were asked to leave. Then she'd gotten sick and died, leaving him with three kids to look after. That's when he'd joined Lyla's camp. At first, he'd worked hard to make sure they stayed. He saw what it was like outside the gates. But then he realized the premium that was put on kids at the camp and realized they were his ticket to an easier life.

So what if he pushed them around a little? The world was hard, better they learn that from him than anybody else. He stumbled over a root and crashed to his knees, picturing his daughters. *Ungrateful brats.* He'd provided for them and they had turned him in. He should have known. They took after their mother.

But Adros, he was supposed to be Brendan's son. He'd grown up strong, big, and he knew the other kids were scared of him. It made Brendan proud. But Adros had stayed behind, too. *Traitor.*

Brendan pushed himself to his feet, cinching his pack tighter around his shoulders. He didn't have a destination in mind. Truth was, he didn't have a clue where he could go. But even as he feared what was to come, he knew one thing for certain—Lyla was going to pay for what she had done to him. She'd taken everything away from him, and he was going to do the same to her.

24

The Unwelcome in front of Miles and Riley were huge, easily eight feet each. They raised their spears.

The scuffle of gravel behind him caused Riley to turn his head. Another Unwelcome was behind them with its spear also raised. But this Unwelcome was a little shorter—only about seven feet tall.

I didn't hear them approach. How did I not hear them?

Riley's mind raced, looking for a way out, but he knew there were no good options here. None, at least, that would result in both Miles and Riley surviving. *Then I need to make sure Miles survives.*

"Humans!" the Unwelcome behind them yelled. "Down!"

Miles appeared too shocked to move. Riley was shocked as well—*they could speak!* But that revelation was nothing compared to the need to survive.

Riley yanked Miles to the ground as a burst of energy blasted from the alien's spear. The blast of light was so close Riley felt the heat on his face. One of the aliens in front of them dropped. Another shot came from the being behind them and the second dropped as well.

Riley rolled to his feet, gaping at the alien behind him.

The alien covered the distance to them quickly. Riley pulled his sword out, but the alien grabbed his arm. "Don't." It looked down at Riley as Miles got to his feet. At least, Riley thought it was looking down at him. With the helmet on, it was hard to tell.

"There are more coming," it said. "You need to run." He released Riley's arm.

Riley stared at the Unwelcome. What was this? A test? A trap? He couldn't figure the alien's angle.

Miles grabbed Riley's arm. "Three more down the road."

Riley glanced back. Sure enough, another three were bounding down the road toward them.

"Run." The Unwelcome ran past them toward the other three. "Run."

Miles yanked Riley off the road and into the trees as the sound of blasters rang out behind them. One blast hit a tree just as Riley passed, sending splinters of wood toward him. But he barreled on, Miles right on his tail and soon the sound of the blasts faded in the distance. But they didn't slow. Together, they sprinted through the woods, changing directions, leaping over downed trees, over upturned earth, staying light on their feet. Riley led the way, no destination in mind except to lead them away from the camp. They ran full-out for twenty minutes, not pausing, not hesitating.

Finally they came to rest in a cliff top that gave them a view of the area surrounding them. Their breathing was harsh, but soon it calmed. Riley strained to look out over the ground they'd covered, but there was no movement, certainly nothing as large as an Unwelcome.

Miles looked up, still bent over from the run. "We good?"

"I think so." Riley didn't pull his gaze from the woods below them. Riley's heart still pounded, but not from exertion. He knew it was fear, not to mention confusion.

"What the hell was that?" Miles asked, his words came out in spurts between gasps for air. "He helped us. They can *talk*."

"No. It has to be some kind of trick."

"What kind of trick? I've never heard of one of them doing that."

Riley had no answer. He'd never heard of one of them doing that, either. "I have no idea."

"We need to go back."

Riley stared at Miles. "Are you kidding? We are *not* going back there."

Miles grabbed his arm. "What if that one is different? What if he can help us? We nearly got caught the last time they came to the camp. And we didn't even know these ones were in the area. We didn't see a ship. There was no warning. What if the same thing happens again, but this time at the camp? People are going to die."

Miles stared into Riley's eyes, and Riley knew he was right. People they cared about would die. The Unwelcome didn't kill adults unless they tried to protect the children in the kill range. And their camp was full of people who would do just that.

Miles continued. "It's only a matter of time before we're caught. We need intel. He might be able to give it to us."

"Or he was hoping we'd lead him to our camp," Riley said. "He was probably counting on that. *That's* the trap."

Miles threw up his hands. "That makes no sense. They already know where our camp is."

"But they don't know we're from that camp."

"Then why not kill one of us? They could still follow the other one."

Riley opened his mouth to answer and then shut it. "That's a good point."

Miles looked over the landscape, and Riley knew he was twisting and turning the situation in his mind, looking for all possible outcomes. "It's possible they had some agenda for sparing us, but I think it's unlikely. That Unwelcome fired on its own kind to save us."

"Or they just staged it. The blasts don't kill them. It could all have been a show."

"It's possible," Miles conceded. "But I think we need to take the chance. Riley, we're dying out here."

"We're doing fine."

"Riley, one bad harvest and people will starve. A fire at the food depot and we'll starve. An attack by a larger group, a tornado swarm erupts in the middle of camp, and we'll lose our camp. So yeah, we're okay right now. But we can't survive a big hit. We've been lucky. But luck is not a strategy."

That was one of Lyla's favorite phrases. She drilled it into them while they trained. For every opponent, they needed a plan, one that could adapt to circumstances, but they could not ever count on getting lucky in a fight.

"We need to change something or we're not going to last. You know that."

And Riley did. The last inspection had nearly caught them. And they'd all made it through last winter, but there had definitely been some hungry days. They needed something. "But it doesn't mean we can trust them. Just because of one incident—"

"It's not just one," Miles said quietly.

Riley's eyes narrowed. "What are you talking about?"

"During the last inspection, one nearly caught me and Dixie. We stepped out on the riverbank at the same time that one stepped out across from us. We could be seen clearly, and it never raised the alarm."

"Maybe it didn't see you."

"*It saw us.* There's no way it didn't see us. And I think it actually helped make sure we weren't discovered." Miles paused. "What if this is the same one?"

"What if it is? So what? It has to be a trap."

"Then why let me and Dixie go? That was days ago. Why not return to the camp, catch us unaware?"

Riley crossed his arms over his chest. "It's a trap."

"By letting me and Dixie go? By saving you and me from the other ones? That's a pretty lousy trap. What if this one is different? Think of all we could learn from him."

"Miles, it is *not* safe."

"Hate to break it to you, Riley, but nothing in our lives is safe. I mean, Dixie had a little cold and it nearly killed her. The Unwelcome have access to technology, probably medicines. If there's a chance one might help us, shouldn't we take it?"

"Even if this one was different, it was three against one. It's probably dead."

"Shouldn't we make sure?"

Riley blew out a breath. He knew Miles was right, but he knew he was as well. The Unwelcome did not want to help them. Everything they had done since they'd arrived confirmed that. But if there was a chance one might ...

Riley sighed. "All right. We go back, see if it's there. But under no circumstances do we bring it back to the camp or indicate we even belong to a camp."

Miles nodded quickly. "Agreed."

"And if I don't like something, we leave. Immediately. No questions asked."

Miles opened his mouth to argue.

Riley stared him down. "I mean it, Miles. No questions."

Miles blew out a breath. "Fine. No questions."

25

Miles trailed behind Riley as they headed back to the ambush site. They'd run away from the road full-out for twenty minutes but were taking care with the return trip. They'd been walking for nearly an hour.

Miles was actually glad it was taking this long. Even though he was the one who pushed to go back, he was nervous. The Unwelcome were dangerous but also an enigma. And now this latest action was just one more question on top of the pile of questions he'd already compiled. He still couldn't wrap his mind around one of the Unwelcome helping them.

Why? What was the Unwelcome's motive? What was it trying to accomplish?

Miles wanted to believe that it was trying to help them, that it wasn't some means to an end. Because if one was willing to help them, maybe others were, too. And that meant real change. But Miles tried to harden himself against that hope. It was good to be optimistic, but it was death to be only optimistic.

Lost in his thoughts, he stepped forward without looking and walked into the back of Riley, who had stopped ahead of him.

Riley turned back to glare at him. "Really?" he mouthed.

Miles shrugged. "Sorry," he whispered.

Riley shook his head, pointing up ahead. The old highway was just a dozen yards in front of them. Riley gestured for Miles to head to the left.

Miles nodded. He carefully crept through the trees until he was about twenty feet away from Riley. Riley gave him a nod, motioning him forward as he did the same. Miles walked carefully, his eyes and ears perked for any noise, any movement. He stopped at the edge of the road, not sensing anything. He looked over at Riley.

Riley looked back at him and shook his head.

Steeling himself, Miles stepped onto the broken road. Up ahead, he saw darker spots on the gray asphalt. He knelt down. It was some kind of liquid.

Pulling a paper from his pocket, he ripped off a small piece and dipped it in the liquid. It was dark red.

He sat back on his heels in surprise. *What?*

Riley walked up to him. "What have you got there?"

Miles showed him the sheet. "It's blood."

"Blood? From who?"

"From the Unwelcome. This is where those two were when the third shot them." Unwelcome had been injured before by their own weapons. It was rare, but humans had occasionally wrestled one away. But the injuries they caused to the Unwelcome were only burns. Blood had never been drawn. So why was there blood here? Did it mean the Unwelcome's weapon could kill the Unwelcome?

"But how can there be blood here?"

"They must bleed, like us." Miles looked down at the blood on the paper. Dark red. He supposed that made sense. Blood was red due to the interaction between the iron in the blood and oxygen. Hemoglobin bound itself to the oxygen, giving it the red color. Did that mean the Unwelcome had the same type of blood as humans?

Miles shook his head, folding and pocketing the paper. He'd look at it through the microscope later. Maybe it would tell them something. "Any sign of them?"

Riley shook his head. "No. But I did see a couple more blood spots. They must have collected any bodies."

Miles nodded. The bodies had always been collected after a skirmish, or maybe if they weren't injured too bad, they walked on their own. To his knowledge, an Unwelcome had never been captured by a human, dead nor alive. "What about our friend?"

"No sign of him, either, although one of the blood spots was most likely him. Three against one are not good odds. And our guy was one of the small ones."

Miles felt disappointment crash through him. He wasn't sure what he had been hoping to find. Maybe the answer to why the Unwelcome had come. Why they were tracking down only certain kids.

It was in his nature to try to figure out mysteries. And an Unwelcome coming to their aid was definitely a mystery. Miles stood. "Guess we should head back."

Riley nodded. Together, they headed back into the trees, an unspoken agreement between them to stay off the road. Neither Riley nor Miles said anything.

Miles was lost in thought, remembering the scene, looking for any other interpretation of the Unwelcome's actions. There was no other explanation. The Unwelcome had helped them. But why?

"Miles." Riley grabbed Miles's arm, his whisper urgent.

Miles stopped, looking to where Riley pointed. A dark liquid had been brushed across a leaf. Blood. Farther in, Miles could make out more traces of blood.

Riley pulled his sword, and Miles did the same. They followed the traces for a hundred yards, stopping at an outcropping of rock. Below, Miles could just make out the sound of labored breathing.

A quick glance at Riley confirmed that he heard it as well. Carefully, they made their way around the rock, each coming from a different side.

The large rock had been lifted by the earth, creating a crevice underneath that was big enough to house two or three humans.

Or in this case, one wounded Unwelcome.

26

The Unwelcome was sitting up, its back against the back of the outcropping, its long legs stretched out in front of it. The thing was tall, at least seven feet, which actually made it rather small for an Unwelcome. Riley had heard tales of them growing to ten feet. Despite its smaller stature, though, this one's shoulders were almost double the width of Riley and Miles's. The top of its helmet was only a few inches from the roof of the overhanging rock.

Even from its seated position, its size was terrifying.

It didn't move as Riley and Miles stared at it, although it wasn't dead. Its chest rose and fell, but the pattern of its breathing was uneven. The Unwelcome's uniform was ripped at the side of its chest, as well as the shoulder. Darker stains were obvious around the rips. The helmet hid its face. Its weapon was two feet to its right.

Miles stepped forward.

"Stop," Riley hissed. "What exactly do you think you're doing?"

"What do you think I'm going to do?" Miles said, exasperation in his voice. "I'm going to check it."

"I won't hurt you," the Unwelcome said, its deep voice sounded strained as if the words were an effort to speak. Riley jerked back, yanking Miles with him. Miles's eyes were huge as they looked at the Unwelcome and then back at Riley.

"They *can* talk," Miles whispered.

But Riley could only nod his head. He was too stunned to do anything more. At the highway, everything had happened so fast that part of him thought he had imagined it. Miles must have felt the same, because they'd both completely forgotten to talk about it. Riley's gaze stayed on the creature as he tightened his grip on his sword. Miles took a step forward, looking like he was going to try and help the thing.

"Miles, back away. He's still armed." Riley had seen how fast these things could move. To the Unwelcome he said, "Kick away your weapon."

The Unwelcome hesitated, and then with a grunt, it shoved the spear away with its foot, lying back heavily.

"Now take off your helmet," Riley said. He wasn't sure why, but he needed to see the thing's eyes, however many there might be. If he could read its face, he'd have a better gauge of what it was planning, what its motivation was. He blanched. *If, that is, it has a face.*

The Unwelcome raised its uninjured arm and unlatched the helmet. He struggled to pull it off with one arm. It was awkward to watch, and Riley knew the alien wouldn't be able to do it.

Miles stepped forward. "I'm helping him."

"Damn it, Miles."

But Miles was already at the alien's side, pulling the helmet off for him.

Miles stumbled back, the helmet in his hands. "Oh my God."

Riley stared, not sure what he had expected. But it wasn't this —the Unwelcome was humanoid. Its head was double the size of a human's, with an enlarged forehead and large eye sockets, even eyelids, that were closed. And around its face was hair—bright red hair. But most striking was its skin color. It was a pale blue-gray.

The Unwelcome opened its eyes and Riley was surprised again. The eyes, although twice the size of a humans, were humanlike with white sclera, blue irises, and even black pupils.

"You're the one who helped us?" Miles asked.

The Unwelcome nodded, closing its eyes. "Yes."

"Why?"

The Unwelcome eyes opened again. "Why would you help someone?"

"Because I'm human," Riley fired back.

The Unwelcome seemed to chuckle, then it winced. "Fair enough. It seemed the right thing to do."

The right thing to do? These monsters had killed who knew how many humans and it was talking about the right thing to do? "Morality doesn't seem to be part of your species' programming."

The alien nodded, closing its eyes. "True."

"Are you hurt?" Miles asked.

It nodded. "Yes."

Miles reached into his pack, pulling out his medical kit.

"Miles, you can't be serious," Riley said.

Miles glared at Riley. "He saved us. It only seems fair to help him."

Riley felt exasperation run through him. "Miles, we can't trust him."

"Yeah, well, if he kills me, be sure to kill him." Miles turned back to the Unwelcome. "I don't think I can cut through your uniform. And I need to stop the bleeding. Can you lean forward, and I'll help you take the top off?"

The Unwelcome nodded, leaning forward with a grimace. Riley was shaken by how human the expression was. Miles struggled to get the shirt off. But the thing was skintight, and Miles only had the use of the one arm.

The Unwelcome reached up.

"Stop!" Riley leapt forward, but the Unwelcome only ripped the shirt down one side. Then it lay back heavily, its chest heaving, its shoulders drooping. Riley stared in disbelief. Knives could not cut through those shirts, and he'd ripped it with one hand.

"Thanks." Miles slipped the shirt off one arm, leaving it hanging from the other arm.

The alien's chest was also blue, with well-developed pectoral muscles and an eight-pack stomach. It was basically a human body on steroids. The skin on its right side was singed as well as its shoulder. Blood oozed from two wounds.

Miles inspected the wounds, mumbling to himself as he grabbed some gauze and water.

Riley watched every move the alien made, ready to jump in if Miles was in the slightest danger. But the alien was as compliant as a doll.

Miles quickly placed a bandage on the lower wound, pulling the alien forward with some effort to wrap the bandage in place. He did the same for the shoulder wound. He pulled out the painkillers and hesitated. "I'm not sure if you can take these."

He looked up, but the Unwelcome didn't reply. Its eyes were closed again. Miles put his fingers to the being's throat.

Riley inched closer. "Well?"

Miles shrugged. "I think he just passed out."

Riley nodded, looking around. The Unwelcome never left one of their own behind. Which meant they would probably be looking for this guy.

He looked back at the being. It hadn't made any aggressive moves, but it might just be waiting until it felt better.

Riley bit his lips, his eyes scanning the forest. They now had an injured seven-foot Unwelcome in their possession. But what the hell were they supposed to do with it?

27

M iles looked at the Unwelcome as he lay sprawled on the ground. Blue skin, large cranial cavity, extremely tall, and well-developed musculature. Miles was beyond fascinated. When he'd bandaged the alien's skin, it had been warm to the touch and soft like human skin. And he could talk? Miles still couldn't believe that.

If this Unwelcome cooperated, there was no telling what they could learn. He looked over at Riley and realized Riley was not as enraptured as he was. In fact, Riley was running his hand along his sword, no doubt wanting to run the alien through with it.

"Look, why don't you head back to camp and make sure no ones missing us," Miles said. "I'll stay with him."

Riley gave Miles a look that suggested he was strongly worried about Miles's mental health. "You actually think I'm going to leave you with an Unwelcome? Are you crazy?"

Miles sighed. "He's injured and weak. I'll be fine."

"Yeah, and animals are at their most dangerous when they're injured."

"How about if we tie him up?"

"With what? These guys are strong, *really* strong. We have nothing that can keep them incapacitated."

Miles glanced around for something, anything that could be used. His eyes fell on the Unwelcome's weapon. "How about his weapon? It can obviously hurt him."

"We don't know how it works," Riley said even as he walked over and picked it up.

"Well, there's no time like the present," Miles said.

The first smile that Miles had seen since they'd found the Unwelcome crept across Riley's face as he looked at the alien weapon.

"Go ahead. Give it a try," Miles urged.

Riley pointed it away from Miles. He turned the spear over. "There's no trigger."

Miles came to stand next to him. He ran his hands along the staff. There was a large groove on the underside of the staff. "I think this might be it."

Riley turned the spear over and pointed it away from them and the Unwelcome. A beam of energy shot from the staff, slicing a tree in half. Riley's mouth dropped open and he fumbled, nearly dropping the staff. "Well, that was cool."

Miles came to stand next to him. "Okay. So all I need to do is hit that button and I'm good. So you head back, cover for us, and I'll keep an eye on our friend."

Riley paused, looking between the staff and Miles's half arm. His eyes met Miles's. "You won't be able to hold it and press the trigger."

The smile dropped from Miles's face, and his shoulders went stiff. "Of course. I should have thought of that."

He swallowed down the resentment. *Once again, everyone needs to do things for the cripple.* He tried to banish the thoughts from his mind, but they stayed heckling him from the corners. He let out a breath. "Okay. I'll head back. I can pick up some medical supplies and you can keep an eye on him."

"How about we just leave him?" Riley countered. "We've helped him. He helped us. As far as I'm concerned, we're even."

"Riley, we were just saying we need to do more. They're still looking for kids like us." Miles pointed at the Unwelcome. "He could tell us why. He could tell us about them. We can't just walk away."

Riley crossed his arms. "Uh, yeah we can."

Miles stared at his brother. He knew Riley was worried more about Miles's safety than his own. But he also knew that if the Unwelcome would talk, it could change everything.

"Look, you've got his weapon, and he's injured. Worst-case scenario, he tells us nothing and we leave him."

"Or kill him."

Miles nodded. "Or that. But don't you think we owe it to everyone to at least see if he can tell us something? Don't we owe it to Maisy?"

Riley's eyes narrowed. "Low blow, Miles."

Miles had known that it was as soon as it came out of his mouth. But Riley would do anything for their little sister. And he hadn't said it just to get Riley to cooperate. When the Unwelcome had arrived, they had killed indiscriminately. Now, they were more circumspect in their choices. But that could change again without warning.

And until they knew *why* they were killing only certain kids, no one was truly safe. Not even Maisy. And like Riley, Miles would do anything to protect her.

Riley broke off his gaze and stared at the Unwelcome. He sighed before looking back at Miles. "You have two hours to get to the camp and back. And you tell no one where we are. Actually, tell someone we're camping out for the night, because Lyla will wonder. We'll question him when he wakes up, and then we'll figure out what to do from there."

Miles struggled to keep the smile from breaking across his face. "Deal."

28

Miles set a fast pace back to camp because he did not want to test Riley on the two-hour time limit he'd set. But Miles slowed down as he approached the main gate, not wanting to draw any attention. He waved at Otto, who was on gate duty. Otto gave him a nod but turned as Annie came to relieve him.

Miles hustled past them both, keeping his head low, hoping not to meet anyone's gaze. He turned onto the main path and then paused. If he headed this way, he'd go right by their home, and more importantly, Lyla's office. He ducked between two cabins and walked along the outskirts of the camp. He made his way quickly to the med cabin. He stepped in, holding his breath, but it was empty.

So far so good, he thought as he walked over to the medicine cabinet. Opening it, he grabbed some extra bandages as well as his suture kit, which was really just a needle and some strong thread.

He paused, looking over the other bottles and jars in the cabinet. Medicines were rare. They used natural remedies when they could. In fact, Simon had found some old texts on Aztec medicines, which had come in pretty handy. But as lucky as they had been, they always seemed to be running low. So he hesitated now. But if the Unwelcome was going to help them, they needed to help him in return.

He grabbed some painkillers and penicillin and promised himself he would only use them after the Unwelcome demonstrated his cooperation.

He wasn't even sure if the Unwelcome could take the penicillin, but he needed something in case his wounds became infected. He grabbed some additional white cloths and some needles. Worst-case scenario, he could boil the rags and lance any infection. He didn't think he'd need it but better to be safe than sorry.

He glanced around, spying his microscope. They'd found it on a scavenge two years ago. He desperately wanted to take it and look at the Unwelcome's blood. But he knew there wouldn't be light enough for that, and besides, he couldn't chance breaking it.

It'll have to wait. He grabbed a few slides, though, carefully wrapping them in the white cloths and sliding them into his pack. Looking around one last time, he nodded. That was everything he could think he might need.

Heading out of the tent, he made his way over toward the kitchen. He could smell dinner cooking. *Smells like venison stew.* He nodded at a few people who'd stopped in to eat early before making his way to the front door. A dozen tables were set up outside the cabin that held the kitchen. Whenever possible, they ate outside. A tarp had even been attached to the kitchen for bad weather.

Pushing open the door, he stepped into its warmth. Shelves lined three of the walls, filled with food reserves and kitchen supplies like baskets, pots, platters, all of them different colors, materials, and sizes. They'd been gathered on scavenge runs over the years.

Emma stood by the big metal table, carving potatoes. Saul pulled a loaf of bread from one of the brick ovens that lined the back of the room. A few volunteers were scattered around doing different chores: washing dishes, taking inventory, peeling vegetables.

Emma smiled when she caught sight of Miles. "Hey, sweetheart. Come to help?"

"Not today, sorry." Miles looked around. "Where's Edna?"

"She went to lie down. She got another migraine."

Miles frowned. "Maybe I should go check on her."

"I just did. She's all right. She just needs to sleep. She gets them all the time."

"If you're sure," Miles said.

"I am, but if we need you, I'll come running."

Miles felt a twinge of guilt that he wouldn't be here, but he also knew Edna did regularly get migraines. After a few hours, though, she was usually back to normal. It should be all right. Besides, Simon could pitch in if it came down to it.

Miles had helped Edna when she'd come down with pneumonia two years ago. He'd stayed by her side for three nights, practically willing her to live. From that moment on, he could ask anything of Emma and Edna and it would be done. He'd never tested that promise before.

Miles walked over to Emma and leaned against the table. "I was wondering if I could get some meals to go?"

Raising her eyebrows, Emma halted her slicing. "How many?"

"Two." He paused, thinking of the Unwelcome. "Actually, three."

Emma's eyebrows remained raised, but she didn't ask any additional questions. "Saul," she barked. "Make up three rations to go."

Saul was easily seventy but had the energy of a much younger man. He made up the third member of the kitchen team. When

Miles had met him, he reminded Miles of a garden gnome he'd seen once. He was short but strong, with a thick head of white hair that reached the bottom of his ears and which, to Miles's knowledge, never moved. And he had these large brown eyes that in anyone else would dominate his face, except that Saul's mouth was equally large. Saul's mouth turned up as he smiled, stepping away from his pile of carrots. "Okey dokey."

Emma looked back at Miles. "Everything all right?"

He nodded. "Yeah. Just taking a little overnighter."

Emma's gaze stayed on him longer than he liked. "Okay. But be careful."

"Will do."

Emma frowned, and Miles knew she was going to ask for more details. But luckily, Saul walked up, holding a pack. "Here you go, Miles." He winked. "A little extra in there for you."

"Thanks, Saul." Miles slung the pack over his shoulder before glancing over at Emma. "Thanks, Emma."

"Have a good night."

Miles escaped outside, feeling guilty. He didn't know why. It's not like he'd lied to them. He'd just omitted. That wasn't the same, right?

Miles once again headed to the perimeter of the camp. He'd been lucky so far not running into Lyla, but he didn't want to push his luck. He picked up his pace and then paused. *Dixie*. He glanced over his shoulder, telling himself she was fine. He'd looked in on her this morning, and she was well on her way to · healthy. But what if something had happened since then? The fear of getting caught warred with his sense of duty.

"Damn it," he mumbled before turning for the Carolinas' cabin.

One stop, then I'm gone. He turned down the first avenue of cabins. At the end was the Carolinas' cabin. People with children were given cabin preference. The Carolinas had been one of the first to get a cabin and tended to take in any little ones that showed up in camp.

He cut across the grass. Five of the Carolina kids were playing tag in front of the cabin. Miles had to dodge out of the way as three-year-old Thad ran backward. Miles grabbed him before he tripped over his own feet and steadied him. "Careful there."

Thad looked up at him with his dark eyes. "Hi, Miles."

A chorus of greetings rang out from the kids, and Miles really wished they'd be a little quieter with their greetings. "Hi, guys. How's Dixie?"

"She's good."

"Feeling better."

"Mama said we have to stay outside until tonight cause she needs rest. When can we go back in?"

Miles hid his smile. "I'm sure you'll be back inside soon. But it is important for Dixie to get some sleep. Sometimes sleep is the best way to heal."

Selma nodded solemnly at his words. For each of these kids, Miles was an adult and always right. "I'll see you guys later," Miles said and headed up the three short steps. He stopped at the door and knocked. "Judith? It's Miles."

The door opened, and Judith Carolina beckoned him in with a tired smile. Her light brown hair was pulled back into a bun, but more than a few stray hairs had managed to work their way free. Her green eyes crinkled at the corners when she smiled, instantly putting Miles at ease. There was something about Judith that was calming. It was probably why she was so good with kids.

"Come in, Miles. Come in."

He ducked in the doorway, his eyes automatically drifting to the back cot. Dixie lay there, looking at him, a small smile on her face.

Miles moved toward her, feeling relieved. Her cheeks had a bit of color in them. He reached down, and her forehead felt cool.

The fever hadn't returned. They still didn't know what had caused it, but it looked like it was gone.

He smiled. "Just checking." He turned to Dixie's mom. "She looks good."

Judith wrapped her arms around him. "Thank you for all you did. I don't know what we would all do without you."

Miles felt a flush crawl up his neck, making him thankful for his dark complexion. "It wasn't anything."

"You stayed with her when I couldn't. You were there when we needed you. We won't forget that." Tears sprang into Judith's eyes. "Oh, I made you something." She stepped into the back bedroom and was back in a moment with a small wooden box. On the lid, his initials were carved with vines and birds rimming the edge. "It's not much, but we wanted to give you something to say thanks."

Touched, Miles took the box, smiling at the little birds. He looked up at Judith. "It's really great. Thank you."

She nodded, and one of the kids outside let out a cry.

Judith rolled her eyes. "Well, that ends the peaceful portion of the afternoon."

Miles laughed, tucking the box into his pack. "I'll check back tomorrow, if that's all right."

"That's great." Judith followed him out to where two of the kids were rolling around on the ground together. "You two cut that out right now."

Miles laughed. "See you later."

Judith gave him a distracted smile before she hurried down the steps to separate the combatants. Miles ducked around the cabin, hoping he didn't run into anyone else.

Hefting the backpack on his shoulder, his eyes darted around. No one seemed to be paying him any attention. He walked quickly down the path before stepping into the trees. With a smile, he headed back toward Riley. Safe. And he still had an hour to get there.

His mind immediately shifted to the task ahead of him, trying to arrange all the questions he wanted to ask. Should he start with the Unwelcome's biology? Or their agenda? What would the Unwelcome be more open to answering?

A hand grabbed his shoulder. "*Where* exactly do you think you're going?"

29

M iles's heart hammered in his chest as he turned around. And then it slowed down. "Petra? What are you doing?"

She raised an eyebrow. "Well, I'm following you after watching you skulk around camp and then slip out." She nodded at his pack. "With a night's worth of provisions."

Miles cleared his throat. "It's nothing. Riley and I are just going to spend the night in the woods."

"Really. And where is Riley?"

"He's, um, he's getting the camp set up."

Petra fixed him with a stare. "You know you're the world's worst liar, right?"

Miles sighed. "So I've been told. Look, yes, we're doing something, but it needs to be kept quiet. So just ... I don't know, pretend you haven't seen me."

Petra looked incredulous. "Miles, do you know I've been trailing you since you entered camp? You have zero awareness. If I let you go wander into the woods alone, you'll either fall into a giant hole or get grabbed by the Unwelcome. Sorry, but I'm coming with you. It's for your own good."

"Petra, no. I'll be—"

She looked at him, unblinking. "I. Am. Coming. With. You."

Miles looked around, but no answer was to be found in the trees. And he knew Petra—once she caught the scent of something, she didn't let go. She was singularly focused. It made her a great warrior. It also meant there was no chance in hell she was going to walk away right now.

"Fine. But you have to promise me that what you see stays between us. No one else can know."

She narrowed her eyes. "What exactly is this big secret?"

"I mean it, Petra. Promise me."

She held up three fingers on her right hand. "Scout's honor."

"Scouts?"

She shrugged. "Boy Scouts. Something my grandpa used to say. It means I promise."

"Okay. Let's go." He glanced back at Petra, but she was not who he was worried about. He sighed.

Riley is going to kill me.

30

R iley watched the Unwelcome sleep. Its giant chest rose
and fell with its breathing. He couldn't believe they were
blue. But the most disarming fact was how human it looked. He'd
figured it would have strange eyes or maybe eat from a mouth on
the top of its head. But it looked like someone had painted its
skin. Besides its size, it looked almost human. He frowned. How
was that possible?

He looked up at the sky and noticed how much the sun had
moved since Miles had left. It was getting close to two hours. He
gripped the Unwelcome's weapon tighter in his hands.

*I should kill him now while he's asleep. Who knows how fast they
heal? It could be back to normal any minute.*

He never should have agreed to this plan. Not any of it. Not
letting the Unwelcome live, certainly not giving the damn thing
first aid. And what the hell had he been thinking letting Miles
head back to camp alone? He was likely to get caught up in a
thought and walk in the completely wrong direction. Or walk
into a branch and knock himself out.

The Unwelcome stirred, a frown on its face. Riley tightened

his hold on the spear. He should just kill the thing. It would be safer all around. His finger inched toward the trigger.

"Riley?" Miles called out.

Riley whirled around. Miles was ten feet away, Petra walking right behind him.

"What the hell were you thinking bringing her?" Riley asked.

"He wasn't thinking anything," Petra shot back. "I didn't give him a choice. Now what's this big—" Her voice cut out as her eyes locked on the alien. "Oh my God. You killed one."

Miles stepped up next to her. "He's not dead."

In a fluid motion, Petra pulled her sword from its scabbard. "Let me take care of that."

Riley blocked her path, even though he didn't necessarily disagree with her reaction. "Not yet."

Petra's eyes caught his. "*Not yet*? What the hell are you waiting for?"

"He saved our lives," Miles said.

Petra sputtered. "Saved your lives? They don't *do* that. They *take* our lives."

"I know." Riley glanced back at the thing. Its chest was still rising and falling, but the rhythm was a little different. Was it waking up? He glanced back at Petra. "But it did. This one might be different."

Miles interrupted. "Look, let's just wait until he wakes up. Then we'll figure out what to do."

Petra eyes went wide, and she nodded toward the Unwelcome. "Well, that time is now."

Riley's gaze flew to their prisoner. It lay in the same spot on the ground, but its eyes were open as it watched them.

31

Miles stared at the Unwelcome. It watched them with its strangely large human eyes, roaming over each of them in turn, before coming to rest back on Miles. "Thank you for your help."

Petra gasped. "It *talks*?"

Miles didn't think Petra's question required at answer. He nodded at the Unwelcome. "You're welcome."

Miles's voice was calm, but inside he reeled at the exchange. He was having a polite conversation with one of the beings that had devastated their world. *Well, devastated it more.*

"Are you up to answering some questions?" Miles asked.

The being nodded, adjusting his position to get a little more comfortable. But both Petra and Riley inched forward as he moved. "Yes."

Miles struggled with figuring out a starting point. He looked over at Petra, who was staring at the Unwelcome with unconcealed hate, her sword clasped firmly in her hand.

Riley had stepped away from the two of them. The Unwelcome's weapon was in his hand, trained on the being. His finger hovered near the trigger.

Whatever Miles came up with, it better be fast. Both Petra and Riley looked like they were just waiting for an opportunity to take the Unwelcome out.

"Your name," Miles blurted out. "What's your name?"

The Unwelcome hesitated. "I do not think you can pronounce it. But I have always liked the name Arthur."

"Arthur? Why that name?" Miles asked in surprise.

The Unwelcome looked at Riley and Petra before his gaze settled back on Miles. "I read King Arthur and Camelot. I liked it."

Stunned, Miles sank down onto a rock opposite Arthur, close but still out of his reach. "Have you read many of our books?"

Arthur nodded. "It was my job to read your literature. To learn as much about you as possible."

"What do you mean? What were you trying to find out?" Riley asked.

Arthur's eyes shifted to Riley with a quick glance at the weapon in his arms. "I am a translator of sorts. My job is to understand your culture, so I could communicate effectively with you. To that end, my job was to read as many of your works of literature as I could find. It was"—he paused—"interesting reading."

"What did you read?" Miles asked, curiosity coursing through him. Wherever he thought his first conversation with an Unwelcome would go, he certainly never imagined it would involve a discussion of literature.

"Everything. Nonfiction, of course." A small smile spread across Arthur's face. "But what I really liked were the fiction books. Have you ever read Louis L'Amour?"

Miles shook his head even as an image of books he'd seen in Frank's cabin flashed through his mind. "I haven't read them. He wrote westerns, though, right?"

"I really liked his books. I was supposed to focus on the nonfiction, but the fiction seemed to tell me more about what humans were like. To me, they showed more of what humans are. I read the classics, Plato, Aristotle, Herman Melville, Chaucer. But I like the more contemporary readings better. I even read some genre called romance." He paused. "Your courting and mating rituals are ... unusual."

Miles darted a glance at Riley and Petra, not surprised to see shock on their faces. He was feeling a little stunned himself. He tried to picture this giant being curling up with a romance novel with a bare-chested man and flimsily dressed female on the cover. He bit back a smile.

"So what did you think when you read them? That we'd be easy pickings?" Petra demanded.

Arthur ignored the anger in her tone, and Miles wondered if it was because he couldn't identify it or because he recognized the precarious position he was in.

Arthur met Petra's eyes. "I was surprised. I had been told humans were selfish, warlike creatures. But your books, they revealed much more complex beings who were capable of great hate but also great sacrifice." He paused. "It was disturbing."

Silence fell and Miles stared at the—what? Creature? Being? Person?

"And so what?" Petra said. "You helped your friends figure out how best to take us down? How to convince us to help you? How to turn our own families against us?"

Arthur nodded slowly. "Originally, that was my goal—along with the others who were assigned the same task as me. But the more I read, the more difficult my task became. Not only did humans seem more complex, but more worthy. I could no longer agree with my leaders' plans."

Miles wasn't sure if he was humanizing Arthur or if Arthur was playing their emotions, but he swore he heard regret in the alien's voice. "And what exactly are those plans?"

Arthur glanced at each of them. "I was not privy to every-thing. But I know removing the threat is only the first stage."

"What's the threat?" Riley asked.

Now it was Arthur's turn to look surprised. "Children between the ages of thirteen and eighteen."

"Why just that age group? What's special about them?" Miles asked, a little shaken to hear the rumors confirmed.

"I was never told that. All I know is children in that cohort are viewed as a threat." Arthur looked at each of them in turn. "Children like you."

There was no change in the tone of his voice, but the hairs on the back of Miles's neck stood up. He forced himself not to back away. "You said that was stage one. What is stage two?"

Arthur looked away. "My people are colonizing your planet. What normally happens to indigenous people if they are not killed outright?"

Miles struggled to see where Arthur was going. But Riley the history buff knew. "They enslave them."

Arthur nodded. "I believe that is their plan. And I cannot go along with it."

"Why not? You had no problem telling them how to kill us before," Petra said.

Arthur frowned, and Miles was once again blown away at how human the expression looked. "I don't know. It just—it feels wrong."

"What were you doing on the road today when you found us?" Riley asked.

Arthur's eyes shifted between Riley and Petra, and Miles stiffened his shoulders in response. "That was my unit. We were doing a sweep of the area."

"So why didn't you let them take us?" Riley asked.

Arthur hesitated. "I heard you talking. You were worried about someone. Concerned about someone else. Over the last few months, I've seen more and more examples of humans caring. I just couldn't be part of your destruction." He nodded toward Miles. "And I saw you protect that girl on the bank when we visited your camp."

"*What?*" Petra yelled.

Miles cringed. He'd only told Riley about that interaction. "I didn't think you had seen us. You left us alone."

"You had a chance to run. Without the girl, you had a shot at making it. But you didn't leave her."

"I couldn't."

"Like I said, you are complex creatures." He paused. "The young girl with you—she was sick?"

"Yes. Why didn't you tell them where I was? Where she was?" Miles asked.

Arthur paused, a frown on his face. "I don't know. I should have. But it seemed wrong. I led them away instead."

Petra looked at Miles, her face pale. "Did that happen?"

Miles nodded slowly. "I had Dixie, but I couldn't reach the cave. I was going to hide her in one of the old downed trees on the bank, but there wasn't enough time. As soon as I stepped onto the bank, an Unwelcome stepped out on the other side."

"You could have been killed," Petra said.

"But I wasn't." Miles turned back to Arthur. "Because of you."

Arthur met his gaze. "Who was it you were concerned about when you were on the road? Dixie?"

Miles glanced at Riley, who shook his head at Miles. Was Arthur looking for information? Maybe, maybe not. As much as he wanted to learn about the Unwelcome, he wasn't ready to trust one with any information, so he ignored the question. "You said the last few months you've seen human interactions. You've been here for five years. Why have humans not affected you before this?"

"For the majority of that time, I was stationed on the ship. I didn't step foot onto the planet until a few months ago."

"Why not?"

"At first, I was providing information by report. Recommending approaches, weaknesses, targets."

From the corner of his eyes, Miles saw Riley's jaw tighten and Petra adjust the grip on her sword. Miles himself felt sick. "What did you suggest?"

"I, along with my colleagues, suggested they focus on families —that that was your weakness."

Petra stepped forward. "Was the trade-in program your idea?"

Arthur shook his head. "No, but at the time I thought it was the right one."

"How could you think that?" Petra burst out, her voice full of pain. "Do you realize how many people you killed? Do you realize the horror of having your own parents turn you in?"

Petra shook with anger. Her parents had tried to turn her in, but she had run away before they could. He couldn't imagine that betrayal. His own mother had died trying to protect his sister. His father—well, that was a different story.

And now he had Lyla, Riley, and Maisy. And they would each die before hurting the other. And he knew that that support, that love, was what had let him survive these years. And what had led him to help other people in the camp. When you're shown love, you share it with others. The Unwelcome had created a way for desperate people to survive. The only cost? Their humanity.

"I only knew what I did of humans because of what I read. On the ground, they told us you were unintelligent beasts. It conflicted with my readings, but I followed my orders. It was only once I saw humans for myself I realized you were more than what my superiors told me. You were what I thought you were." He gave them a small smile. "You were complicated."

"So what," Petra said, "now you expect us to believe that you've turned your back on your own kind? And you want us to help you out, bring you back to our camp, show you where we are?"

Arthur shook his head. "No. I told you because I thought you should know. I do not expect anything from you. To be honest, I did not expect what I have received so far."

Silence fell. Miles studied Arthur, who had closed his eyes again. Arthur's bandages had become bloody again, which meant he did not seem to heal any faster than a human. He looked over at Petra and Riley. Both still watched Arthur with suspicion.

Miles sat back. Realistically, Arthur was saying all the right things to gain their trust. But if he'd studied human behavior, he'd know that. Yes, he'd saved them, but they didn't know why. And he wasn't sure they could trust what he said. But maybe there were other things they could learn.

"How are you feeling?" Miles asked.

Arthur opened his eyes. "I'm sore. And I feel like my left side is on fire."

"Will you heal from this?"

"Eventually, as long as the wounds do not become infected."

"Do you heal faster than humans?"

Arthur shook his head. "I do not believe so."

"May I look at your wound again?"

"Absolutely not!" Riley yelled.

"No chance," Petra said at the same time.

Oh, how nice. They agree on something. Miles held up his hand. "Look, either we're helping him or we're not. So which is it?"

"We're not," Petra said.

He looked at Riley. "Riley?"

Miles could tell Riley was trying to figure out what was in the best interest of the camp. He wasn't oblivious to the potential benefits of having an inside view on the Unwelcome's plans.

Finally Riley spoke. "We help him for now. But you do not answer any questions about us or the camp. He provides information and we help. He stops and so do we."

"Riley ..." Petra said.

"I know, Petra. I know. But we won't let him out of our sight."

Riley looked at Arthur. "And if he does anything even slightly threatening, we will end him."

Arthur met his gaze and nodded. "I understand."

Miles grabbed his med bag and walked to Arthur, but Arthur kept his eyes on Riley and Petra. And Miles couldn't blame him, because obviously those two were just waiting for an excuse to make good on Riley's threat.

32

L yla walked down the path toward the school. *Right on time,* she thought as kids ran out of the tent.

A chorus of "Hi, Lyla" rang out as child after child sprinted past her.

Lyla smiled. "Hi, everybody."

Maisy walked out of the tent next to her friend Sabrina Carolina. Lyla waved, and Maisy walked over, giving her a hug. "Hi, honey. How was school?"

"Good," Maisy said. Maisy had only started talking a year after they had saved her. She still didn't talk a lot, but Simon had assured Lyla that was by choice, not because of any cognitive difficulties. Maisy pulled back to look up at Lyla as Lyla pushed back Maisy's strawberry-blonde curls. She remembered running along the river, seeing Maisy being tossed by the water, and finally grabbing her. At that moment, Maisy had been someone she needed to save, and then a short time later she became someone she couldn't live without.

They started to head back to the house hand in hand. "I wanted to talk to you about something." Lyla explained about

Alyssa and Rachel coming to live with them. "I'm not sure how long it will be, but it might be a while. Are you okay with that?"

Maisy leaned into her. "They're nice."

Lyla smiled. *Maisy's seal of approval.* "Great. They're getting their stuff. When they come back, how about if you show them around?"

Maisy nodded.

"And how about tonight, we all sit down to dinner and play UNO?"

Maisy looked up at her. "But the boys are gone."

Lyla stopped and looked down at her with a frown. "What do you mean gone?"

Maisy shrugged. "Miles told Sabrina's mom they were going to camp overnight."

Lyla stared at her with her mouth hanging open. What was going on? Miles and Riley knew they weren't allowed to just take off like that without talking to her first. She trusted both of them, to a certain extent. But they were still at an age when stupid ideas seemed brilliant.

Lyla kissed the top of Maisy's head as they reached their home. "Okay, Frank's inside. When Rachel and Alyssa get here, can you show them where they'll be staying?"

Maisy grinned. "Okay. You're going to find the boys, aren't you?"

"Oh, you bet I am," Lyla said.

Addie walked up with the two girls. The girls' hair was wet and they wore clean new dresses. Lyla forced herself to smile. "Hi, girls. Did you get everything?"

They nodded. "Maisy, can you show them where they will be sleeping?"

Maisy smiled at them, stepping between them and taking both of their hands. "Sure. Come on. Your room has a window with real glass."

The girls headed inside with Maisy. Rachel stopped in the

doorway and looked back at Lyla with a shy smile. "Thank you." Then she disappeared inside.

Lyla watched the empty doorway, a feeling of rightness in her chest. Banishing anyone, even Brendan, was never easy. But already Lyla could see the weight lifted from the girls' shoulders. It was a good start.

She turned back to Addie. "Did everything go all right?"

Addie curled her lip. "Yeah. But that tent was disgusting. I sent Jamal to get started on washing their things while I gave the girls a bath." Addie paused. "There's some old bruises on them."

"I wish I could say I was surprised. I should have gotten them out sooner."

"We had no proof."

"I know. It just kills me." The girls appeared in the window above them and their laughter could be heard clearly.

"I think they're going to be all right," Addie said.

Her conversation with Maisy came back to her. "*They* might be, but I may kill Riley and Miles."

"Uh oh. What did they do now?"

"Apparently they decided to camp out for the night without letting me know where they are going to be."

Addie winced. "Well, that was stupid of them."

"I'm going to go look for them."

"I'll grab Jamal and we'll help. Meet you at the front gate in five."

"Thanks." Lyla headed for the cabin as Addie headed off to find Jamal.

She quickly explained to Frank about where she was headed, and he agreed to stay with the girls until she returned.

Five minutes later, Lyla was heading to the front gate.

Boys, you better not be doing anything stupid.

33

"So what planet are you from?" Miles asked. Arthur had fallen asleep after Miles had checked his wounds again and he'd only just reawakened.

While he'd slept, Petra had argued they should kill him before he regained his strength. Miles had argued they'd already gotten information and they should wait and see what else they could learn. Miles knew Arthur's injuries were serious and probably painful, although truth be told, he couldn't be sure he felt pain and wasn't acting.

But he wanted to find out everything he could, because that information could be very helpful, and Riley had amazingly agreed with him. "But once he stops being helpful ..."

Miles nodded, understanding. So as soon as Arthur's eyes opened, he'd spoken.

Arthur licked his lips. "A planet outside your solar system."

Miles frowned. "So it must have taken you a long time to get here."

Arthur shook his head. "A few years."

"So your ships must be fast."

Arthur frowned. "I don't know."

"How do you not know?" Petra asked.

Arthur hesitated, and Miles had the feeling he wasn't sure if he should reveal something.

"Can I have some water?" Arthur asked instead.

Miles hesitated for only a moment before handing him the water sock.

Arthur lifted it with his good hand and took a long drink before handing it back. "Thank you."

Miles thought about going back to Petra's question but then thought maybe once they got him talking, he'd be willing to reveal more. "We've seen Unwelcome who are different heights. Why is that?"

"Our origin planet had less gravity than yours does. The taller of my people that you've seen are older and spent more time on our planet."

"Huh." Miles had read about the effect of lower gravity on astronauts.

"Is that possible?" Petra asked.

Riley nodded. "Yeah. Reduced gravity would allow the bones to lengthen, unhampered by the weight of a stronger gravitational pull."

Miles looked at him in surprise.

"What?" Riley demanded. "I read."

"I didn't say anything," Miles said, hiding his smile.

"What about your hair?" Petra asked. "Are you all redheads?"

Arthur shook his head. "No. We have black, blonde, brown, and some lose their hair. Our skin tones are similarly varied. My skin is on the lighter side."

"You have races," Riley said, his eyes wide.

Arthur opened his mouth and then shut it with a frown before he spoke. "I suppose that's true, although we've never spoken of it that way."

"Why not?" Miles asked.

"Because the Naku never classified us that way."

Petra frowned. "The Naku? I thought you *were* the Naku,"

Arthur's head jolted up. "We—" Arthur swallowed, his eyes becoming unfocused.

Miles stepped toward him. "Arthur?"

A blur of motion was all the warning they had before Lyla sprinted from the woods, tackling Miles away from Arthur. She rolled to her feet, her sword out. "Run, Miles!"

Miles scampered to his feet. "No!" He threw himself in front of Arthur. A sick sense of déjà vu crawled over him as Lyla swung her sword.

34

Y ears of training were all that kept Lyla from running Miles through. She pulled the sword away at the last second, the tip coming just inches from Miles's chest.

Fear hammered through her own chest at how close she'd come to killing him. "What are you doing? Get away from it."

Miles put his hands up in front of him. "It's okay. He won't hurt us."

Lyla stared at him in disbelief. Her heart had nearly stopped when she saw Miles kneeling next to the Unwelcome. When its hand moved, she didn't think; she just reacted.

What the hell was going on? Miles was her smart one. She reached out to pull him away when the being's voice stopped her cold.

"He's telling the truth."

Lyla felt her mouth fall open. They talk? She stepped to the side to get a good look at the Unwelcome. She knew her eyes were wide as she took in its form and the injury to its side. *They're blue*, was all she could think. She glanced back at Riley, who held the being's weapon. "Did you do that?"

Riley shook his head. "No. His people did that to him."

Miles put up his arms. "Lyla, Arthur doesn't mean—"

Lyla whirled on him. "You *named* him? Have you all gone nuts?"

"Just let me explain," Miles pleaded. Lyla looked into his eyes and saw the sincerity there. But she also knew Miles had a good heart, a trusting one. She glanced back at the being, who regarded her in silence. The being whose brethren had destroyed millions, including Lyla's sister.

"Miles, please step away from that thing," she said quietly, her control starting to slip.

Miles must have realized how precarious Lyla's temper was at that moment, because he took four large steps back.

Lyla let out a breath, feeling a little calmer. She nodded toward the Unwelcome's weapon in Riley's hands. "Can you use that thing?"

"Yes."

"Then keep it trained on him, and if he so much as twitches, shoot him."

Riley nodded, his back straightening and his grip tightening on the spear.

Lyla looked at Miles. "Talk."

Miles began to speak quickly, telling her that the being had saved him and Riley when they were ambushed on the road. Then he told her how they had backtracked and found him. Then he explained about the river with Dixie. Lyla felt her heart pound even harder, the idea of nearly losing her boys terrifying her more than anything.

"But we haven't told him anything," Miles said. "He's been the one telling us stuff."

Lyla stared at him in disbelief. How could he be so naive? She looked at Petra and Riley. She expected better of them. Lyla counted to ten, trying to tamp down her anger. Finally, at least a little calmer, she looked at Miles. "You have confirmed for him what camp you are from. You have confirmed there are multiple targets there. You have confirmed that we have been actively hiding targets. You've told him we have a camp, that there are people there you care about, how far away it is, and in what direction."

Miles jaw fell open. "No, we didn't."

"You left to go to the camp, right?"

Miles nodded.

"He knows how long it took you to get there and back. Did you at least head off in the wrong direction before heading back?"

She saw the awareness dawn across Miles's face. She glanced over at the other two as well. Both of them looked a little paler.

She couldn't leave the being alive. It was too big a risk. They didn't even know how they communicated. It could have already contacted its people.

Lyla advanced on the being. She wasn't ready to call him Arthur. "When are your people coming for you? When will they be at the camp?"

"I haven't communicated with them. But they may come searching for me."

Addie appeared on the top of the rock outcropping. From her vantage point she could not see the Unwelcome. "Oh, good, you found them."

Grinning, Jamal appeared next to her. "And they're all still breathing. Excellent restraint."

"Yeah, well, we'll see about that," Lyla grumbled. "You two need to get down here."

Addie and Jamal walked around the outcropping. Jamal looked from person to person, lifting an eyebrow. "What's the big —holy crap!" He leapt back, reaching for his sword.

Addie reached for hers as well, looking between Lyla and the Unwelcome. "Lyla, what the hell is going on?"

"Apparently these guys took it upon themselves to befriend a wounded Unwelcome." Lyla quickly ran down what she knew.

When she finished, Addie glared at the three teenagers. "Are you three insane?"

Lyla nodded. "Yup."

"It's blue. Did anybody else notice it's blue?" Jamal asked.

"Jamal," Addie said, her voice hard.

"Right, um. Well, maybe they're not insane," Jamal said.

"What?" Addie and Lyla said at the same time.

Jamal put up his hands. "Hey, hey, I'm not saying what they did was smart. But it's done now. So maybe we should see if it, um, does he have a name or speak?"

Miles nodded. "His name's Arthur. And he's been helping us."

Lyla felt like she was going to explode. "Helping you? What is wrong with—"

Jamal raised his voice. "*If* Arthur can provide us with any information, maybe we should hear what he has to say."

Everyone was quiet when Jamal finished speaking. Lyla had kept her attention on the Unwelcome while they had been speaking. Its face had remained expressionless except for a grimace every now and then. And sweat had begun to develop on its brow.

Both responses could be due to pain. But they knew so little about these things it could also be due to some sort of long-distance communication from other Unwelcome.

Lyla didn't take her gaze from the being. "Tell me why I should let you live."

He said nothing for a moment, then shook his head. "You shouldn't. I'm too big a risk. It's safer for you all if you kill me now."

Addie stepped forward. "I'm game."

"Hold," Lyla said, watching the creature. The being was right. Killing him was the right call.

"He can tell us things." Miles stepped next to her. "Think of all we can learn."

"He can kill us, too. Think of how dead we can be," Addie said.

Lyla's eyes drifted toward the creature's injury. It did look bad, and it obviously had been caused by an Unwelcome's weapon. "How bad is he injured?"

"He's burned pretty bad on the one side, and he doesn't have much use in that arm, either."

Lyla nodded. Miles was right. They could learn from him. But Addie was right, too. The sooner she decided, the better. Because time was against them. "Jamal, go grab some rope."

35

J amal disappeared to grab rope from one of the stashes of
emergency gear they kept littered around the area outside
the camp. With the way the weather changed here, it was
too easy for someone to get caught unaware, with help too
far away.

While he was gone, no one said a word. Lyla was so angry at
the three teenagers in front of her that she didn't trust herself to
speak. All the horrible things that could have gone wrong flew
through her mind. She had trained them, lectured them, done
everything to prepare them. And then they went and did something so monumentally stupid she questioned whether they had
learned anything at all.

Lyla turned to stare at "Arthur." He appeared unthreatening,
except for the strength he exuded even in his weakened state. But
she had to admit the idea of being able to get some answers was
tempting.

But not like this.

They'd move him farther from camp, and the camp would be
put on a heightened watch. The first sign of an Unwelcome ship
near the camp and Arthur would be dead. But until then, Lyla

would interrogate him. Addie now held the Unwelcome's weapon, keeping it trained on Arthur.

It only took Jamal a few minutes to return with the rope, and Lyla quickly helped Jamal tie Arthur's arms. The rope had been wound from Arthur's wrists, around and around, all the way to his shoulders. Lyla was taking no chances. Even with the extreme rope tying, though, she was worried. These things were so strong.

Arthur said nothing as Lyla and Jamal finished up. Lyla wound the rope back across his shoulder, unintentionally scraping his burn. Arthur sucked in a deep breath. Lyla almost mumbled sorry before pinching her mouth closed. *Like hell I'm apologizing.*

She tied the rope, ignoring a second small gasp of pain Arthur—*no, the creature,* she reminded herself—emitted.

Miles had sat quietly and watched as Jamal and Lyla tied up Arthur. And with each wind of the rope, he knew they were making a mistake. They needed to talk to him as an intelligent being, not a captive.

At the first flinch of pain, Miles tightened his fists. At the second, he jumped forward. "You're hurting him."

Addie growled, not taking her gaze from Arthur, her finger uncomfortably close to the trigger of the Unwelcome's weapon. "And what do you think he'll do to us if he gets loose?"

Frustration rolled through Miles. "He hasn't tried to harm us. The opposite, in fact."

Lyla glared at him. "Miles, you've made your feelings clear, but you are not in charge. In fact, you three need to head back to the camp *now*. Do not tell anyone about this."

Miles shook his head. "I'd like to stay."

Riley tugged on his sleeve. "Miles, let's go."

Miles whirled on him. "But—"

"Miles," Petra said sharply. "We need to go."

Miles looked between the two of them. "Fine."

Riley opened his mouth and then closed it.

"Tell Frank I'll be late," said Lyla, "and you three are restricted to the camp until further notice. We'll discuss the rest of your punishment when I get back."

Riley and Petra nodded, but Miles met Arthur's gaze. Arthur nodded. "Thank you for your help, Miles."

Addie started at his voice, and Jamal paled. Miles nodded and followed Petra and Riley into the trees. The three of them were silent as they walked back to the camp. They walked for ten minutes before Petra spoke. "What do you think they'll do with him?"

"Question him. See if he has any information that can help us," Riley said.

"And if he doesn't?" Petra asked.

Riley shrugged.

Miles stopped. "We need to go back. She'll kill him. She'll—"

Riley got right into Miles's face. "Hey, that's Lyla you're talking about. She's saved all of us I don't know how many times. And you know she is fair. She won't kill him just because. She'll only do it if the camp is at risk. So what the hell is your problem?"

Miles deflated in the face of Riley's arguments. "I don't know. I just feel like Arthur is an opportunity. And Lyla doesn't seem to see that."

"No," Petra said as they all resumed walking. "Lyla sees threats first and guards against them. But if Arthur proves not to be a threat, then she'll see the opportunity. Riley's right—you need to trust her."

"I do, more than anyone." He sighed. "I just want to be the one who talks to Arthur, who learns what he knows." Miles shook his head, going quiet, not sure how to put what he was feeling into words. Petra and Riley were the best of the young Phoenixes.

No one doubted the important roles they'd play in keeping the camp safe in the future.

And Miles had to admit, he was jealous of that. He knew being the camp doctor was important, but he spent most of his days reading medical books or bandaging cuts. And he was winging it most of the time.

He just wanted to do one thing that would make the whole camp say, "Wow, look what Miles did." And even as he thought it, he knew it was a stupid, egotistical wish. But it was hard being the kid with half an arm. People were always trying to help him. And he knew he should appreciate it more, but it just made him want to do something no one else could do. To prove he was more.

"Guys, wait," Riley said, reaching out to grab Miles's arm.

Petra instantly went on alert. "What is it?"

"I don't know. The forest just got quiet." Riley pulled out his staff.

Petra and Miles did the same. Miles looked around but didn't hear anything.

"Get down!" Riley yanked Miles toward a Douglas fir and all but threw him under it. Petra dove under another one as Riley crawled in next to Miles.

Nothing happened for a long minute, Miles opened his mouth to ask Riley a question but Riley clamped a hand over Miles's mouth, his eyes wide. "Look," he mouthed, nodding to where they had just been standing.

Miles stared but didn't see anything. Then a shadow blocked out the sun. Miles looked up, starting to shake as an Unwelcome ship slowly flew over them.

36

Lyla, Jamal, and Addie escorted Arthur another forty minutes away. There was an old quarry littered with mine shafts that Lyla thought would work to hold him until she figured out what to do with him. Arthur walked in front of them, his arms wrapped behind his back. He swayed every once in a while, and Lyla wasn't sure if that was because his balance was thrown off by the position of his arms or a weakness from his injury.

His bandages had shown spots of blood when they'd started to walk, and now they were drenched in blood. Lyla felt no sympathy. These things were killing kids without any sympathy. They'd killed God knew how many in that goal.

As horrible as all those deaths were, though, she wasn't focused on the deaths of those children. Ever since they'd begun to walk with their prisoner, there only one death that remained in the forefront of her mind—Muriel's, her sister.

For years, Lyla had beaten herself up for not guessing what Muriel was going to do. She'd imagined scenario after scenario where she'd prevented Muriel from running out into that clearing to lead the Unwelcome away from Lyla and Riley. Over time, though, she'd come to realize that that was Muriel's decision. She'd decided to sacrifice herself to protect Lyla and Riley. If the positions had been reversed, if Lyla had been closer to the entrance of their hiding spot, Lyla would have done the same thing.

Her sister, although not the fighter Lyla was, had her own strength. And Lyla had come to realize it was a disservice to her sister to constantly question what could have been done differently. Because at the end of the day, Muriel had done what she set out to do. She had saved her son and her sister. So now when Lyla thought of her, she simply said a silent thank you.

But right now, all that hard-won acceptance had gone out the window, and she was angry all over again. Images of Muriel flowed through her mind. She pictured the joy on her face when Riley had been born, the promise she had elicited from Lyla to always protect Riley.

Lyla dug her fingernails into her palms. She had promised Muriel she'd take care of him. And then Riley had gone out searching for an Unwelcome. The thought of everything that could have gone wrong terrified her. She could have easily lost both of her boys today, as well as Petra. Ahead, Arthur stumbled, falling to his knees. Lyla put up a hand, and both Jamal and Addie stopped.

"Get up," Lyla said.

Arthur nodded, still resting on one knee before pushing himself to his feet. He didn't say a word, just took a deep breath and kept walking.

"How much further?" Jamal asked.

"Two minutes," Lyla replied.

"Addie?"

"I'm good." Addie held the Unwelcome's weapon and had not put it down the entire walk. Lyla knew her arms had to be aching. No one inquired how Arthur was doing. She knew Miles thought he was willing to help, but as far as Lyla was concerned, they had no goodness in their hearts. She wasn't even sure they had hearts.

The old quarry came into view as they crossed over the remnants of the chain-link fence that had once encircled the entire site. Inside the fence, much of the area was still just rock. But nature had been slowly reclaiming the space, with trees sprouting through the ground. There were dozens of old shafts across the area. Some were impassable. Others went farther than Lyla was willing to venture. But she knew of at least a dozen that were passable and connected with an underground river. If the Unwelcome did show up, they would be able to escape through one of those tunnels.

"Jamal, go check out shaft four," Lyla said.

Jamal jogged ahead. Lyla tensed, expecting Arthur to try something now that he had only two guards. But he didn't. He simply stopped walking and asked quietly, "May I sit?"

Lyla hesitated for only a second. "Yes."

Arthur sat down heavily with a sharp intake of breath. He leaned back against a tree, closing his eyes. Lyla frowned, watching him. *I don't think he's faking.*

Jamal appeared in the entrance of the mine and waved them forward.

"Break time's over. Let's go," Addie said.

Arthur didn't stir.

"Hey!" Addie yelled.

Arthur started, his eyes popping open. "What?"

"On your feet," Addie said.

Arthur nodded. He leaned forward, resting on his knees. Then using the tree, he slowly got to his feet.

"Head to the opening," Lyla instructed.

Arthur started forward at more of a shuffle than a walk.

"Check if the dynamite room is usable," Lyla called to Jamal as they approached. He ducked back into the old tunnel.

Montell and Lyla had found and explored the mine shafts a few years back. Inside the shaft to the right was a room carved out of rock that Frank said had been used for storing dynamite.

There was a heavy metal door at its opening with large metal loops outside that could be used to secure it.

Jamal reappeared and jogged over to them, giving Arthur a wide berth. "I checked the room. It's solid and the door works."

"Good. Let's get him in there." When they reached the entrance of the shaft, Lyla nodded toward it as Arthur stopped. "In."

Arthur hesitated at the dark entrance.

"Afraid of the dark?" Addie asked with a bite.

"A little," he said before stepping in.

Lyla stayed behind him but out of striking distance. She didn't worry about him escaping down the shaft. It had been sealed off years ago by a cave-in. Besides in prime condition, Arthur could probably move a few rocks but not now.

The sunlight only penetrated ten feet into the tunnel. But Jamal had lit a lantern farther down the tunnel, providing some light.

"In there." Lyla nodded to the door to the right. "Against the back wall."

Arthur briefly hesitated at the dark opening. Jamal grabbed the lantern and brought it closer. It illuminated the dark room, revealing walls of rock.

Arthur stopped in the middle of the room. But as the lantern illuminated the space, he walked to the rock wall at the back and slid down to the dirt floor.

Lyla and Jamal shoved the heavy iron door shut and slid a rod of metal through the loops on the door, securing it in place.

Addie blew out a breath, lowering the Unwelcome's weapon. "Well, that was stressful."

"Yes, it was," Lyla agreed, looking through the metal bars at the top of the door. Arthur had fallen on his side, his eyes closed once again.

"So now that we've got him here, what exactly is the plan?" Jamal asked.

Lyla put a finger to her lips nodding to the door before leading them back to the entrance of the shaft. "You two are heading back to the camp."

"What?" Jamal exclaimed.

"Tell Frank—and *only* Frank—what is going on. And make sure you double the guards and half the shift time. I don't want anyone getting tired and missing something."

Addie crossed her arms over her chest. "We are not leaving you here alone."

"Look, you two are going back. I need you there if the Unwelcome show up."

"And if they show up here?" Addie demanded.

Lyla nodded toward the Unwelcome's weapon. "Then I'll handle it. You need to explain things to Frank. Tell him where we are. I'm going to let Arthur rest for a little while, and then I'll start questioning him. We're okay for tonight, but tomorrow bring some food and we'll see where we go from here."

"Lyla, we can't leave you—"

"You *can* and you *will*. This is not a request; it's an order. Four Phoenixes are on a scavenge, another two are sick. The camp needs you there. And I need to be here."

"What if he tries something?"

Lyla looked back toward the room that held the injured Unwelcome. "Then he dies."

37

The Unwelcome ship moved overhead slowly, without sound. That was the part of the ships that scared Riley the most—the lack of noise. He held his breath, as if even breathing would result in them getting caught. He watched the ship as it moved out of sight. Next to him, Miles was equally silent, his hand over his mouth. Neither of them moved, even when the ship was gone from view. One tree over, Petra stayed still as well. For thirty minutes, they stayed where they were, none of them even daring to move.

"What do you think?" Petra asked in a loud whisper.

"I think we're okay," Riley said.

"Probably," Petra agreed, although she did not move from her hiding spot.

"They have to be looking for Arthur."

Riley nodded. "Yeah."

"Okay, well, I'm done lying here." Petra crawled from under the fir tree, brushing off the pine needles that clung to her clothes as she stood. Miles and Riley exchanged a look before slowly climbing out themselves.

"I didn't hear the camp alarm," Petra said.

Riley glanced back toward the direction where the ship first appeared. "It didn't go off. Maybe they didn't see it. It wasn't coming from the direction of camp."

"That's a good sign," Miles said.

Riley turned to look at him in disbelief. "A *good* sign? Are you kidding?"

"It means they don't know where Arthur is. He doesn't have a tracker on him. He hasn't contacted them. They're *searching* for him. It means he was telling the truth."

"It means it's *possible* he was telling the truth," Petra said.

"We should go tell Lyla," Miles said, turning back. "She needs to know—"

Riley grabbed his arm, pulling him forward. "*We* need to go back to camp. Lyla is already mad at us. If we disobey her again ... well, I don't even want to think of what creative punishment she might come up with."

Miles cringed, no doubt thinking about her last one. Riley and Miles had skipped out on working in the fields one day to go fishing. Lyla had been waiting when they returned. They had pleaded that they had just needed a little time off. Lyla agreed. Then she had put them in charge of all the Carolina kids for three days and nights, claiming that their parents needed a little time off as well. All things considered, Riley would have preferred to run until his feet fell off. It seemed like there was always one of them talking, two or more of them fighting, one of them crying, and one of them trying to get themselves killed. He had been beyond exhausted when the three days were up.

Miles looked back in the direction they'd come. "You think she's all right?"

Petra snorted, pushing past him. "She's fine. It's probably Arthur you should be worried about."

38

A rthur did not wake up for hours. Lyla was beginning to wonder if he ever would. If he didn't, that would save them the trouble of figuring out what to do with him. But even those thoughts sounded cold-blooded in her mind. The creature had saved Riley and Miles. He'd saved Miles twice. She should be grateful for that, and she was. She just wasn't ready to trust the thing.

Jamal had returned a short while ago. He'd brought food, water, and news. Riley, Miles, and Petra had seen an Unwelcome ship, but it had not gone near the camp, although Frank had doubled the guard on duty as Lyla ordered. The ship appeared to be searching for Arthur, but it had not been seen near the quarry.

Jamal nodded to the door of Arthur's holding cell. "I don't think he has a tracker. They would have been here by now."

"I suppose," Lyla said.

"So what do you want to do?"

"I'll stay here tonight. Can you and Addie keep an eye on the kids?"

"Of course."

"And then you guys can head here tomorrow and I'll get back to the camp."

Jamal left a short while later, decidedly reluctant. But first he'd helped Lyla leave some food and water in the cell.

Lyla was dozing when she heard movement from the cell. Her eyes popped open, and the Unwelcome weapon was in her hand as she quickly got to her feet. She glanced through the bars and saw that Arthur had managed to sit up. He looked up. "How long was I out?"

"A few hours."

He nodded. "Is it night?"

"Yes." The mineshaft was bathed in shadow, with only two lanterns providing any illumination.

He leaned back, closing his eyes. "I am guessing you have questions for me. I am ready."

Lyla paused. While Arthur slept, she had been thinking about what exactly she wanted to know. And there was only one place to begin. "What are your plans?"

Arthur opened his eyes. "My plans?"

"Your people. What are they trying to accomplish? What do the Naku want?'

"I cannot speak of them."

Lyla narrowed her eyes. "You said you'd answer questions."

He shook his head. "You misunderstand. I physically cannot speak of them. We all have implants. If we attempt to speak of them, it is painful, extremely painful."

"What do you mean an implant?"

"It is a piece of hardware they have implanted in our brains when we are young." He paused. "As children, we had many procedures performed on us."

The image of children, granted small blue children, tugged at her heart. She tried to harden herself against it, even as she found herself asking, "What kind of procedures?"

Arthur shifted, wincing slightly before he began to speak.

"Our planet, as I mentioned, has less gravity. It is the reason for our size. But generally less gravity makes bones brittle, and space travel further weakens the bones. If we were left in a pure state, we would be tall but not as muscular. We would be a shadow of ourselves."

"So how are you so big?"

"They incorporated particular chemicals into our food that forces muscles to grow. And they graft carbon into our bones at a young age. The carbon was created so that it would spontaneously grow with us, making our bones strong enough to support the extra weight of the muscles."

"How old were you when they performed those operations?"

"On our planet, the days were longer. A year was equivalent to two in Earth time. By your measurements, I was five years old. They do not want to waste the resources on a child who will not survive. If someone made it to five, there was a good chance they would make it to adulthood, and so that is when the surgery was performed."

Lyla was quiet for a moment. "How many children made it to age five?"

Arthur met her gaze. "One in twenty."

She gasped. "What?"

"Our planet was not an easy one. The atmosphere was thick, and breathing problems were common. Death was a part of life. To have the surgery, as painful as it was, meant the Naku had taken an interest in you. They poured resources into you, and it meant you had a chance."

"What about education?"

"Most of my people are not educated. Education leads to free will, and they do not want—" He choked, seeming unable to get a breath, his eyes growing large.

"Arthur?"

He sucked in a huge breath of air. "I'm all right. But perhaps we could stay away from that topic."

She studied him. It almost seemed as if his breathing had been cut off when he'd spoken of those in charge. "How did you learn to read?"

"I was bred to be a bridge to alien species. I was educated along with only a few dozen others."

"Do they feel as you do? Are they sympathetic to the plight of humans?"

"I do not know. Because of what we have learned, we are never allowed to speak with the other translators. None of the Unwelcome communicate much beyond what is needed for our jobs. It is"—he paused—"frowned upon."

"That must have been lonely."

He didn't say anything, just nodded his head.

"Are there any women in the Unwelcome? The ones I've seen all look male."

Arthur met her gaze before looking away. His chest heaved for a moment. "There are women. Some are taken to the breeding pool. Some are soldiers."

In Lyla's mind, she ran through all of the Unwelcome she had seen, but none had shown any physical indications of being female. "I must not have seen any of the female soldiers, then."

"You've seen females. They look no different than the males." He paused. "Their reproductive organs are removed when they are young, and they are given steroids and growth hormones. They are indistinguishable from the males."

Horror crawled over Lyla. Who were these people? "That's ... that's so cruel. How could you do that to one another?"

Surprise flashed across Arthur's face. "We do not. It is the Naku who are responsible."

Lyla frowned. "But I thought you *are* the Naku."

"No. My people have no formal name. We are simply servants."

"And the Naku are ...?"

"Our overseers."

39

O*ur overseers.* The words stayed in the back of Lyla's mind over the days as she questioned Arthur. It had now been almost two weeks since Arthur had been brought to the tunnel. Lyla had spent the most time here, at least during the day. They had not told anyone else at camp about him, save for Frank.

Lyla had been in charge of interrogations. He had shared a great deal, although any attempts to learn more about his overseers, the Naku, resulted in only pain. He'd even passed out once in an attempt to answer the questions put to him. They'd just finished another marathon question session, and Lyla was feeling drained. She had left the door to the cell open with the understanding that Arthur must not attempt to even stand or she would shoot. He had stayed against the back wall across from the door, but she could tell even that small change had brought him some relief.

"I would like to ask you a question, if I may," he said.

Lyla tensed. There was a truce of sorts between them now, but she would not let her guard down. She kept waiting for him to try to pry information about her camp, her people, the Cursed.

"It is not about your camp," he said quickly. "It is about your culture, the human culture. It is something I have not been able to understand, and I have spent considerable time trying to."

"What is it?"

"Knock knock jokes."

Lyla stared at him, thinking she had misunderstood. "What?"

"Well, most jokes I do seem to understand. They are just ... strange. For most, it is easy to understand what the punch line is. But for knock knock jokes, it is particularly obvious or the punch line is not funny."

Lyla wasn't sure what to say to that. How did one explain a joke? After all, the explanation tended to ruin the joke itself. She kept her face expressionless as she leaned back against the wall, her arms over her chest. "Answer my questions first."

Arthur looked at her and then nodded his head slowly, his disappointment obvious. "Yes, yes, of course."

"Will you remember me tomorrow?"

Arthur frowned. "Of course."

"What about in a week?"

"Yes, my memory is very good."

"How about in a year?"

"I will never forget you, Lyla."

"Knock knock."

He frowned, tilting his head, looking puzzled. "Who's there?"

Lyla raised an eyebrow. "I thought you said you'd never forget me?"

Arthur's mouth fell open. Then a smile spread across his face as his shoulders began to shake. Then Lyla was the one who was shocked as a deep belly laugh erupted from him.

Lyla tried to stay stoic, but his laughter was infectious. Soon she was holding her stomach and laughing just as hard. It wasn't just the joke but the release of tension. She looked across the space at Arthur, who smiled brightly at her, laugher still quaking through him. And for the first time, she smiled back.

The laugh Lyla and Arthur shared seemed to change the dynamic of their conversations. But the truth was, none of her conversations with Arthur had gone as planned. To start with, they weren't supposed to be conversations but interrogations. But Arthur had answered everything she asked. He seemed straightforward. But she wasn't sure she could trust her impressions. She felt he was being honest, but every single thing she knew about the Unwelcome told her she'd be a fool to believe that.

She blew out a breath, glancing through the bars the next morning. Arthur glanced up at her. "Good morning."

"Good morning," Lyla said without thinking, then berated herself for being polite. It was just difficult to be cold when he was so cooperative. "Back against the wall, please."

Stop being polite! she yelled at herself.

Arthur walked to the back corner and knelt down, facing the wall.

Lyla opened the door, watching him carefully for any movement, but he stayed where he was.

Lyla picked up the two bowls, one with water and one with food, on the rock ledge to the left of the door.

She'd just stepped back when the floor shook violently. *Earthquake.* She dropped both bowls, grabbing onto the wall to keep herself upright. It felt as if the floor was alive, shifting and writhing under her feet. She crashed to the ground, unable to stay standing.

From the corner of her eye, she saw Arthur get one leg under him. And she realized he'd been waiting for a moment like this. Lyla tried to crawl to the door, knowing she needed to get it shut before Arthur reached her, but the world felt like it was coming apart.

Part of the tunnel ceiling crashed to the ground outside the room. Large chunks of rock fell in the doorway. She'd have to move them to get the door shut. Behind her, Arthur got unsteadily to his feet. Fear charged up Lyla's throat.

A rock slammed into her shoulder and she cried out. The ceiling above her began to come apart. Rocks pelted her as she held on to the trembling ground.

Arthur lunged toward her with a roar. And there was nothing she could do to stop him.

40

Brendan's right ankle was still smarting from the fall he'd taken a week ago. He limped along, trying to figure out his next move. But the truth was, he didn't have one. Ever since he'd been kicked out of the camp, he'd been living from moment to moment. He'd eaten the food they gave him when he left within two days. And he'd only found some here and there. He did find a rabbit in somebody else's trap that he'd stolen after a week. That had been the first time his stomach had felt full in a long time.

He hitched up his pants, wishing he had some rope to tie them tighter. He'd lost weight. His stomach didn't growl anymore from hunger. It was more of a constant gnawing in his swollen belly. He needed to get food soon. He was getting really weak, and he knew that before long, he wouldn't be able to walk much more.

Voices sounded from the creek bed to his right. Brendan paused, trying to figure out what to do. People could mean trouble, but they also most likely meant food.

I'll just take a look and then decide. He crept closer, leaning against a tall oak to peer out when a hand clasped down hard on his shoulder and yanked him back. "Just what do you think you're doing?"

Brendan was whirled around. A muscular man missing a few teeth leered down at him. Brendan put up his hands. "I wasn't doing anything. I promise. I was just hungry."

The man scoffed, pushing Brendan in front of him. "Let's go."

The man kept a hold on the back of Brendan's shirt as he prodded him forward. Branches scratched him as he was shoved through two juniper bushes. He tripped over his feet and landed hard on his knees on the bank of the creek.

A group of six people stood staring at him. All of them looked hard, but their clothes were clean and none looked hungry, which meant they were most likely from another camp.

A woman in front stepped up. "Who's this?"

"Some guy spying on us in the bushes." He nudged Brendan in the back. "Says he's hungry."

"Where are you from?" the woman demanded.

"I, uh, nowhere."

The woman grunted. The man handed her Brendan's pack. "This was all he had on him."

The woman rifled through it. "Not much here."

"I don't mean any trouble. I was just hungry, that's all."

The woman narrowed her eyes, pulling out a water skin. "This is from Attlewood."

Brendan looked up and then looked away. But in that glance, he recognized one of the men. He traded with Attlewood from one of the camps to their north.

The man stared at him, and then recognition dawned. "You're the one they kicked out for beating his kids, aren't you?"

"He what?" the man who'd grabbed him demanded.

Brendan whirled around, seeing the anger on the man's face. "No, no. It wasn't me."

"Sure it wasn't." The man reached down and grabbed him, yanking him to his feet.

The rest of the group looked unconcerned as the man hauled him back down the creek.

"What are you going to do with me?"

"Show you your future." The man pulled him along. Brendan tried to keep up, but he wasn't as fast and kept getting dragged along the ground. The man barely slowed. For five minutes, he pulled him along until they reached the edge of a twenty-foot cliff.

Brendan's eyes went large as the man held him at the edge. "No, don't! Please!"

"Is that what your kids said?" the man demanded. "I had two kids. Some asshole like you took them and gave them to the Unwelcome."

"I would never do that. Never."

"Sure you wouldn't." The man's voice was laced with derision.

"Please, I'll do anything."

"Great. Fly." He shoved Brendan off the edge.

41

L yla braced herself, knowing when Arthur reached her it was the end. The earth trembled under her, and in her mind she said goodbye to Riley, Maisy, and Miles.

She screamed as Arthur reached her. But he stopped right behind her and didn't touch her. Instead, he stayed hunched over her, protecting her from the falling rocks. It felt like forever as she lay there while the earth trembled.

But finally the world stilled. Lyla's limbs were numb from all the shaking. She looked up to where Arthur knelt above her, his eyes closed, his mouth a thin line.

"Arthur?"

He didn't move, didn't open his eyes, but his forehead was creased. "Crawl out. Quickly, please."

Lyla wasted no more time. She pulled herself out and turned as Arthur dropped himself to his side. She blanched at the sight of his back. The ropes had protected some of it but there were still some deep gashes from where the rocks had struck him.

Those injuries would be on my back if Arthur hadn't protected me.

He sucked in a breath through his teeth, and Lyla marveled at his strength and his actions. He had saved her. Just like Miles and

Riley said he had saved them. He opened his eyes and scanned her face. "Are you all right?"

Lyla nodded slowly. Why had he done that? If he had let her get killed, he could have escaped. Was this just an attempt to win her trust? "I'm okay. How about you?"

A grimace crossed his face. "I have been better."

She hesitated for a moment before reaching down and grabbing his arm. "Let me help you."

Arthur struggled to his feet, swaying as he stood upright. Lyla hesitated and then pictured Arthur's face as the rocks crashed down on him.

Damn it. She pulled out her knife and cut the ropes binding his hands. He let out a breath as he flexed his bleeding arms. He swayed again and blinked hard, his eyes unfocused. The room was covered in rocks, and he didn't look like he could maneuver his way around them.

Lyla took one of his arms and draped it over her shoulders. She stumbled a little as his weight fell onto her.

"Sorry," he mumbled. Together they made it out of the room. A little farther back, her bedroll lay untouched; the ceiling here had held. She led him there. She tried to lower him gently to the ground, but his weight was too much and he slammed into it.

Lyla winced at the drop. But Arthur just let out a grunt and fell onto his side, closing his eyes. Lyla went and grabbed the med kit. She knelt down next to him and looked at his back. The wounds weren't as deep as she first thought, but his back was still a mess. She quickly cleaned the cuts with water and then covered them in bandages.

She bit her lip, staring at the bandages Miles had placed on his other wounds. They hadn't been touched since Miles's ministrations.

"I'm going to have to change your other bandages." She hesitated. "It's going to hurt."

He met her gaze and nodded, closing his eyes again.

Lyla removed the bandages. They had fused to the wounds and in removing them she had reopened the cuts. But she cleaned them, put on some antiseptic ointment, and then re-bandaged them. Hands shaking, she sat back.

"Thank you," Arthur said softly. She glanced up and saw his eyes watching her.

She backed away. "Uh, you're welcome." He closed his eyes. She waited a few minutes but realized he had fallen asleep. He shivered. She grabbed her blanket, placing it over him.

She looked back down the tunnel and with a shock realized she had left the Unwelcome weapon just outside the room. At any point, Arthur could have grabbed it. She pushed some rocks off of it. Rocks that she would have been under if not for Arthur. She dug out the weapon and inspected it. It didn't seem damaged. In fact, it didn't even look scratched.

She carried it back to where Arthur lay. He was snoring slightly. She sat across from him. Why had he saved her? What was his end game? Why had she untied him?

And what exactly was she supposed to do with him now?

42

W hen Brendan woke, his whole body ached. It was dark, and he tried to roll to his side, but all he managed was a groan.

"Shh, shh, rest easy," a voice said. His head was lifted gently and chicken soup filled his mouth. Despite the pain, he grabbed the hands to keep the cup at his lips.

"Easy, easy now," the man said. He pulled the cup away. "That's enough for now. Now you need to sleep."

"No, no," Brendan mumbled even as his eyelids responded to the man, closing on their own.

For the next three days, Brendan was in and out of consciousness. He felt like he blinked and it was daylight. He blinked again and it was night. He couldn't seem to keep his eyes open for very long. But each time he awoke, the man was there, and so was the soup. On the fourth day, he awoke and blinked his eyes wide open. He felt better, not good, but better. He looked around. He was in a small cabin. He raised his right arm, which was covered by two pieces of wood wrapped in fabric. His right leg had the same treatment.

"Afraid you broke those two when you took that fall. It was lucky I came along when I did."

"Yeah," Brendan said with a swallow. "Thanks."

The man nodded at him. "I'm David."

"Brendan."

"Well, Brendan, looks like you might be staying awhile. Are you hungry?"

His stomach growled in response. And Brendan couldn't believe his luck. Someone upstairs was definitely looking out for him. "Yes, David, I am."

43

After the earthquake, Lyla had left the cell unlocked. She knew she was taking a chance, but she was going with her gut. She didn't think Arthur would hurt them, and she also didn't think he had anywhere to go.

Addie and Jamal had even scrounged up some old stuffed chairs and brought them into the tunnel. Lyla and Arthur sat in them now.

"So when you arrived on our planet five years ago—"

Arthur cut in. "We did not arrive here five years ago. We've been here for seven years."

"What?"

"We created New City five years ago. But we had been on your planet for almost eighteen months prior to that. Your gravity is different. Our ships have less gravity than your planet. Our bones were infused with carbon when we were young to keep them strong, and our suits actually dampen the effect of your gravity, but we still needed time to adapt."

"Adapt how?"

"In all ways—our spatial orientation, hand-eye coordination, our balance. And many of us were violently sick the first few months."

"So where were you?"

"In a high region. I believe you once called it Mount McKinley."

Lyla pictured the tall mountaintop she'd seen in a book belonging to her grandfather. "That's the highest point in North America. I didn't even know it still existed."

"It does, although the water has risen around it. It is not as far above sea level as it once was."

"Is that where you read about humans?"

"Yes, some. But I had been reading about you for much longer."

"How much longer?"

"In your estimates, it would be ten years."

"You knew you were coming ten years ago?"

Arthur shook his head. "*I* did not know. I just knew I was expected to learn."

"Expected? By who?"

"The—" Arthur's mouth was open, but no sound came out.

He began to shake and then fell out of his chair.

Lyla leapt to her feet. "Arthur!"

He continued to shake for a minute, his eyes rolling back into his head.

Lyla cursed herself for putting him through that. Of course the Naku were the ones who expected him to learn. Over the last few weeks, Arthur had struggled to try and tell her about them. But each time, his reaction grew more damaging.

Lyla crouched next to him, not sure what to do. "Arthur?"

He let out a little groan. His eyelids flickered a few times before he opened them. He struggled to sit up.

Lyla put her arms around him, helping him. "You need to stop trying to speak about them. We'll find another way to get information."

"But I wish to help."

"I know. And you will. But not this way." At first, when he'd had these reactions to questions about the Naku, she had wondered if he was faking it. But his pulse rate shot up, sweat broke out across his body, and he seemed to almost seize up. If he was faking, he was incredibly talented. "Why are you sharing all of this with me? I don't understand that. You're betraying your people."

Arthur shook his head. "No. They have already been betrayed by themselves. This is not who we are, not who we are meant to be. My people have been enslaved for as long as we can remember."

By the Naku. Lyla heard the words as clearly as if they had been spoken out loud. The Naku were there on the edge of all of their conversations. Lyla wanted to know who they are. But more than anything she wanted to know what they looked like. Removing Arthur's helmet had humanized him, humanized all of the Unwelcome. They were no longer the boogey monster.

But the Naku ... Lyla had no concept of them. As far as she knew, no one had seen them. Everyone thought the Unwelcome were the Naku. But Lyla was getting the feeling that the Unwelcome were victims as well.

And Lyla had to admit, she didn't like how that made her feel. Not that she thought any of the other Unwelcome would be willing to sit down over a cup of tea and discuss their issues, but still.

She stood up and began to pack the dishes they had used. Arthur knelt next to her, carefully packing the rest with her. Finally, he held on to the pack. "I was thinking, if you think it's all right, I could walk with you. Not all the way back, of course. But just a little bit."

Lyla looked up into his face. Despite his size and strength, Arthur was more of a gentle giant that a raging beast. And right now she was only getting one emotion off of him—loneliness. It must be difficult to be on his own so much. He hadn't had much companionship throughout his life. And now that he had a taste, he seemed to loathe the silence he'd formerly lived in.

She nodded. "I'd like that."

44

It had been almost a month since they had found Arthur. Lyla spent almost every day at the mine, at least for a few hours, before Addie and Jamal took over. But they still would not let Miles visit. He'd argued that he should go check Arthur's wounds, but none of them would budge. He'd thought about following them one day to see where they'd taken him, but he knew that he had no chance of being able to follow them without getting caught.

Finally, though, this morning, Lyla had said he and Riley could go with her when she relieved Jamal. Riley was walking up ahead with Lyla while Miles hung a little farther back, trying to once again figure out what to ask Arthur. Lyla had shared some of what he had told them about his home planet and his time on the ship. Miles was beyond fascinated but also horrified. It did not sound as if Arthur had led an easy life.

They stepped through an opening in the old chain-link fence around the old quarry. The rock face was dotted with dozens of openings. He'd never been here before. In fact, this was the farthest from camp he'd been in his entire life.

Riley looked around. "Which one is—"

Laughter sounded from the shaft directly ahead of them. Lyla smiled, heading forward, but Riley and Miles stayed where they are. Miles looked at Riley, who looked back at him, his eyes large. "Is that Arthur laughing?" Miles asked.

"And Jamal, too."

With one last look, the two of them hurried forward. They stepped into the opening, and Miles blinked a few times to adjust to the dimmer light. Jamal and Arthur were in the dynamite room, a checkers board between them. Lyla sat perched on a rock near them.

Arthur glanced up with a smile. "Miles, Riley. It is good to see you." He got to his feet and walked over, extending his hand. Miles's mouth fell open, and without thinking, he extended his own hand. Arthur shook it and turned to Riley. Riley shook his hand as well.

"Do you shake hands on your planet?" Riley asked.

"No." Arthur glanced back over his shoulder at Jamal. "But Jamal said it was the way you greeted people here. Did I do it wrong?"

"No, no," Miles said quickly. "You did it just right. We're just surprised is all."

"Oh, well, Jamal, Addie, and Lyla have been teaching me some human interactions while I teach them about my people and home world."

"You're not locked up?" Riley asked.

"We've come to an understanding," Lyla said, exchanging a smile with Arthur that nearly floored Miles. They were *getting along*? He wasn't a prisoner?

"Okay, enough," Jamal said. "I'm about to kick Arthur's butt all over this board. So you all will just have to wait to chat with him until I'm done."

Arthur nodded at Riley and Miles with a little nod. "Excuse me." He returned to his spot across from Jamal.

Miles moved forward, sitting on a rock next to Lyla. He leaned against her and smiled as they watched Arthur beat Jamal in checkers.

45

B rendan had spent the first week of the month he spent with David sleeping a lot, his body needing to recover. The cabin David had brought him to was a one-room cabin with two twin beds, an old scarred wooden table with three chairs, and a wood-burning stove. David had taken care of Brendan, giving him a chance to heal. He'd kept him fed and seemed to not have any problem tracking down food when they ran low. Brendan had begun to think of David as his guardian angel.

But as he'd gotten better and slept less, he realized his guardian angel was more of a tormented angel.

"No, no. I didn't mean it. I didn't know. I would have protected you," David begged as he crouched in the corner staring at an image only he could see. Each night, David received a visit. As the day began to draw to a close, he would tense, anticipating the night to come.

For the last few weeks, Brendan had watched the drama unfold before him. But tonight, he thought it was time he became part of the play. He sat up. His leg hadn't been broken. The knee had only been sprained. He could walk with a little pain. He grabbed the crutch by the bed and began to hobble over to David, careful in the dark. David never put on lights at night.

"What does she want, David?" he asked as he got closer.

"To protect them. She always wants to protect them."

Brendan knew David had worked for the Unwelcome when they had first arrived. He'd worked in their science advancement building. But he had left after an incident. Brendan was sure the incident was what he relived every night.

"Protect who?"

"All of them, but her especially. She died so they couldn't reach her." David looked up above him. "I didn't tell them. I didn't tell them. I kept your secret."

"I think she wants help in keeping her secret. I could help. I could help keep her secret safe."

David looked at Brendan before his gaze flew across the room. He backed up even farther against the wall, as if he could push himself through it. "He's here. He's angry."

Oh no. David did not have only one ghost haunting him. He had two. From David's ramblings, Brendan had eventually realized that the other ghost was the child he had turned in to gain entrance to New City.

Even though he knew David was hallucinating, Brendan couldn't help but glance over his shoulder to check. And the air itself always seemed to grow colder and more still whenever David experienced his visitation.

Ignoring the goosebumps that had broken out across his skin, Brendan spoke calmly. "No, no. He can't hurt you. He wants you to let me help the lady, too."

David's gaze strayed across the room before he nodded. He pulled a piece of paper wrapped in a plastic case from his pocket. He placed the case in Brendan's hand. "We must protect her. It is what she wants."

"Of course, of course." Brendan frowned down at it. He

thought it might be a picture, but he couldn't see anything in this light.

David curled back away from him, muttering to himself, and Brendan knew he would be like that for hours. He made his way back to his bed, placing the plastic on the table next to the bed. Then he climbed slowly back in and dozed until dawn. Each time he awoke, he checked to make sure the plastic case was still there and that David hadn't reclaimed it. It was still there, and David was lost to his nightmares in the corner of the room.

When the first rays of sunlight came up, Brendan picked up the case and quietly made his way to the door. He unlatched it and looked at David, who mumbled in his sleep but didn't awaken. Brendan slipped out the door, closing it quietly behind him. He walked to the end of the small porch and lifted the case, angling it to avoid the early morning shadows. It *was* a picture.

Must be his ghost, he thought as he peered into it. It was an old photo, frayed at the edges with creases in it. Brendan had expected to see a younger David, but he wasn't in the shot. Instead, the photo was of two young girls. Brendan peered closer. Then his jaw dropped and his breath halted. It couldn't be. He studied the photo, but there was no mistake. It was *her*.

Brendan sat down heavily, staring as the sun rose in the sky. David came out of the cabin and Brendan composed himself, making sure his face betrayed none of his shock, only compassion. He held up the photo.

"I think you should tell me about these women."

46

Miles was still stunned at the freedom Arthur was being given. But he and Riley and even Petra managed to visit him another four times over the next month. Miles grilled Arthur about his biology, Riley wanted to know the best way to take an Unwelcome down, and Petra only wanted to know one thing—why they wanted kids their age dead.

Arthur happily shared what he knew of the first two, but he couldn't answer Petra's question. He simply didn't know the answer.

Today as Miles stepped into the shaft, he called out, "Arthur?"

Lyla had decided that Arthur could remain on his own without a guard at night. Miles didn't think Arthur was very keen on the idea. Miles had the impression he liked the company. And from what Miles knew about his upbringing, he could understand. Companionship, friendship, was not something encouraged. In fact, if it was observed, the Unwelcome involved were reassigned.

Arthur had spent a few nights alone over the last week. Jamal came out a few times and stayed with him. Not as a guard, but just to keep him company. Lyla had even spoken about figuring out a way to bring him back to the camp. But that was not something that would happen for a while. Getting everyone in the camp to accept him was going to be something that required a great deal of planning. But Miles hoped they could figure out a way to do it.

Miles walked through the tunnel, but Arthur was nowhere to be found. He noticed that a few mismatched chairs had been placed inside the dynamite room. He frowned, heading back to the entrance, and spotted Arthur walking across the clearing toward the tunnel, a table above his head.

He spotted Miles and smiled. "Miles, look what I found!"

Miles stepped out of the tunnel. "Where'd you find it?"

"A maintenance shed." Arthur walked past him and carefully maneuvered the table through the doorway of the dynamite room. He flipped it over and then lowered it to the ground. He pushed lightly against it and it looked pretty solid. "I thought it would be nice to have a table when we are eating."

"That's great. In fact, I brought some lunch. So how about we test it out?"

They ate their lunch sitting at the table, and Miles could see how proud Arthur felt at being able to offer Miles a more comfortable place. It was amazing. They were amazed at the Unwelcome's technology, and yet it was something as simple as being able to sit at a table and eat that brought a smile to Arthur's face. Miles had learned that none of the Unwelcome had possessions. Everything belonged to the Naku.

Arthur finished up the last of his lunch, wiping at his mouth. "Thank you, Miles. And please thank Emma and Edna for me. I truly appreciate their efforts."

Miles ducked his head. Emma and Edna knew something was up with all the food that was being sent outside of camp, but they didn't know about Arthur. He actually thought they might be a good place to start with getting the camp on board with him. "Sure."

"I've been thinking about what Petra has asked." Arthur paused. "I may have some information."

Miles sat up. "You do?"

"I can't be sure. But I remember that when we arrived at New City, many were killed. You know that. But some were taken initially, and they were tested."

Miles leaned forward. "Tested how?"

"All ways—genetic screening, blood, physical abilities. It was thorough."

Miles swallowed. "And what did they find?"

"They found you, or at least, people your age. The testing stopped and our raids began to focus only on children between certain ages. They never told us why."

Miles sat back. "But there has to be a reason."

Arthur was quiet for a moment. "The only reason to focus on a specific group would be if you offered a threat."

"A threat? What kind of threat could we possibly offer? I mean, you have more strength, more speed. Your height alone makes it difficult for an adult to take you down, never mind a kid."

"And yet, you are the ones we have been told to target. There must be something to it."

"But what?"

"I know that when they tested, they were particularly interested in your blood."

"Our blood?"

He nodded. "If you are looking for an answer to why the Cursed have been targeted, I think the answer can be found in your blood."

47

B rendan stared at the walls of New City. He'd heard the
stories of it, but he never expected it to be so large, so clean,
so foreign. Two Unwelcome stood on either side of the main gate,
checking that everyone who arrived had a bracelet.

Brendan felt his pulse quicken at the sight of them. This
could go horribly wrong, but he would not spend the rest of his
life in a little shack with a crazy man for company. He patted his
pocket, where the picture still lay wrapped in its plastic case. He
had taken it from David last night while he slept and then slipped
out the door with all the food he had been able to find.

Over the last few weeks, he'd gotten David to tell him more
and more about his time in New City. And more importantly, why
the woman in the picture was so important.

David had been reluctant to discuss her at first, but Brendan
was persistent, staying calm even when he wanted to shake the
man, and his persistence paid off. David had spoken of his last
day working at the Advancement Building. How he'd seen the
woman's body fall as he'd sprinted down the stairs. He had made
it to the first floor in time to rush to the edge of the water and see
her body get pulled under by the force of the falls. But her head

had stayed above the water, staring at him, accusing him for a split second before she completely disappeared.

And he'd known what she wanted. He'd sprinted back up to her cell and taken the picture she had hidden under her bunk. And then he'd left New City.

But no matter how far he went, he could not leave the woman behind. She would not let him. She started to appear to him at night, along with the boy he'd traded in to get access to the city.

Brendan took a breath and then headed to the front gate. People were being waved through after their bracelet was tapped. Brendan walked up to a woman in a bright-blue velvet robe. "Excuse me, ma'am?"

She turned, looking down her nose at him, curling her lip. "There are no jobs available."

"No, no. That's not why I'm here. I need to speak with someone in the Advancement Building."

Her derision lessened only slightly. "And why is that?"

"Because I have information on a subject that the Naku are very interested in."

48

I *think the answer can be found in your blood.* Arthur's words rolled through Miles's mind as he headed back to the camp that night. Arthur had given him a sample of his blood before he left, and now Miles wanted nothing more than to see what it told him. He hurried through the camp entrance.

"Miles!"

He looked up at Riley's yell.

"Hey," Miles said, not slowing.

"What's going on?"

"I spoke with Arthur." He quickly ran down what Arthur had told him. He'd just finished when they stepped inside the med cabin. He quickly opened the door to the cabinet. His microscope lay on the bottom, and all of the supplies lay with it, but everything on the shelves had toppled out of their holdings. Miles gaped. "Someone's been in here."

"Ah, shoot. No. We had an small earthquake while you were visiting Arthur. I checked the cabin but not inside here."

Miles reached down and pulled the microscope out. *Please be okay.* He placed it on the desk and looked through it. The lens was a spiderweb of cracks. "Damn it."

"How bad is it?"

Miles waved him forward. Riley peered in. "Oh. That's bad."

Miles nodded, rustling through his pack for the slide he'd created from Arthur's blood. "But maybe it can still tell me something."

Miles placed the slide on the stage and peered through the eyepiece, trying to see something between the cracks in the lens. Then he placed the slide he'd made of his own blood. He switched it again.

"Well?"

Miles stared into the microscope. The lens was cracked, but even so, he thought he saw something. Was there a color difference? He switched back in the other slide. He sighed. *This is useless.*

"Well?" Riley asked.

"I don't know. I mean, they look the same from what I could make out, but this microscope has obviously seen better days. But the samples *should* be different. With the right microscope, maybe we'd be able to see something. If we could get a higher-powered microscope, I could compare Arthur's blood samples and maybe we could figure out a way to fight them."

Riley's eyebrows rose. "With blood?"

"Disease has been a weapon for centuries, both intentionally, like with the Native Americans, and unintentionally, like when Europeans first arrived in Australia. The diseases they brought with them wiped out most of the indigenous people because they'd been isolated from the rest of the world. Arthur's people are from a different planet. There have to be diseases here they're not inoculated against."

"Even if there are, how would we know? You have a cracked microscope. And don't you need books or something to figure that out? Never mind a way to access the diseases?"

Miles nodded, his mind whirling. "The first step, though, is figuring out the differences. I bet the old university would have a decent microscope."

Riley narrowed his eyes. "You can't seriously think Lyla's going to let you go there."

"What? This could help all of us, not just in this camp, but humans. This could be the key."

"*Could* be. You don't know that for sure. The university is a two-day walk from here. Lyla's let up on some of the security increases she put in place since we found Arthur but she's never going to agree to let you go all the way out there."

"If we took the horses, it would take less than one day to get there."

"Miles, it's a long shot at best. And I don't think things are dire enough to risk someone's life by sending them through hostile territory. You'd have to go through the wild lands, which is full of unaligned people. You'd also have to cut through Old Meg's territory. I just can't see that happening. Not right now. And not you, not a Cursed."

"But *I* have to go. There could be books there that would help and supplies we could use."

"Hey, I get it. But I just don't think that's going to happen anytime soon."

All Miles's daydreams about uncovering the Unwelcome's biology disappeared with Riley's words. He was right. "I guess."

Riley clapped him on the shoulder. "Look, it's a good idea. Maybe we can ask everyone to keep an eye out for a new microscope when they go on a scavenge."

"Yeah, you're probably right." He glanced back at the microscope, a nagging feeling that the blood was the key. But Riley was right. A trip to the old university wasn't in the cards anytime soon.

"Come on. We need to go train. We don't want Lyla taking away our ability to go see Arthur."

"Yeah." Miles stood and followed Riley to the door. He

paused, looking back at the damaged microscope. A deep sense of foreboding fell over him, and he had a feeling that sometime soon, they were really going to regret not making an effort to learn more about the Unwelcome's blood.

49

His tea was still too hot, so Chad nibbled on a biscuit while he waited for it to cool. He looked out of the glass wall at the falls behind the Advancement Building. It was truly a beautiful sight. There were no camps to visit today, thank God. How those people lived that way was beyond him. He ran a hand down his velvet robe. He would never be able to live without the sumptuous fabric again. But then again, that was not something he had to worry about.

His father had taught him how to get by in this world. How to make yourself indispensable to the people that mattered. And Chad had taken those lessons to heart and made himself, if not indispensable, at least very handy to have around.

Of course, I don't actually work for people, he thought with a smile before taking a sip of tea. He sighed with pleasure. *Just right.*

The intercom buzzed, and he punched the blinking button. "What is it?"

"Sir, there is a man here who is demanding to speak with you."

"Me, specifically?"

"Not by name, but he says he can only speak with the person in charge."

Chad drummed his fingers on his desk. "And why should I care what he wants?"

"He says he has information about an incident from five years ago. Something about a suicide?"

Chad sat straight up, knocking his desk and spilling some of his tea. The incident had been the one blight on his record of service with the Naku. "Send him in, along with a guard."

"Yes, sir."

Chad frowned. How could someone know about the incident? All those involved were still here. All except David.

He looked up, expecting to see David's dark hair, but instead a man who was a good few inches shorter than David and who looked to be in ill health appeared in the doorway. Chad pulled out his handkerchief, putting it to his mouth, not wanting to catch whatever diseases the man was surely carrying. *Or fleas.* He held up his hand. "That's close enough."

The man stopped only a few feet in the room. An Unwelcome stood directly behind him. "Um, are you the man in charge?"

"Yes. What is it you needed to tell me?"

"Well, um, I need to show you something first."

Chad leaned away from him. "What?"

The man pulled out a small plastic case from his pocket. "This."

Chad hesitated before waving the man forward. "Put it on the edge of the desk."

The man hurried forward, and a wave of body odor flew toward Chad with his movements. Trying not to gag, Chad waved him back once he'd placed the object on the desk. Using a tissue, Chad pulled the case over. He glanced down at it. It was a picture of two girls.

Chad looked up, irritation rolling through him. "What is this? I don't have time to—"

"Look at the woman on the right. Don't you recognize her?"

Blowing out a breath, he stared at the woman. She looked vaguely familiar. Something about her eyes. Blue eyes staring at him from a stretcher full of hate floated through his mind. He reared back. "Where did you get this?"

"From David. He took it from her cell."

That weasel.

"But I'm not here about her. I'm here about the other woman in the picture."

Chad's head snapped up. "What about her?"

The man smiled. "I know where to find her."

L yla stood up and stretched. "Well, I should get going."
Arthur nodded. "Of course. I've kept you longer than you had planned on staying. I am sorry for that."

"No, I was enjoying myself," she said, amazed at the truth in her words.

"Could you wait just a moment? I have something I would like to give you."

"Sure."

Arthur stood up and walked down the mineshaft, disappearing from view. Lyla looked around, wishing they could find somewhere else for him. He shouldn't have to hole up in the dark like this, hidden from the world.

Arthur reappeared with three wooden figures in his arms, each about a foot tall. One was a rabbit, one a bear cub, and one was a fox. He handed them to her. "For your girls."

Lyla took them, looking at each one in wonder. The carved faces were so sweet and so lifelike. She looked up at him. "When did you do these?"

Arthur shrugged, a small blush appearing on his cheeks. "I

was looking for something to do. I thought your girls might like them."

"Like them? They will love them." Lyla smiled.

Arthur smiled in return. "I hope I get to meet them someday."

"I do, too," Lyla said, and she meant it. She placed the statues in her pack, carefully wrapping them in her sweater to make sure they didn't get damaged. "Thank you, Arthur. This was very kind."

"No, thank you, Lyla. When I helped your sons, I never imagined it would lead here. I thought I was signing my death warrant. I am glad I was wrong."

"I am, too." She looked into his eyes, and time passed slowly. She stepped back quickly, her heart pounding as she looked away. "Um, well, I'll see you tomorrow, okay?"

"Okay."

Normally he'd walk part of the way back with her. But they were expecting a trading group to come in today or tomorrow, so it wouldn't be safe for him to wander around.

So she headed out of the shaft and into the bright sunlight alone. She took a deep breath, feeling Arthur's gaze on her as she crossed through the boundary fence. She hated that he was alone so much. And she wondered when exactly he had gone from being someone she feared to someone she was concerned for.

51

Brendan swatted at a bug that crawled over his leg. He hated being out here. Crawling around in the woods like some kind of animal.

He'd been here for four days, waiting for his chance, but it had never materialized. He broke into a cold sweat thinking about the Unwelcome that had dropped him off half a day's walk from here. He didn't want to think what would happen to him if he didn't deliver. He thought for a moment about just running, heading west as far and as fast as he could.

But he glanced down at the metal wrapped around his wrist. Chad had had the Unwelcome place it on him as soon as he'd agreed to their terms, and he had no doubt they could track him through it.

No, running wasn't an option. Besides, he wanted his reward. He was sick of struggling. And without his kids to barter for food, it was only going to be that much more difficult. When he came through, he would be living on easy street.

Voices reached him, cutting into his thoughts. He sunk lower into his hiding spot. Three teenagers appeared, water buckets in their hands. Finally. He picked up a rock, and as they passed, he tossed it at the large boy in the middle.

The boy looked over his shoulder with a frown. Brendan straightened enough for the boy to see him. Adros's eyes went wide. Brendan waved him over.

Adros swallowed hard, his head turning between his two companions, who'd kept walking.

Josh stopped and looked back at him. "What are you doing?"

Adros rolled his shoulders. "Shoulder's acting up. You guys go on. I'll be right there."

Josh shrugged and followed Shane.

Brendan waited until he couldn't hear the boys any longer and stood. "Hello, son."

Adros glanced over his shoulder before turning back to him. "Dad, what are you doing here?"

"What? I can't check in on my kids?"

Adros's gaze shifted to him before it shifted away. "Uh, I guess."

"So how are you? And the girls?"

"The girls are okay."

"Good, good. I was worried about them. You, too. I miss you guys."

Adros's mouth fell open for a moment before he closed it. "Um, well, we're good. Lyla's taken the girls in. And I'm with Shane's family."

Brendan's anger spiked at the mention of Lyla, and he struggled to keep a lid on it, but he must not have done a good job because Adros took a step back. Brendan blew out a breath. "You know, that's good, real good. I know I messed up. I never should have touched the girls, or you. I'm real sorry about that."

Adros just stared at him before he shook his head. "Dad, I can't get you back into camp."

Brendan waved his words away. "Not asking you to. I need to earn my way back, and I plan on doing that. And maybe then I can come back. Listen, it's been a little rough out here, though. Do you think you could bring me some food?"

Adros's relief was palpable. "Food, yeah, sure, no problem. But I'll need to finish the water duty so no one knows."

Brendan tried not to bristle at the fact that Adros didn't run to get him food immediately. And he also didn't seem concerned about where he'd been these last weeks.

Adros picked up his buckets. "I'll meet you at the old oak in about an hour, okay?"

Brendan smiled. "Great. Thanks, son."

Adros paused, looking confused. "Um, you're welcome." He disappeared into the woods after his friends.

The smile dropped from Brendan's face. *Ungrateful brat.* He'd learn exactly who was sorry the next time he saw him.

It was closer to two hours before Adros appeared at the old oak. Brendan glared at him, and Adros stumbled back. "S-sorry. I had to sneak food from the kitchen."

Brendan counted to ten internally before smiling. "No problem. I appreciate it."

Adros hesitated for only a second before handing Brendan the pack. "Um, it's ham. I got some of the gravy you like, too."

Brendan grabbed the pack and quickly dove into the food. He was starving. He'd barely eaten anything since he'd left New City.

He sat back when he was done, the edge taken off the hunger, but it was still there, reminding him why he needed to do this. Not that he needed much of a reminder. He licked the tin that had held the gravy clean.

Adros had stood silently the whole time Brendan ate, shifting from foot to foot. He glanced back in the direction of the camp. "So, I should get going."

"Not yet." Brendan placed the pack down and pulled his knife from the sheath at his waist and started cleaning his fingernails. "There's something we need to discuss first."

"Um, okay."

Brendan looked up from his nails. "I need you to get Lyla banished from the camp."

Adros's mouth dropped. "What? No, I'm not doing that. I couldn't do that." He slammed his mouth shut, glaring. "You haven't changed, have you? I don't know why I thought— You know, it doesn't matter. Goodbye, Dad." He turned to head back to the camp.

Brendan narrowed his eyes. "If you don't, your sisters are dead."

Adros stopped walking, his whole body tensing. He faced Brendan. "What did you say?"

"Get Lyla banished or your sisters are dead."

"You can't touch them. They're safe inside the camp."

"*I* can't touch them. That's true. But what about the Unwelcome? I don't think your Phoenixes will be able to stand up to them."

"They've come to camp before. And they've never—"

"But those times they didn't know where the cave was."

Brendan let the words lie between them. And he watched his son's face fill with anger as he stepped forward and pulled his staff. "Then I guess I need to make sure you can't talk to anyone."

Brendan held his knife in front of him. "I already have. And unless you get Lyla out of that camp, the Unwelcome will know where to find all of you."

Indecision warred across Adros's face, and Brendan knew he was trying to find the lie in Brendan's word. But he'd never find it, because there was no lie.

Adros lowered his staff. "Why? Why would do this?"

"Because that bitch deserves everything that is coming to her."

Adros shook his head. "What? You're going to try and kill her? She'll kill you before you can even raise your arm."

Brendan narrowed his eyes. "Oh, she'll get what's coming to her. Don't you worry about that."

Adros stared at him, his gaze hard. "How am I going to get her kicked out? It's *Lyla*."

"The same way she got me kicked out."

"Violence? Lyla's never laid a hand against anyone in camp except during training."

"No, *she* beat you—repeatedly."

"No, she didn't."

Brendan held out his hand. "Give me your staff." Adros hesitated.

"The Unwelcome will come. You, your sisters, every kid in the age range will become little piles of dust. Or you can send Lyla out of the camp." He paused, his voice hardening. "Now hand me your staff."

With a shaking hand, Adros handed it over. And Brendan saw the fear he'd been looking for in Adros's eyes. He smiled. "Turn around."

"Don't do this," Adros pleaded.

"*Turn around.*"

Adros watched him for a moment before turning around.

"Never forget, Adros. Even when I am not nearby, I control you." He swung the staff.

52

The sound of laughter drifted down the stairs, making Lyla smile. Alyssa and Rachel had been a little shy at first but Lyla had really seen them bloom the last few months since Brendan had been gone. The girls had been overjoyed at the little wooden statues. Alyssa had rubbed the little bear's head over and over as if it was real. When they'd asked, she told them a friend had made them for him. And she really hoped that one day they could meet him.

She glanced out the window, but there was no sign of Miles or Riley. They'd gone to see Arthur again. When they'd first taken him, she never could have imagined she would allow the boys to see him again, never mind visit him unsupervised. They'd come a long way. And the boys were the reason for that. They had been the ones who had found him, helped him, convinced Lyla to keep him alive. Miles and Riley had gone and grown up on her when she wasn't looking. And it made her both proud and sad.

Miles even had an idea as to why the Unwelcome were targeting the Cursed. He believed there was something in their blood. But the answer to why that would be required a microscope. The only place Lyla thought they might be able to find a microscope was at the old university. But they'd have to travel through Old Meg's territory and the wild lands. She wasn't quite ready to take that step. Right now, she had the Phoenixes on double guard duty, in case the Unwelcome were still looking for Arthur. So she couldn't spare people for a possibility, intriguing as it was.

She had, however, given Miles her blood to test against when the time came. She was hoping that action would appease him for a little while. Plus, she had directed the scavenge groups that had left over the last few days know to keep an eye out for a microscope. It *would* be amazing if he could figure out why the Cursed were being targeted.

Through the window, she saw Frank hurry toward her house, Edna right behind him. She frowned, not liking the look on his face. She hurried to the door and had it open before he had a chance to knock. "What's wrong?"

Frank paused midstep. "Lyla, I need you to come with me. Edna, go stay with the girls."

Edna looked at Lyla, tears in her eyes.

"What's going on?" Lyla asked.

Edna opened her mouth to speak, but Frank shook his head. "Go on, Edna."

Edna glared at Frank and then hugged Lyla tightly. "I don't believe a word of it," she whispered before hurrying into the house.

Lyla watched her go in confusion before turning to Frank. "What on earth is going on?"

Frank's eyes looked a little wet as well. "Just come with me. Please."

He looked so lost. It tugged at Lyla's heart. "Of course." She fell in step next to him. Neither spoke as they headed toward the stables, crossing the training circle, which was empty.

They rounded the stable, and a crowd had gathered near the well. Otto's head stood above the others, and he looked mutinous.

She realized the rest of the Phoenixes were there, at least those
not on duty. But there were another two dozen people and more
coming in from the fields and the kitchen area. The crowd parted
as it caught sight of her and Frank. And Lyla caught some of the
not-so-hushed whispers.

"I don't believe it."

"Of course she did it. She hated him."

"Guess the rules don't apply to her."

The comments only added to her confusion.

Frank led them into the center of the group, where Otto
stood, his arms crossed over his massive chest. And sitting on the
ground in front of him was Adros. His left eye was swollen and
pain was etched across his face.

Lyla gasped, hurrying forward. She knelt down next to him.
"What happened? Who did this to you?"

Adros wouldn't meet her gaze. His voice shook as he spoke,
whisper soft. "You did this to me."

Lyla reared back. "What?"

Frank stepped forward. "Adros said you cornered him in the
woods. That you were angry at Brendan and took it out on him."

"Adros, why would you say that?" She reached out a hand for
him. Adros cringed away.

"Keep her away from him!" someone yelled.

"She didn't do anything!" Otto yelled back.

Soon the crowd was yelling at one another, half defending
her and half accusing her. Lyla tried not to be hurt by those who
believed she was capable of beating a child, even a very large one.
She studied Adros. Someone had obviously hurt him. But why
would he say it was her?

Shoving started somewhere in the crowd, yanking her attention back to the tense crowd of people surrounding them. Lyla
knew they were only moments from a full-fledged brawl.

"Silence!" Frank yelled. "Now!"

It took a moment, but everyone quieted.

Lyla stood, and Frank turned toward her. "Lyla, do you have anything to say?"

"I didn't do this."

Frank nodded, his relief obvious.

One man pushed through the crowd, stepping in front, his arms crossed over his chest. "So that's how it goes? She says she didn't do it and we ignore the boy?"

Lyla stared at Sheldon. Her gaze narrowed before it shifted to Adros on the ground and then over the crowd. She had a victim claiming that she was the one responsible for his injuries. If it were anyone else he had accused, his word would have been enough. But because it was her, her people were fighting back.

And that couldn't be allowed to happen. The camp would splinter, maybe not immediately, but eventually. And her escaping punishment, even if it was unwarranted, would be the catalyst for all of it.

Lyla met Frank's graze, and she saw his eyes widen. He shook his head, but she spoke before he could. "No. Adros has made an accusation and it will be respected. The rules apply to me as well as well as anyone else. I did *not* do this, but I cannot prove that." She stopped a tremor working its way through her, and she felt ill at the words she was about to say. "I will leave the camp."

The crowd exploded. The Phoenixes yelled they wouldn't accept it, others yelled she should go, and some yelled, it seemed, just to yell.

But she held up a hand. "The decision is made." Her head held high, she started to walk through the crowd.

Otto stepped in front of her, clearing a path. Montell fell in behind her as Addie and Jamal flanked her sides. The crowd mumbled as she passed, and she struggled to keep the tears back. Jamal started to speak, but she shook her head. "Not yet."

He gave her an abrupt nod. Lyla kept her face composed, but her mind raced. Why had Adros said it was her?

And what on earth was she going to do now?

53

Lyla asked Addie and Jamal to stay outside a moment when they reached her house. They both looked like they wanted to argue, but they agreed.

Lyla shut the door and leaned against it, her head bowed. *I've been banished. How is that possible?* She stayed where she was, trying to control the emotions raging through her. She needed to be in control to get through the next few minutes. Taking a deep breath, she pushed off the door, then opened it, letting Addie and Jamal in. Footsteps sounded on the stairs and Edna appeared. She hurried across the room and hugged Lyla tight. "I don't believe a word of it."

Lyla gave herself a moment to enjoy the comfort and then pulled back. "But unfortunately not everyone shares your opinion."

Edna wiped the tears from her cheeks. "Well, they're idiots. I hope you set them right. Accusing you. It's—"

Jamal's voice was absent its usual lightness. "Edna, Lyla agreed to be banished."

Edna's eyes went wide, turning to each of them in turn. "You can't be serious."

"It's true. She did," Addie said.

"Well, why the hell did you go and do that?" Edna demanded.

Addie crossed her arms over her chest. "I'd like an answer to that as well."

Despite the anger in her voice, Lyla could see the tears in her best friend's eyes. Lyla sighed. "Guys, you saw Adros—"

"But you didn't do that," Jamal cut in.

"No. But someone did. And Adros is saying it's me. Meanwhile, the camp is rumbling. You saw them. It looked like the whole crowd was about to throw down. My accepting banishment avoided that."

Jamal ran a hand through his hair, looking like he wanted to hit something. "Yes, but you are exiled! How the hell can—"

Addie yelled at the same time. "That's insane! You can't just—"

Lyla put up a hand, and they both quieted. "I don't plan on staying in exile. But my going will give the camp a chance to calm down, and then you guys and Frank can figure out what's going on. And then I can come back."

"They can investigate with you here," Edna said.

"No, they can't. The camp's been unsettled. The rules have to be followed. The rest of the camp has to see that we are not above the rules. This is the only way."

"I don't like it," Addie said.

Lyla sighed. "Me, either. Now can you guys grab me some food stores? I'll put together a pack and meet you at the front gate. And Edna, do you think you, Emma, and Petra could stay here with the kids? We just got Rachel and Alyssa settled, and I think it will be easier for Maisy if she stays in her room."

"We'll take care of them, even if—" Edna's hand flew to her mouth, her eyes filling with tears.

"This is *not* goodbye. I'll be back," she promised, and Edna nodded.

Addie and Jamal's gazes were no more reassuring, so she just turned and headed for the stairs to speak with the girls while tears pressed against the back of her eyelids. *This is not goodbye,* she repeated to herself. But her legs felt heavy and her chest felt tight.

But it really does feel like it.

54

Saying goodbye to the girls nearly shattered Lyla. Rachel and Alyssa had stood silently, clinging to each other as tears rolled down their cheeks after Lyla hugged them. Then Lyla turned to Maisy. Maisy hadn't screamed or cried. She had stood silently, shaking, her eyes bright with tears. Then she'd flung herself at Lyla.

And she had refused to let go. Nothing Lyla said had worked. No words of comfort, no promises of return could get her to release her hold.

Finally, Lyla had just carried her downstairs along with her pack. And it had taken both Frank, who'd arrived while she was upstairs, and Edna to get her off.

And that's when the screams had begun. Even now as she walked with Frank, they echoed through her mind. For a moment, she had thought of taking the girls. Edna had even suggested she and Emma would go with them. And then it would be Addie and Jamal, followed by Otto, Montel, and Shayna. Soon the camp would be emptied of its cooks and protection. And Lyla couldn't do that, as much as she wanted to. Besides, it was safer for all of them to stay inside, especially the kids.

"We'll all make sure the kids are all right," Frank said.

Lyla just nodded, not trusting herself to speak. But they were approaching the gate and there were things that needed to be said. She pulled her emotions back, locking them away. "I'll need you to talk to Riley and Miles."

"Where are they?" Frank started, as if he'd just realized that they'd missed everything.

She squeezed his arm. "Visiting our friend. And Frank, you need to make sure they don't do anything stupid. I don't know why Adros accused me, but if Riley or Miles gets into a fight with him ..."

"I won't let that happen. And I *will* get to the bottom of this."

"I'm counting on it."

They stopped just before the gate. Addie and Jamal stood there with the other Phoenixes. Lyla looked at each of them. "Remember your duty. This changes nothing. We protect all those within our walls."

"Even Adros?" Rory asked, his mouth set in a firm line.

Lyla nodded. "Especially him." She didn't think Adros had done this out of spite. He looked too devastated, too guilty. No, it was more than those bruises that were paining him.

Jamal took Lyla's pack, and Addie placed the food supplies in. Then he handed it back. His hands shook. "That should see you for a few days."

"I packed an extra water skin, just in case," Addie said, her voice trembling and tears cresting in her eyes. One slipped over onto her cheek.

Lyla hugged her tight. "It will be all right."

Addie laughed. "Shouldn't I be comforting you?"

"You know me, always taking charge." She turned and hugged Jamal.

Then she faced Frank, struggling to keep her emotions in check.

Frank's voice was rough. "I *will* find out what's going on."

She hugged him quickly. "I know." Then she walked quickly toward the gate before her tears broke through again.

She focused on placing one foot in front of the other, aware of the audience watching her leave. She kept her shoulders straight. *Just to the trees. Just make it to the trees.* She let out a shaky breath, and then she was hidden from the camp by the trees.

But she didn't stop. She kept walking, giving herself false finish lines to make her legs move, even as the tears trailed down her face.

When Lyla left the camp she didn't have a destination in mind. She had wandered for a while, torturing herself by replaying Maisy's reaction and imagining what the boys' reaction would be.

But then she got ahold of herself and realized she needed a plan. She needed a place to stay where she'd be safe from the elements and she could set up a camp. And it immediately became clear where that should be—in the mine with Arthur. She could continue to pick his brain about the Naku and the Unwelcome. And she'd be able to see Riley and Miles. Plus, it would be nice for both of them not to be alone.

Unfortunately, she had gone in the wrong direction. Changing course, she realized she'd come to the highway farther up than where they normally crossed to head to the mine. If she'd been thinking clearly, she would have headed there right away so she could intercept the boys. But she hadn't, and there was no changing that now. Still, she picked up her pace, the irony that she was now seeking out Arthur to help her not being lost on her.

And she had to admit, there was a comfort in the idea of spending her time away from camp with him. After all, it looked like they both could use a friend right now.

55

B rendan had climbed a tall tree to watch Lyla leave the camp. He'd felt a smug satisfaction at the sight of her walking away alone. She looked small, tiny, beaten. Her Phoenixes had lined the way, but even they could not stop her from leaving.

He smiled. *I did that. She thinks she's so smart. But who's the smart one now?*

He stayed in his perch, watching her with binoculars as she made her way through the woods. As luck would have it, she headed straight for him. He'd stayed silent when she'd gotten closer. But she'd passed by, unaware that she was under observation.

She moved slowly, not seeming to have any particular desti-nation in mind. Then she'd stopped for some water and sat on a fallen tree for a while. When she stood, she changed direction, heading toward the old highway.

She was moving faster now, and Brendan quickly climbed down. He knew if he cut a parallel path to her, he'd hit the highway as well. And that was fine. He didn't need to catch her.

He just needed to be there when somebody else did.

He tapped one of the buttons on his bracelet and hurried toward the highway.

56

"Okay, Miles." Riley pointed to the camp entrance. "You have talked about the ramifications of the blood differences for the entire walk. How about we give that a rest for a little bit?"

"But don't you get it? This could explain so much about them. It could tell us what their weaknesses are. It could change everything!"

Ever since Arthur had suggested the Naku were interested in the blood of the Cursed, Miles had been unable to think of anything else. He'd scoured the medical texts he'd had to see what he could learn. There hadn't been much. There was one line of research though that might relate. In the Before, researchers had begun to investigate if exposing older cells to younger blood could reverse some of the signs of the aging process. The research had not been completed when the asteroid hit.

But the Unwelcome weren't interested in *all* younger humans, just a select subset. Besides, the Unwelcome weren't trying to take blood from the Cursed. They were destroying them, which meant, as Arthur said, they feared something about them.

Miles knew that the answers could only be found through an

examination of the blood. He had Arthur's blood, Riley's, and Lyla's. He just needed a way to compare all three. And he couldn't seem to think of anything else these days. The answers could be right there in his med cabin.

Riley, though, wasn't quite as fascinated by the possibilities as Miles was. "Look, I get that, and as soon as you learn what those weaknesses are, I am all ears. But right now, my ears are bleeding from this conversation."

Miles cringed. "Sorry. I get carried away."

"And we are all lucky you do. Just maybe spare the rest of us the minutiae."

"Minutiae? That's a big word for a small mind."

Riley shoved Miles as they passed through the entrance. "Not small—just not science obsessed."

Miles grinned. "Tomato tomahto."

Riley shook his head with a smile and met the gaze of Coral, the Phoenix on guard duty. She looked away, her face and body language radiating stress. Riley frowned, noticing almost everyone within their line of sight was watching them.

"Is it me or is everybody watching us?" Miles asked.

"Thank God!"

They both turned as Petra hustled up to them.

"What's going on?" Riley asked. But Miles just scanned the faces of the people around them. Their expressions ranged from angry to sad to concerned. Something big had happened while they were gone.

Petra glared at a group of people that had stopped to openly stare at them. They quickly continued on their way, whispering amongst themselves. "Come on." Petra grabbed each of their arms and pulled them toward the kitchen. She only let them go when they were behind it and there was no one in sight.

"What the hell, Petra?" Riley asked, rubbing his arm.

"It's bad, guys."

At the seriousness in Petra's voice, Miles glanced at Riley, whose face reflected his concern.

"It's Lyla." Petra explained about Adros and the punishment.

Miles stood rooted in place, torn between disbelief and anger. Adros had always been a bully, but Miles had seen him with his little sisters. He knew he wasn't always a jerk. But why would he do this? Was he just trying to get back at Lyla for banishing Brendan?

Riley's response was less introspective. "You can't be serious. Who the hell would believe that?"

"Lots of people, apparently," Petra growled, glaring at a man who stepped out from the kitchen. He wisely headed back inside.

Miles shook his head. "We need to talk to her. This can't—"

"She's gone," Petra said quietly. But her words had the impact of a thunderclap.

Miles felt the world tilt. "What?"

"It happened almost an hour ago," Petra said.

Riley's body was rigid, his fists clenched tightly at his sides. "Where's Adros? I'm going to kill him."

Petra blocked his way. "Someone *did* beat Adros. I heard Frank speaking with Jamal and Addie. They're going to find out why Adros is lying."

Someone had hurt Adros, and he said it was Lyla. In his gut, Miles knew Brendan was somehow behind this. But no one had seen him since he'd left.

Riley blew out a breath, staring over Petra's head. Miles could feel his anger. And he was worried that Riley might take his anger out on Adros. "Well, at least they believe her. And they'll find out what's going on."

"A lot of people believe her. Some of the Phoenixes even threatened to quit. Addie managed to talk them out of it. But everyone's worked up."

Miles shook his head, agreeing with the Phoenixes. Lyla was

dedicated to this place. Yet one false accusation and it was all for naught.

"We need to find Lyla," Miles said.

"She left through the main gate," Petra offered.

"Okay. Then let's go," Riley said.

Miles followed him for a moment before he stopped. "Wait. She might have left that way, but I don't think she kept going in that direction. She'd go somewhere that she could be found when this is all over."

Riley reversed directions and headed for the gate that they'd just entered through. "You're right. And there's one place we visit regularly."

57

The walk through the woods was renewing Lyla's confidence. She had a plan. She would use this time to learn all she could from Arthur. And then once Frank learned who was behind the attack on Adros, she would be back in the camp with her family and with a better picture of the nature of the threat the Unwelcome offered.

The memory of Maisy being carried away by Edna drifted through her mind, and shudders ran through her. But she shoved the memory and the feelings away. There was no point in torturing herself with things that were beyond her control. *I'll come back to you, Maisy,* she promised before locking her image away.

Forcing herself to focus on Arthur, she ran through what she knew about him. Strong, of course, but no faster than a human, although they could leap longer distances due to their suits. And while their skin was no tougher than a human's, their suits and uniforms made them impervious to both knives and guns.

Except for that one time. Lyla remembered the warmth that had come over her right before she had plunged her knife into the Unwelcome. When she'd explained what had happened,

Arthur had been shocked. He agreed the only explanation was that the suit must have been defective, although he had also never heard of that being the case.

How you ran, Lyla, it wasn't natural. No human can run that fast. It's not possible.

Lyla shook her head as if to wipe away the memory of Jamal's words. He'd said them after she'd outpaced him to get to Cal who had taken kids from the camp. The rest of the Phoenixes had been tired, that was all. *I had extra adrenaline because it was the kids in danger.* Although there had been fifteen kids who Cal had grabbed, the fact that three of them had been hers had added an extra layer of fear that coated her as she ran.

But that's not related. That was just ... strange. She dismissed the line of thinking. It wasn't relevant to anything except to how hard she would push herself for her kids.

Speaking of which ... She glanced around, straining to hear anything from the surrounding woods. Even though she knew there was only a slim chance of it, she was hoping she would intercept Riley and Miles on the way back to camp.

She'd angled her path toward their usual route but so far, she'd neither seen nor heard any sign of them.

Leaving without saying goodbye had been difficult. But rules were rules, and she needed to leave quickly. The camp had been too on edge, and she'd worried what would happen if she stayed too long. She just hoped they figured out Arthur was where she would go.

She started at the thought and the feeling of security that accompanied it. *He's an asset, not a friend,* she warned herself. But she had to admit, she enjoyed the man's company.

Not man, alien. She found herself reminding herself to keep her distance the more time she spent with him. But he just seemed so open.

The snap of a branch pulled her from her thoughts. Her head whipped to her left, and she slowed her pace, straining to hear. There was a rustle of leaves, and then another a branch snapped.

Definitely not the boys. They would never be so careless. She edged toward the sounds, pulling her sword from its sheath. Humans and Unwelcome weren't the only predators to worry about in these woods. She moved closer as a light wind blew, bringing with it the stench of strong body odor.

Human, then. But she still didn't know how many.

Carefully, she crept forward and peered around a wide-trunked maple. Her lip curled in distaste, and then everything clicked. Anger roared through her as she stepped out.

"You bastard."

58

Brendan whirled around, his heart pounding.

Lyla strode toward him. "You did this, didn't you? My God, he's your son."

Brendan straightened his shoulders. "No. You took him from me. He's not my son. Not anymore."

"You beat your son to get back at me? What kind of monster are you? But why would Adros—" She paused, her eyes growing even angrier. "You threatened him, and probably his sisters, too."

Brendan sneered. "Not just them, but every single kid in the camp. One word to the Unwelcome and they'll be dust." He snapped his fingers. "Just like that."

As soon as the words left his mouth, Brendan realized his mistake. If he thought Lyla looked angry before, it was nothing compared to how she looked right now.

"What did you say?" she asked quietly.

Brendan stumbled back, pushing the button on his bracelet over and over again.

Lyla bounded to him in three steps, grabbing his wrists. "What is this?" She stared down at the bracelet, her eyes growing large.

In a strength born of fear, he yanked his arm away and shoved her. Then he sprinted away, his legs already aching at the action.

Behind him, he knew Lyla was already giving chase, although he couldn't hear her. Adros had once said that she made no more noise than a ghost when she moved. Brendan had berated him for making the woman into more than she was.

But he could feel her silently zeroing in on him. And he knew that if she caught him, he was the one who would be a ghost.

59

S hocked by the alien markings on Brendan's bracelet, Lyla wasn't prepared for the shove. She flew back, bracing her fall with a slap of her hands.

He's working with them. Oh my God.

She launched herself to her feet and took off after him. She needed to learn what he had told them. The whole camp was in danger.

He was only twenty feet ahead and ran awkwardly, favoring his left leg. He burst out of the trees and onto the old highway. Lyla was right behind him. She leapt, tackling him at the knees. He went down with a scream.

She brought her knee up hard between his knees, and he cried out again. She pushed the side of his face into the cracked asphalt.

"What did you do? What did you tell them? What does that bracelet do?"

"See for yourself." That's when Lyla felt the presence behind her. She rolled off Brendan, yanking him up in front of her as a shield—a shield between her and the five Unwelcome advancing on her.

She'd been so focused on catching Brendan she'd failed to check her surroundings. She'd failed to see the Unwelcome ship parked on the highway twenty yards away.

60

Miles, Petra, and Riley moved quickly through the forest. Even though there was no immediate danger, Miles knew that each of them felt the need to see that Lyla was all right with their own eyes.

They were about two hundred yards from the highway when Riley put up a hand, and they all stopped. Miles stepped up next to him. "What is it?"

"I don't know. I thought I heard something."

A yell sounded from straight ahead. Riley and Petra exchanged a glance before each pulled out their staffs. Miles did the same a second later. Riley put a finger to his lips and pointed at Petra and then to his right. He did the same to Miles toward his left.

Miles moved silently, his heart pounding. He trained with the young Phoenixes, but it was rare for him to have to use those skills. He kept Riley in his peripheral vision, and he could just make Petra out as well. He moved forward at their pace.

Ahead, someone was moving noisily through the woods. Riley reached a large maple and stepped past, then his gaze shifted to the ground. He reached down and picked up a necklace.

Even from his distance, Miles recognized it. It was on old penny that had been flattened and a lion stamped on it. He'd found it on a scavenge one day.

And given it to Lyla.

61

Lyla held Brendan tightly in front of her as she faced the Unwelcome. She knew in her gut that Brendan had called them here, although she had no idea how he had managed it.

"What do they want?" she hissed in Brendan's ear.

"You," he spit out, blood dripping from his cheek.

She frowned. "Why—"

An Unwelcomed leapt forward, yanking Brendan from her hands and tossing him away. Then it reached for Lyla, wrapping its fist in her shirt and lifting her off her feet.

"You are not taking me," she growled, feeling the warmth steal over that she hadn't felt since the last time she fought an Unwelcome.

And won.

She slammed her boot in between the Unwelcome's legs before running up his chest, kicking him under his chin, which snapped his head back. She flipped up and out of his grasp. The Unwelcome flew back, crashing onto his back. Then the other Unwelcome surged.

Lyla jumped, slamming her boot into the first who reached her. It windmilled back into another two. The fourth came at her from the side, reaching for her. She slapped its hand away, stepping to the side and burying her right hook into its ribs. Her left slammed into the kidneys, and then she stomped on the back of its knee. She grabbed its shoulders and twisted as she yanked back, sending it sprawling.

A dart landed in her neck, and she yanked it out. Two others rushed her, a third scrambling to its feet behind them. She slipped the first's reach, but her vision was dimming and her movements growing heavy. She ducked a second grab but was too slow. It grabbed her shoulder. She reached up to put it in a wristlock.

But her limbs were no longer listening to her. Her hand dropped and her knees gave out. And then everything faded to black.

62

L yla's necklace. Riley ran a thumb over the familiar face. A yell sounded again and Riley's head whipped up. *Lyla.*

Riley launched himself to his feet and sprinted forward, barely aware of Petra and Miles racing toward him. Ahead, he saw the edge of the woods and slowed. He could hear the sounds of a fight.

He reached the edge of the woods and peered out in time to see Lyla dropkick an Unwelcome into two others. His jaw dropped as she dodged another before taking it down as well.

Then she slapped at her neck and yanked out a dart as four of the five got to their feet. She stumbled.

Riley lunged forward. "No!"

Someone tackled him at the knees from behind. He barely got his hands in front of him in time to avoid slamming his nose into the ground. A hand slapped over his mouth. "Be quiet," Petra hissed.

Riley tried to buck her off, and then he felt another weight on him—Miles.

On the old highway, an Unwelcome picked Lyla up and carried her to the ship. The other Unwelcome followed him, along with one limping human—Brendan. They walked up the ramp, then the door closed, and the craft lifted off.

Riley watched as it picked up speed. Petra removed her hand and rolled off him. Miles sat back and stayed on the ground.

Riley leapt to his feet, whirling around with a growl. "Why did you do that? She needed our help! We could have *helped* her."

"They would have killed us!" Petra yelled.

"You don't know that! We could have—"

"They took her," Miles said, getting slowly to his feet.

"I know! Why did—"

"No!" Miles yelled. "They *took* her. They didn't kill her. Not one of them pulled a weapon. Why?"

Riley went still, his anger draining, replaced by confusion, realizing Miles was right.

"And what does Brendan have to do with this?" Petra asked. "I think it's way too much of a coincidence that Adros shows up beaten, Lyla gets banished, then she gets grabbed, and what? They agree to give Brendan a lift?"

Riley looked between the two of them, his anger cooling and his ability to think clearly returning. Petra was right. If he had run out there, all he would have done was get himself killed. And Brendan showing up. No, that was not a coincidence. "Why do you think they took her?"

Miles shook his head. "I don't know. Arthur did say they grabbed people initially, but they stopped that. So why take Lyla?"

"Well, my money's on Adros having answers," Petra said, and Riley approved of the anger in her voice.

"We need to tell Frank and speak with Adros. Let's get back to camp." Riley strode back the way they came, Petra right behind him. But Miles stayed where he was.

Riley stopped and looked at him. "Miles?"

"You guys go. You don't need me for that."

"What are you going to do?" Petra asked.

"Speak to Arthur. If anyone can shed some light on why she was taken and where, it's going to be him."

It was a good idea. Riley looked at Petra and said, "I'm going with Miles."

"I can walk to the mine without an escort," Miles said.

"I know." An image of Adros's smug smile appeared in Riley's mind. "But I think it's a good idea for me to stay clear of Adros for a while."

63

The walk to the mine was silent. Riley stared at the ground, looking like he wanted to kill someone. Miles was feeling pretty murderous himself right now. He was still trying to wrap his mind around everything they'd seen. The Unwelcome had taken Lyla. Brendan had somehow set her up. And even with all of that running through his mind, there was something else that stood out more. He glanced at Riley from the corner of his eye. "She fought them."

"Of course she did. Lyla would never go down without a fight."

"No. I mean she was *able* to fight them. She kicked one of them *across* the highway. That guy had to be over two hundred pounds. How the hell did she do that?"

"She ... adrenaline. Or maybe she managed to get some momentum behind him or something."

"Riley, the one fact that everybody agrees on when it comes to the Unwelcome is that you can't fight them. You can get them off balance, but you can't actually do any damage. It would be like trying to move an oak tree by yourself. So *how* did she do it?"

Riley shook his head, his expression troubled. And Miles saw just how scared he really was. "I don't know, Miles. Maybe Arthur will." He nodded toward the cave.

Arthur stood highlighted in the doorway, the shadows making his blue-gray skin appear even darker. His bandages were gone and he stood with his legs braced, his hands on his hips. He looked like the god Poseidon from a book Miles had seen as a kid.

Arthur inspected the two of them as they approached. He frowned. "Something's wrong. What is it?"

Yet again, Miles was surprised at how adept Arthur was at reading human expressions. He supposed he shouldn't be, but there was only so much you could learn from books. He was very intuitive.

"It's bad, Arthur." Riley walked past him and then stopped short. Two old club chairs and a loveseat now sat in an alcove to the left. Two large rocks served as side tables.

Arthur gave him a sheepish smile. "I, uh, I thought it might be more comfortable with more places to sit. Lyla said it was all right."

Lyla's name stabbed at Miles's heart, and he sucked in a breath.

Arthur's head jerked toward him. "Is she hurt?"

Riley opened his mouth, but no words came. So Miles was the one who spoke. "She was taken."

Arthur listened silently, not saying a word while Miles recounted what had happened, allowing Riley to see the whole incident through Miles's eyes. And Arthur picked up on the same issue as Miles.

"She fought against them?" Arthur asked. "She *moved* them?"

"Yes. If there hadn't been so many, I think she might have been able to get away. They tranqed her."

Arthur frowned. "That shouldn't be possible."

"Lyla's a good fighter. You've never seen her," Riley said defensively.

Arthur shook his head. "Even so, she might get lucky with one. But she took down four? You humans cannot take us down. It's like a rabbit taking on a grizzly bear. The weight differential alone is insurmountable."

"Well, she managed. And they took her," Riley said. "Why? You said that you took people when you first arrived, right?"

Arthur nodded slowly.

"But they're not still taking people, right?" Miles asked.

"I'm not sure."

"Not sure?" Riley demanded.

"We don't talk amongst ourselves. But I overheard snippets of conversation, reports, really, that once New City was established, humans were being taken and brought into the city."

"What do they do to them?"

"I ... I don't know," Arthur said. "But I can guess ..."

"Experimentation," Miles said softly.

Arthur nodded. "Yes."

An image of Lyla strapped to a lab table, screaming, stabbed through Riley's mind. "Where? Where would this be happening?"

"The Advancement Building in New City."

The thought of Lyla in their hands, as their lab rat—it made Riley sick. "We can't let them do that. We have to go after her."

"It won't be easy. New City is well fortified. There are two hundred Unwelcome there at minimum and more on the mother ship that hovers over the city."

Miles's jaw fell open. "Two hundred?"

"It doesn't matter. Lyla wouldn't leave us there. And I'm not leaving her there," Riley said.

Arthur stood up. "Then I am going with you."

"You can't," Miles said. "If they catch you—they *know* you're AWOL."

Arthur frowned. "AWOL?"

"Absent without official leave—it means you left the Unwelcome without their permission," Miles said.

"We do not have that term. We do not go with AWOL. You are either with them or you are dead. There is no other category. They probably think I am dead. They won't be looking for me any longer. And you will need someone to guide you through the city. I can do that. How else will you find her?"

"He's right." Miles eyed his bare chest. "But I don't think you walking in like that will exactly help you blend in."

Arthur looked down at his chest. "I will need a shirt."

Riley shook his head. "Well, yours is ripped beyond help. It's not going to work."

"There are barracks located on the outside of New City. I can get a shirt there."

Riley watched him. He trusted Arthur—for the most part. And the truth was, he *was* going to need a guide. He couldn't exactly search every building in New City until he found her.

"We might be able to get one of Otto's cloaks for the walk down there. If he kept the hood up, he might not be noticed," Miles said.

Riley nodded, even though he wasn't sure he agreed. Hiding what Arthur was was not going to be easy. Otto was the biggest guy in the camp but even he was at least six inches shorter than Arthur. It was probably impossible to hide him. But it didn't matter. Because they needed Arthur to get Lyla.

So I guess we just hope for the impossible.

64

They left Arthur outside the camp as they made their way back in. They would grab some things and head out again. Riley wanted to head straight to New City, but he knew that they would need supplies. They had nothing on them. But he was aware of every minute ticking by.

Riley had just stepped out of the kitchen with a full pack when Petra and Miles joined him. Miles had gone to find her. They needed one person in the camp to know where they were going.

Riley looked at her. "What are Frank and the Phoenixes doing?"

"They're going to do recon and then come up with a plan."

Riley shook his head. "Lyla may not have that time. We need to go get her now."

"I know. But we can't just walk in there blind," Petra said.

"We're not going blind," Riley said.

Petra frowned. "How do you— Arthur."

"He's agreed to go with us," Miles said. "To help us get her out."

"Well, that changes things, doesn't it? But you're sure he won't change sides once he's back around his people?" Petra asked.

The same thought had been rolling around in the back of Riley's thoughts. But he had been tamping down that worry ever since it had popped into his mind. "He'll be fine."

"What about the camp's rescue mission?" Miles asked.

"It will be too slow," Riley said. "They won't be able to get into New City. They won't have Arthur to help them."

Petra looked between the two brothers. "Should we tell them about Arthur? Maybe if they knew we had an inside man ..."

Riley shook his head. "No. Addie doesn't fully trust him yet, Frank hasn't met him, and whatever Phoenix we send with him will not trust him at all. We'd be back at square one, wasting all our time convincing people he's trustworthy. It won't work. Not to mention Arthur would have to be comfortable with them as well."

"Yeah, but if we walk into New City, or even try ..." Petra shook her head. "We'll be targets. We're the Cursed."

Riley nodded. He knew what a risk it was to go into the city. And he knew how long the odds were of them coming out safely. He loved Miles, but he was not exactly a man of stealth. Petra was, but he didn't want to risk anyone else's lives. "Which is why you two should stay here. I'm going to go with Arthur alone."

Petra's eyebrows practically turned into one continuous line as she glared at Riley. "Absolutely not." She nudged Miles. "Tell him."

Riley prepared his arguments in his mind—all the reasons why he and Arthur should go alone. But he didn't need any of them.

"Actually, I'm not going to New City," said Miles.

Petra gaped. "What?"

Riley felt his own mouth open. "Um, okay."

"No, not okay," Petra said. "*Why* aren't you going?"

"Because I think there's somewhere else I need to be."

65

Petra had left to see what else she could learn about the camp's plan, and in her words, to leave the brothers to get their acts together. Riley had gone to see if he could snatch a shirt or cloak from Otto's tent. But before he left he made sure Miles knew they were not done with their conversation.

Miles disagreed. Ever since Arthur had said Lyla had most likely been taken to the Advancement Building, he'd known what he needed to do—get to the lab at the old university. Now Miles quickly made his way to the med cabin. He was hoping he could gather the supplies he needed and be gone before Riley could track him down.

Miles pulled out the box that Judith had given him from the cabinet. He was currently using it to hold extra bandages. He opened it and placed the vials with Lyla's, Riley's, and Arthur's blood inside. He wrapped them tightly in the bandages before wrapping a piece of twine around the box to keep it closed. Then he placed the box in his pack, anticipation rolling through him. He had three samples—one human adult, one Cursed, and one Unwelcome. He'd compare the three and see what he found. He knew the reason why the Cursed were being targeted, why Lyla had been grabbed, would be in those samples. He could feel it in his bones. This was important. And it was also something only he might be able to do.

He hitched the pack onto his shoulder. The answers to his questions could very well be in that box. He headed for the door. *So now it's time to go get them.*

The door opened as he reached out a hand to grasp the door handle. He had to jump back to avoid getting hit by it as Riley stormed in. Miles struggled not to groan.

Oh crap.

Riley crossed his arms over the chest, blocking the doorway. "What are you doing? What did you mean when you said there was somewhere else you need to be?"

Miles had been thinking about it ever since Arthur had mentioned that the Unwelcome were testing people's blood. If they were still experimenting, if they went to all the trouble to get Lyla, then there must be something special about her. And if Arthur was right, the answer was in the blood.

"I'm going to the lab at the old university. I need to do this, Riley."

"Are you crazy? You can't go there by yourself."

"Yes, I can. I'll take a horse. It will speed up my travel time, and the camp can't spare anybody right now. Besides, I'm the only one who knows what I'm looking for. There are books there that might help me figure this out. I won't know what they are until I see them."

"This is crazy. Lyla's already in danger, and now you're running off to put *yourself* in danger."

Miles crossed his arms over his chest, too. "I'm not putting myself in danger. We need to know why they took her. We need to know what's different about our blood. Without that, we will be right back in this same situation with someone else being taken. We need to figure out what's going on. And right now, I'm the only one who can. I need to do this."

Miles could sense Riley waffling. But he also knew Riley's stubbornness would not allow him to agree without putting up a fight. "You don't need to do this. You want to do this."

Miles paused. "Yeah. You're right. I want to do this. I want to help. Just like everybody else."

"Miles, you help all the time. Without you, half the people here would have died from the flu last year."

Miles shook his head. "But I need to help now. We need to know why they are targeting us, why they targeted Lyla. And I think the answer is in our biology. And if that's true, I am the only one who can figure it out."

"Yeah, but you can only figure it out at the lab. A lab we're not even sure exists. Which is miles away in unfriendly territory."

"Riley, I can do this. And I'm going to."

Riley stared at him before looking away, his jaw tight. Miles stayed quiet, knowing Riley was on the edge of caving.

Finally, Riley turned back to him, his tone grudging. "I'll let you go, but only if you take one of the Phoenixes with you."

Miles opened his mouth to argue, but Riley cut him off. "That's not negotiable." His voice softened. "I'm not doubting your skills, Miles—just your attention span. You'll get lost in some thought and not even notice someone or something is creeping up on you. You need another set of eyes."

Miles wanted to argue. But he knew Riley would never let him go otherwise. And he also knew he was right. "Fine."

Riley nodded, turned away, and took two steps. He stopped and then made his way back to Miles and pulled him into a hug. "Be careful."

Miles hugged him back. "You, too."

They released each other, giving one another an embarrassed smile. "And listen, if you run into Meg, do not lie. She can sense them. Honesty is your only chance with her." Riley waited for Miles to nod his agreement. "Okay. See you later?"

"Yup," Miles said.

He watched Riley walk down the path toward the training ground. Shaking off his concern, he headed to his tent. After packing a bag quickly, he headed for the western entrance.

He knew he'd promised Riley he'd take someone with him, but that would leave the camp with one less Phoenix to defend it. He couldn't do that, no matter how right Riley was. He would just make sure his mind didn't wander. He rounded the last cabin in his row and came to a stop.

Petra stood there, holding the reins of two speckled Appaloosa. She arched an eyebrow as he came close. "You were trying to sneak off, weren't you?"

Miles sighed. "Look, if anyone comes with me, we leave the camp more defenseless. It's not right."

"Miles, if you are right, you may help more than just our camp. You may help all of us. Your little research trip is more important than defending the camp. The more we learn about why they're targeting us, the better chance we have of figuring out a way to beat them."

Arguments that countered Petra's words filled Miles's mind. But then he took a look at her face. Her jaw was set. He knew that look. He was never going to change her mind. "Fine, you can come."

She snorted, handing him the reins to one of the horses. "As if there was *ever* any question of that."

66

Riley hated the idea of Miles going outside the walls without him. But Miles was right—what he was doing could be really important. And besides, it's not like Riley had a right to argue that Miles's mission was too dangerous. After all, Riley was the one heading to the place where he would most likely be killed on sight.

"Riley, hold up a minute," Frank called.

Riley stifled a groan. He'd really hoped he'd be able to slip out of camp without running into anyone else. But as he watched Frank approach he realized this might actually work out for the better.

Frank stopped in front of him. "I wanted to speak with you and Miles."

Riley glared at him. "We know already," he said, his voice clipped. "Petra told us."

Frank put a hand on Riley's shoulder. "We don't believe what Adros said. But we need to figure out why he said it. And Petra told us about Lyla. I already have a team getting ready to head out and do some recon. How are you?"

Riley had planned on acting angry and then saying he needed

some time to cool off as he headed out of the walls. But he realized he didn't have to act angry—he already was. "*How am I?* Lyla has done everything she could for this place. She has put herself on the line time and time again. Do you know how many times I have seen her fall exhausted into her bed only to get right back up as soon as someone needs her help? And this is what she gets for her commitment? You let them banish her?"

"She chose to—"

"To what, Frank? Keep the camp calm at her expense? Don't you see? She's been doing that since she became a Phoenix. She puts herself last. And you let her do that. And now the Unwelcome have her! They have her, Frank, and every single person in this camp who let her walk out that entrance is responsible for that." Riley spun on his heels.

"Riley, wait."

"No. You don't want Lyla here, and I don't want to be here, either."

"Don't do anything stupid."

Riley whirled back around. "Me? No, I'll leave the stupid decisions for the *adults*."

Frank winced, and Riley felt a twinge of guilt but not enough to apologize. "Riley—"

"Just leave me alone, Frank. I won't do anything stupid. I just don't want to be here right now." He stormed toward the entrance.

Frank let him go, and the Phoenixes at the entrance just nodded at him. Riley didn't slow as he headed into the trees. He didn't slow his pace even as Arthur fell in step beside him. He didn't say anything to Arthur, and Arthur didn't ask. He simply handed Arthur the shirt and cloak he'd taken from Otto's.

They walked in silence for more than an hour, and Riley let his anger wash through him. They had banished her, and now she had been grabbed. After all she had done, they had turned their backs on her. He stewed and stewed, his anger eating him up. Finally, though, he knew he was doing nothing but expending energy he might need later. He shoved his feelings aside and took a breath.

"Hey, Arthur. Sorry. I'm just so—"

He turned around, but no one was there.

He was alone.

67

"Arthur?" The giant Unwelcome was gone. "Arthur?"

A yell sounded from twenty feet away. Riley sprinted forward as Arthur lifted Adros into the air. "Arthur, no!"

Arthur turned his head to look at Riley, Adros still dangling in the air. "You know this human?"

"Yes, he's—" Riley's words choked in his throat, struggling against his anger at Adros. "He's from the camp. He's the one who lied about Lyla."

A growl emitted from Arthur's throat that raised the hairs on the back of Riley's neck, never mind what it did to Adros. Riley almost felt sorry for him—almost.

"He was following us."

"P-put me down!" Adros yelled.

Arthur looked over at Riley, his eyebrows raised. Riley blew out a breath and waved his hand. "Put him down."

Arthur dropped him on the ground without warning.

With a yell, Adros landed with a thud. He rolled onto his side and scampered away from Arthur. Riley had to give him credit for not running away screaming. Adros glanced at Riley. "You're *friends*?"

"Sort of. What do you want?"

"I heard. Heard about Lyla."

Riley stepped forward. "Heard *what*? That she was banished? Because from what I hear, you had a ringside seat for that one."

Adros's cheeks burned, but he didn't back away. "I know. I'm sorry. But that's not what I was talking about. I heard about the Unwelcome ... and Brendan."

Riley rolled his hands into tight fights, the need to hit Adros quickly beginning to override his ability to hold himself back. "And what? You came to gloat?"

"No, no! You don't understand. My father ..."

"Your father what?"

"He threatened my sister, me, every kid in camp. He was going to tell the Unwelcome where we were if I didn't blame Lyla."

Riley shook his head in disgust. "So you just did it. How did you even come by your injur—" His words cut off as Lyla's words floated through his mind. *Do you really think the girls were the only ones he abused?*

Adros studied the ground, and Riley studied him. One half of his face was a mass of bruises that would only get darker with time. His lip was split and one eye was swelling. And he was favoring his left side.

"He did that to you, didn't he?" Riley asked quietly.

Adros didn't answer, but Riley didn't need an answer. He knew he was right. And just like that, his anger at Adros was gone. Riley hated Brendan, but he hadn't been raised by him. He couldn't imagine Lyla or his mother ever raising a hand against him. Being raised by someone like that, it would make you terrified of that person, no matter how big you got.

"I heard what Petra said about Lyla. I didn't know. I swear I didn't know. I thought I was protecting—" His words cut off and he took a breath. "I didn't know, Riley. I swear it."

Riley studied him for a moment before nodding. "Okay. But

do me a favor when you go back to camp: Make sure no one knows you saw us, okay? Especially Arthur."

"Arthur? Him? How did—" Adros shook his head. "You know, not really important, I guess. And I'm not going back to camp."

"Where are you going?"

"With you." He glanced at Arthur before his gaze returned to Riley. "Uh, I thought you might need some help. So I'm coming with you. I owe you. I owe Lyla."

"Who told you I was going anywhere?"

"Come on, Riley. Lyla was taken. There is zero chance you would sit back and just wait for someone else to help her." Adros glanced around. "I'm just surprised Miles isn't here."

"There was somewhere else he needed to be."

Adros met Riley's gaze for a moment before nodding. "Then you definitely need my help. You can't get her out by yourself."

Arthur grunted.

"Or with just one other, um"—he looked at Arthur and then quickly looked away—"person?"

Riley opened his mouth to argue against the idea but then shut it. Truth was, he could use the help. And as much as he and Adros didn't get along, he was a fighter. He could help. "All right. You can come. But if you do anything that threatens Lyla or Arthur—"

"I won't. I swear. But, um"—he lowered his voice—"are you sure we can trust him?"

Riley tried not to roll his eyes. Arthur could hear every word Adros was saying. "Right now, I trust him more than I trust you."

Adros stared back at Arthur in awe and fear, and it gave Riley a small sense of satisfaction to seem him tremble. "Um, okay."

"Come on. We've wasted enough time." Riley started to move quickly through the woods.

Adros jogged up next to him. "Hey, uh, just one more question."

Riley gritted his teeth. "Fine. What?"

"Why is he wearing Otto's shirt?"

68

F lashes of consciousness were all Lyla experienced. She recalled forcing her eyes open to see artificial lights above her and the sense of movement. The next time her eyes opened, she felt cool air on her face as she was pushed on a stretcher. Finally she woke for good. She was in a cell. A rock wall, cool to the touch, was behind her. A concrete wall was on either side, and a wall of bars, like in an old-time jail, was in front of her. There was a bucket to her left, which she assumed was a toilet, and she lay on a concrete bunk that jutted out from the rock wall.

She sat up, her head aching, her thoughts fuzzy. What happened? She tried to remember, but it was like there was a block. Bit and pieces began to trickle in. She had been banished. And then the Unwelcome were there ... and Brendan.

Why was Brendan there? She grabbed her head. *Why can't I remember?*

"Ah, you're awake. Good."

She looked up and saw a man standing on the other side of the bars. The hallway light seemed awfully bright. She squinted to bring his features into focus. "I know you."

He smiled. "Yes. We met a few months back when I visited your camp."

His name snapped into her brain. Chad Keyes, the Naku's liaison. "Where am I?"

"At the Advancement Building in New City. It is the most technologically advanced building in the world."

Lyla glanced at the bucket. "Really?"

"Well, we can't really waste those resources on someone such as yourself."

"And *who* am I?"

"A person of interest. Or at least, you're related to a person of interest."

Lyla frowned. "What are you talking about?"

"Your sister, of course."

Lyla's thoughts jolted. *Muriel?* "My sister? She died five years ago. The Unwelcome killed her."

"Not exactly."

Lyla got to her feet slowly, even though her knees felt wobbly. She made her way to the bars. "What do you mean *not exactly*? An Unwelcome shot her."

"True. But you see, that is exactly where the story gets interesting. She was shot, but she didn't die."

Lyla stared at him, her mouth falling open, her mind still feeling cloudy. "You're lying. That's not possible. Anyone who gets touched by that ray dies."

"Apparently the Naku believed the same—all until your sister. Oh, she had a burn all right. But she did not turn to ash like she should have."

Lyla backed away, shaking her head. "No. You're lying. She died. No one survives an Unwelcome blast. I don't know why you're doing this, but I'm done with this conversation. Go play your mind games with someone else."

"I am telling the truth. Your sister did not die when she was struck by the Unwelcome's weapon. You look just like her. You two have the same exact eyes. Her name was Muriel, right?"

Lyla went cold. "How do you know her name?"

"Why, she's where this all began. She is *why* we knew who to target."

Lyla shook her head. "This is some sort of trick. I'm not falling for it."

"I thought you might say that." Chad crouched down and slid something across the cell floor toward Lyla. Lyla wanted to stay where she was, to not give him the satisfaction of seeing her curiosity. But even as she was telling herself to ignore the object, she found herself kneeling down to pick it up.

The lights in the cell blared to life and she blinked hard, covering her eyes to avoid the brightness of the lights. After a few seconds, her eyesight adjusted, and she looked at the object in her hand. Her heart all but stopped. It was the picture her grandfather had taken of her and Muriel when they were kids. It was the last photo he had in his camera. Her grandfather had kept it with him until he died. And then Muriel had kept it on her. How did Chad have it? It should have been incinerated when Muriel died. "I don't understand."

Chad sighed, picking a piece of dirt from his robe. "Apparently, when they shot Muriel, she was wounded. They were surprised. So they brought her back to New City."

Lyla felt vomit rise in her throat. *She was alive and I left her.* "What did you do to her?"

"Well, they had to find out why she survived. There was something in her blood. They were going to probe her mind, but she resisted. They began questioning her about her family, looking for others with her blood type." He looked at her and smiled. "They were looking for you."

Shock had robbed Lyla of her voice.

"Of course, they didn't know that. And your sister, she was tougher than she appeared. When she realized what they were looking for, she protected you the only way she could." He went silent, watching her expectantly.

She didn't want to give in to his theatrics. But she had to know. "What did she do?"

"She threw herself out of a window."

Her vision dimmed, her knees went weak, and she grabbed onto the wall.

"But it was all for naught, wasn't it? After all, here you are. Well, I suppose that's enough of a chat for now. I'll let you get some rest. We'll begin questioning in the morning. The tranquilizer they used on you has some short-term memory effects, but it should be well out of your system by morning. So get a good night's sleep. After all, tomorrow is a big day." He headed down the hall, disappearing from view.

Lyla sank heavily onto the mattress. Muriel had been alive. She was taken to New City.

Chad's smug face appeared in her mind. *She threw herself out of a window.* Lyla rushed to the bucket in the corner and vomited. All the contents of her stomach came up. And even when it was empty, she continued to dry heave.

Finally, she pushed back from the bucket. Too shaky to stand, she curled her knees into her chest.

Muriel was alive. I left her behind. Oh God. Tears rushed down her cheeks. *I'm so sorry, Muriel. I'm so sorry.*

69

The land Miles and Petra were crossing was beautiful. They were in a deep valley. A small river flowed a few hundred feet to their right. The sky was turning pink against the hills in the background. Miles inhaled deeply.

"What are you grinning at?" Petra asked.

"This ... It's nice."

And it was. In fact, the whole trip had been really enjoyable. He'd seen all sorts of wildlife, including a herd of wild horses, which had flowed over the hills in one majestic wave.

He'd never gone too far from the camp boundaries. The truth was, Arthur's tunnel was the farthest from camp he'd ever been. As the camp doctor, he'd always known he'd needed to stay close.

But it was because he was the doctor that he was the only one who could do this. Simon could handle things back at the camp while he was away. And for the first time, Miles felt free, light. He'd never realized how much his position in the camp was weighing him down.

Even with the beauty surrounding him, though, he was all too aware of the horror of Lyla being taken. In the back of his mind, an image of her being carried into the Unwelcome's ship lurked.

"You know we're coming into Old Meg's territory. You need to quit looking at the scenery and look for guys hidden in the trees."

"I know. But I don't see why I can't do both. Besides, it helps keep me from thinking about everything else."

Petra's face softened. "Oh. Sorry. You're right. I didn't—"

He waved away her words. "No biggie." But even as he said it, he imagined Lyla on a lab table with Unwelcome surrounding her. Then he imagined Riley being cut down by the same Unwelcome as he stormed into the room. He tightened his grip on the reins.

"Let's get them some water. And there's a full moon tonight, so hopefully we'll be able to ride well after the sun's gone down."

Miles nodded, turning his mount toward the river.

A jackrabbit skittered across the plain ahead as a hawk circled above. *Move, little guy*, he urged as the hawk dove for the ground. The rabbit's feet were a blur of movement, the hawk no less fast as it aimed directly for him. With a dive, the rabbit flew through a hole in the ground. The hawk's claws swiped and just missed him.

"Yes!" Miles yelled.

Petra raised an eyebrow. "What are you doing?"

Miles pointed toward the hole. "You didn't see that? That little jackrabbit beat the—"

Petra grinned.

"You did see that. You stink."

Petra laughed. "And you are too gullible. I swear—"

Thundering hooves cut off her reply. Six horses burst out of the small copse of trees on the other side of the river.

Petra yanked on the reins, turning her horse back in the direction they came. "Move, Miles!"

Miles got his horse turned around, but not as quickly as Petra. By the time he did, the horses had already plowed through the river and were coming up fast behind them.

He leaned forward, his horse's mane flying as he urged the

horse to go just a little faster. Petra was two horse lengths ahead of him when she pulled hard on the reins.

He looked up in time to see another three riders heading straight at them.

They were boxed in.

70

M iles's eyes went wide. But Petra just reached behind her, pulled her sword, and charged. She swung at the first rider, who ducked, but her back swing sliced the thigh of the second. The third was too far out of her reach. But it didn't matter because she was past them before he could do anything.

Miles wouldn't be able to do the same. He needed his full arm to hold onto the horse. His sword attachment was attached to the horse behind him. And besides, he'd need time to snap it in place. He leaned down lower, squeezing the horse with his thighs to urge it forward. He veered to the right around the riders, feeling the ones behind him following. He turned and saw Petra had turned around, heading back for him. He turned back just as his horse's front hooves left the ground to clear a downed tree. Not prepared, Miles was thrown back. He slammed onto the ground and rolled, the air knocked out of him.

He ended up on his stomach and got to his knees. He gulped, but no air entered his lungs. Spots began to dance before his eyes before he took his first full breath.

He looked up at the horses that ringed him. A man smiled as

he slid off his horse. And Miles recognized him—Gil, one of Cal's men who'd disappeared after Cal had been killed.

Gil smiled. "Well, look who we've got here."

"Miles!" Petra yelled.

Before he could reply, Gil grabbed Miles by the hair, yanking his head up, but his words were for Petra. "Get off that horse or I kill your friend here."

"Get out of here, Petra!" Miles yelled even as she slowly slid off her horse.

"Petra?" Gil eyed Petra as she walked toward him. "Well, well, didn't you grow up real pretty?"

One of Gil's men grabbed Petra, pulling a knife and holding it to her throat. Miles gritted his teeth. "Leave her alone."

Gil yanked him up higher. "What did you say, cripple? Have fun with your friend? Why thank you. I think we will." Gil shoved Miles's head forward. He crashed into the ground, landing on his half arm with a grunt.

Gil walked up to him and kicked him in his ribs. "Look at this, boys. We got us a cripple here who thinks he's a hero."

"I really don't like that word." Miles rolled to his feet.

Gil glared at him. "Where you think you're going, boy?" His men snickered.

"I don't like that word, either," Miles said with a glare.

"What you going to do, take me down one handed?" Gil laughed. "Tell you what, I'll make it fair. I'll hold my hand behind my back, how about that?" He leaped around, one hand behind his back, the other pawing at the air.

Miles glared. "I'll take you down either way."

"Ho ho, big talk. Let's see if you can back that up."

"Kick his ass, Miles!" Petra yelled.

"Shut up." The man holding Petra pushed the knife in tighter. Miles only spared her a glance, knowing he needed to keep his focus on the man in front of him.

Gil skipped to his right then stopped, tossing his knife

between his hands. "Ooh, what you going to do? What you going to do?"

Miles ignored Gil's taunts and his stupid grin as he circled to his left. But he also didn't let it fool him. He knew Gil wouldn't hesitate to gut Miles. Miles just wasn't sure he had it in him to do the same back.

Gil feinted forward and then to the left, stabbing at the air with a laugh. Miles kept out of his reach.

"Come on, Gil. It's getting late. Finish this guy and let's go," one of the other guys growled.

Gil shrugged. "Sorry, kid. Looks like my boys are in a hurry. But don't worry, we'll take care of your pretty friend for you." Gil feinted again, going low, but then he brought his knife up quickly to Miles face. Miles anticipated the move. Lyla had made him repeat the counter to it over and over again, dozens of times.

Miles blocked the blow, landing a kick at Gil's knee, straightening it. Gil screamed, swinging wildly with his right. Miles blocked it with his half arm, stepping in and pushing Gil's wrists back toward his shoulder as he grabbed his stump, locking Gil's arm between them, and then he stepped behind Gil with a little twirl.

Gil's feet flew up, and Miles felt and heard his shoulder dislocate. Gil landed on his back with a scream and Miles slammed his foot into his face. Gil's eyes rolled into his head.

One of the men stepped forward. "What the—"

Petra gripped the hand holding the knife to her throat and turned, slamming an elbow into the face of the man holding her. He stumbled back, and she kept hold of his knife hand, twisting the wrist to a ninety-degree angle and forcing him face down into the dirt. She yanked his arm toward the middle of his back and then stripped the knife from his hand, ignoring his scream of pain as she kicked him in the head. Petra lunged for Miles and they stood back to back as the other seven men circled them.

"Miles?"

"Yeah?" He didn't take his gaze from any of the guys in front of him.

"Don't be nice."

He nodded. "You, either."

She snorted. "That's never been *my* problem."

Horse hooves pounded through the valley, and everyone turned to see a dozen horses bearing down on them.

Oh no. They've got friends. Miles had thought there was a chance they could take the seven guys surrounding them. Lyla was a big fan of multiple-attacker drills. But another dozen was asking a little bit too much.

"Shit, it's Meg," one of the men muttered. "Let's get out of here."

The seven attackers turned tail and ran for their horses, leaving Gil and the other injured man behind. They wasted no time turning their horses and running flat-out across the open ground.

Miles turned to watch them. "Uh, what the hell?"

Petra's gaze locked on the incoming riders. "Guess they don't like Meg."

Neither Miles nor Petra moved. Their horses had run off, so they wouldn't get very far anyway.

"What should we do?" Miles asked.

The first of the riders reached them. Petra put her hands up. "Pray?"

Miles put his hands up as well. "Oh, good, I was worried we didn't have a plan."

71

Miles and Petra stood side by side as the horses pulled to a stop only a few feet in front of them. All the riders wore deep-magenta tunics over their clothes, all except one. She wore a flowing white peasant blouse with a sash the same color as her people's tunics.

None of the riders smiled at Petra or Miles. But none made any moves toward them, either. Then the horses parted to allow the rider in the peasant blouse through. Old Meg, leader of the Valley people, came forward. Her long white hair reached her waist and was held back in a low ponytail.

Miles had heard the legends of Old Meg. She ruled her territory with an iron fist and had a legion of soldiers loyal to her. From the name, he'd expected her to be old and grizzled. But she wasn't. Her hair was white, true, but her face wasn't lined. He didn't think she was more than forty.

She inspected Miles and Petra and then looked at the two men on the ground before she spoke. "You two responsible for that?"

"Yes," Petra said, her chin jutting up.

For a moment Miles thought he saw a smile, but when she

turned to him he was sure he'd been mistaken. "What about you? You help?"

Miles nodded, not really sure what to say.

"He took down that one." Petra nodded toward Gil.

Meg's eyebrows rose. "You took down Gil, huh?"

"Yes. They tried to steal our horses and ..." He glanced at Petra, but she glared at him in response, so he shut up.

Meg nodded. "I see. Where are you two from?"

Petra stayed silent, and Miles's mind raced. But he was not very good at lying. "We're from Attlewood."

Meg frowned for a moment, then tilted her head. "You're one of Lyla's kids."

"I'm Miles."

Meg studied him. "The doctor. Who's your friend?"

"Petra."

"And what brings you two to my valley?"

"No, Miles," Petra whispered. But Miles knew Meg would not let them go without the truth. "We're trying to get to the old university."

"Well, sounds like there's a story in that. You two will come back with us. I'd like more comfortable surroundings to hear it." She turned to her men. "Let's get these two their mounts."

"What should we do with Gil and his gang?" the tall man next to her asked.

Meg looked at Petra, meeting her gaze, and she read something there that made her nod. "I don't accept the existence of men who think rape is an option in my valley. Kill these two and send a group to hunt down the others."

"Yes, Meg." He bowed.

Meg turned back to Miles and Petra. "Shall we?"

"Yes, ma'am," Miles said with a bow of his head, because he knew her words were *not* a question.

72

I t was only a fifteen-minute ride to Old Meg's camp. The camp was surrounded by a fifteen-foot wall, a mixture of wood, metal, and barbed wire. A large gate stood open for them, with two sentries wearing the same magenta tunics on either side as they rode through.

Miles wasn't sure what he expected to see beyond the mish-mash of a wall, but it wasn't this. It was like stepping back into medieval times. Animal hides had been cured to create huts with fur doors. People peeked out of them. A few kids ran up and Meg smiled down at them.

Most people wore tunics and leggings, although unlike Meg's riders, these tunics were all different colors and patterns. But the color magenta was everywhere—window coverings, flags above homes, wrapped around poles.

A large chicken coop and a barn could be seen in the distance. He sniffed, following the scent to a pig being slow roasted over a fire. They wound their way past a blacksmith, a butcher, and a forge. Each adult they passed paused what they were doing as Meg approached and bowed.

Ahead there was a stream that cut under the fence, emptying into a pond. He frowned, looking at the construction where the creek met the river. It was made of wood and turned with the force of the water.

I've seen that before ... Then it came to him—a water wheel.

He smiled, recognizing that they were using it to power a millstone.

Meg caught Miles staring at the wheel. "What do you think?"

The smile was still on his face when he turned to her. "I think it's ingenious. Do you know that could even produce electricity?"

Meg raised an eyebrow. "How?"

"The principle works the same as the millstone. You need about a three-foot drop and a flow of twenty gallons per minute, but it looks like you have that. Then you need to just connect a simple coil generator. It won't give you enough to power the whole camp, but it could help you with a few things."

Meg grunted. "You're a smart one, aren't you, Miles?"

He bowed his head again. "Um, no, I just read a lot."

"Hm, I think maybe it's more than that," Meg said before she nudged her horse ahead of him.

Petra took her place. "Hey, brainiac," she whispered.

"What?"

"Stop showing how smart you are. We want her to actually let us *go*, not keep us."

"What? She wouldn't do that."

"Old Meg has been known to keep what she wants."

Miles blanched. "Right, sorry."

Petra shook her head. "I know you can't help yourself. It's what makes you you. Just try to be a little less you for a little bit, okay?"

Miles nodded. Ahead, Meg stopped next to an actual house with two turrets and rock siding. It looked like a small castle. Meg strode inside, the guards at the doors opening the double doors for her. Miles and Petra pulled their horses to a stop and disembarked.

A boy no more than ten ran up to them, holding out his hands. "I'll take them."

Miles and Petra handed over the reins. Meg's second waved them forward. Miles and Petra exchanged a glance and then headed for the door that Meg had disappeared through. Miles took note of the guards that stayed outside. Petra's words floated through his mind. *Old Meg has been known to keep what she wants.* Swallowing hard, he stepped inside.

Being Meg's camp had Miles in a medieval state of mind, so he had expected the inside of her 'castle' to be dark and foreboding. So he'd been pleasantly surprised at the bright light that greeted him, even in the foyer and along the long hallways He glanced up and saw that skylights made from real glass ran from the front door down the hall, ending at a set of double doors.

A young woman in her twenties with her hair pulled back and wearing another magenta tunic walked in from the sitting room to their right. She gave them a shy smile.

"If you'd follow me, please." She headed down the hall without waiting for a reply.

Miles stepped forward, but Petra gripped his hand for a moment and gave it a quick squeeze. She looked into his eyes. "Be careful," she whispered before following the woman.

Miles's heart began to pound. *Don't act too smart and don't lie,* he reminded himself as he walked past the six guards lining the hall. Two more guards opened the double doors at the end of the hall as the young woman and Petra reached them.

Miles hurried to catch up with them. He was by Petra's side as the doors fully opened. His mouth fell open, and Petra seemed frozen in place. It was an actual throne room. Ivy grew on the wall straight ahead of them and Meg sat on a chair with a tall back on a raised dais in front of it. A frayed red carpet ran from the doorway to the base of the dais twenty feet away.

Meg waved them forward. Petra tugged on Miles's sleeve to get him moving. He hustled forward. There were another four guards in the room and no other people. The young woman bustled in from a door to their right and headed for the dais, a large tray with a pitcher, mug, and fruit on it. She placed it on the table next to Meg with a bow.

Meg nodded. "Thank you, Isolde."

The woman gave her a small smile and then quickly retreated. Meg waited until the woman shut the door behind her before she spoke. "So, tell me, son of Lyla, what brings you two to my valley? I'm surprised Lyla would allow it."

Miles swallowed, coming to a stop at the guards that stood on either side of the red carpet in front of the dais. "She wouldn't if she knew."

Meg raised an eyebrow. "So you left without her knowledge? You don't strike me as a rule breaker." Her gaze shifted to Petra. "You do, however."

Miles took a breath. "She was taken by the Unwelcome."

The amusement dropped from Meg's face. "I am sorry to hear that. She was an incredible fighter, and I respected her as a fair leader."

"She's not dead," Petra said. "They took her to New City."

Meg frowned. "The Unwelcome don't take prisoners."

"We thought the same thing. But we've learned that Lyla is not the first. We believe the Unwelcome are searching for something. Something in the blood of the people they take. I think it might be why they've targeted the Cursed."

Meg leaned forward. "In the blood? And what is that?"

"I–I'm not sure," Miles said. "But we were on our way to the old university to see if I could find a better microscope. Mine is too cracked. I believe the answers might be there."

Meg sat back. "What do you think they are looking for? You must have some idea. You wouldn't come all this way if you didn't."

"I–I think it might be some sort of weapon or defense against the Unwelcome. I can't think of any other reason why they would take her. And I think it might be related to why they only kill those of a certain age."

Meg studied Miles, and he began to feel uncomfortable beneath her gaze. But he didn't look away. "I believe you are telling me the truth. You do believe that answers are in the blood."

Miles felt relief flood him. Well, at least she wasn't going to kill him for lying.

"Once you have found your answers, what will you do with them?"

"Bring them back to our camp," Petra said. "Hope that they will help us fight the Unwelcome."

Meg nodded, her hand on her chin. "I see."

Silence descended, and Miles became absurdly aware of his own breathing. It sounded so loud in his ears. He took a small step closer to Petra. She didn't look at him, but her fingers brushed lightly against the back of his hand.

Meg rapped her scepter on the ground. "I agree your mission is important. And you should be allowed to continue."

"You're letting us go?" Miles asked.

Meg's gaze locked on him. "Do you really think you can figure it out?"

Miles straightened his shoulders, looking her right in the eye. "Yes."

She watched him for a moment longer before giving him an abrupt nod. She turned to her second in command, who stood to the right of her chair. He was a tall, muscular man with thick dark hair pulled back into a low ponytail and a scar across his cheek. "Lewis, you're to accompany them. Make sure they get there and back."

"Back?" Petra asked.

Meg nodded. "When you figure this out, you bring your answers to me. And *only* me."

73

R iley, Adros, and Arthur made good time to New City. It was getting dark as they arrived, which was perfect, because darkness gave them a little extra cover. For all his brave talk and his determination to get to Lyla, Riley knew how dangerous it was to come here. There was a cold ball of fear that had only grown in his chest the closer they got to New City. When he'd first caught sight of the city, that cold ball of fear had taken his breath away.

Riley had heard descriptions of the mother ship above New City, but seeing it was entirely different. He had never seen anything like it in his life. It was so much worse than what he'd imagined. The size alone was terrifying, never mind the sight of all those smaller ships flying to and from it. It looked like a second city hovering above the one on the ground. Lights blinked from underneath its dark exterior, and he could just make out a bay where ships were landing.

New City itself was mind altering. Truth was, he'd never seen block upon block of buildings. He'd certainly never seen any above two stories tall. It was like they were stepping into a different world.

"Oh my God," Adros mumbled from next to him.

"Come," Arthur said. "We can't stay here too long."

Riley nodded, following, but he kept glancing back at the large ship. *Please don't let them have taken Lyla up there.*

There was a storage warehouse at the outskirts of the city. Arthur managed to sneak in and grab a full uniform without being detected. Riley and Adros had waited outside, growing increasingly nervous until Arthur reappeared wearing a new shirt. The uniform he'd grabbed was a little looser than what the Unwelcome normally wore. Riley didn't like to think of how big the guy that fit the shirt had to be.

With great reluctance, Arthur had put the helmet back on as well. And it was hard to remember it was Arthur underneath there. But if they got caught, there'd be no way to explain Arthur walking around without the helmet on. Now the three of them lay flat on a hill overlooking the Fringe, the neighborhood Adie and Jamal had first visited years ago when they'd met Max Turner.

"So what exactly is the plan?" Adros asked.

Riley glanced at him. He looked a little pale and was sweating pretty hard, only partly from the long walk. But he had to admit, Adros hadn't voiced a word of complaint the whole journey here, even though Riley had caught him wincing every once in a while. Whatever Brendan had done to him, it had hurt and still did.

Riley nodded toward the homes. "Two blocks from the tree line, you see that white house with the rocking chair out front?"

Adros nodded. "Yeah. Why?"

"The guy who lives there is named Max. He works for the Unwelcome."

"Can we trust him?"

"From what Addie says, he doesn't *want* to work for them, but his grandson is inside. And so he stays nearby."

"You think he'll help?" Arthur asked.

268

R.D. BRADY

"I hope so." Riley looked back at the house. "Because if he doesn't, I don't know what we're going to do."

The streets had been deserted for hours before Riley felt it was safe enough for him and Adros to creep into the Fringe. Arthur stayed hidden in the trees close to Max's house. Riley didn't think showing up with an Unwelcome would exactly inspire Max to trust them.

Riley's whole body was tense, and his eyes darted around. If anyone saw them, they could raise the alarm. Adros was equally tense next to him. Luckily they were both large, which meant they could pass for older. So instead of skulking in the shadows, they walked with feigned confidence, as if they had every right to be there. But a cold sweat had broken out along Riley's back.

They reached the front door of Max's house and paused. They had passed a handful of people on the way here, but no one had said anything or seemed suspicious of them. But now was the big test.

He didn't hear anything inside but he still hesitated. It was possible Max had changed his mind about staying outside New City and had moved on. Or if he was here, he could raise the alarm to get himself passage inside. It had been a year since Addie had last snuck into the Fringe to visit him and learn what he knew.

"What are you waiting for?" Adros hissed.

Riley pictured Lyla's unconscious body being carried into the Unwelcome ship. *Now or never.* He knocked on the door. It remained quiet for a moment.

"Knock again," Adros said.

"Just wait." Shuffling sounded from behind the door and then a man's voice. "Who's out there?"

"I'm a friend of Addie Hudson. She said to come see you."

The door opened a crack, and a man with bright blue eyes and white hair peered out at them. His eyes went large. And he opened the door all the way. "You're Cursed. Quick, get in here." He stepped back, and Riley and Adros hesitated for only a moment before stepping inside. Max stepped into the doorway, glancing at the street before closing the door and locking it with a shaking hand. He turned at face the boys. "Addie sent you?"

Riley nodded, waiting. He didn't want to hurt the man if he didn't have to, but he also couldn't chance the man raising the alarm.

"What was she thinking? If anyone saw you—" He paused, his eyes going wide. "Is she all right?"

"She's fine."

"That's good. That's good. You can stop looking at me like I'm going to yell. I won't turn you in."

"Why not?" Adros asked, his tone belligerent.

"Not all people are bad, son. Now come on back and have a bite to eat. You must be hungry." Max walked past them to the kitchen.

Riley followed, and after a second, Adros did as well. Max stood over by a cooling box and pulled out some dishes. "You boys eaten recently?"

"A little," Riley said.

"Got some salmon here. It will take only a minute to grill up."

"Salmon?" Adros asked.

"It's a fish. Real good with butter. Sit, sit."

Riley still felt nervous, but he was tired and he didn't get any sense of a threat from Max. And besides, this was the plan. Find Max, get his help, and get to Lyla. He pulled out a chair and slumped into it. Adros sat next to him. The smell of the fish had Riley's mouth watering by the time Max set it in front of him and Adros.

Max pulled out a chair across from them, a mug in his hands and a small plate of salmon in front of him. "Go ahead. It's good."

Riley waited, for a moment wondering if Max had drugged the food. But he'd watched him closely and hadn't seen him make any suspicious moves.

"Man, that's good." Adros nudged him. "You really need to try this."

Riley shook his head. Apparently food overrode any of Adros's other concerns. Riley took a tentative bite and smiled. "That *is* good."

"Go on. Finish up. I've got some cobbler for dessert."

Adros's eyes lit up. "Cobbler?"

Riley abandoned all pretense and just tore into his food. Twenty minutes later, they'd finished the cobbler as well. And Riley actually felt full. He couldn't remember the last time he'd felt full. "That was really good. Thank you."

"You're welcome. Now, what are you boys doing here? I can't believe Addie would send two Cursed in here."

Riley spoke quickly, not wanting to lie to Max about who had really sent them. "We're looking for somebody."

Max frowned. "Who?"

Riley paused. "My aunt. The Unwelcome took her yesterday. We think she's in New City."

Max's lips became a tight line. "I'm sorry, son. But I'm not sure what you're planning on doing about that. You can't just walk into New City. No one can just walk in, but especially not two boys your age."

"I need to find her. Addie said you work for the Unwelcome. I was hoping you could tell us a way into the city. Or where they might have taken her."

Max was quiet for a moment. "Is it just you two going in?"

"There's one more," Riley said quickly.

"You know its suicide going in there, don't you?"

Riley didn't break Max's stare. "She'd do it for me."

Max studied them for a moment over the rim of his cup. "I'll make you deal."

Adros frowned. "A deal?"

Max nodded. "I'll help you if you help me."

"Help you with what?" Riley asked.

"Get my grandson out of New City."

Riley's mouth gaped open. "I–I don't know if—"

"Look, I think I know where they took your aunt. There's a building inside. It's set up for experiments. I've seen other people there."

"How do you know this?"

"I'm a plumber. I go where I'm needed. Last year, they finally assigned me inside. I've been paying attention."

Adros leaned forward. "You said you had a grandson inside. Do you know where he is?"

"He's on a work detail."

Riley frowned. "How old is he?"

"Eight."

Riley shared a confused glance with Adros. "But I thought all the kids who were brought inside were given homes," Riley said.

Max scoffed. "That's what they say. But turns out that not all the people willing to trade in kids for an easier life want the responsibility of raising kids. When they can't find homes for the kids, they put them to work."

"They're slaves," Adros said.

Max nodded. "Yes."

"Do you know where your grandson is?" Riley asked again.

Max nodded quickly. "Yes. I've seen him. But I can't get to him. Not on my own. But I do have a plan for getting him out. I just need some help."

"You're sure you know where my aunt is?"

"They bring humans in from time to time. You hear talk. And there's only one place they'll bring them. So I'm pretty confident she'll be there."

Riley didn't know what to do. He knew Max had been out here for years trying to find his grandson inside. But the chances of successfully rescuing Lyla and Max's grandson seemed even slimmer than the already long odds they were facing.

Riley looked at Adros, who stared back at him. Things just got a lot more complicated. But he couldn't blame Max for wanting to get his grandson out. Hell, the idea of kids being used for slaves made Riley want to get them out, too. But two breakouts, that was a lot. And as soon as one was found out, they'd raise the alarm. Which meant both had to happen at the same time.

"We can do this, Riley," Adros said.

Riley turned back to Max. "Max, I think it's time you met our friend."

"Friend?"

"Yeah. He's the reason we're going to be able to do this." Riley paused. "Just promise not to freak out."

74

The meeting between Max and Arthur went better than expected. Probably because Max seemed on the verge of passing out, which had kept him quiet.

Riley had gone to collect Arthur, and Adros had let them in. When Riley stepped back into the kitchen with Arthur, Max rose from his seat, his face going pale. "You tricked me. You're turning me in. You—"

"No, no, no," Riley said quickly. "He's our friend. He's helping us."

Max sunk back into the chair, his eyes wide, still shaking.

"Arthur, take off your helmet," Riley said.

Arthur quickly removed it, and by some miracle, Max's eyes went even wider. His breaths came out in little pants.

"Max, I know this is shocking, but he *is* actually on our side. He saved me and my brother more than once."

Arthur strode forward. "It's a pleasure to meet you, Max." He extended his hand.

Max reared back. Arthur folded his hand slowly and stepped back.

"Arthur, take a seat," Riley said.

Max continued to stare at Arthur. Adros leaned over to him. "Look, I get it. I don't really trust him, either. But I trust Riley, and if he says Arthur is good, then Arthur is good."

Max looked between all three of them. "They're blue."

Riley smiled. "You know, I think that's the first thing everyone says when they meet him."

Max gave him a nervous smile.

"Look, I know it's a lot to take. It took me a lot to come around as well. But he's not like the others. And what I said was true—he did save us, and my aunt as well. And he can help us inside. He can get to places we can't."

Max nodded slowly. "O–okay."

Riley plowed ahead, not wanting Max to focus too much on Arthur when he needed to focus on how to get them inside. "Good. Now let's hear this plan of yours for your grandson, and then we'll come up with one for Lyla as well."

And we'll pray that splitting our forces will allow us to get everybody out safely ... somehow.

75

R iley, Adros, Arthur, and Max talked late into the night, working out the details before they all called it a night. Max thought Lyla was being held at the Advancement Building, which was on the edge of the city, right next to the falls.

Arthur had never been inside it, but Max had. He'd even caught a glimpse of the cells. He said they reminded him of a castle dungeon.

So now, as Riley lay down to get some sleep, all he could picture was Lyla strung up in some cold, damp dungeon. He tried to shut off the line of thought, but the images kept slipping through. He knew he needed a good night's sleep. Mistakes could be easily made when tired. But he had been unable to rest. Even when he had managed to doze off, it had been an uneasy sleep. It was long before dawn when Arthur stepped into the room and carefully made his way over to the side of Riley's bed. He knelt down. "I'm going."

Riley sat up, rubbing his eyes. Last night they had agreed that Arthur would need to sneak out before anyone in the Fringe woke up and before the shift change happened at the wall. Arthur believed it would the easiest time for him to slip into New

City. Max had told him about a few unoccupied buildings he could hole up in until the rest of them got inside.

"Be careful, Arthur."

"I will be." He paused. "Thank you for trusting me."

"Thank you for helping us."

"I'll meet you inside in four hours."

"Four hours," Riley echoed. Arthur quickly left the room, and a few moments later, Riley heard the soft click of the front door closing behind him. He lay back down and closed off his mind, replaying every step of the day to come. If all went well, they'd be back in camp by nightfall. But so much could go wrong. He tortured himself for a few minutes longer with all the ways their plans could be derailed.

Enough. He forced his worries from his mind and focused on his breathing. *It will be fine. All will be fine.* He felt his body start to relax. *It will work. And Lyla will be back at camp tomorrow.* He repeated the phrases over and over, and finally, sleep claimed him.

76

M ax took off just after dawn to grab some uniforms for Riley and Adros. Riley was a little worried that he might turn them in. He still didn't seem to like Arthur, but he returned without incident.

Now Riley pulled at the front of the jumpsuit. It was a beige one-piece with a zipper up the front. It was a little tight, especially with his regular clothes on underneath. Max was a lot smaller than either Riley or Adros.

"I can barely move in this thing," Adros grumbled. The arms of Adros's suit were tight, and Riley worried if he reached too far he might split the thing.

"Just be careful," Riley said. He handed him a navy-blue cap that signified they worked for the plumbing division.

Max stepped into the room. "You two good? We need to get going. They don't like if we're late."

"We're ready." Riley tugged the cap onto his head, wondering if Arthur was all right. He was going to go in through an Unwelcome entrance. That was probably the most dangerous part of the plan. He couldn't use his own ID because it would set off alarms. So he needed to grab someone else's. And if he got caught, they'd never be able to pull off any of the rest of it.

Shoving down the rising panic, he grabbed the utility bag Max handed him. Adros slung his over his shoulder.

We've got this. Arthur will get through. We'll get Lyla, and we'll get Max's grandson. Everything's going to be fine.

But his hand still shook as he reached for the handle, and he prayed neither Adros nor Max noticed.

77

M iles and Petra got started just before dawn the next morning. Meg had insisted they stay the night. She'd given them an empty hut and a full meal. And she posted two guards outside the hut.

Given the fear coursing through Miles and the anxiety about Meg's decree, Miles had been sure he would be unable to sleep. But he had slept like a log, and Petra had to shake him awake the next morning. He'd stumbled from bed and eaten a quick breakfast before getting on his horse.

Lewis was waiting for them by the gate, along with two other men. A teenage girl a little younger than Miles and Petra hugged him tight before she joined two other girls, who were even younger. They all looked too much alike and too much like Lewis to be anything but his daughters. He ran a hand over each of their cheeks before swinging himself up to his saddle with a practiced ease that Miles envied. With a glance over at Petra and Miles but not a word, he led them through the gate, setting a fast pace. And he hadn't said anything beyond the bare minimum for the entire ride.

It was only an hour's ride to the university, and the sun was in the sky, giving everything a pink glow. Miles took a swig of water as Petra rode abreast of him. "There."

Miles nodded. They'd seen a few old signs for the university as they'd ridden. More and more had appeared over the last hour. And now the remains of the arch over the main entrance to the campus came into view.

"Once we get in, where will we be going?" Lewis asked.

Miles looked over at the man. He was a serious man, strongly built, and he didn't talk much. His partners were less serious. Aaron and Ham were only a few years older than Miles and Petra but had chattered and bickered nonstop on the way here. Miles could not figure out why Meg had chosen them for this particular mission. Maybe she thought it would help them get more experience or something.

"We need to find the science buildings. I'm not exactly sure where they'll be, but Frank said campuses used to have big directories with maps of the campus. I'm hoping some of those might still be standing and can point us in the right direction. If not, we'll have to search."

Lewis met his gaze and gave an abrupt nod.

"Search the whole place?" Ham whined. "Are you kidding?"

"That'll take forever," Aaron said.

Lewis glared at them. "And if it's what needs to be done, we'll do it, right?"

"Yeah," Ham muttered.

"Fine," Aaron grumbled, before giving Miles a dirty look.

Miles looked away. Petra moved her horse closer to his. "Don't worry. We'll find the building."

Miles nodded, but he knew that finding the building was the easiest part of this mission. Finding something in the blood—*that* was going to be the tricky part.

78

As they walked through the Fringe, Riley had expected someone to call them out. But no one did. Everyone was just going about their own business. Everyone wore the same uniforms. The only thing that differentiated them were the baseball caps—a different color for each type of work. As plumbers, they wore blue. Housekeeping wore yellow. Janitorial wore green and so on.

Now Riley, Adros, and Max stood on line at the work entrance. A concrete wall twenty feet high ringed New City. There were only six entrances in—two work entrances for humans, three entrances for Unwelcome, and the main entrance, which was heavily fortified. The work entrance was manned by an Unwelcome, eight feet tall. He scanned the lines but didn't seem to be particularly interested in anyone. Max explained the Unwelcome only interceded if there was a problem at the gate. But as long as people had IDs and uniforms they tended to leave them alone.

Still, Riley felt sweat lining his back as they got in behind three women in uniforms with red caps. They'd waited until the line had died down, and now they would be the last in. The women chatted, not stopping as they slid their IDs through and headed into New City. Max slid his ID in and stepped through. Riley and Adros hustled in after him. They didn't stop but continued down the high-walled path. The path had a low ceiling. Riley frowned, trying to figure out why that would be. No Unwelcome could fit without doubling over.

Then he glanced at the walls and saw the small holes, only about an inch in diameter, carefully drilled into the walls every six inches. He swallowed, realizing it must be a security measure, and part of him really did not want to know what came out of those holes. Ahead, Riley could see the three women had reached the end of the path and turned right.

Riley tensed, waiting for the alarm to ring out, but it remained silent. He let out a breath and gave Adros a nervous smile.

"Holy crap, this is tense," Adros whispered. Riley nodded.

Now we just have to worry about Arthur. And Riley was worried. Arthur had to go through an Unwelcome entrance. But if he used his badge, he would set off alarms immediately. They thought he was dead. *And if he got caught ...* Riley swallowed. *I hope you're all right, Arthur.*

The low ceiling kept Riley from seeing anything beyond the end of the path. From inside the tunnel, it appeared to dead end at a brick wall. But now as Max led them to the right, Riley got his first unobstructed view of New City.

The city was arranged in orderly blocks. Buildings, some twenty stories tall, sprouted up here and there, but most were between three and five stories. Some had balconies with little dining sets. Most had large, wide windows with flower boxes. Everything looked brand new and so clean it was startling.

"We need to keep moving," Max said.

Riley realized he and Adros had stopped dead while they gaped at the city in front of them. Adros wore a dazed expression on his face that Riley was pretty sure was on his own. He tugged Adros's sleeve to get him moving. They followed behind Max.

Riley knew his mouth was hanging open, but he couldn't seem to shut it. New City was pristine, with concrete sidewalks so clean they were practically white. Carts driven by other people in uniforms occasionally drove by. Buildings lined the neatly laid-out streets. It looked like the asteroid had never happened here.

Other people wandered by, most in similar one-piece uniforms, although inside the city walls, there were different colors. There was some people though that wore mustard yellow tunics. None of them wore caps either. Riley frowned watching a group of three workers skirt around one of them on the sidewalk. "What's with the yellow guys?"

Max didn't look over at the man. "Don't look."

Riley averted his gaze but could feel the man's gaze rove over him.

Once they were passed them, Max's shoulder's relaxed. "He's a McGovern."

"What's that?" Adros asked.

"The McGovern's are I guess a religion. Jason McGovern was the first human to not be killed by an Unwelcome. He threw himself in front of one, his hands up and the Unwelcome didn't shoot. From that moment on, McGovern and his followers have sworn their loyalty to the Unwelcome. They turn in other humans for any hint of disloyalty or rule breaking. If you see one, keep your head down and your eyes averted."

Ahead another man in mustard yellow turned around a corner. Riley watched as more people scampered out of his way. "Do they get special privileges?"

"No. They're just true believers in the betterment of humanity through colonization," Max said.

"They approve of all this?" Adros asked.

"With every beat of their tiny little hearts," Max said. Riley wasn't sure what to say to that but Max's words took some of the awe out of his thoughts as they walked through New City. They walked the rest of the way in silence. No one glanced at Max,

Adros, or Riley as they hurried past on to their own work assignments and there were no more McGoverns.

But even though he was dressed the part, he felt like everything about him screamed outsider. Everyone here was soft, fleshy. He couldn't remember the last time he'd seen a fat person. Besides Brendan, he realized, he actually never had. Not in person, at least. He'd only seen pictures.

His hand strayed to his stomach. Perfectly flat, not an extra ounce anywhere. He looked around and he was disgusted, but part of him couldn't help but be envious. These people didn't have to run for their lives every day. They didn't have to train to protect themselves and the people they cared about. They were protected.

Max caught sight of Adros and Riley's expressions and nodded. "Plumbing, electricity, transportation, there's even a movie theatre and restaurants."

A man walked by carrying a bakery bag and a cup with steam coming from it. A combination of sugary sweetness and freshly brewed coffee rolled over Riley, and he could not remember ever smelling anything so good. But his mouth slammed shut as he remembered how all this had come to be and what each of these people had done to get here. This place it was built on death. And it ran on death.

"Half our camp nearly starved two winters ago," Adros growled.

Riley nodded, his own anger mounting. These people had traded in children for their own security. A woman walked by with a small child holding her hand. And Riley couldn't help but notice mother and child looked nothing alike. Disgust rolled through him.

"You two need to calm down," Max whispered urgently. "You look like you're about to start a fight."

Riley took a breath, trying to calm his breathing. He uncurled the fists he hadn't realized he'd clenched. He also rolled his shoulders, trying to loosen them up. Max was right. He felt like punching the next person who walked by him. "Adros."

Adros glared at him. "I know. I'm working on it," he said through gritted teeth.

Riley glanced around, trying to keep himself calm, but the scene was so unreal. The place was bustling, even in the early morning. Street sweepers pushed brooms along paths. A coffee cart was set up on the first corner, a pastry cart on the opposite. Storeowners were opening their doors. There was a shoe store, a drug store, a restaurant, and a clothing store.

"Close your mouths, boys. You're supposed to have seen this before."

Adros slammed his mouth shut, but his eyes stayed wide. "This is—"

"Crazy," Riley finished for him, watching a shop owner with a very large belly struggling to reach over his display of shoes to turn over the open sign. All he could picture was the hungry look on the half the camp's faces last winter. How Maisy had whispered she was hungry late at night, like it was a sin to admit it. He clenched his fists again. *Bastards.*

Two Unwelcome appeared at the end of the street, and Max headed for the pastry cart. Riley and Adros averted their heads and followed him. Max handed them each a pastry, and they stepped to the side. Riley and Adros kept their backs to the Unwelcome.

"Eat," Max said, taking a bite and trying to act casual as the Unwelcome came closer. The Unwelcome slowed down, and Riley could feel their eyes on them, but then they passed by without stopping. Riley let out a breath as they rounded the corner and disappeared. He took a bite of the pastry and nearly fell to the ground. It was so good. He had to force himself not to gobble it down.

"Heads up. Here comes another one," Adros said. Riley took another bite as he glanced over his shoulder. A seven-foot Unwelcome stepped into the street from a doorway. Riley narrowed his eyes, noticing that the Unwelcome's shirt was a little looser than most. The Unwelcome paused, scanning the street before heading toward Riley, Adros, and Max.

"Riley," Max said, a warning in his voice.

"It's okay. I think that's Arthur."

The Unwelcome walked over to them, not stopping. "Follow me."

"Casual, guys." Riley took another bite of his pastry as he slowly started to follow Arthur, keeping his steps unhurried. Adros and Max followed behind him. They stayed about a block behind Arthur. He walked for another block before slipping into an alley.

Riley, Adros, and Max slipped into it just a few seconds later. The Unwelcome stood with his hands on his waist, waiting for them.

Riley went still, a sudden fear filling him. "Arthur?"

The Unwelcome nodded. "It's me."

Riley let out a breath. "You scared me for a minute. Everything go okay?"

Arthur hesitated. "I had to take a badge."

"How'd you do that?" Adros asked.

"I had to knock out another Unwelcome."

"When he wakes up, he'll raise the alarm," Riley said.

"No. He won't wake up for hours."

"What if someone finds him?" Adros asked.

"They won't do that, either. I put him in a storage crate at the back of a storage closet. When he does wake up, it will still take hours for him to get out."

Riley nodded. "Okay."

"We don't have to worry about cameras?" Adros asked.

Arthur shook his head. "No. They don't worry about humans fighting back. Everyone who's here wants to be here."

Max nodded. "He's right. I've never seen a single camera."

Riley was glad Max seemed to have lost some of his fear of Arthur. "Everybody knows the plan, right?"

If Max was right, Lyla was being held at the Advancement Building, located right on the edge of New City, right next to the falls. The falls were a new creation that the Unwelcome had added to the landscape—a two hundred-foot waterfall. It powered the entire city. There was a large bridge over the falls. That's where they would meet up and make their escape.

Max's grandson was part of a cleaning detail. As luck would have it, it was only a few buildings over from where Max believed Lyla was being held.

"We'll meet you at the rendezvous point," Riley said.

Adros nodded, shifting from foot to foot. "Okay."

"Adros, you good?" Riley asked.

"I'm good. I'm good. We're doing the right thing."

"Max?" Riley asked.

"I'm good, too. And thank you. For helping me."

"You got it. Okay. So this is it. We'll see you in two hours."

"Two hours." Adros nodded before heading off with Max. Riley watched them go, hoping that everything went all right.

"You ready?" Arthur asked.

Riley straightened his shoulders, forcing away his doubts.

There was no time for doubts. Now it was time to act. He nodded. "Yes. Let's go get Lyla."

79

The campus had not survived well. Miles didn't think that the destruction was due to Mother Nature, though. Many of the buildings were scorched, so that all that was left were their metal frames.

"What happened here?" Petra asked.

Lewis looked around, his jaw tight. "After the asteroid, students took up residence here. There were dorms, a cafeteria stocked with food, and a wall with gates encapsulating the whole campus. A lot of families came and joined their sons, daughters, brothers, and sisters. For a few years, it was all right. But then, like with everywhere else, resources got used up. And people began to fight over what little was left. This was the result of that fight."

Miles studied the older man. "You were here."

Lewis nodded. "My older sister went to school here. My parents and I came up here to get her, and then my mother decided we should stay until we figured out a plan."

"Did they ... are they ...?"

Lewis met his gaze, giving him the briefest of smiles. "They are all back at Meg's camp. We left when my parents realized the direction the campus was heading. We linked up with Meg's mother a few weeks later and have been with her camp ever since." He looked around, the memories playing across his face. "But a lot of good people lost their lives here."

Petra watched him for a moment before turning to look at the shell of an old dormitory. "A lot of good people are still losing their lives. That's why we're here."

Lewis gave her a nod.

"Do you know which are the science buildings?" Miles asked.

Lewis shook his head. "I was really young back then. My parents didn't let me explore." He spurred his horse a little farther forward. Miles watched him go, wondering what was going through the man's mind.

"Hey!" Ham came racing up from between two buildings. He and Aaron had split off on their own as soon as they entered. "I think I found that directory thing."

Ham had indeed found the directory a few buildings over, in front what had once been an administration building. It was left largely untouched by the fires that had consumed the dorms. The directory had been a freestanding sign in front of the building, encased in glass. The glass was long gone, but the map itself was made out of plastic and had stood up to the test of time.

Miles studied the map and pointed to a site. "This area of campus holds the science buildings. It looks like there were four separate buildings—chemistry, biology, physics, and astronomy. Let's try the biology building first."

They made their way to the science buildings, which were all in a square facing one another. Each of the buildings was twelve stories high. The glass along the first and second floors of all the buildings were shattered, but it didn't look like any of the buildings had been burned. They tied their horses to an old flagpole. Petra helped Miles strap on his sword attachment.

Aaron chortled at the sight of it. "What the hell you going to do with that thing?"

Petra glared. "Run you through if you don't shut up."

"Hey, who do you think—"

"Aaron," Lewis barked.

Aaron kept his gaze on Petra. "What?"

"Stay with the horses. I don't want us to lose them."

"Yeah sure, whatever," he grumbled, walking back to them.

Lewis indicated Miles's attachment. "Smart. Can I take a look at that later? We've got a guy who lost his arm two years ago. Maybe we could put something like that together for him."

"Yeah, no problem," Miles said.

They headed into the biology building, Lewis leading the way and Petra bringing up the rear. The first two floors had been ransacked. Everything not tied down had been removed or destroyed. Miles began to lose faith that they would find anything useful inside. But when they hit the third floor, the damage was less. By the time they reached the sixth floor, the damage was almost non-existent.

And then at the seventh floor they hit pay dirt—it was all labs. Miles smiled as he stepped into a room with long metal tables and three microscopes.

Miles put his pack on one of the tables. "This is good. I'll use that table over by the window."

"Okay. You get started. Ham and I will clear the rest of the building and then check the buildings around to make sure we're alone." Lewis looked at Petra. "You'll stay with him."

She nodded. "Yup."

"Good. We'll be back." He headed out the door.

Petra turned to Miles. "What do you need me to do?"

"Grab that microscope and bring it over to the window," he said as he started to unpack his bag. He smiled.

Time to get to work.

80

Adros and Max had split from Riley and Arthur about ten blocks from the Advancement Building, but they did not head right there. Max stopped and did two plumbing jobs along the way, so as not to rouse suspicion. Adros had stood next to him, trying to look like he knew what he was doing.

Now, Adros and Max walked quickly along, their bags of tools occasionally jangling. Adros tried not to wince each time. He knew it was no big deal. A plumber walking with a bag of tools was normal, but he hated anything that drew attention to them.

"That's the building." Max nodded toward a three-story building ahead of them. There was no sign outside the building to indicate what it was used for. But it was the engineering building where they kept the plans for the city and where a few human engineers worked. It was a stroke of luck that the cleaning detail was sent there that morning. One, it was close to the Advancement Building and two, it was almost always empty. The engineers were not in great demand and often didn't show up unless there was a specific project they were needed for.

"So you're sure there won't be any Unwelcome?"

"There shouldn't be. The cleaning detail is all kids. Humans are in charge."

Adros shook his head, a sour taste in his throat. Humans were the overseers. He knew he shouldn't be surprised. After all, everyone had to turn in a kid to get into New City, and yet somehow he was. Surprised and disgusted.

They crossed the street, waiting for a golf cart to drive by. Max nodded at the driver, but Adros kept his gaze on the building. They reached the glass doors and opened them, stepping into a small foyer. There was an information desk, but no one was behind it.

"So only three humans are with the kids, right?"

"Yeah. Always three."

Adros knelt down behind the desk and placed his bag there. He pulled out a long wrench. Max placed his next to Adros's and also pulled out a wrench.

Adros stood. "Okay. Let's go find your grandson."

81

After splitting with Max and Adros, Riley and Arthur holed up in a vacant apartment a few blocks away from the Advancement Building. Max's grandson wouldn't be in place for another hour, and they needed to coordinate their rescues.

But unlike Max, they did not have a good reason to wander the city. So they decided that it would be safer to just stay put. Yet while it might be the safer option, it certainly wasn't the easier one. Riley was practically climbing the walls from the minute they stepped in the front door. He'd spent some time searching the apartment. It was fully furnished with plush carpeting in the bedroom and a shiny new kitchen. Riley opened the oven and a cooling box, checking them out. There were a few machines in the kitchen that he did not understand, but everything looked clean, high tech, and modern. And every piece in there made him angry.

Done with his inspection, he paced the floor of the empty apartment, counting down the minutes. He'd had to continually talk himself down from rushing out the door to find Lyla. His mind worked overtime imagining what she was going through.

"We need to stick to the plan. It is the safest way to get her out," Arthur reminded him as he watched Riley pace.

"I know, I know," Riley mumbled.

Finally enough time had passed, and they were on their way.

Riley kept his head down as he walked next to Arthur, who gripped Riley's upper arm. Riley had stripped off his uniform and was wearing his regular clothes. There were handcuffs placed across his wrists. Arthur had broken them so they would not lock, but they would pass a quick inspection.

The Advancement Building was up ahead. It had been built at the same time as the falls and was actually built into the cliffs just below the city. They had already walked down the steep stairs that led to the entrance. There were labs dominating the front of the building, but the back was built into the rock face, and that's where they kept the subjects. He glanced at the bridge suspended above the Advancement Building. It connected New City to the hydro-electric power plant powered by the falls, which, according to Arthur, supplied the majority of power to New City. He'd also seen wind turbines along the coast, solar panels on every roof, and even fake trees whose leaves acted as mini-wind turbines.

How nice. They don't want to damage the planet—only its inhabitants.

Riley swallowed as they grew closer, the sound of the falls ruling out any chance of conversation. Which was just as well. Arthur couldn't talk to him now. They'd already passed four Unwelcome. Riley tensed each time, but they didn't even look at him.

Ahead, the entrance to the Advancement Building loomed. There were clear glass doors, but everything else about the building was dark. Black glass covered the front. Arthur had explained that inside you could see through perfectly, but from outside, nothing could be seen.

Just as they want it.

Arthur wasn't sure if the people in New City knew about the experiments. He doubted it, although even if they did know, Riley didn't think they would care very much. Protecting themselves seemed to be the residents' primary motivation, not looking out for others.

Arthur gripped Riley's arm a little tighter as they approached the front doors. Riley winced. "Ow."

But Arthur said nothing, and his grip didn't loosen. Ever since they had entered New City, Arthur's posture had straightened and he'd talked less. Riley prayed he wasn't having second thoughts, that being around his people was not making him rethink helping them. Arthur said that he would never be accepted by his people now that he had betrayed them. But maybe turning in a camp and revealing a plot to release kids and a prisoner would buy him some good will.

The Unwelcome at the door nodded as Arthur and Riley passed. Arthur tugged Riley to the right as they passed through the doors. He paused for a moment, glancing around the foyer. Three humans in white coats hurried past, coffee mugs clutched in their hands. They didn't even glance at Riley. Two Unwelcome stood waiting for the elevator and stepped inside as soon as the doors opened.

Arthur pushed Riley toward the stairwell and through the doorway. Once inside, he released his grip on Riley's arm. "Are you all right?"

Riley rubbed his arm, some of his doubts lessening. "Yeah." He paused. "Are you?"

Arthur was silent for a moment. "It is more difficult being here than I thought it would be."

"Have you changed your mind about helping us?"

"No, no. But I wish my brothers and sisters understood as I do where we have gone wrong. Maybe one day I will be able to show them. But that is for another day. Today, we free Lyla. And maybe tomorrow we see about freeing my people."

Riley had never thought about the Unwelcome from that perspective—that they had, in essence, been brainwashed into thinking the humans were unworthy of consideration. He didn't like how it made them seem like victims. Because right now, he needed them to be his enemy so he could do what he needed to do. So he closed those thoughts off in his mind to be examined at another time. Today he'd worry about the humans. Tomorrow he could worry about the Unwelcome. "Lead the way."

Arthur nodded, beginning to climb the steps. Through Max's access, they knew Lyla was being held on either the fourth or fifth floor. Max's access didn't tell him that exactly, but it did tell him that those floors were off limits, which only happened if there was someone there. The stairway was quiet as they ascended. Most people used the elevators.

On the third floor, voices sounded outside the door. Riley and Arthur hustled back down to the second-floor landing, ducking out of sight just as the door pushed open. Two humans stepped out and began heading up the stairs.

"She's not cooperating. And I am not going near her—not after last time."

"I don't understand it. It's not like she'll be able to hold them off. They will get what they want from her."

"She'll learn soon enough. A representative of the Naku is coming in this afternoon to read her. She won't be able to stand against that."

"I almost feel sorry for her."

"Well, I don't. I feel sorry for my nose." Their voices disappeared as they opened another door and disappeared inside.

Arthur leaned down. "Do you think they were talking about Lyla?"

Riley grinned. "I'm sure they were." The idea that she was still fighting, that she hadn't given up, made him inordinately pleased. He'd worried they'd broken her. That he'd find her and she wouldn't be Lyla, not anymore. But apparently they hadn't broken her yet.

"Let's go." Riley picked up his pace, jogging quickly up the stairs. He stopped on the landing outside the door to the fourth floor.

Arthur handed him the cuffs. "Put them on."

Riley quickly slipped them over his wrists. Arthur grabbed Riley's bicep with one hand and the handle with the other.

Riley let out a breath. "Here we go."

82

Getting to work hadn't happened as quickly as Miles had hoped. One microscope had a shattered eyepiece, so that one was of no use. Another was missing the focus knobs. They managed to track down two others that looked to be in good condition in another lab, but they were all dirty, and they had to spend some time finding some cleaner. While they'd been searching for that, Miles had come across an office with some textbooks on blood analysis. He'd brought them all back to the first lab so he could go through them.

Now he was finally ready to begin. Miles started with Arthur's blood. He knew he should approach this rationally, have a plan, and follow a procedure. But he'd been dying to look at Arthur's blood ever since he'd taken that first vial and made that first slide.

He slipped a slide underneath the first scope and looked through. He'd been shifting between two scopes because he'd been unable to find a scope with all objective lenses intact. Everything was blurry, and he adjusted the focus knob before the cell came into view. He studied the sample with a frown. It looked normal. He didn't know what he'd been expecting. Arthur was a humanoid, so he'd known his blood would be similar to a human's, but he thought something would jump out at him. Doubt began to creep in. What if this had all been a big waste of time?

No, not yet. I am not doubting yet. He took a breath and pulled out his notebook. *Okay, characteristics. Let me start with that.*

Miles stared at the microscope, moving between different slides, noting observations but not letting himself get distracted by anything but what was in front of him. He glanced back to the first slide of Arthur's blood and frowned. *There should be something here. Something different. Maybe I'll see something under the higher magnification.*

His eyes were beginning to burn, and he felt the beginning of a headache stirring behind them as well. He grabbed Lyla's slide and slipped it onto the stage of the second microscope. Adjusting the focus, he looked through the eyepiece and saw small dots littering her blood. But then he noticed the nucleus—it was slightly altered, as if there was a bulge at one end.

That's not right. He pulled the slide out as the door flew open.

Miles whirled around, his elbow knocking into the tray with the slides as Ham stumbled in the door, Aaron chortling as he pushed in behind him.

"Hey, I found some beers!" Ham thrust a six pack into the air.

Miles tried to grab the tray, but he was too slow, and it crashed to the ground. "Damn it," he grouched, looking up at Ham.

Ham shrugged, his words slurred. "Sorry, doc."

"Which slides were those?" Petra asked.

Miles pictured the strangely shaped nucleus only noticeably different at the higher magnification. "Arthur's and all of Riley's. I thought I grabbed Lyla's, but it must have been Arthur's. I finally saw a difference in the nucleus. Which makes sense because Arthur is a different species. But I saw something in it. I need another sample." He reached for the box where he still had some of Arthur's blood left.

"No need for that." Ham stumbled across the room toward them. He belched, pulling out his knife.

Miles reared back. "What are you doing?"

Ham snorted. "Chicken." He sliced the blade across his palm. Blood pooled along the cut. Ham made a fist and blood began to drip onto the floor. "Well, take your damn sample."

"Um ..." Miles fumbled to open the desk drawer and scrounged around inside, his hand finally closing around a slide. He turned to Ham and put the slide under his hand. Three drops landed on the clear glass.

"Uh, thanks," Miles said.

"Wimp." Ham pulled a dirty handkerchief from his pocket and wrapped his hand in it. Miles opened his mouth to say something but then shut it. Ham probably wouldn't appreciate hearing about the infection he could get from the germs crawling all over that handkerchief. Ham had his hand down, blood dripping on the floor, but if he passed out on them that could be a problem. "Um, you should hold your hand up. It'll slow the bleeding faster."

He grinned, pointing his hand upwards. "You're the doc."

Miles turned back to the microscope. He placed Ham's slide in and glanced through. It looked like a normal human sample.

"Well? Is he human? I'm guessing no," Petra said.

Miles smiled. "As far as I can tell." He took the other slide from his pack and placed a drop of Arthur's blood on it. He placed it on the stage and examined it. *That can't be right.* Quickly he replaced Arthur's slide with Ham's.

"What is it?" Petra hovered near his elbow.

He looked up at her, shock flowing through him.

"Okay, Miles, you're beginning to freak me out here. What is it?"

Feeling his mouth hanging open. He shut it and shook his head, trying to clear it. "It's the samples. They don't make any sense."

"What do you mean?"

"Just before Ham came in, when I first looked at the samples with the more high powered microscope, I saw a difference. But here"—he gestured to the slides—"there's no difference. His blood sample and Arthur's are the same." He sat back, stunned. "They're the same."

"How's that possible? You're sure you saw a difference before, right?"

Miles nodded, too numb to say anything. Had he just imagined it? Was that why he'd seen a difference?"

"Check Lyla's," Petra said, her voice quiet.

Miles grabbed Lyla's slide, his heart beginning to pound. *It was Arthur's slide where I saw the difference. Not Lyla's.* But his hands still shook when he placed Lyla's slide on the stage. Taking a breath, he peered through the eyepiece. And he saw it—the slightly misshapen nucleus and the small dots in the blood.

He sat back, his mouth hanging open.

"It's there again, isn't it?"

Miles nodded numbly.

"So what does it mean?" asked Petra.

"If I didn't know any better, I'd say Lyla's nuclei are slightly misshapen when compared to a human's."

"So it's slightly misshapen. That's not a big deal, right?"

"Actually, it's a really big deal. I mean, the difference is small but noticeable. If I didn't know any better, I'd say out of all the samples, Lyla's was the one that indicated the alien."

"You're not suggesting she's not human, right?"

Miles looked up at her, feeling lost. "I don't know what she is, but her blood—it's not human."

83

Adros and Max searched the first and second floors without any luck, which meant the kids had to be on the third floor. Adros paused on the landing outside the third floor. He could hear voices and movement on the other side of the door. He glanced back at Max. "You ready?"

Max looked a little nervous, but he nodded. "Yes."

Adros inched the door open. The hall was ten feet across, and the voices were coming from the left. He peered around the door. Two men and one woman stood in the hallway. Kids were moving quickly from large carts that had been positioned in the middle of the hall to the rooms. One kid, who couldn't be more than six, had a limp and struggled to reach a roll of toilet paper on top of the cart. One of the men walked over as the kid reached it and shoved the kid. "Move faster. We're not spending all day here."

The kid stumbled, catching himself before he fell but wincing as he landed heavily on his bad foot. But the kid didn't say anything to the man. He just snatched the toilet roll and disappeared back into the room. The man walked back to the other two adults and all three laughed.

Adros jerked his head back, taking a breath, memories of his father filling his mind. He remembered one time before they'd settled at the camp. He'd tried to take some of his dad's food stash while his dad was passed out. His hand had just reached into the pouch when his father's hand reached out and gripped him. Without a word, he'd backhanded Adros, sending him flying. Then his father had grabbed the pouch and, gripping it to his chest, fallen back to sleep. Adros had only tried to get the food because he'd been so hungry, and worse, his sisters had been hungry.

Adros looked at Max, who met his gaze with a nod. And just like that, their plan had changed. They weren't just getting out Sean. They were getting all of the kids out.

"Okay. They're there. You go first."

Max paused for only a second before stepping out into the hallway. Adros pushed the brim of his cap down before stepping out behind him. Max walked casually down the hall. The man who had pushed the kid looked up. "What are you doing here?"

"We got a call about a problem with one of the toilets."

The woman frowned. "We didn't hear anything about that."

Max shrugged. "Hey, I just go where I'm sent, you know?"

"The kids are cleaning in there. You'll have to wait."

"It's no problem. They won't be in my way."

A small boy with blonde hair and big brown eyes stepped out of the bathroom, and Max went still, his eyes growing large. The kid stopped, too, his mouth falling open. "Grandpa?"

"What the—"

Adros slammed his wrench into the back of the man's head before whipping around and catching the woman. Both dropped. The third man tackled Adros around the waist. The two of them crashed back, Adros on the bottom.

"Get the kids out!" Adros yelled, trying to avoid the man's punches.

He managed to trap the man's arms and sent an elbow into the man's chin. The man's eyes rolled back in his head and Adros shoved the guy off of him. He whirled as movement from the floor caught his attention. The woman had gotten to her knees, blood running down the side of her head. She held a device in her hand. Adros kicked her wrist and she cried out. He yanked the device from her hand. It was a rectangular box with buttons on it. A small screen displayed a message: *Security on the way.*

Shit. "Max, we need to go!"

Max reappeared from the bathroom. A little girl no more than four was in his arms. Another four kids were behind him, ranging in age from four to eight. All looked malnourished with bruises and a haunted look on their faces. Adros's stomach clenched, recognizing the look. His sisters had the same one.

"One of them called for help. We need to move."

"There's two more kids in the other bathroom."

"You get moving. I'll grab them." Adros sprinted into the other room. Two girls jumped up, their eyes wide.

"Hey, it's okay. I've come to get you out of here."

The girls looked at one another, both shaking. Adros stretched out his hand. "Trust me. Please."

The girls hesitated for just a moment before running toward him. Adros scooped them both up and sprinted into the hallway. Max was halfway to the stairwell when footsteps rang out from the stairs—heavy footsteps.

"Max!" Adros yelled.

But Max had heard them as well and yanked the kids to a stop as an Unwelcome stepped into the hallway.

84

M iles checked the slides over and over and over again. And the truth was, the only difference he saw was in Lyla's slide. Had he messed up the samples? Was it actually Arthur's he was looking at? Had he mislabeled them?

The door opened again, and Lewis stepped in. He glanced over at Miles and Petra before turning to Ham and Aaron, his face hardening. "What the hell do you two think you're doing?"

Ham tried to sit up straight and failed spectacularly. "We, uh, found some beer—"

Lewis snatched the bottle from his hand and dumped it down the nearest sink.

Ham stumbled forward. "Hey—"

"Get downstairs and take care of the horses. Now."

Aaron grabbed Ham by the collar and pushed him out the door. Miles would be surprised if they made it to the horses. They'd probably find them sleeping it off in the stairwell later.

Lewis shook his head as he headed over to them. "Sorry about that. They're young. Young and stupid."

"Still older than us," Miles mumbled.

Petra turned her head toward him. "What did you say?"

"That they're older than us."

"Miles, you need to check Lyla's slide against the Cursed."

Miles stared at her. "What are you talking about?"

"Ham. He's older than us. You've been comparing Arthur's slide to Lyla's and Ham's. Riley's were destroyed. You need to compare those samples to the Cursed, to us." Petra held out her hand. "You need to try my blood and then yours."

Miles turned back to the table and picked up his knife. "You're right." He glanced over at Lewis. "Would you also be willing to ..."

Lewis wound his way around the tables. "If it will help."

Miles stared at the microscope, his idea forming more clearly in his mind. "It will. I think it will."

85

Miles stared at his notes. *This makes no sense.* He'd gone back through all the blood types and carefully examined everything. Double checking he hadn't messed up any labels. He'd thought he was onto something, but now, now he just didn't know what he was looking at. He did see markers in three of the samples—his, Petra's, and Lyla's. But Lewis, Ham, and Arthur had none. If he was right, and there was something about the Cursed's blood, then Lyla's shouldn't have any markers. She was too old. But she did, and yet they were different than what he was seeing in his blood. Hers were more spread out. His and Petra's were larger, but there were very few.

On a hunch, he carried over the more powerful microscope. "Okay. Let's try this again."

He ran through each of the slides, going through the same process but at a stronger magnification. Everything was the same, except he could see the markers more clearly in his and Petra's blood. It was as if there was a protective bubble around a grouping of darker spots. They looked like they were a dark blue. He sat back. So what did that mean?

He shook his head. What he wouldn't give to have someone

who actually knew what they were doing to look at these. He was basically pulling bits and pieces from what he'd read.

This is crazy. I don't know why I thought I'd be able to figure anything out.

He pulled over Lyla's slide and placed it on the stage. He blew out a breath. If it weren't Lyla's, he'd swear he was onto something. But since she showed similar markers, maybe it was just a factor of the environment. Ham, Lewis, and Arthur all grew up somewhere else. Lyla, Miles, and Petra had lived together for the last five years at least.

He looked through the eyepiece, adjusting the focus, and frowned. *What is that?* Then his mouth fell open as he finally understood what he was looking at.

Lyla's blood had the same dark blue dots, but hers weren't grouped together in a protective bubble. They had spread throughout the blood, as if they'd been activated. He sat back, his hand to his mouth, his mind racing furiously. Was that why they wanted her? Whatever was in Riley, Petra, and his blood was exposed within Lyla's system. He frowned. But how would the Unwelcome know that?

He sat back, running his hands over his face. *Okay. Think this through.*

He and Petra had the same markers, but they hadn't been released. Lyla's had been released. And Arthur didn't have them at all. He frowned.

What the hell does that mean?

Lewis walked into the room. He made his way over to Miles and Petra, handing them each some jerky and an apple. "Thought you two might be hungry."

"Starved." Petra took her portion. "Thank you."

Lewis nodded, holding out the other one for Miles. "Miles?"

He took it absentmindedly, placing the food on the counter.

"I take it it's not going well," Lewis said.

"I don't know. I don't really understand what I'm looking at."

He remembered Addie and Jamal joking with Lyla about her inhuman running ability. His gaze flew back to the microscope, his mouth falling open. Could it be?

"Miles?" Petra stood looking at him, her brow furrowed.

"I think I know why the Unwelcome took Lyla. I know what the weapon is."

"What is it?" Lewis asked.

"Her."

86

The heat beat down. Lyla reached a hand down to the water, which was up to her thighs, bringing a handful up and dropping it on the back of her neck. She was in the lake, just off shore. Riley, Miles, and Maisy were all there, playing in the water. Addie and Jamal were in a canoe to her right, splashing water at one another. On the shore, a barbeque had been set up. Emma and Edna were grilling something. A waft of smoke drifted toward her and Lyla took a deep breath, her stomach growling in response.

That smells good. She could see the other Phoenixes milling around, some sitting in groups. Everyone was smiling, having a good time.

Lyla ran a hand through the water, turning her face to the sun. These were the kind of days she loved—lazy summer days.

A fly buzzed around her head, and she swatted it away. But it wouldn't leave. It just buzzed more incessantly with each wave of her arm.

"Go away." The fly was beginning to annoy her and reduce her peaceful mood. The sky flashed, and the scene changed. Unwelcome stormed through the beach, firing their weapons as everyone scattered in a screaming frenzy. But in another flash, it was gone.

Lyla frowned, the lake suddenly feeling cold. Miles swam past her to the shore. She looked at him, and then there was another flash and she was sitting next to his bed, waiting for him to wake up, his stump bleeding slightly.

She frowned. *You were never at this camp. Neither was Maisy.* Clouds rolled in, blocking the sun. *This isn't real. None of this is real.*

Her eyes flew open. Artificial lights shone brightly overhead. One wall had a long lab table lined with equipment. Another one held the door. The third had a window overlooking the falls.

She was in New City. A monitor beeped somewhere to her right, but she couldn't see it. She was strapped to the bed. She struggled against the bindings that held her down, but there was no give, and her strength was not what it should be. She glared at the IV in her arm. She'd been hooked up to one ever since the first group of white lab coats had shown up in her cell this morning.

"My, my, you certainly came out of that quickly." Chad stepped into view as the beeping stopped. "But just as well. I would have had to have pulled you out if you hadn't taken yourself out. How did you do that?" He stepped closer to the stretcher.

She smiled sweetly at him. "Take off these bindings and I'll be happy to tell you."

"Ah, I think we all know what will happen then. Why, you broke poor Trintan's nose."

"Pity that's all I broke."

"Always tough, aren't you? Well, we'll see how long that lasts when the Naku arrive. Because you see, they were surprised, unprepared, for your sister. For you they've prepared. They are not going to wait. They are bringing their strongest reader. I've heard what happens to the people he reads." He smiled. "It's not pretty."

Lyla said nothing.

"You know, I've been wondering how reading minds could be so destructive. I have a theory. Would you like to hear it?"

"No."

"See, I don't believe that answer. I think you *want* to know what's to come. And being you and I are such good friends, I'll tell you my theory. At first, I thought the Naku's ability was a passive sort of ESP. That they could see what was inside someone's head, as if looking through a window.

"But I've realized that's not quite accurate. They are not looking through a window at all. They climb right through it. The Naku enter a subject's brain and rifle around for what they are looking for. They are a physical presence inside the subject's mind. And as with any physical object, they take up space, damaging whatever they touch. Creating pathways that weren't there before and destroying ones that were."

He leaned down, his voice barely above a whisper. "So I would advise, my dear, that whatever they want to know, you tell them, and quickly. Or say goodbye to this world, because when they are done with you, you won't be able to understand it at all. You'll stare drooling at a wall, never speaking again." He kissed her cheek.

Lyla wanted to wipe it off, but with her arms restrained, she couldn't. Chad stepped back and looked in her face. "Ah, there it is. I was wondering when I would see it."

Lyla snarled. "See *what*?"

He patted her hand. "Fear."

87

P etra stood staring at Miles, her hands on her hips. "Lyla's a weapon? Have you lost your mind? Seriously, did Ham or Aaron slip something into your food? Because once I get ahold of them—"

Miles grabbed Petra before she could storm off. "Look, humans have a specific blood type."

"And?"

"And Lyla's is different. Plus she has these little blue dots that are scattered throughout her blood." He paused. "I think the Cursed have those same blue dots but they aren't spread out —not yet."

"Not yet? There's something in our blood that's going to what, explode?"

"In a way."

"That is *not* comforting, Miles. I mean, Lyla doesn't seem any different than the rest of us, so maybe it doesn't have any ..." Her words dwindled off as she looked at his face. "What? What are you thinking?"

"You remember when Cal grabbed all us kids?" he asked.

"Yeah, of course."

"Addie and Jamal said she ran so much faster than the rest of the Phoenixes. And do you remember when she showed up? She wasn't even breathing hard."

"I don't remember that," said Petra.

"Well, she wasn't. And then she took out the Unwelcome—the same way she took down the Unwelcome at the old highway. So maybe whatever's in her blood allows her to do that."

Petra paused looking at him. "Which mean maybe someday we can do that."

Miles smiled. "Which means we can fight them."

Petra smiled back at him before her face froze and the smile dropped from her face. She grabbed her pack from the table. "We need to go. Now."

"What? What's the rush?"

"Miles, they have Lyla. They are going to figure this out. We need to get her out of there. We need to send *everyone* to get her out of there. They're going to kill her."

"But they didn't. They took her."

"Yeah, to figure out what the deal is. But once they realize she's just like the rest of the Cursed ..." Petra met his eyes.

He started to shove everything back into his pack. "We need to go."

Lewis stood, his sword in front of him, blocking the only way out. "Yes, right back to Meg."

88

The hallway was empty as Arthur opened the door, although a murmur of voices could be heard from down the hall. Arthur once again had Riley by the arm and nodded straight ahead. If Max's information was correct, the cells should be right behind the door in front of them. They walked forward and Arthur reached for the handle.

"What are you doing here?" A man in a white lab coat with matching white bandages over his nose stood staring at them. "There are no subjects due today."

Riley wasn't sure what he should do. Should he speak? Not speak? Should Arthur speak? Did these guys know the Unwelcome could talk? Riley hadn't heard a single Unwelcome speak since they'd arrived. He could feel Arthur tense next to him.

"Great, then tell this giant to let me go," Riley growled, trying to pull his arm from Arthur's grip.

The man frowned, moving toward them. "Shut up, mouse. Let's get him in a cell and then I'll call down and find out what's going on." He pulled on the card hanging around his neck and ran it through the keypad. The light above the pad blinked green.

Riley looked up at him and grinned. "Thanks." Pulling his

arm from the shackles, he slammed the man's face into the edge
of the doorframe. The man let out a yell, and Riley was happy to
see blood burst from his nose. He shoved the man inside and
Arthur quickly stepped in behind them, closing the door.

The man scampered along the floor, holding his nose. "What
are you doing?"

"I'm looking for someone. A woman. Dark brown hair, blue
eyes. She was brought here yesterday."

The man cringed. "She's not here."

Arthur stormed forward and picked the man up, and Riley
was able to read the name on his lab coat—Trintan. "Then where
is she?" Arthur demanded.

Trintan began to shake even more at Arthur's voice.

"You heard him. Where is she?" Riley asked.

"In–in the procedure room. They're preparing her for the
Naku's arrival."

"When are they arriving?" Arthur asked.

Trintan just stared at him.

"When?" Riley demanded.

"Less than an hour."

"Where's the procedure room?"

"The sixth floor."

Riley looked up at Arthur. "Put him in a cell."

Arthur carried him by the throat and tossed him into a cell
away from the door. Trintan slammed into the back wall with a
thud and crashed to the ground with a cry. Riley looked at the cell
door. "This thing should lock automatically. But we'll need to
gag him."

"We won't need to." Arthur stepped into the cell and grabbed
Trintan again, punching him in the face. He ripped the badge
from around his neck and then he dropped him unconscious to
the floor. Riley slammed the door shut as Arthur stepped out.

"Okay. On to the sixth floor."

"Who's out there?" a voice called from down the cellblock.

Riley paused, wanting to rush up the stairs to Lyla. But it could be someone else besides Lyla locked up in here.

"Hold on," he said to Arthur before heading down to the cell. "Hello?"

"Oh, thank God." A figure rushed to the bars.

Riley reared back, his nostrils flaring. "You."

Brendan recoiled, his lip curling, but then common sense, or more likely desperation, took hold. "Riley. You have to help me."

"I don't have to do anything."

"You can't leave me here. You're not like that. You're good. You're human."

Arthur stepped up behind him. "You know this man?"

"This is Brendan."

In a blink, Arthur had reached through the bars and yanked Brendan up by the neck. "You did this to her."

Brendan clawed at the hand around his throat, but he was no match for Arthur's strength. Riley was content to let Arthur squeeze the life out of him. *But then we're no better than him.* He put a hand on Arthur's arm. "Let him go."

Arthur held him for a second longer and then released him.

Brendan collapsed to the cold tile floor, gasping for breath. Using the bars, he pulled himself up. "Thank you, Riley. I knew you wouldn't let him kill me."

"No, I wouldn't. But I did that for Arthur. I don't want your death on his conscience." He headed down the hall.

"Don't leave! What am I going to do?"

Riley walked back to the cell. Brendan smiled, reaching out a hand. "Thank you. I knew you-"

Riley grabbed his hand, yanking him forward into the bars. He face hit with a bang. Riley reached through grabbed him by the back of the head and slammed his face into it again. Brendan didn't even have time to cry out before he dropped to the ground unconscious.

"What should you do? Rot,." Riley strode toward the hall, Arthur right behind him.

As they reach the door leading to the main hall, Arthur put out a hand, blocking Riley's way. "I think I should go alone."

"What? Why?"

"If the Naku are coming, they'll send out an advance team to make sure the facility is secure. If they aren't here already, they will be soon. It's too dangerous. I'll get Lyla."

Riley shook his head. "It's just as dangerous for you. I'm going."

"Riley—"

He pushed Arthur's arm out of the way. "We're wasting time."

89

A dros slid the girls to the floor behind him as the Unwelcome leveled its weapon at Max and the kids.

"No!" Max dove in front of the kids, flattening them to the ground just as the Unwelcome pulled the trigger. The beam barely missed Max.

Adros's mind went blank for a moment, and then rage surged through him, along with a feeling of warmth that started in his chest and spread throughout his body.

"You bastard!" He charged at the Unwelcome, tackling the monster at the waist. The Unwelcome thumped to the ground and Adros kneed him in the groin before slamming a fist into his side. He straightened, stomping his foot into the Unwelcome's stomach, and then he wrenched the weapon away from it. He turned the weapon over, found the trigger, and pulled it. The Unwelcome's side erupted in blue light and burned.

Adros stumbled back.

"More are coming!" one of the kids yelled.

Adros looked up as three Unwelcome stormed toward them. "Get them out of here, Max!" Adros yelled as he pulled the trigger again and again.

Max wasted no time ushering the kids toward the stairwell. But he hesitated in the doorway. "What about you?"

Adros didn't turn from the oncoming Unwelcome. He caught one in the chest and the being dropped—all ten feet of him. The floor shuddered as he hit.

The other two paused, giving Adros enough time to catch one in the leg. The third dove into an alcove. "I'll meet you at the rendezvous. Now go!"

Adros kept up a barrage of cover fire as he heard Max's footsteps quickly retreating. He didn't dare turn his attention from the hiding Unwelcome. But he could see the Unwelcome he'd tackled pulling himself along the floor, trying to get to safety.

I tackled him. I took him down. How the hell did I do that?

But he had no time to answer that question, as more Unwelcome appeared at the end of the hall. *Time to go.* He ducked into the stairwell, slamming the door shut. He glanced at the piping near the door. Reaching up, he yanked a three-foot-long piece off the wall.

Adros's mouth fell open. Then he quickly shoved the metal piece through the loops in the door. "That should slow them down for a minute," he mumbled before hurrying down the stairs after Max and the kids. His whole body shook, and he knew it wasn't because of the fight.

It was because he had been *able* to fight.

How did I do that?

90

P etra gripped her sword, staring at Lewis as he stood blocking the only exit from the lab. "Get out of the way, Lewis. We don't have time for this."

"You are going back with me to report to Meg."

Miles looked between the two of them, noting the tension in each of their frames. *They're going to kill each other.* Miles stepped between them before either of them could take a swing. "No. Wait."

Petra looked at him in disbelief. "What are you doing?"

Miles's heart pounded as he turned his back on her to plead with Lewis. "Let us go. Please."

"Why would I do that? I have orders from Meg."

"I know. But my family is in danger. And this information could mean the difference between life and death. I will write everything out for you. I will give you all of the information. I think we all need to have it. But we cannot go back with you. I need to get to them."

Lewis stepped forward. "Why do you think I'll betray Meg?"

"Because I think you're a good man. And I think you know we don't mean you any harm or any of your people any harm. And you know"—Miles hesitated, praying this was the right approach —"you know what it's like to get there too late to save the ones you love."

It had been a guess, but Miles knew from Lewis's reaction that he had been right on the mark. His jaw clenched, but Miles's couldn't tell if it would be enough. He couldn't read him. He couldn't tell if he had gotten through to him or just destroyed any chance he and Petra had of getting back to Attlewood.

Lewis's sword lowered until it pointed at the ground. "Tell me everything you know."

Miles spent an hour writing everything out and answering all of Lewis's questions. Lewis was less shocked than Miles or Petra had been. Or maybe the man was just more practiced at schooling his emotions.

"And you think this is why people your age are being targeted?"

Miles nodded. "Yes, although I can't understand how it happened. I've only checked my blood and Petra's versus yours, Ham's, and Lyla's. But it all comes up the same."

Lewis had insisted on seeing the slides himself, so Miles had set it up. After he'd viewed them, Lewis sat back silently.

"Lewis?"

"It was the ash," he said softly.

"What ash?" Petra asked.

Lewis ran a hand through his hair and then over his mouth. "When my wife was pregnant, she was so worried about the ash that was always in the air. We didn't know why it was there. But it was in the air for three years, and we still found it in the ground water for another two years beyond that."

"Five years," Miles said. "One of your daughter's is Cursed."

"Sarah. She's fourteen."

Miles put his hand to his chin. *An ash that covered the world for five years.* "It's possible. And this ash, it was everywhere?"

Lewis nodded.

"So did they ever figure out what caused the ash?" Petra asked.

"Not that I know of. My father thought maybe a volcano or another asteroid had caused it. It appeared, and then years later, it stopped. But we had no way of knowing what caused it, not really."

Miles wasn't so sure about that. Someone must know. The Unwelcome must know.

Lewis shook his head as if to clear it of thoughts. "Now run through all of this again. Starting at the beginning."

Miles nodded. "First I compared the two samples, and I thought I had messed up labeling them." Miles spoke for another thirty minutes, going over everything again.

Finally, Lewis seemed satisfied. He put Miles's notes in his pocket. "Okay. I'm good. You two should get going. Stay to the east of the valley. There's a small canyon there. It will cut a lot of time off your travel and the patrols won't be out that way this late."

Miles held out his hand. "Thank you, Lewis. And if you ever need me, you will have my help."

Lewis shook his hand. "I may call you on that."

"I hope you do."

Petra shook his hand as well. "How will you explain our absence to Meg?"

Lewis actually grinned. "I'll say you slipped out while under Ham and Aaron's watch. They're passed out downstairs. I'll say I searched, but I just couldn't find you."

"Thank you," Petra said, and Miles could tell she really meant it.

Lewis helped them carry some of the books and two microscopes down the stairs. They passed by Ham and Aaron, who were indeed passed out in the front lobby, leaning against one another.

After securing their gear to the horses, they mounted them quickly. Lewis stood back. "I hope you two get there in time. God speed."

Miles nodded at him and set them off at a gallop, Lewis's words ringing through his mind. *I hope you two get there in time.*

Miles lowered his head, urging his mount to go faster. *We'll get there in time. We have to.*

91

After sharing his information on the Naku's process for retrieving information, Chad had stepped out of the lab, leaving Lyla alone. And for once she was grateful to Chad because she needed the time alone to get her emotions under control. The picture Chad had painted had left her terrified. She strained against the restraints holding her but she was still too weak. She was barely able to move her arms. There was enough medical equipment in the room that even in her weakened state she would be able to defend herself. But she needed to get free first. *And then what?*

Muriel had managed to keep from revealing anything to the Naku but only by killing herself. She must have known they were getting close. That wasn't an option for Lyla, because she was trussed up like a turkey. Frustration welled up in her. Where the hell was that strength she'd had when Brendan had led them to her? Whatever Chad had given her had dampened it.

A noise sounded from outside the door, and Lyla tensed. She'd heard the lab techs talking about an advance team for the Naku. She said a quick prayer that she could keep her composure. She knew she would eventually break under the Naku's onslaught, but she just hoped she kept her dignity. They were going to take enough from her. She couldn't let them have that as well.

More noises came from down the hall. She frowned when she heard a thud against the wall. Then the door opened and two lab techs flew into the room. An Unwelcome stormed into the room after them, stopping short at the sight of Lyla. What the hell? Had one of them gone nuts?

It rushed over to her and she pulled back.

"Lyla, it's me."

"Arthur?"

He nodded, pulling on one of her restraints and snapping it off.

"Behind you!" Lyla yelled as two more Unwelcome appeared in the doorway. Arthur yanked a lab tech from the floor and, using him as a shield, rammed him into the two Unwelcome, forcing them out of the room. More sounds of fighting came from the open doorway. Lyla reached over and yanked the IV from her arm. Then she unlatched her other arm before reaching down and removing the restraints from her legs.

Swinging her legs over the side, she lowered herself to the floor. Her knees buckled. She grabbed onto the bed as the room swam.

The discharge of multiple Unwelcome weapons sounded from the corridor. *Arthur.* She pushed herself upright, the fog in her mind beginning to lift. She rolled her neck as she felt her strength returning. *Okay.*

An Unwelcome appeared in the doorway, its back to Lyla as it shot into the hallway. It was much larger than Arthur. Grabbing the needle that had just been in her arm, Lyla sprinted forward. She leapt up and launched herself onto its back. In one swift movement, she plunged the needle into its neck, right between the uniform and helmet.

The Unwelcome jerked. Lyla jumped off, twisting the Unwelcome's shoulder as she did. Off balance, it toppled to its side with a thud. She slammed her foot into the base of its spine and then yanked its weapon from its hand. Without hesitation, she turned and fired it point blank into its chest.

Movement yanked her gaze to the doorway as a man appeared. No, not a man. Still a boy, at least in her mind.

"Riley!" She scrambled over to him, pulling him from the doorway and hugging him quickly before glancing past him. She wanted to yell at him, hug him again, and ask him a million questions all at the same time. But there was no time for any of that. Five Unwelcome were in the hall. One was holding them back.

"We need to help Arthur," she said.

"The staircase is right behind him. We're heading there and then going up."

"Up? Shouldn't we be going down?"

"No. We have a plan."

She stared at him. There was no smile on his face. He was dead serious. And she realized she'd been right the first time. A man had been standing in the doorway. She squeezed his hand.

"Then let's get to it."

92

Lyla was alive and standing next to him. Riley's relief was threatening to overwhelm him. But he shoved it aside because they were not in the clear yet.

She nodded down the hallway. "I'll cover you. You head for the stairwell. And then you cover me."

He got into position, preparing to sprint. "Got it."

"Ready? Go!" Lyla pulled the trigger over and over again as Riley sprinted for the doorway. He bulldozed right through it like it was a tackling dummy from practice. "Through!" he yelled back.

He leaned out and started firing as Lyla sprinted toward him. She dove into the stairwell, rolling quickly to her feet.

Riley took aim down the hall at another Unwelcome trying to charge. "Arthur! Come on!"

Arthur didn't look back at him as he stomped an Unwelcome rushing him in the chest. "I'll cover you. Go. Get to the roof."

"No. You are coming with us. Stick to the plan!" Riley yelled.

"Arthur, come with us," Lyla said. "We're not leaving without you."

Arthur hesitated for only a second before he turned and ran

for the stairwell. Lyla leaned out of the opening, continually firing at the Unwelcome and keeping them back.

Arthur ran through the doorway and Riley slammed the door shut.

"Go! Run!" Arthur yelled as he slammed something onto the back of the door.

"What is that?" Riley yelled as he tore up the stairs, Lyla at his side.

"You need to go faster," was Arthur's only response. Below them, the door opened. Arthur vaulted forward, pushing both Riley and Lyla against the wall as an explosion rang out.

93

A dros tore down the stairs from the Advancement Building. He knew the Unwelcome would find a way out soon. Or call for reinforcements. Either way, he really needed to get into gear. He bolted out of the door at the first level.

Sprinting across the empty foyer, he burst through the front doors. He angled left, not slowing down. A street cleaner was pushing a broom and Adros clipped him. The man crashed to the ground. Adros did not say sorry. He did not feel sorry.

You're all sick bastards.

He pounded down the street. People scattered, watching with open mouths as Max ran by with the kids. Adros did a quick head count—six. They were all there. A little boy fell, landing hard on his chest. The same boy with the limp from the hallway. Adros barely slowed as he scooped the boy up.

The boy let out a scream.

"One of the good guys," Adros yelled. "Hold on."

Max paused at the entrance of the bridge.

"Go! Go!" Adros yelled, because behind him he could hear the pounding of feet. The whole road seemed to tremble under their onslaught.

Adros looked over his shoulder and his eyes went wide. He stumbled but stayed upright, his arms tightly wrapped around the little boy. He swung the boy to his back so he could use his arms. "Hold on."

Adros rounded the turn onto the bridge, the boy still perched on his back. And Adros himself nearly stumbled.

The bridge was empty.

No Arthur. No Riley. No Lyla. No escape. He glanced behind him. Six Unwelcome were coming up fast, and across the bridge, another three were heading for them from the hydro-electric plant.

The boy tightened his grip on Adros's shoulders, and a renewed sense of purpose filled him as he pictured his father. He was going to protect these kids.

Or die trying.

94

Lyla's ears were ringing, and she was having trouble focusing. Riley shook his head next to her. Slowly, sound returned as she turned to Arthur, who lay on the ground. "Arthur!"

She rolled him over and pulled off his helmet. His eyes were closed and blood dribbled from his nose. "No, Arthur, no."

Riley reached down for one of Arthur's arms. "We need to go."

Lyla grabbed his other one and they hoisted him between them. His weight fell on her, causing her to stumble. And then she felt the warmth flow through her. She straightened, Arthur's weight no longer as much of a problem, and she noticed Riley straighten as well.

They sprinted up the stairs. Lyla paused at the last floor, but Riley shook his head. "No. Keep going."

Arthur groaned in between them, and Lyla said a silent thank you that he was coming around. They reached the top of the stairs. Riley kicked open the door, revealing the roof and an Unwelcome ship sitting there. An Unwelcome sprinted down the open ramp and opened fire. Three more appeared behind him.

They took cover behind an air vent. Lowering Arthur to the ground, Lyla looked at Riley. They had lost their weapons in the explosion. "I need you to draw their fire, okay?"

Riley looked back at her and then up at the bridge. A group of people were sprinting full-out down the hill toward it. "That's Adros and the kids. We need the ship. We're meeting them on the bridge."

Adros had a kid in his arms as he sprinted forward, and behind them, three Unwelcome gave chase. *Oh no.* Attached to the building was a ladder that connected to the bridge. "Make for the ladder," said Lyla. "Help Adros and the kids. I'll keep these guys from you."

"You'll need help."

She stared into his eyes. "Together, then. But when you're clear, you run for the ladder, okay?"

"Okay."

Arthur stirred next to them, blinking his eyes a few times.

Riley placed a hand on his shoulder. "Arthur, we're going for the ship. Stay here until it's clear."

Lyla peered out at the oncoming Unwelcome, her stomach tightening in fear. "On the count of three. One, two, three."

Riley bolted from their hiding spot to the left. Lyla sprinted for the Unwelcome closest to her on the right. She rolled as the weapon's charge flashed above her, and she slammed her fist into the being's groin. She kicked out at one knee from the ground and then looped her leg around the other, shoving it to the ground. With a yell, he crashed.

Another Unwelcome turned and opened fire. She dove behind its comrade as a third sprinted for her. *Shit, shit, shit.*

The Unwelcome rounded the downed alien in front of her. Lyla slammed her feet into the downed alien, sending it sliding across the roof, right into the second one's legs. It wobbled mid-run.

And that was all Lyla needed. Keeping the unstable alien

between herself and the other two, she stomped her foot into its chest, feeling its bones crack. Another stomp and its knee shattered, and it dropped to her eye level. She twisted her hand and slammed the side of it right in between the helmet and uniform and felt the neck break. It dropped, and she yanked its weapon, opening fire on the last one.

"Go, Riley!" she yelled.

He sprinted for the ladder, only slowing to grab an Unwelcome's weapon. Lyla shot each Unwelcome, not willing to take the chance that they would stay down. Then she ran back to Arthur, who was just stumbling to his feet.

She grabbed him around the waist. "Come on. You know how to fly this thing, right?"

He stumbled but kept his balance. "Yeah."

"Then let's get it on the air." She hurried him across to the ramp and watched Riley reach the top of the ladder and disappear from view.

You've got this, Riley.

95

The Unwelcome had just reached Adros as Riley rolled over the side of the bridge. Adros ducked the first swing and caught the Unwelcome with a kick to the gut. Not that it moved him.

"Adros, down!" Riley yelled.

Adros dove out of the way as Riley brought the Unwelcome weapon around and pulled the trigger. The shot caught the Unwelcome dead center, and it fell back. Adros got to his feet as Riley began to fire at the other Unwelcome.

"Riley!" Adros tackled him to the ground as the blast of an Unwelcome's weapon came from behind.

The weapon rolled out of Riley's hand. "We need to disarm them," Riley said.

"Got it," Adros said.

Riley grabbed the weapon and pushed it into Adros's hand. "Here. Get this to Max."

Adros gave him a nod before rolling to his feet. Riley got to his feet as Adros opened fire, running across the bridge. A small girl slipped out of Max's grasp. In an instinct born of pure terror, the girl sprinted away from him. "No!" he yelled.

Then she was hit by an Unwelcome's blast, which reduced her to dust.

A cold anger rolled over Riley. He turned to the Unwelcome, narrowing his eyes.

You're dead, he thought as a warmth began to spread from his chest out through his limbs. And then he was sprinting across the space, dodging the blasts of the Unwelcome's weapons. As he was about to reach the Unwelcome, he spun, slamming a back kick into the Unwelcome and sending it flying ten feet.

Riley gaped, as did the other Unwelcome. But then he smiled, turning to the Unwelcome three feet away. "You're next."

96

The Unwelcome ship stood waiting, its ramp open. Lyla and Arthur sprinted for it. Arthur didn't even wait. He just bowled up the opening. Taking a breath, Lyla followed. Once up the ramp, thuds sounded from her right.

She ran down a short hallway and stepped into the cockpit. Arthur held a creature up, a growl in his throat. Lyla started. It wasn't an Unwelcome. Its skin was a pale gray, almost white. It was only four feet tall and extremely thin with sagging skin. Its skin was wrinkle upon wrinkle, lapped over one another. There were so many it was hard to make out its features. But she could just see the two small nostrils above a tiny mouth in the middle of its face and yellow eyes that somehow managed to convey contempt despite the situation.

Arthur growled again, clutching the creature's white shirt tighter, but then Arthur's face went blank. He carefully lowered the creature to the floor. And in that moment, Lyla knew she was looking at a Naku.

"Arthur!" she yelled, but Arthur didn't move. The Naku, however, turned, its face full of malevolence. And Lyla felt a presence trying to push inside her mind. At the same time, Arthur crashed to his knees with a scream, his hands holding his head. *Oh, no, you don't.* Lyla leveled the weapon and blasted the creature in the chest. The blue glow engulfed the creature but did not harm it. It smiled.

Lyla threw the weapon aside. *Okay, then.* She sprinted forward, thrusting her hips forward as she slammed her foot into the creature's chest. With a squeal, it went flying across the cockpit. Arthur's hands dropped from his head. He looked up.

"Arthur?"

"I'm okay. It didn't have time to do much damage."

"It's a Naku, isn't it?"

"Yes. It didn't hurt you?"

"It tried. Hold on." Lyla strode across the cockpit as the Naku tried to get to its feet. She grabbed the Naku and yanked it up by the shirt, then slammed it into the wall. Its mouth fell open and its eyes pulsed before its head fell to the side.

Lyla frowned, releasing the creature. It collapsed in a heap at her feet. She stepped back. "What happened?"

"They're very fragile. That's why they created us."

Lyla turned her back on it and nodded to the instrument panel. It was a flat surface with hundreds of lights. Lyla had no idea what any of it meant. "Can you fly this thing?"

Arthur stumbled to the pilot's chair. The ship was already running. He hit a few buttons and the ship listed sideways. Lyla grabbed onto the back of Arthur's chair as they went airborne. A few seconds later, they were landing on the bridge. She was already sprinting away from the cockpit before they had touched down.

She ran down the ramp, taking in the scene in a single glance. Max was hunkered down, five kids behind him while Adros and Riley took on the Unwelcome.

"Get the kids in the ship!" she yelled at Max as she sprinted forward, throwing herself into the fray. Lyla shoved an Unwelcome away and turned, landing a round kick on the approaching

Unwelcome's knee. She slammed her other foot into its groin and its legs buckled. Spinning, her back kick took it off its feet, and it landed on another two who were coming up on them.

"Let's go!" Max yelled from the ramp on the ship.

Arthur charged down the ramp and let out a yell as he threw an Unwelcome over his shoulder, and the Unwelcome landed on the edge of the railing and then tipped over the edge. She saw Adros flip an Unwelcome over his shoulder. The Unwelcome crashed into another, both hitting the ground heavily.

"Adros, help Max get the kids strapped in."

Adros nodded before sprinting for the ramp. Movement farther down the bridge caught her attention. She squinted, moving closer to the railing. "Riley?"

Two Unwelcome swung at Riley. Riley ducked and hit with amazing speed. Then one caught him on the side of the head with a hook to the face. He stumbled back. Lyla's vision dimmed as he slammed into the railing. And then the force of the hit took him up and over the side.

"Riley!" she screamed, running to the railing. Riley's body fell over the falls, two hundred feet down, before disappearing in the churning water below. Lyla grabbed the edge, readying to vault after him. "No!" Unwelcome blasts hit the railing, forcing her back.

Answering blasts from behind her answered them, and she lunged for the railing again. "Riley!"

Strong arms wrapped around her and pulled her back. "Lyla."

Tears streamed down her cheeks as she struggled against Arthur's grasp. "Let me go!"

"Lyla, we have to go."

"Riley. I have to—"

"He's gone, Lyla." Arthur's voice was filled with sorrow. "There's no way he could have survived that fall. He's gone."

Lyla turned around, staring into Arthur's face, looking for some sign that he was wrong. But there was none. And in her mind she saw Riley fall, saw his body disappear under the churning water.

And it was as if someone had turned off a switch. Her vision blurred and she collapsed, unable to stand. "Riley," she croaked.

Arthur picked her up, his arms under her shoulders and knees. He cradled her to his chest. "I'm sorry, Lyla."

She leaned into his warmth, but she felt cold. So very, very cold.

Riley ...

97

A dros had managed to strap all the kids in by the time Max bounded up the ramp. "They're coming!" he yelled.

"Okay." Adros checked and made sure the kids were all accounted for. Occasionally, a child would sniffle, but no one seemed to talk. Adros was pretty sure they were in shock, and he had no idea what to do about that, so he kept telling them they were safe, and he really hoped he wasn't lying to them. He'd counted them over and over again because he needed something to do. And he kept replaying that one little girl getting turned to ash.

He ran a shaky hand over his face. Where the hell was Riley? He should have been right behind him.

A heavy thud on the ramp made Adros jump, and he let out a relieved sigh when Arthur's head appeared. But that relief quickly shifted the concern when he saw Lyla in his arms. He'd just seen her fighting. She'd been fine. He ran up to him. "Is she hurt?"

Arthur shook his head, his face strained, his voice heavy. "No. It's not her. It's Riley."

"Riley? Where is he?"

Arthur met his gaze. "He fell from the bridge into the falls. He's gone."

Adros felt like the air had been sucked from his lungs. His legs shook so hard he had to reach out for the wall. Riley was gone? Riley? Adros had always competed against him and never won. Riley, who seemed to always make the right choice. Riley, who had headed into this stupid city to save his aunt.

And he would have been safe at home if Adros hadn't spoken to his father. If he had told someone what his father was planning. It was probably a bluff anyway. Brendan was never going to send the Unwelcome to the camp. But even if he hadn't been bluffing, there could have been another way. *If I had trusted someone ...*

Guilt and shame poured through him. *I did this. If I had finally stood up to him, if I had told someone what he said, none of this would have happened.* Now he owed Riley more than he could possibly repay. He owed Lyla. He reached for her, even as his hands shook. "I'll take her. You need to get the ship in the air."

Arthur hesitated.

Adros swallowed hard. "I'll take care of her. I promise."

Arthur nodded, handing her over. Adros was surprised at how light she was. She always seemed so tough, so sturdy. But right now, she weighed nothing. A tear slipped down her cheek, and Adros stumbled at the sight of it. He carried her to an empty seat and sat her down, buckling her in. She didn't say a word. Didn't move a muscle. The only thing that moved were the tears that dropped down onto Adros's hands as he finished the last of the straps. He stepped away, but she reached out, grabbing his hand. "Stay."

He sat next to her, strapping himself in. "I'm sorry, Lyla. I'm so sorry. For all of it."

She squeezed his hand but said nothing as tears trailed down her cheeks. Adros looked up at the ceiling, trying to keep his own tears back.

I'm sorry, Riley. I'm so sorry.

98

L yla stared at the ceiling as Arthur piloted the ship. Adros sat next to her, his hand wrapped around hers. She kept torturing herself by replaying Riley disappearing beneath the water over and over again. She shut her eyes against the image, but it didn't help. It was branded in her mind.

The ship shifted, and Lyla could tell they were landing. They could only use the ship for a short while. It would be too easy to track. So they'd drop off the kids, and then Arthur was going to backtrack and ditch it, then catch up with them.

The ship touched down in a clearing, and Lyla took a breath. Opening her eyes, she turned to Adros. "We need to get the kids out."

"I'm on it." He quickly unbuckled and started helping some of the smaller kids out of their seats. Max did the same. Lyla felt like she was moving in slow motion, and it took her a while to unbuckle herself. By the time she was done, Arthur had shut down the engine and opened the ramp.

Forcing herself to focus on the task at hand, she turned to the kids looking at her. "Okay, guys, we're getting out here." She led the way down the ramp, the kids following quietly.

Lyla led the kids away from the ship, into the trees, waiting for Arthur to join them. The kids started at the sight of Arthur.

"Hey, hey, it's okay," Adros said before they got too worked up. "He's a friend. He's a good guy."

Lyla looked at him in surprise. Apparently Adros had done a lot of growing up in a short time. He looked at her with a nod. She gave him a small smile before turning to the kids. "Okay. We're going to bring you guys to our camp. It will be safe there. It's about two and a half hours from here."

Max stepped forward, his hand on the shoulder of a boy who shared his eyes. "Thank you. All of you, for what you've done. And I'm so sorry for—"

Lyla cut him off, not able to hear that right now. "Arthur and I will ditch the ship. Adros, can you lead them?"

"Yes. But I can go with Arthur."

Lyla shook her head, her resolve slipping as she looked at all the innocent faces in front of her. She pictured Riley when he was born, the first time she had held him. Sucking in a breath, she tried to keep her voice even. "No. I'll do that. You get everyone back home, okay?"

"Okay." Adros turned to the kids, picking up a little girl who was only about four and swinging her onto his shoulder. "All right, guys, let's get moving." The kids fell in line behind him as he headed for the trees. Max held the hand of the small boy as he brought up the rear.

Lyla watched them all disappear, feeling numb.

"I could ditch the ship myself."

She turned back to Arthur, who peered down at her. "I know. But you said there was a rendezvous point—" Her voice broke, and she took a breath to calm herself. "That you had planned on meeting up at if you got separated. And I just need to be sure."

Arthur stared into her eyes for a moment and then nodded. "Then we'll make sure."

Lyla looked away from his knowing gaze and took a breath,

trying to keep her tears back. She knew it was a false hope. Because Arthur was right—no one could survive those falls. But it was Riley. And she *needed* to be sure. After all, she'd thought Muriel was dead as well. And she had been left behind. She would not make the same mistake with Riley.

Besides, until they reached the rendezvous point and confirmed that he wasn't there, she could believe he might still be alive. And that was the only thing keeping her upright at the moment.

Because she didn't know how she was going to carry on when that hope was wiped away. She wasn't even sure she could.

99

Petra and Miles rode toward camp, but they had to go around Meg's land. But even with that detour, the canyon Lewis told them about cut hours off their time. They were back in familiar land in just a few hours. They slowed as they got closer to the camp.

Miles's mind had churned the entire ride, making him wish he had access to better equipment and the skills to use them. He knew that finding the unusual markers in their blood and Lyla's was only the tip of the iceberg. There was still so much that was unknown.

A small rock hit his thigh. His head jolted up to look at Petra, who glared at him, a finger to her lips.

"Listen," she mouthed.

He could just make out the sound of movement and then the low sound of voices. Petra slid off her horse, and Miles did the same. They led their horses farther away.

"Stay here," Petra mouthed.

Miles shook his head.

"Stay here," she mouthed again, this time through gritted teeth.

"Fine," he hissed.

Petra rolled her eyes at him before disappearing into the trees. Miles leaned against his horse's neck, absentmindedly running a hand along the underside of her jaw.

Two short whistles sounded, and Miles stood up straight. Friendlies. He grabbed the reins of both horses and led them forward. He could hear voices. He stepped back onto the path and five little kids startled at his sudden appearance, horses in tow.

"Hey, hey, it's okay. This is Miles," Adros said.

Miles looked at him in surprise. "What are doing out here? And who are all these kids?"

"I was just about to tell Petra." Adros paused. "You might want to tie up those horses."

Something about Adros's tone sent a shiver of foreboding through Miles. Without a word, he attached the reins to a low-lying branch. Carefully composing his face, he turned back to Adros. "Okay. Talk."

Miles listened in disbelief as Adros told him about travelling to New City with Riley and Arthur. But as Adros spoke, the sense that Adros was building to bad news wouldn't leave him. He finally cut into Adros's speech. "Where are Riley and Arthur?"

"We had to split up. Riley and Arthur went to get Lyla," Adros said, meeting Miles's gaze for only a moment before looking away.

"What happened?" Petra demanded.

Max stepped forward. "I'm sorry. Riley ... he didn't make it."

Miles stared at the older man, not understanding his words. "What do you mean he didn't make it? Is he still back in New City?"

Adros turned to Miles, his eyes holding a world of grief, and the meaning behind Max's words slammed into him. He sucked in a breath, his vision dimming at the edges. "What happened?"

Adros's tone was somber. "We were fighting the Unwelcome. There was a bridge over the falls. Riley went over the edge."

Petra's face went white. She stumbled over to Miles and gripped his hand, but he barely felt it. The image of Riley falling burned its way into Miles's mind. Riley was gone? He couldn't be gone. His mind seemed to shift between disbelief and soul-crushing grief.

"What about Lyla?" Petra asked.

"She went with Arthur to dump the ship and then go to the rendezvous, just in case."

Miles felt disconnected from the words Adros was saying, from the words Miles was thinking. But he shoved through the molasses in his mind to try and figure out what to do. And he had one thought—get to Lyla. "I need to get Lyla. Where's the rendezvous?"

Adros winced. "Miles, he's gone, man."

"I know. But if he's gone, then Lyla she's going to need—" His words cut off, and he swallowed hard. Tears sprang to his eyes, picturing what Lyla must have looked like right after Riley had died. As tough as she was, as many responsibilities as she had, he knew each of them—Maisy, Miles, and Riley—were the most important parts of her life. And if Riley was gone, she was going to need him.

That need to help Lyla was all that was holding his grief at bay. That and the hope that Lyla would tell him it was all a horrible mistake. "Where's the rendezvous?"

Adros gave them directions. "Do you want me to go with you? Show you the way?"

Miles shook his head. "No. You need to get these kids back to camp. Warn Frank that the Unwelcome might be coming."

"If you're sure ..." Adros said.

"I'm sure." When Riley had headed to New City and Miles to the lab, they'd both been so angry at Adros. But Miles could see the toll the last two days had taken on his old tormentor. The

Adros standing in front of him now was a far cry from the Adros who'd pushed his books to the ground only a few months ago.

Miles looked over the group of kids who'd sat down to rest while Adros and he had been talking. Adros had risked his life to save them—complete strangers. Yeah, this Adros was someone new. And Miles hoped he stayed around and didn't let the old Adros slip back. "You did good, Adros, saving these kids. Riley would have approved."

Adros met Miles's gaze, and Miles felt Adros's grief like a sucker punch to the chest. He sucked in a breath as Adros gave him a quick nod and headed away, his shoulders stiff.

Petra nudged his shoulders. "You want to ride?"

A numbness was steeling over him. *Riley's dead.* He swallowed. "Yeah, but there's no rush."

100

The rendezvous point wasn't all that far from where they'd seen Adros, at least not on horseback. Miles got onto his mare's back, but then he just sat there, staring off at nothing, picturing Riley falling. Tears pressed against the back of his eyelids. It wasn't possible. It just wasn't.

"Miles," Petra said quietly.

He wiped a tear that had fallen onto his cheek. "I'm coming." He nudged his horse forward. Luckily, his horse did not need much direction, because Miles just sat in the saddle, numb. His limbs all felt heavy and at the same time disconnected. Riley was gone. It wasn't possible. Riley was so strong, so full of life. It couldn't be true. It just couldn't.

Miles pulled at the collar of his shirt. It felt tight, like it was cutting off the air. What was wrong with the air?

Petra pulled her horse to a stop. "Miles?"

"There's no air. There's no air," Miles said, looking around. Where were they?

Petra was at his side in a flash, pulling him from his horse. Miles's breaths came out in pants, and he couldn't seem to focus. And his chest felt so tight.

Petra held his biceps tightly. "Miles, I need you to look at me. Look at me. Now, Miles. Look at me."

Miles's gaze strayed around. He couldn't seem to focus before he finally found Petra's pale green eyes. They stared into his. He felt his knees weaken and his eyes fill with tears. "He's gone, Petra. Riley's gone."

Petra put her hand on his cheek, her own eyes shining with tears. "I know."

And those two words slashed through the wall holding back his grief. He crashed to the ground. *Riley.*

Petra's arms wrapped around him as she, too, fell to the ground, her tears falling on his neck. And together they sobbed for their brother and friend.

101

I t was silent. That was the first thing Riley noticed. In his life, silence was never a good thing. Silence meant danger was near. His eyes shot open and he reared back at the strangeness around him. He was lying on a rocky surface and it was murky. He held up his hand and realized he was in water. *I fell.*

He was sore, but he didn't think anything was broken. He pushed off just as a school of fish swam by. He jerked back in surprise and then let out a scream as an eel slid over his shoulder.

Panic surged through him as water poured into his mouth. *I'm going to drown.* But the need to breathe never came. And the water in his mouth didn't bother him. He frowned, realizing he'd swallowed the water and nothing had happened. He sat treading water at the bottom of the lake, and he was fine. Just fine.

How is this possible?

Bubbles floated past him, coming from his neck. He reached up and felt three slits on either side of his neck. He jerked his hand back, his heart pounding, but then he couldn't keep himself from reaching up again. Gills. He had gills.

Okay, I have gills. That's ... weird and not at all terrifying.

He pushed off the bottom of the lake. As he approached the

surface, he slowed, staying under the water. He could see the tumult from the falls and knew the shore was to his right. But he didn't think getting out right here would do him any favors. Disbelief and more than a little panic etched his thoughts.

Besides, I have gills. Might as well make use of them.

He headed away from the falls, keeping along the shore, trying to figure out how he was going to catch up with everyone while a larger part of him wondered when he'd wake up. But if this was a dream, it was the most realistic dream he'd ever had.

He remembered the fight on the bridge and then falling. *I must be dead*, he thought as he swam on. *This is where you go after you die.* A piece of seaweed got caught around his arm. He stopped to pull it free and watched it float away. If this was the afterlife, it was awfully strange.

He swam quickly, amazed at how fast he was able to move through the water. They had planned to meet up at a spot two hours from the camp. Hopefully they'd still be there. If he ran hard, he could hopefully catch up with them. And the longer he swam, the more his mind cleared. He wasn't dead. This wasn't heaven. He wasn't dreaming, either. This was real. Somehow, some way, all of this was real, which meant he needed to get on shore.

For a moment he worried the gills would make it impossible for him to leave the water. But he had to hope they were only a temporary affliction.

And if they aren't? a voice whispered from the back of his mind. But Riley shut the voice down quickly. Although the terror of that possibility stayed at the back of his mind as he swam.

Riley stayed under the water at the edge of the shore, trying to work up the nerve to step out. *It's going to be fine.* He knew he needed to get moving. He was already going to have to sprint for the rendezvous point, and even then he might not be able to catch them. But he kept picturing himself flopping on the shore like a beached fish.

Because a fish was exactly how he felt. He felt as if the water was where he belonged. Even his skin had taken on a different texture. Usually if he stayed in the water too long, his skin would get all prunelike. But his skin was smooth, *too* smooth. His skin had the texture of the eel that swam over his shoulder. And he couldn't tell exactly because the light was really dim, but he even thought it had taken on a gray cast.

Enough. I need to move. I'll just go up there and sit in the shallow water until I know for sure. Swimming closer to the shore, he stayed under the water, even as he was forced to stop swimming, and walk along on his hands. He pictured Petra with her hands on her hips. *You big chicken.*

Rolling his eyes, he pushed himself upright out of the water. For a moment, he gasped, his vision darkening as the air choked him. His lungs screamed as the air met the water there. He turned on his side and coughed up what felt like a bucketful of water, his throat burning.

Then the pain faded. He sucked in his first lungful of air. He stumbled to the bank, then lay on the ground, panting. He reached up and felt the gills recede until all that was left was smooth skin. *Thank God.*

He held out his arms. They were a gray color, tinged with green and shiny. He pulled his hand closer to his face to examine webbing that was now between his fingers. *So that's how I swam so fast.*

But as he watched, the webbing split down the middle and the skin disintegrated. And the gray cast to his skin began to pink up. In a few seconds, his skin was back to its normal color and the webbing was gone.

He sat up, patting down his chest, his legs, making sure everything was where it was supposed to be. And he realized he wasn't hurt—at all. He didn't think he even had any bruises. He'd fallen over two hundred feet and he didn't even have a bruise to show for it. Shock was slowly stealing over him at the transformation and his current condition. He shook his head as if he could shake away the sense of unreality.

Deal with it later. Find everybody else first.

He looked around slowly. No one was around, and he didn't recognize where he was. He looked up at the sun, trying to get a sense of where he was. In the distance he could see the ship hovering above New City. He started at a slow jog, but soon his worries about Lyla, the kids, Arthur, Max, even Adros, had him picking up his pace until he was sprinting through the trees. But like in the water, his breathing remained even.

It's nothing. It's normal, he told himself even as he realized he had never run as fast before in his life.

102

The ship had auto pilot. Lyla sat strapped into the same seat she'd been in before they dropped off Adros, Max, and the kids. Arthur was going to slow it down enough that he could jump and then let it continue on its way up the seaboard, away from the camp. Hopefully that would keep the Unwelcome from following them, at least immediately. Lyla knew that they would come for the camp. She just hoped Adros and Max would get there with enough time to warn everyone.

In her mind, she went over all the details, depending on which scenario played out—the Unwelcome arriving at the camp before she got back, the Unwelcome arriving just after she returned, or hopefully, the Unwelcome arriving long after they'd abandoned it. The mental exercise was helping ground her. Giving her something to focus on, other than the ever-expanding pit that had started to develop in her chest when Riley had gone over the railing.

Lyla looked up as Arthur appeared. "It's on auto pilot. It's going to slow almost to a stop for five seconds. We need to jump then." The ramp at the back started to lower. "I'll have to carry you for the jump."

She nodded as she unbuckled herself and stood. "Okay."

The wind whipped through the cabin, making talking impossible. She followed Arthur down the ramp, holding onto the railing so as not to get pulled out. He reached out a hand for her. Without hesitation, she placed her hand in his. He pulled her to him, wrapping his arms around her. The ship noticeably slowed. Arthur leapt.

Lyla buried her head in his chest, closing her eyes. They hit the ground and Arthur rolled, keeping her protected in his arms. When he stopped rolling he was on his back, Lyla lying on top of him.

"Are you all right?" he asked.

She raised her head and looked into his face. She knew he wasn't just asking about the jump. "No. But I will be."

Even as she said the words, she knew that they were a lie. Riley dying—there would never be anything all right about that. She rolled off of him and stood up. "Which way?"

He nodded to their left as he stood. "Through here."

Lyla followed him through the woods. She had to jog to keep up with his long stride. He offered to slow down, but she knew time was of the essence. Part of her also knew that even trying to find Riley was an exercise in stupidity. He was gone. She took a stuttering breath, clawing back the grief that wanted to overwhelm her.

"Not yet, not yet," she mumbled quietly. She needed to be sure. She needed to know that she had not left him out here. *Not like Muriel.*

They walked for an hour without speaking. And when Arthur finally did, Lyla's head jerked up at the sound of his voice. She'd been thinking about Riley as a kid, when Muriel had been alive, as well as Riley's father and grandfather. It had been tough. They had been barely surviving at times, but together it had felt right. *And now I'm all that's left.*

"Lyla," Arthur whispered.

She went still as she heard it. Someone was running. Lyla swallowed as hope bloomed in her chest. But if it was Riley, he would *not* be running. He'd be limping at best. She nodded to Arthur and indicated she was going to a tree ten feet away.

The person running would pass right between them. She quickly made her way over to the large maple and ducked behind it. Slowing her breathing, she scanned the area to make sure there wasn't someone else coming up on them while the runner distracted them. But she sensed no one else.

The footsteps drew closer, then slowed. Whoever it was knew they weren't alone. Lyla tensed, crouching down. The person's footsteps were barely audible now as they moved cautiously forward. Lyla squinted, trying to make them out in the forest.

Then a face peeked out from behind a tree.

Lyla's heart slammed to a stop. She shoved out from her hiding spot, practically tripping over her own feet in her haste, her eyes filling with tears, even as she knew it couldn't be him. That her eyes, her mind, must be playing tricks on her. "Riley?"

Riley peeked out again from behind the tree, his mouth falling open. And then he was sprinting for her, wrapping his arms around her and pulling her off her feet. Lyla clasped him to her, tears streaming down her cheeks. "You're here. You're alive. You're alive."

He twirled her around with a laugh. Finally he put her down, and Lyla wiped at the tears on her cheeks before reaching up to wipe the ones on his cheeks away. She kept her hand on the side of his face. "I thought I lost you."

"Not quite yet." He smiled, his eyes bright.

Arthur cleared his throat. And Riley turned to him with a grin. "Hey, Arthur."

Arthur hesitated for only a moment before pulling Riley off his feet and into a hug. Riley let out a yelp but then laughed as Arthur lowered him down. "It is good to see you, Riley."

"You, too, big guy."

Lyla frowned, looking him over. "I don't understand. You don't look injured at all."

"I'll tell you the whole story, but maybe we'll walk and talk, because I think we need to get back to the camp as fast as possible."

103

The gate tower came into view first above the trees. Adros looked up in relief. Leading the kids here had been rough. The kids jumped at every shadow and rustle. And their paranoia was contagious.

But more than that, Adros felt the guilt weighing him down. Miles had been really decent when Adros saw him. Hell, he'd even told Adros he'd done a good job. But Adros knew how close Riley and Miles were. Two biological brothers couldn't be closer than those two. Miles had been shocked and in disbelief, but Adros knew the reality of what had happened would hit him soon. And he'd realize all of this had been set into motion by Adros's actions.

Lyla was taken because of him, and now Riley was dead because he hadn't stood up to his father. There was no changing that. And the relief he felt when he saw the towers dissipated just like that. The camp wouldn't want him around. Not after what he'd done.

"Oh, thank God," Max said. "That's it, right?"

Adros shifted the little girl in his arms. Her name was Shelly. She was really thin, like Alyssa and Rachel. And that thought led to more guilt piling on top of him. He should have protected them more. He should have told Lyla or Frank. *So much pain could have been avoided if I had just manned up.*

"Adros?" Max prompted.

What had he asked? *Oh, right.* "Yeah. That's it. That's the camp."

"They won't have any problem with the kids and myself being here?"

Adros shook his head. "No. They're good people. You guys will all be welcome here."

Max clapped Adros on the shoulder. "We couldn't have done any of this without you, son. You're a real hero."

Adros swallowed as the gate came into view. Frank and Montell were walking toward them. The guard tower must have notified them of their approach. "No, Max. I'm not," he said, quietly moving ahead.

Adros tried to read Frank and Montel's body language, but neither showed him anything. Adros figured they'd be mad. After all, he'd accused Lyla of assaulting him and then disappeared from camp.

Frank crossed his arms over his chest as Adros reached him. "Adros, where have you been? And who are all these kids?"

Adros nodded back to Max and the kids. "This here is Max Turner from the Fringe, Addie's friend. And these are the kids we freed from New City."

"Freed? And who's we?" Montell asked.

"Me and"—he swallowed, a wave of grief hitting him—"Riley. Lyla's safe, too. She's farther back."

"Lyla?" Frank smiled broadly. "Thank God. She's all right?"

"She's fine." Adros met his gaze and looked away.

"Who isn't fine?" Frank asked quietly.

Adros took a breath, picturing Lyla's tear-stained face. "Riley. He didn't ... he's not ..." Adros's voice broke, and he just shook his head, not able to get the words out.

Frank nodded, looking away, a tremble in his chin. "I see. I had a feeling he'd gone and done something stupid."

"Max!" Addie yelled as she ran through the entrance. They all turned to watch Addie hug Max tight. And Adros was glad to have the chance to get ahold of himself. And he thought Frank and Montell appreciated the distraction as well.

"What are you doing here?" Addie asked.

"It's a long story," Max said.

"And we'd like to hear that story. Let's get these kids settled, and then you and Adros can tell us what's been going on. Meet me at Lyla's house." Frank clapped Adros on the shoulder before heading into the camp.

The little girl Adros had been holding for most of the trip walked up, slipping her hand into Adros's. "Adros? Are we safe here?"

"Yeah, Shelly, you're safe here." He picked her up and headed for the gates, knowing the walk to Lyla's house was going to be tougher than the one from New City.

104

Miles knew he should feel embarrassed about crying in front of Petra, but he wasn't. Riley deserved tears. His loss shouldn't be glossed over with strong words and composed faces. And besides, Miles felt Riley's loss down to his bones. What other choice did he have but to mourn?

Petra ran a hand over Miles's head. "What do you want to do? Head to the camp or catch up with Lyla?"

"Lyla," Miles said, getting to his feet. "We need to find her. This is going to be tough for her."

"For all of us," Petra said, hugging him tight before heading for her horse. And then they were on their way. Neither of them spoke, both lost in their own thoughts. Miles thought about when he'd first met Riley. Riley had been his first friend in years. And since that point, Miles had known that Riley always had his back, as did Lyla, and even Maisy, in her way. They were one unit. And now that unit was irreparably changed.

Ahead, Petra pulled her horse to a stop. Miles's horse stopped of its own accord, jolting Miles from his thoughts. Petra pulled her sword from its scabbard. Miles tensed.

"Good job, Petra." Lyla stepped from the woods in front of them with a smile. The smile threw Miles off. Did she not know? He slid off his horse. "Lyla?"

She walked over and hugged him tight. "Oh, it is good to see you."

He hugged her back, taking a shuddering breath.

She pulled back looking at him. "Miles? What's wrong?"

"It's ... it's about Riley."

"What about me?" a voice called.

Miles whirled around as Riley stepped out of the woods, Arthur right behind him. Petra slid off her horse. "Riley?"

But Miles didn't say anything. He just sprinted toward Riley and pulled him into a hug.

"Hey, hey, what's going on?"

Miles stepped back, wiping at his eyes. "We ran into Adros. He said you fell off a bridge. That you were dead." Miles inspected him. He didn't even have a bruise. "I guess he was mistaken."

Riley looked at Lyla before turning back to Miles. "He wasn't mistaken."

"But why would Adros think you were killed? You don't even look scratched," Petra said as she joined them.

"I should have been killed from the fall. But I wasn't. And something really weird happened when I was under the water."

"What?" Miles asked.

"I could breathe underwater."

"That's not possible," Petra said.

"I would agree with you, except that I did," Riley said.

Lyla stepped next to Riley, putting an arm around his shoulders. "I don't know how he survived that fall. I'm just thankful he did."

Miles felt Petra's gaze on him. "I think you should tell them what you discovered," she said.

Riley looked between them. "At the lab? You made it? What did you find?"

"I think I found the reason you survived the fall."

105

Montel, Otto, Addie, and Jamal were waiting with Frank when Adros arrived with Max at Lyla's house. Each of them had grinned at Adros and shook his hand, telling him what a great job he had done. And with each utterance of praise, Adros felt worse and worse.

Frank made the introductions to Max and then asked for a rundown of what happened. Adros took a breath and held nothing back. He told them about Brendan finding him in the woods and then his threat. He told them about finding Riley, going to New City, the eventual rescue, and Riley's fall.

Addie had sucked in a breath, her hand flying to her mouth as he recounted what Arthur had told him.

Jamal shook his head. "Is there any way he could have survived? We could send out a search party. He could be hurt, but—"

Max shook his head. "The bridge was about two hundred feet above the water. Even if he somehow survived the impact with the water and missed the rocks, the water there just pounds everything into submission. No one could survive that. I'm sorry."

The room fell into silence. "And Lyla? She's coming behind you?"

Adros nodded. "Her and Arthur."

Montell spoke up. "Who's this Arthur?"

Addie and Frank exchanged a look. But Jamal was the one who spoke. "He's a friend. A really tall, really blue, really alien friend."

Frank cut in before Montell could ask any more questions. "We can talk about that another time. Right now I think we need to prepare for the Unwelcome. Lyla and Arthur were sending the ship away, but we know they'll head back here. They know where she's from. Where she'll come back to. Everything needs to be ready. We may need to move the camp. The Jingle kids need to be secured, along with the food and meds. Hopefully they'll just look around and leave."

Adros and Max exchanged a glance.

"What?" Addie demanded.

"They took Lyla for a reason," Adros said. "They think there's something about her that's different. And we made a *really* big noise when we left. I don't know if they get angry, but if they do, when they show up here, they're not going to just look around. They're going to want to do some damage. We need to be prepared for that."

Frank nodded. "Okay. Let's get as many people out of the camp as we can, as much supplies as we can. Everyone needs to help out. Adros, get Shane and take the kids to the cave."

Adros stood. "I'll get Shane. But if there's a fight, you're going to need me here."

Frank shook his head. "I appreciate it, but the Phoenixes—"

Adros cut him off. "Can't do what I can do. Something happened in New City, to me, to Riley. We're stronger, faster. I don't know why, but we can fight the Unwelcome, not just get them off balance. You need me here."

Frank looked at Max, who nodded back at him. "I saw it with my own eyes. I wouldn't have believed it otherwise."

Frank was quiet for a long moment. "Okay. But get the kids secure in the cave first, all right?"

"Yes, sir." Everyone stood and headed for the door.

"Adros, wait," Frank called.

Adros tensed, turning back. "Yes?"

Frank walked over to him with a wince, his limp more pronounced. "What happened to your father?"

Adros shrugged. "I don't know. Last I saw of him he was going into the Unwelcome ship—with Lyla being carried in."

"What you did—"

Adros nodded. "I know I shouldn't be here. But I'd really like to help. As soon as the fight's over, though, I'll go. I promise."

Frank shook his head. "Your father put you in a very difficult spot. You chose poorly but understandably. And you tried to make up for it. You are a part of this camp, Adros. You don't have to prove that in the fight to come. Don't do anything stupid, all right? We already lost Riley. I don't want to lose you, too."

"But—"

"You're not going anywhere, Adros. We need you here. Your sisters need you here. All right?"

Adros's throat felt tight, so all he could do was nod.

"Good. Now get the kids safe and then get back here as fast as you can, okay?"

"Okay." Adros headed for the door, feeling some of the weight lift from his shoulders. But not all of it. Because he knew Frank was wrong. He had to prove something in the fight to come. Maybe not to Frank or the camp but definitely to himself.

106

Miles made Riley recount everything he could remember after falling off the bridge. But then Arthur interrupted. "But it began before that. You were able to fight us off. No human should be able to do that."

Miles looked between Lyla and Riley. "Did either of you notice anything? Any sort of change or feeling or—"

"The warmth," Lyla said. "When I tracked down Cal, when I was on the old highway, whenever these skills have manifested, I always feel this warmth spread through my limbs. At first I attributed it to adrenaline."

"I felt that, too," Riley said.

Petra frowned. "So that's the trigger?"

Lyla shook her head. "No, I think that's the sign that the process had been initiated."

"But what causes this? There is no record of humans having such abilities," Arthur said.

"I did find some markers in our blood. They weren't in people who are not Cursed." Miles frowned, looking at Lyla. "Except you. The markers are in your blood as well. Although I don't really understand why."

"They must have been in Muriel's as well. That's why they kidnapped her," Lyla said.

"Wait—*Mom*? What are you talking about?"

Lyla looked stricken. "God, Riley, I'm sorry. With everything, I forgot to tell you. Your mom—she didn't die right away. She was struck by an Unwelcome weapon, but she didn't turn to ash. They took her to New City to find out why."

Riley's paled noticeably. "She survived? She was alive?"

Lyla nodded. "They wanted her to tell them about her family. She refused. She took her own life to keep them from getting to us."

Riley's mouth fell open. "She sacrificed herself for us twice."

Lyla reached over and squeezed his hand. "She loved you. She loved me. She protected us the best way she could."

Riley nodded, but Miles could see how shaken he was.

"She sounds like an incredible woman," Arthur said quietly in the silence.

"She was," Riley said. And no one said anything for a few moments. Then Riley finally spoke. "Okay, so, Miles, if I understand this all correctly, you're saying you think we are no longer human."

"I don't know if I'd go that far. Maybe just modified humans. But I'm betting if I checked your blood right now, it would look just like Lyla's. I mean, you could breathe underwater. You had actual gills. Not to press the point, but you know normal humans can't do that, right?"

"But how?" Lyla asked. "And why just the Cursed and me?"

"Lewis, Meg's second in command, says he thinks it might have been the ash that was around when all of us Cursed were babies," Petra said.

Lyla nodded, her tone thoughtful. "That stuff was everywhere —the food, the air. I think it's as good an explanation as any."

"Do you know where the ash came from?" Miles asked.

Lyla shook her head. "No."

Petra frowned. "But how exactly does it work, though? I mean, I have the markers in my blood, but they haven't been activated. I don't have any special powers. Trust me, I would *love* that."

"I don't know. There must be some sort of trigger." Miles turned to Lyla. "Did you feel anything different when your powers first activated?"

"I felt that warmth spread throughout my limbs, but I don't know what the trigger was."

"Riley?"

"Uh, I don't know. I guess it was on the bridge. When the kids were in trouble."

Miles mind raced. "Lyla, you were racing to save us. That was the first time you felt it. Could that be it?" he mumbled.

"Could what be it?" Riley asked.

"Different emotional states result in the release of different chemicals in the human body. Dopamine is associated with happiness, depression, apathy. Serotonin is associated with alertness or calming behavior. Oxytocin reduces stress. There are dozens that are associated with different emotional states. I wonder if the drive to protect is associated with a neurotransmitter, that when released, unlocks the ability."

Arthur stood up. "I think you all need to go."

Miles jolted at the abrupt change in conversation, but Riley got to his feet, looking around, instantly on alert. "Why? What's wrong?"

"If you are right, and the Cursed all have powers that allow them to fight us, to fight the Naku, then the Naku will waste no time in destroying you."

"They've tried. I don't see why—"

"No, destroying *you*. They know what camp you are from." He looked at Riley. "They know Lyla is from there, you are from there. They know your powers have manifested. We have probably thrown them off with the ship we sent on, but it won't take them long to track it down and then change course."

"And find a dead Naku." Lyla leapt to her feet. "He's right. We need to go. We'll double up on the horses." Lyla looked at Arthur. "Or maybe triple."

Arthur shook his head. "The horse would not be able to support my weight. I will only slow you down. You four need to go. I will come as fast as I can."

Lyla nodded. "He's right. Riley with me. Petra, you and Miles. Let's move."

Miles sprinted to the horse with Petra, knowing that the scientific conversation could wait. Right now, they needed to go protect the people they cared about.

107

L yla rode hard for the camp with Riley. Petra and Miles were right on her tail the whole way. Even as all the scenarios ran through her mind, she couldn't help but think of what Miles had found out.

Is it possible? Do the Cursed somehow have abilities? But why? And where did they come from?

She thought that Lewis was probably right about the ash being the source of the abilities for the kids. But what about Lyla? She'd been born well before the ash. *So how did I get them? And did Muriel have them as well?*

But the bigger question was: What activated them? From what Lyla saw, Adros had them, as did Riley. But Miles and Petra didn't, although according to Miles, their blood showed they had the potential.

But was this all just a big guess? Miles was smart, but he was looking for a difference. And because he found one, he assumed that was the explanation. It was entirely possible it was unrelated.

But even as she thought it, she knew it was *she* who was grasping at straws, not Miles. She had fought the Unwelcome. First when Cal had taken the kids, and then again when they'd ambushed her at the old highway. Something had caused that. And as Addie had pointed out years ago with the Cal incident, Lyla had been able to do something that no human could do. A chill ran over her. *Because I'm not entirely human anymore.*

Lyla looked up as the fence for the camp came into view. She shoved all her questions about herself, her abilities, and what it all meant to the side. Those were questions for some other time. Now it was time to make sure the camp was safe. Three blasts sounded across space, and she reined in her horse sharply, searching the sky.

"There!" Petra yelled, pointing behind them. And sure enough, an Unwelcome ship could be seen in the distance, heading right for the camp.

108

The woods were quiet as Adros led the group from New City to the cave. Shane had gotten the rest of the Jingle kids and should already be there.

"Adros," Max panted from behind him, "we need to slow down."

"We can't. Not until we're at the cave." Adros glanced back. The kids were struggling, and Max's face was pale at the end of the procession. *Damn it.* Adros slowed a little, but inside he was itching to flat-out run. He needed to get the kids to the cave so he could get back to the camp. The Unwelcome could arrive at any minute.

Jack, the oldest boy in the New City group, looked up at him. "We can do it."

Adros gave him an abrupt nod. "Good."

Adros turned, but saw a grimace of pain flash across Jack's face. He turned back. "Jack? What's wrong?"

"Nothing. I'm fine," he said quickly.

Adros was tempted to let it go, but he couldn't. "Tell me."

"He hurt his ribs," Susie, the girl walking next to Jack, said.

"Shh." Jack looked at Adros and swallowed hard. "It's not bad. I'm fine."

"Let me see." Adros nodded to his shirt.

Jack hesitated and then reluctantly pulled up his shirt. Adros gasped, and Jack quickly pulled his shirt back down.

"When did that happen?"

Jack wouldn't meet his eyes.

"Last night," Susie said. "He dropped his soup and asked for more."

The kid's chest was a mass of purple bruises, some really dark. He had to be in a lot of pain. "Why didn't you say something?"

"If we say something, we get punished more, and if we're too hurt, we get put in the tower."

"The tower?"

"Below the bridge."

The Advancement Building. Oh my God. They experimented on kids. Adros gaped and saw tears streaming down Jack's cheeks. "I'm sorry. It's okay. It doesn't hurt."

And for a minute, it wasn't Jack standing in front of him, but Adros standing in front of his father. And Adros did what he wished his whole childhood his father had done. He knelt down in front of him. "Hey, hey, it's okay. No one's going to hurt you. You were really brave walking all that way without complaining. You did a great job."

Max caught up with him. "Are we—"

"We're slowing down. The kids need a break."

109

M iles held on to Petra as she raced their horse up the path leading to the camp. The gates were closed, but they opened as Lyla sped toward them. She didn't even slow her horse down as she dashed through the entrance. Petra was right behind her.

Lyla brought her horse to a quick stop inside the gate. She and Riley were off the horse before Petra had even brought her and Miles's horse to a stop. Otto came running from over by the training ground. "Lyla?"

Lyla whirled around just in time to be caught in Otto's hug. "Thank the gods. We'd heard you were—Riley?" Otto went still, looking between Riley and Lyla. "But Adros said ..."

Riley grinned. "I'm not a ghost. And I'm all in one piece."

Otto grabbed Riley into a hug and twirled him around like he weighed nothing. "Otto! Otto! I'm not dead, but you keep hugging me like this and I will be."

"Sorry, sorry." Otto wiped at his eyes after setting Riley down. "I'm just really glad you're not dead."

Riley smiled. "Me, too."

Miles slid off the horse. "Sorry to break this up, but remember the Unwelcome?"

Lyla turned to Miles and Petra. "You two get to the cave."

Petra stepped forward, shaking her head. "But Lyla—"

"Your abilities have not manifested. We don't know if they will. Until then, you are at the cave, all right?"

"But—"

"Now, Petra."

Petra's back snapped straight and she nodded. "Yes, ma'am."

With a nod, Lyla turned to Otto. "Where's Frank?"

"At your house," Otto said,

Lyla nodded at Riley. "You're with me."

"I'll be right there," Riley said. Lyla nodded before she and Otto headed off.

Miles looked at Riley. "Be careful."

Riley nodded. "You, too."

"Yeah, we'll be really careful hiding out in the woods," Petra mumbled.

"Hey, you know she trusts you. She just needs to know you're safe. And all the kids."

"Yeah, yeah. But it would be nice if my super powers kicked in," Petra said.

"I'm sure they will," Riley said.

Petra rolled her eyes. "Whatever. Miles, let's go."

Miles nodded and looked at Riley, not sure what to say. Finally he decided to go with what he felt. "Look, I mourned you once. I don't want to do that again, okay?"

Riley nodded. "Okay."

110

Lyla sprinted up the stairs to her house as the door flew open. "Lyla?"

She grinned, still running as Frank caught her in a hug. "Thank God."

She pulled back, looking at him. And his smile disappeared. "We heard about Riley, and I'm so—"

"Heard what?" Riley asked as he vaulted up the steps.

Frank's mouth fell open. "But Adros—"

"Was mistaken. I'm good, sort of."

Frank stared at him for another long moment before shaking himself from his shock. "Right, well, we have Unwelcome inbound."

Montell stepped out of the house, the four Unwelcome weapons they had gathered over the years but never used in his arms. They didn't want to give away they had them, and they were only for extreme situations. This one definitely counted.

"Okay, so what's the plan?"

Frank took a spear from Montell and handed it to Lyla. "Defend the camp."

There were a lot of double takes at Riley as he headed for the front gate next to Lyla at a jog. "I think we're going to have to come up with a good explanation about how you're walking around," Lyla said.

"Why not the truth?"

She raised an eyebrow. "That you survived a two-hundred-foot fall, grew gills, and then ran full-out for an hour like you were out for a stroll?"

He blanched. "Yeah, you're right. We're going to need to come up with something."

"Uh huh," she said. But all levity dropped as they approached the front gate. The Unwelcome ship had landed and they would be at the gates any minute. Lyla would be in one guard tower. Riley would be in the other. She hugged him to her. "I mourned you once. Don't make me do it again."

"Miles said the same thing."

"Well, they say family tend to think alike."

"I'll be careful. But you need to be as well."

"I will."

He gave her a smile and then jogged toward the other tower. And once again she was struck by just how much he'd grown up. But it didn't reduce her fear for him.

She forced herself to turn toward the other tower. She'd trained him, and hopefully with his extra abilities he'd be fine. *He will be fine,* she told herself as she climbed the ladder on the outside of the tower.

Shayna reached a hand down, helping Lyla up the last two rungs of the ladder. "I'm glad you're back." She pulled Lyla into a hug.

"Me, too," Lyla said.

Shayna looked around. "I know it's not the time, but I have a feeling there's a lot going on around here that I don't know about. Promise me when this is all over you'll read me in?"

"You have my word." Lyla's gaze strayed to where eight Unwelcome were marching toward the front gate, a man in a deep-violet robe in front. If Chad's nose was any farther up in the air, Lyla was pretty sure he'd be unable to see where he was going. She curled her lip in disgust.

Shayna followed her gaze. "Friend of yours?"

"Something like that." Lyla did not take her gaze away from Chad. He'd been there when Muriel died. He had planned on letting Lyla be turned into a brainless zombie.

You will not hurt my people, she promised, feeling a sense of warmth roll through her. And she smiled, welcoming the sensation.

The Unwelcome contingent marched toward the gates, which opened as they arrived. Frank stood waiting in the middle of the open space on the other side of the gate. Otto and Montell stood at his sides.

"I don't like this," Shayna said quietly from next to her as she looked down.

"Me, either," Lyla said.

This was the part of the plan she liked the least. So much could go wrong. The Unwelcome could just start shooting and no one would be able to get to Frank, Montel, or Otto in time. But they needed to start this way, in case there was any chance violence could be avoided.

The Unwelcome fanned out behind Chad as he came to a stop only a few feet in front of Frank. Lyla held her breath.

Chad scanned the space. "Where is she?"

Frank crossed his arms over his chest. "Where is who?"

Chad narrowed his gaze. "Don't play games with me. Your precious leader has already caused me enough of a headache with the Naku." Blood dripped from Chad's nose, and he quickly reached up with a tissue to stem the bleeding.

Guess I did cause him quite a headache. Lyla hoped the bloody nose was a side effect of the Naku's invasive interrogation technique. Lyla felt no guilt for Chad's pain, only annoyance that the Naku hadn't killed him. *Although I suppose I should thank them for allowing me the opportunity to do it myself.*

"Where is she?" Chad asked again, his voice making him sound more petulant than demanding.

Frank glared at him. "Last I heard, *you* had taken her. We have not seen her since then. But if she's escaped you, I can't exactly work up any rage on your behalf."

Chad narrowed his gaze. Lyla tensed. Then Chad headed back to the entrance. Lyla held her breath. Was that it? Were they just going to leave? She watched Chad's progress to the gate. *Keep going,* she urged.

But he paused as he reached the entrance. Then he turned around, casting a scathing look at the camp and the few occupants in view. "Kill them all."

111

A s soon as the words left Chad's mouth, Lyla pulled the trigger on the Unwelcome's weapon. The first blast found its mark on a ten-foot Unwelcome nearest Frank. A second blast crashed into the other Unwelcome on the other side of him, thanks to Riley.

Frank ducked behind a cart next to him as an Unwelcome let out a blast, setting the cart ablaze. Otto and Montell wasted no time slamming their staffs into the knees of the injured Unwelcome and wrenching their weapons away from them. Using them as shields, they took aim at the other Unwelcome.

Lyla was pulling the trigger as fast as she could manage, but it wasn't fast enough. Angel darted across open space, trying to reach shelter, but an Unwelcome blast caught him before he could. Engulfed in a blue light, he was there, and then he was dust.

Lyla handed the weapon to Shayna. "Keep firing."

"What are you going to do?" Shayna asked as Lyla stepped onto the edge of the tower.

"What I can," Lyla said, stepping off. She landed in a crouch and rolled to her feet. The thirty-foot jump—a jump which would destroy anyone else's kneecaps—had no effect on her. She sprinted forward at a run. Twirling as she approached the Unwelcome closest to her, she slammed a sidekick into its lower back. It arched, its hands flying back. She grabbed it by the neck and yanked it to the ground. Pulling out her knife, she plunged it into its neck.

Grabbing its spear, she whirled around, spying Frank behind the cart. "Frank!" She tossed the spear. He grabbed it, turning in time to catch the Unwelcome behind him.

"Lyla!" Montell yelled from her right. She whirled around and dove, sensing the Unwelcome behind her, but she wasn't in time. She felt a blast slide across her ribs as burning pain engulfed her.

112

It took them another ten minutes to get to the cave, but Adros didn't mind the extra time. Shane appeared in the cave entrance only a few seconds after they spotted it. He hurried out to them. "I was getting worried."

"We had to slow down a little bit. Everybody here?"

Shane nodded. "Yeah. Plus a few extras."

"Extras?" Adros said as he followed Shane inside. People lined the tunnel—all the older members of the camp or those who couldn't fight for one reason or another.

"Wow." Adros looked around. "You weren't kidding. Look, can you get these guys settled? I need to—"

"Adros?" His sister Rachel stepped out from the crowd, Alyssa tucked behind her like always.

He had barely seen them since they had moved into Lyla's house. And he hadn't seen them at all since Brendan had ... He cut off that line of thought, not wanting to think about it.

Rachel took a tentative step forward.

"Look, I'm going to get these guys settled. I'll see you," Shane said, directing Max and the rest of the kids farther into the cave.

Adros stared at his two sisters. Even in the dim light, he could tell they looked so much better than he had ever seen them. They weren't as slim and had some color in their cheeks.

"Hi, girls. Are you okay?"

Rachel moved closer to him. Adros knelt down so he wasn't towering over them—that always made them nervous. Alyssa ducked around Rachel and stepped up to Adros. He was surprised by her boldness. She put a hand on his cheek and rubbed her thumb over the bruise on his cheekbone. "Dad did this?"

Adros nodded, touched by the sweetness of the gesture and the concern in her voice.

Alyssa's eyes filled with tears, and she hugged him tight. "I'm sorry."

Her tears fell onto his neck, and he held her back just as tight. When he spoke, his voice was thick. "I'm sorry, too. I should have protected you guys more. I should have done more."

Rachel hugged him from the other side. "No. You were just like us. Lyla explained it to us. And we know you protected us as best you could. Even when she left, she told us you didn't mean it. That someone had hurt you and not to be mad at you because it wasn't your fault."

Gratefulness tugged at his chest. *Another thing to thank Lyla for.* She could have castigated him, and he would have deserved every word of it. Instead she'd made it so his sisters looked at him with compassion, not hate.

Alyssa pulled back. "Are you leaving again?"

Adros looked at his sisters, at the people in the cave who were looking away to give him and his sisters a little privacy, and then he looked back out the cave toward camp. He turned back to his sisters. "No. I'm staying right here."

113

Riley's breath caught as he watched Lyla leap from the other guard tower. But then she was on the ground and moving with a speed he could barely comprehend. Next to him, Angela balked. "Oh my God."

Riley handed her the Unwelcome spear as the feeling of warmth spread over him. With one hand on the edge of the opening, he threw himself over the side. He hit the ground with a roll, but his momentum was too strong, and he did not roll to his feet as gracefully as Lyla. He sprawled, practically tripping over his own feet, as he landed behind two Unwelcome.

No time to be embarrassed, he swept out, burying his shin into the side of the taller one's knee. The Unwelcome buckled, and Riley was on his feet as the other turned toward him. Using the Unwelcome's momentum, he stepped in to him, continuing the creature's momentum around as he clasped its arm to his chest and twirled. The Unwelcome's feet came up off the air, and Riley released it, sending it flying into the side of the camp fence.

He back kicked the other one, turned, and landed a round kick on its knee, which lowered it enough to slam the side of his palm into the creature's throat.

Placing his hand under the creature's chin, he moved its chin up and over, sending it crashing to the ground.

He grabbed the discarded spear as it crashed, unloading it point blank in its chest. Ahead, he saw an Unwelcome chasing after a group of campers. *Oh, no, you don't.* Riley sprinted after them. He paused for only a second as he neared and pulled the trigger, catching the Unwelcome in the thigh. It stumbled to a stop. To his left he saw another Unwelcome giving chase to another two people. Rory sprinted for them.

"Rory!" Riley threw the spear at him. Rory plucked it from the air and continued after the giant.

Riley sprinted after the one he'd injured, dodging a blast and tackling the thing at the hip. It felt like hitting a wall, but he didn't stop shoving through like a train as he wrapped his hands behind its knees and yanked.

The Unwelcome toppled backward. Riley didn't slow. He stomped on the creature's groin and chest, and he literally ran him down. Yanking the creature's weapon away, he placed it on its chest and pushed the trigger. He stumbled back as a hole appeared, smelling of burnt hair, skin, and plastic.

He turned to follow Rory when a bellow sounded from the front gates, followed by a yell.

"Lyla!"

Her side burning, Lyla fell onto her other side, breathing shallowly. *Oh crap, that hurts.* A roar filled her ears followed by her name being yelled. Steeling herself, she pushed herself up as Arthur tackled the Unwelcome who had shot her. The two of them hit the ground with a trembling thud.

Arthur kneed the creature in the groin and then the chest. He ripped the creature's helmet off. Surprise flashed across Arthur's face right before he elbowed the Unwelcome in the chin with a force that wrenched the Unwelcome's chin to the side with a sickening twist. The Unwelcome went still. Arthur climbed off him, rushing to Lyla's side.

"Get away from her!" Otto yelled, raising a spear at him.

"No! No!" Lyla scrambled to her feet, ignoring the pain lancing through her as she ran between Otto and Arthur, her knees shaking and the world dimming at the edges. "He's a friend, Otto. He's a friend."

Otto lowered the spear, a confused expression on his face.

"Lyla." Arthur picked her up as her knees gave way. Lyla let herself sink into Arthur's arms. "Hey."

He smiled down at her. "Hey."

R iley sprinted to the front gate, his heart pounding. The Phoenixes were inching toward a towering figure, his blue skin looking even more luminescent in the sunlight, as he stood above a figure on the ground.

Riley came to a halt as Arthur reached down, and Riley recognized who he held in his arms. *No.* He sprinted toward them. "Arthur? Is she all right?"

Lyla winced. "I'm fine."

"She was hit in the side," Arthur said.

Otto moved closer, looking between Lyla and Arthur. "What ... what's going on?"

"Otto, this is Arthur. He's a friend of ours. He helped me save Lyla from New City."

"O–kay." Otto looked between Lyla and Arthur, his mouth slightly open and his brow furrowed.

The Unwelcome on the ground stirred. Riley moved quickly, placing the spear on his chest.

"Wait!" Arthur yelled.

Riley paused, not taking his eyes from the creature. "What?"

"Don't kill her. Please."

R.D. BRADY

Riley did a double take, just noticing the longer lashes the creature had, and the more pronounced cheekbones.

"Who is she?" Lyla asked.

"My sister. My twin."

Riley gaze flew to him. "What?"

But Arthur didn't answer him. Instead, he walked to Otto. "If you would ...?"

"Uh, okay," Otto said, taking Lyla from him. Riley turned his gaze to the Unwelcome on the ground. Her hair was cut close to the scalp, but now he could see the red in it. *His sister?*

Arthur quickly walked to Riley. "Please, Riley."

"She's coming to."

Arthur reached down and punched her across the face. She stopped moving. "That will keep her asleep for a little while."

Riley's mouth fell open. Did he just punch his sister? It wasn't just that he had hit his sister, but that it was *Arthur*. Violence really didn't seem to be in Arthur's nature.

"Let her live, but keep an eye on her," Lyla said. "Otto, put me down. I'm feeling better."

Otto shook his head. "Lyla, you were shot. You shouldn't—"

She placed her hand on his arm. "It's all right. Let me down."

Otto hesitated but then gently lowered her to the ground. He kept an arm around her waist for a moment to make sure she could stand, but then released her. "Otto, keep an eye on Arthur's sister. Try not to hurt her if you can avoid it. Riley and Arthur, with me."

"Where are we going?"

Lyla's eyes arrowed to slits. "After Chad."

116

C had stood in the gateway after he'd instructed the Unwelcome to kill everyone in the camp, waiting to see the humans cower. Then the first blast of the Unwelcome spear had rung out. He'd stumbled back as two Unwelcome crashed to the ground. And then Lyla had appeared like a superhero from the comics he'd read as a kid.

Chad had not waited to see what happened next. Those old comic books told him exactly what would happen. He fled toward the ship, tripping over his robes in his haste. He raised them above his knees as he ran, but they kept getting caught on branches. Fear poured through him, sweat dripped down his back, and his breathing became more labored with each blast that sounded from behind him. *I should have brought more guards.*

But even as death sounded behind him and he ran away as fast as he could, he knew there was no saving him now. If Lyla did not find him, the Naku would. Either way, he was a dead man walking.

Yet even knowing that, he ran. He got turned around for a little bit and had to backtrack, but then he saw the Unwelcome ship in front of him. He let out a breath. It was a small reprieve.

But he could lock himself inside and maybe figure out some way to—

A blast tore into the tree next to him. He screamed and jumped back, tripping over a low-lying holly bush. His robes got tangled, and it took him a few precious seconds to extract himself. He got to his knees as two feet appeared in front of him.

He looked up into a face without an ounce of compassion in it.

"Get up," Lyla said. Behind her, a boy who looked like her and an Unwelcome stood. *They're blue*, was all Chad could think as he stared at the giant.

Chad put his hands up. "Now, let's just think about this for a moment."

"Think about it?" Lyla kicked him in the face.

He screamed, his face throbbing as he fell backward. Cradling his face, he rolled onto his side.

"Get. Up," Lyla said through gritted teeth.

Tears streaming down his face, Chad struggled to think through the pain. Something hard rolled around in his mouth, and with horror he realized it was a tooth. He swallowed the coppery taste of blood and nearly gagged.

A hand grabbed the back of his robe and yanked him upright, slamming him onto his feet. He swayed for a moment before regaining his balance.

"Are there more Unwelcome coming?" Lyla asked.

"Why should I tell you?" Chad demanded. The loose tooth flew from his lips and his words came out mumbled.

Lyla stepped toward him, her eyes blazing. "Because you want to live."

Hope sprang inside Chad. "You'd let me live?"

"If you speak truthfully. Are there more coming?"

"No, no. I didn't want to raise the alarm. It is only the Unwelcome with me. Although more will come later when we don't report back. But that's hours from now."

"So it's just the eight."

Chad paused, not sure if he should speak. But if there was a chance she was going to let him live ... "There's fourteen."

"What?" The young man stepped forward.

Chad flinched away from his anger. But Lyla held up a hand, her voice clam, almost soothing. "It's all right. Where are they?"

"We know about the cave. We sent the other six to it."

"You two go," Lyla said, not taking her eyes from Chad. The Unwelcome and the young man disappeared quickly back toward the camp.

Chad let out a sigh of relief. "I believe I will need some medical attention."

Lyla nodded. "Of course. Is there anyone on the ship?"

Chad shook his head. "No. But there is a first-aid kit."

Lyla glanced around the forest.

Chad tensed, listening as well. "Is something wrong?"

Lyla laughed, turning back to him. "Is something wrong? You have sentenced how many children to their deaths? You sentenced my entire camp to their deaths. So yes, something is wrong."

Chad backed away, his body beginning to shake. "But–but you said—"

With a growl, Lyla kicked him in the chest. He flew backward, slamming into an oak. The world swayed, and his vision became dark at the edges as she stalked toward him.

He crawled on his feet away from her. "You said you'd let me live."

"I lied." She kicked him in the ribs. The force sent him in the air and flipped him, sending him back to the earth on his back. Pain rocked through him and he cried out.

"But–but ... you can't. You're one of the good ones."

Lyla pulled out her sword. "And what will you do if you are allowed to live? Crawl back to your overlords and beg for another chance?"

Chad cringed away from the anger in her eyes and the truth in her words. He shook his head. "No, no. I would never—"

"Never what? Sentence innocent people to death? End lives with less thought given to them than what shoes to wear that day?"

"No, no, you don't understand—"

"Oh, I understand. I understand you have no conscience, no guilt over the lives you have destroyed. And on behalf of the humans whose lives you have taken, I sentence you to death." Lyla plunged her sword into his chest.

Chad gasped, his whole body buckling at the shock of the pain. She pulled her sword out and the pain doubled. Blood gurgled up his throat.

He reached out a hand, not wanting to die alone, but she was already walking away. She didn't even turn to look at him.

The forest was silent. He looked around and then saw a face. A little boy with blonde hair appeared through the trees, followed by a little girl with dark skin and dark hair. Then a man, and then a woman. Soon crowds of people streamed toward him. He didn't recognize any of them. But they all recognized him.

"Murderer."

"Killer."

"Traitor."

All the ghosts of the people he'd had killed crowded around him, pointing fingers and yelling at him. He tried to close his eyes, but one of them held them open. One man plunged his hand into his wounds and Chad screamed.

And a small girl with bright blue eyes leaned down to whisper into his ear. "Don't worry. You will die. But we control how fast. And each of us is going to take a turn."

117

M iles glanced back through the trees behind him. "How long before the Unwelcome reach the camp?"

"Any minute. We need to move faster." Petra paused. "You sure you don't know how they turned their abilities on?"

Miles shook his head. He'd been going over it and over it. It had to be some sort of chemical that turned it on. He thought it was something related to heightened emotion, the desire to protect more than anything. But as to what that chemical would be or how to access it, he had absolutely no idea.

Petra swatted a branch out of her way. "How the hell did Adros of all people turn his power on? I mean, he's not exactly altruistic."

Miles had to duck as the branch swung back at him. He pictured Adros when they'd last seen him. He hadn't been the same Adros. Whatever had happened in New City, or maybe what his father had done to him, seemed to have profoundly changed him. "I don't know. I think maybe there's a whole other side to Adros that we haven't seen yet."

"I guess," Petra said, although from her tone, Miles knew she put very little stock in that explanation.

They walked for another five minutes in silence and finally rounded the curve that led to the cave. Miles nodded ahead when he saw it. "We're almost there."

"Yeah, we're—" Petra whipped around. The sound of heavy footfalls could be heard clearly through the silent woods behind them.

Petra grabbed Miles's sleeve and yanked him toward a group of three boulders. As far as hiding places went, it was great, as long as the Unwelcome didn't walk around it.

Miles crouched down low as Petra pulled out her staff. Miles did the same. Petra looked at his half arm. "Where's your attachment?" she whispered.

He winced. "Still on the horse."

She looked at him like she wanted to yell at him but nodded instead, her lips tight. They both tensed as the footsteps approached. Miles held his breath, waiting for them to change direction. But they didn't. They kept going. Miles peered out and saw them heading away.

Heading straight for the cave.

"They know," Petra whispered, her voice filled with horror.

Miles kept his gaze on their hulking figures, which cast even longer shadows across the ground. Everyone in that cave was now a sitting duck.

Petra stood. "We can't let them get to the cave."

"How are we going to stop them? I saw at least four. Maybe one we could take down, but four—"

Petra's face and voice showed no sign of fear, only conviction. "We're not going to stop them. We're going to slow them down to give the people—the *kids*—in the cave a chance to escape. That's all we can do."

Miles swallowed, knowing what she meant, and he pictured Maisy—her smile, her laugh. She was only eight years old. She deserved a longer life than that. A longer life than his other sister, Kayla, had had. He nodded. "Let's go."

118

Miles moved quickly along the ground, running parallel to the path the Unwelcome were taking to reach the cave. Petra had moved to the other side so that they could flank them. *As if that's going to help,* a voice mocked from the back of Miles's mind.

Miles clamped down on his doubts. He knew if Maisy was killed and he lived because he hid away, he'd never be able to live with himself. A hundred yards ahead, he saw his destination. The ground had been turned over from an earthquake years ago, which had forced tall shards of rock through the ground. Miles stretched out his stride, his breathing notching up as he sprinted for the rock formations. Not giving himself a chance to doubt, he leapt for the rock, landing four feet above the ground. Scrambling on all fours, he moved quickly to the edge. He peered over. He was ten feet above the ground.

The ground trembled at the quick approach of the Unwelcome. Sunlight glinted off a blue helmet, and Miles ducked down. The rocks jutted up on either side of the path. He didn't see Petra across from him, but he was sure she was there. He lay flat, his heart racing. Sweat rolled down the side of his face, slipping into his eyes. He didn't dare wipe it away, afraid the movement would pull attention to him.

From the corner of his eye, he watched the Unwelcome approach. They didn't move their heads, just looked straight ahead. Which was good, because Miles's hiding spot was practically eye level with the first Unwelcome that passed. They marched by, two by two, and he realized there weren't four. There were six.

Even as the pure insanity of his next move rushed through his mind, he started to rise, still keeping low and inching toward the edge. The last two marched past, and Miles lunged from his perch. He wrapped his arm around the being's neck. The plan had been to wrench him to the side. But Miles's sweat-slicked arm slipped. He ended up scrambling just to hold on. The Unwelcome stopped and turned quickly, trying to swing him loose before it reached over with one giant arm and grabbed the back of Miles's shirt.

Miles was up, over, and flying through the air before he could even scream. He landed with a thump, air rushing from his lungs. The being raised its weapon and pulled the trigger. Miles rolled, feeling the heat of the blast as it crashed into the ground right where he had lain a second before. But he didn't have time to think about that close call, because when he'd rolled, he'd rolled right into a second Unwelcome.

119

The Unwelcome peered down at Miles, who felt his own eyes go wide. The Unwelcome didn't pull out its spear but raised his foot. Miles rolled as he stomped onto the ground. The ground shuddered in response, and Miles could only picture what his chest would have looked like. Heart pounding, he continued to roll, hearing a blast of an Unwelcome spear somewhere near the other rock outcropping, and he prayed that Petra was okay.

Miles slammed into a rock as a feeling of warmth spread through his limbs. The Unwelcome towered over him, his leg raised. Miles pictured Lyla, Riley, Maisy and said goodbye as a tingling ran down his arm—the arm that was no longer there.

Miles threw his hands up to keep the creature's giant foot from crushing him, closing his eyes with a yell. His hands wrapped around the foot and halted its forward momentum. His eyes flew open in shock.

Wasting no time, Miles slammed his heel into the creature's other leg and was rewarded with the snap of a kneecap. The creature stumbled heavily to his side and Miles shoved on the foot he still held. The Unwelcome pitched to the side.

Miles leapt to his feet, twisting the spear from the creature's arm, which had flung wide. He flipped the spear and pulled the trigger twice, emptying it into the creature's chest. And he looked down at his left arm—his *complete* left arm. He rolled his fingers, not believing what he was seeing.

"Miles! The cave!" Petra yelled. His head jerked up. One other Unwelcome was down. Petra was fighting with one—*fighting*. Not backing away, but trading blows. She was poetry in motion. Adros fought another. Miles wasn't sure when he had shown up.

But that left one more. A dark-blue blur barreled down the path, heading straight for the cave. Miles dropped the spear, knowing its length would only slow him down, and right now he needed all the speed he could muster. Miles kept his gaze on the figure as he bolted for it, moving faster than he had ever run in his life.

The cave entrance was thirty feet in front of the Unwelcome, but apparently it decided not to wait until it got there. It began shooting into the dark entrance. Screams sounded from inside. Miles lengthened his stride, his arms pumping. "No!"

The Unwelcome turned at Miles's yell, but Miles was already airborne. His knee slammed into the creature's chest. It flew backward, its spear flying, letting off a blast that crashed into the rock face above the cave entrance. Rocks broke off, sliding down to cover the entrance.

Miles landed in a crouch and sprang for the Unwelcome, but it hadn't fallen with Miles's hit, and it dove out of the way. Miles and the Unwelcome circled one another. It was about nine feet tall, more than three feet taller than Miles. But Miles didn't care. It had weaknesses. It had vulnerabilities. Miles faked a punch for the creature's throat. Its hands flew up to protect itself, and Miles drilled the ball of his foot into the creature's hip. It doubled over. Miles yanked on the back of the creature's helmet and the helmet came off in his hands.

Miles gripped the helmet, and with a backswing, caught the

Unwelcome in the jaw. It flew off its feet, landing with a thud. Heaving, Miles advanced on it, but it was out. He paused. He knew he should kill it, but he couldn't bring himself to do it, not like this.

Pounding feet sounded behind him, and Miles whirled around, his fists up. "Whoa." Riley slid to a stop. Petra, Adros, and Arthur did the same.

"He's still alive." Miles nodded to the Unwelcome on the ground.

But none of the others replied to his statement.

"Miles, your *arm*," Riley said.

Miles held it up, feeling the tingles running along it. "Yeah. I know." The arm began to become transparent and disappeared as the adrenaline wore off. Seconds later, his arm once again ended just below the elbow. All the faces looking at him wore the same stunned look, and Miles was pretty sure his was the same.

"How's that possible?" Riley asked as he tore his gaze from Miles's arm to meet his eyes.

"I guess the same way you were able to develop gills." A yell sounded from inside the cave. Miles's head jerked toward it. "They're trapped. We need to help them."

"I will help." Arthur moved quickly to the cave entrance, Adros with him.

Petra stepped over to the fallen Unwelcome, the Unwelcome spear in her hands aimed at the creature. "What about him?"

"It doesn't feel right killing him," Miles said.

Petra gave him an incredulous look. "Are you kidding?"

"I'm just saying, it seems wrong. We should see if he's willing to talk."

Riley laughed.

Both Petra and Miles turned to him. "What?" Petra demanded.

"This conversation—it sounds awfully familiar." He nodded

to where Arthur was moving incredibly sized boulders out of the way.

"Yeah, well, I doubt they're all like Arthur," Petra said.

"True, but let's just make sure. If he wakes up and tries anything, shoot him," Riley said, heading for the cave entrance.

Miles watched him go and then turned to Petra. "I'm going to go help. You got this?"

"Yeah." Miles turned to go.

"Miles?"

He turned back. "Yeah?"

"You did great. I know how scared you were." She paused. "I was, too."

"You felt it, right?" he asked.

She nodded. "I think maybe we need to change our name from Cursed."

"What do you suggest?"

She smiled. "Blessed."

B y the time Lyla reached the cave, the fighting was well over. Her side ached, but the pain was manageable. Ahead, she saw five Unwelcome littering the path. She stopped and checked, but none of them were breathing. She let out a sigh of relief at the fact that she did not see any of her people on the ground near them.

That relief was short-lived, though. Three of their people had been killed when the Unwelcome had fired into the cave. Shane was one of them. Lyla could see the news hit Adros hard. But he still stayed at the cave entrance, helping people out over the rocks. The injured were pulled out first. Most had only minor injuries like gashes from falling rocks, but Saul had broken his leg. Nothing was life threatening. Miles moved between patients, bandaging, holding hands. Lyla's throat swelled up as she watched him. He was an incredible kid.

Arthur was at the front of the cave, helping people through. More than one person stood staring at him in shock. Lyla smiled at their looks.

Guess I don't have to worry about breaking the news about

Arthur's existence to them. They were actually taking it better than she had when she'd first seen him.

Arthur disappeared into the cave and then reappeared with Edna in his arms. Edna stared up at him, her mouth hanging open. Arthur was either oblivious to her reaction or ignoring it. He smiled down at her. "You must be Edna. I love your biscuits."

"Um, thank you?"

"You're welcome." He gently placed her on the ground as Lyla reached them.

"Are you all right, Edna?" Lyla asked.

Edna continued to stare at Arthur. "Um ..."

"I believe she may have sprained her ankle," Arthur said. "But I do not think it is too bad."

"Um ..."

"I will take you over to your wife. She will ease your pain, I'm sure." Arthur picked Edna up, whose eyes grew even wider, and headed over to where Emma sat, her arm wrapped in a makeshift sling.

Lyla put a hand to her mouth, watching them, trying not to laugh.

"Well, Arthur's certainly made himself at home," Frank said as he came to a stop next to her.

"So he has," she said, watching him for a moment longer before turning to Frank. "What's the damage?"

"We lost seven at the camp. Here?"

"Three. Shane was one of them."

Frank blanched. "Damn. So what do we do now?"

"We need to go. The Naku are looking for me. But they are also going to be looking for Riley and Adros. They'll come here first with more. We need to move everybody. It's not safe."

Frank nodded. "We'll split up. Go out in groups."

Lyla spotted Montell and Otto heading toward them. She waved them on. "Let's get Montell and Otto to break up the Phoenixes, grab every able-bodied person and break down the camp. Food, medicine, and weapons are the priority. We'll head to Site Alpha."

Years ago they'd established secondary sites that they could fall back to in the event that the camp became unlivable. They'd planned for this moment, and now it was time to put that plan into action.

"I'll get them started." But Frank stayed where he was, looking around. "We defeated them. For once, we took them down."

"Yeah," Lyla said, watching Petra, Riley, Adros, and Miles and knowing they were the reason why. "But we started something here. And it's only going to get tougher."

"Probably. But we'll face it. We'll overcome." He clasped her hand. "Together."

She squeezed his hand back. "Together."

Frank headed off to intercept Montell and Otto. Lyla knew he'd handle things. The million and one things she needed to do flew through her mind. But then a little face that she loved more than life itself popped through the opening, looking around fearfully.

Lyla jogged over, and Maisy let out a cry when she saw her. Lyla dropped to her knees, and Maisy plowed into her, hugging her tight while she sobbed. Lyla's side ached from where Maisy's legs touched her burn, but she didn't move an inch. She'd take the pain if it meant holding her girl again. Because at the end of the day, that was what was important.

Family.

EPILOGUE

On the mother ship, a female Avad screamed as the labor pains took hold. Xantar pushed to the observation window to watch. The blue female was extremely tall and thin with long dark hair. The breeder's bones were reinforced with carbon, but steroids and growth hormones were not administered to breeders. There was no need for these ones to be strong. In fact, the maternal instinct was so strong that physical strength would only lead to an uprising.

Three Naku stood around the woman, watching her labor, monitoring her vitals. Her heart rate was elevated. The labor was proving difficult. Labors often were for the slaves. The woman's hips were often too narrow to allow the child to pass through naturally. But operations were rarely performed to remove the child. They destroyed the females' ability to have future pregnancies.

And then the Naku had no choice but to destroy the female.

So they let the labors progress as long as possible before taking that step. The female screamed again, sweat rolling down her cheeks. Xantar tilted his head, watching her. So much pain. It was the aspect of the slaves he had to admit he admired—their ability to handle pain and continue on. The Naku had no such coping mechanisms. It was why the slaves were developed—to protect the Naku, allowing them to grow their intellectual gifts.

Aek looked up from where she monitored the fetal heart rate inside the delivery room. *Will you need to operate?* Xantar asked.

Aek shook her head, hearing his words as easily as if he had spoken them out loud. And that was when the other two Naku rushed to the end of the table. A few seconds later, the baby's cry sounded throughout the room.

Xantar didn't smile as he watched the bundle get carried to the waiting table, wrapped in a white blanket. Aek paused for just a moment as she reached the child, and then she drew seven vials of blood. She handed them off to a waiting assistant, who hurried them from the room.

Aek stared into the eyes of the other Naku, who took a step back with a nod. The slave reached her arms toward the child, crying. But Aek ignored her. She picked the child up and walked toward the observation window.

Xantar frowned, watching her progress. From the corner of his eye, he saw Irit inject a clear liquid into the slave's IV line. The slave's eyes went large before she fell back, the beeping of the monitor going silent.

The death had no impact on Xantar as he watched the bundle in Aek's arms. Aek turned the bundle so he could see. A baby, its eyes still closed, lay bundled in her arms. Its smooth skin was unmarred.

And pink.

His gaze flew to Aek, who nodded. *It has begun.*

No, not yet. There should have been more time, a full generation, at least. He felt Aek's gaze on him, waiting for instructions. *Tell no one.*

And this? Aek nudged her small chin toward the baby.

Xantar curled his lip. *Destroy it.*

ACKNOWLEDGMENTS

Thank you for taking a chance on my new series. I know jumping into a new series can be a risky endeavor. Hopefully, if you've made it to this point that means you enjoyed it. If you have a chance, please leave a <u>review</u>. Reviews are one of the best ways to get a book into the hands of a new reader. And a new series always needs help, so if you have the time, I would really appreciate it. You can leave a review <u>here</u>.

A giant thank you to my Beta Reading Team. Your insight has been so incredibly helpful in this process. Thank you for taking the time to help me out. I truly appreciate it.

Thanks to the creative staff at Damonza for the incredible book cover. I loved it so much, that I used a variation of it for all three books in the series.

Special thanks to Crystal Watanabe and her editing team at Pikko's House. I could not do it without you.

And as always thanks to my support team at home. You guys make everything better, especially me. I love you.

ABOUT THE AUTHOR

R.D. Brady is an American writer who grew up on Long Island, NY but has made her home in both the South and Midwest before settling in upstate New York. On her way to becoming a full-time writer, R.D. received a Ph.D. in Criminology and taught for ten years at a small liberal arts college.

R.D. left the glamorous life of grading papers behind in 2013 with the publication of her first novel, the supernatural action adventure, *The Belial Stone*. Over a dozen novels later and hundreds of thousands of books sold, and she hasn't looked back. Her novels tap into her criminological background, her years spent studying martial arts, and the unexplained aspects of our history.

If you would like to be notified about her upcoming publications, you can sign up for her mailing list. Those who sign up will receive a free e-book copy of *B.E.G.I.N.* and other freebies over time. Email addresses are never provided to any other sources.

BOOKS BY R.D. BRADY

<u>D.E.A.D.</u>

<u>The Unwelcome Trilogy</u>

Protect

Seek

Proxy

Be sure to <u>sign up</u> for R.D.'s mailing list to be the first to hear when she has a new release and receive a free short story!

16319017R00253

Made in the USA
Middletown, DE
23 November 2018